Angela Knight

The Forever Kiss

"Battling vampires, a protective ghost and the ever present battle of good and evil keep excellent pace with the erotic delights in Angela Knight's *The Forever Kiss*—a book that absolutely bites with refreshing paranormal humor." 4½ stars, RT Top Pick

—*Romantic Times BOOKclub*

"*The Forever Kiss* flows well with good characters and an interesting plot. How can you help but like the handsome Cade who ignores his own pain to protect and love the mortal woman? … The story has a fresh look at vampires that dispel some of the myths and the romance is very scorching between the protagonists with many love scenes.

"If you enjoy vampires and a lot of hot sex, you are sure to enjoy *The Forever Kiss*."

—*The Best Reviews*

"I found *The Forever Kiss* to be an exceptionally written, refreshing book. Immediately readers are drawn into this story by the very steamy love affair between Cade and Valerie. Angela Knight has written this cast of characters wonderfully. Ms. Knight has captured Valerie's internal struggle so well, that readers also feel undecided; if she helps Cade her life is forever altered, but if she doesn't can she live with the repercussions? … I really enjoyed this book by Angela Knight. As a new-to-me author, Ms. Knight goes straight to my 'auto-buy list'. 5 angels!"

—*Fallen Angel Reviews*

"*The Forever Kiss* is the first single title released from **Red Sage** and if this is any indication of what we can expect, it won't be the last. Angela Knight fans have known for years what a talented writer she is and now there will be others will get a chance to read her. Ms. Knight sucks you in (pun intended) from the beginning and doesn't let go until the last page. The love scenes are hot enough to give a vampire a sunburn and the fight scenes will have you cheering for the good guys."

—*Really Bad Barb Reviews*

Angela Knight
The Forever Kiss

THE FOREVER KISS

Red Sage Publishing, Inc.
P.O. Box 4844
Seminole, FL 33775
727-391-3847
www.redsagepub.com

ISBN 0-9648942-3-8

Printed in the U.S.A.

Layout and book typesetting by:

Quill & Mouse Studios, Inc.
2165 Sunnydale Boulevard, Suite E
Clearwater, FL 33765
www.quillandmouse.com

Forword

I would like to dedicate this book, my first, to the many people who made it possible.

My publisher and friend, Alexandria Kendall, and my editor, Claire, who worked so hard to help me make it the best it could be.

To all of those who wrote asking when it was going to be published. I hope you find it worth the wait.

To the wonderful S.P.s of my Yahoo! e-loop, who waited for it for two years, if not with patience, at least with humor and encouragement.

To Diane Whiteside, my critique partner, who read each and every draft and made great suggestions about improving it.

To my sister, Angela Patterson, who gave me critiques and encouragement on everything I wrote long before I ever had a single word published.

To my parents, Paul and Gayle Lee, who believed in me when I was a nine-year-old writing my first opus, "The Mouse Who Went to the Moon," published in pencil.

And most of all, to my own hero, Michael, and to my son, Anthony, future author, who provided me with inspiration and love.

Chapter One

"I need you tonight." His voice emerged from the darkness, a low male rumble of heat and hunger. "Will you give yourself to me?"

Valerie Chase sat up in her tumbled bed. The cowboy stood just outside the open French doors, watching her from the balcony as moonlight spilled around him. The brim of his white Stetson shadowed his face. It always had. She'd never seen his features clearly, not in all the years she'd dreamed of him.

His white cotton shirt stretched over broad shoulders and tucked into the worn jeans that hugged his long, muscled legs. Moonlight glinted on the star of a Texas Ranger pinned to his leather vest. He wore two gun belts crossed over lean hips, the holstered Colt revolvers forming a seductive frame for the thick, impressive ridge of his erection.

It was the way he'd always looked in her dreams, her cowboy fantasy, her dream lover. Her hero.

"Come in," she said softly, and felt her nipples tighten.

He started toward her with that long, pacing panther stride of his. As he moved, his clothes melted away, revealing the hungry jut of his cock.

Her mouth went dry. Her sleep shirt vanished. She wasn't sure which of them had made it disappear.

Then his hands were on her, warm and long-fingered and skilled as he took her mouth in a deep, famished kiss flavored with desperation. Her own hands found brawn and heat as he slid onto the bed, his weight pressing her deliciously into the mattress.

"I couldn't stay away," he whispered, his voice hoarse.

She gave him a wicked smile. “Good.”

He laughed, the sound midway between a chuckle and a groan of hunger. “Vixen.” As if starved, he bent his head to sample her lips, the angle of her jaw, the curve of her collar bone, stringing a line of hard kisses and gentle bites along her skin. Fire poured through her veins to pool low in her belly.

“God, I missed you.” Closing her eyes, she fisted her hands in his short, silky hair, not even noticing when she knocked off his Stetson.

“Not as much as I missed you.” He lifted his head to look at her. Even without the shadowing hat, she couldn’t see him clearly, though she could feel the love and the need in him. “There’s nothing I wouldn’t do for you. Nothing.” His low voice vibrated with a fierce determination that made her frown.

“What’s wrong, Cowboy?” She caught his face between her hands. “What aren’t you telling me?”

“Nothing, darlin’.” She could hear the strained smile in his voice. “I’m just a dream, remember? I’m not even real.”

Before she could protest, he dropped his head to her breasts. His tongue flicked the stiff points as his teeth scraped delicate flesh.

“You sure don’t feel like a dream,” she moaned, dropping her head back on the pillow as lush, glittering pleasure built beneath her skin. Her legs fell bonelessly apart. “Then again, maybe you do.”

He stroked down her thigh to find her sex. “Mmmmm,” he purred. “Don’t wake up.” Long fingers slipped inside in one possessive thrust. “At least, not yet.”

Her eyes slid closed. Instinctively, she dug her fingers into his powerful shoulders, seeking an anchor against the pleasure that swamped her with each caress and kiss. “Are you sure…” She sucked in a gasp. “…sure this isn’t real?”

“It’s as real as we’re going to get.” He sounded bitter. Before she could ask why, he buried his head between her thighs. She cried out in shocked delight as his wet tongue stroked her clit, teeth gently nibbling as he reached for her nipples to tease and pinch.

Relentlessly, he devoured the tender folds until she felt an orgasm building like a cresting wave. She pumped her hips, trying to grind the climax into breaking, but it hung suspended just out of reach.

Then he stabbed two fingers into her, flicked a skilled thumb over her clit, and brought her crashing home. She screamed.

As if that was the signal he'd been waiting for, he tore himself away from her, sat up between her thighs, and took her knees in both big hands. Dazed, Val looked up at him. His cock stood high and hard as he spread her wide. He released one knee just long enough to aim himself. She felt the silken head brush swollen, creamy lips. He angled his hips and drove into her in one breathtaking thrust.

"Oh, God!" she gasped, her fingers fisting in the sheets as he began to shaft her hard.

"Come for me again," he growled. "I want to watch you."

As he bucked against her, every nerve in her body seemed to detonate. Convulsing, Val screamed the only name she knew for him. "Cowboy! I love you!"

"I. Love. You." Jolting her hard with his last thrusts, he threw back his head in a guttural roar. Still shuddering, she looked up, eager to watch his raw male pleasure as he climaxed.

Instead, her deliciously erotic dream became a nightmare.

As Val stared, stunned, the canine teeth in his open mouth grew longer, sharper. She froze, ice washing away the heat.

When he lowered his head to look at her, his eyes glowed red over menacing fangs.

"Cowboy?" Her voice shook. A scream of betrayal and disbelief built in her throat.

He didn't answer. Still buried deep inside her, he lowered his head….

Val catapulted off the bed expecting to feel Cowboy's fangs tear into her skin. Her ears still rang with the echo of her own screams. Racing for the bedroom door, she threw it open and flew out into the hall.

Hands clamped around her shoulders. She yelped and swung a wild fist.

"Hey, watch it!"

The cry yanked Val from the dream's grip. Her eyes focused to find Beth staring at her, dark hair tumbling around her shoulders, fright and annoyance mingling on her young face. "You're asleep, dammit," her sister said, giving her captured shoulders a little shake. "Wake up!"

A dream. It had been a dream. "Cowboy was going to bite me."

Beth rolled her eyes like the teenager she was. "So what else is new? And since when do you mind?"

Val sagged against the hallway wall as her terror drained away, leaving behind weak knees and a brassy taste in her mouth. "He was a vampire."

"Oh, babe." Beth reached out to scoop a lock of hair out of Val's eyes. "You must be freaked, if you're seeing Cowboy as monster material. Come on, sweetie — let's fix some chocolate. I think we need to talk."

Cade McKinnon jolted awake, frustrated fists gripping the sheets. The head of his erection brushed his flat belly, and his fangs ached. The room would have appeared pitch black to human eyes, but his vampire vision easily made out the empty elegance of Ridgemont's mansion, the polished mahogany and expensive crystal.

Valerie was gone. Not that she'd ever been there to begin with.

And he'd terrified her, dammit. Their last time together shouldn't have ended in fear, but he'd lost control of both the Hunger and the dream.

Reaching for Valerie's mind without feeding first had been a mistake, but he'd had to see her, touch her, one final time. Knowing he'd never have another chance, he'd wanted to capture as much of her as he could. Silken skin, long muscled legs, velvet pink nipples, the dizzying musk of her scent, the hot, salty feast between her thighs.

With a groan of frustrated hunger, Cade rolled onto his belly. Once, twice, again, he ground his hips into the tangled linen sheets, imagining her tight and slick around him. Throwing back his head, he came with a growl, his fingers clamping the soft fabric of the pillow.

Heart bounding, he collapsed, the taste of bitterness and loss in his mouth. Finally he shook off the depression and rolled out of bed.

It was time to get ready for the last night of his life.

"He doesn't even exist," Val said, hands still shaking faintly as she sliced slivers from a chocolate bar into a saucepan of milk. She and Beth stood in the apartment's wonderfully normal kitchen with its cheery strawberry wallpaper and cream counter tops. Unfortunately, her vibrating instincts kept insisting Cowboy was somewhere just out of sight, all sex and fangs and menace. She breathed in, trying to settle her jangling nerves with the scent of chocolate and simmering milk. "He's just the world's longest running dream. Hell, I lost my job this week —I have real stuff to be upset about. Why do I feel so damn betrayed?"

"Well, for one thing, your own personal knight in shining armor is not supposed to turn on you." Beth perched on the counter next to the stove, swinging her tanned legs as she watched the cocoa preparations. "Anyway, I'll bet you had the nightmare because of the job."

"Maybe." Stirring the chocolate, Val studied her sister. Beth was a tall girl, barely eighteen, her elfin face dominated by perceptive brown eyes. A loose red shirt skimmed down her rangy, athletic body to the tops of her thighs. Like almost everything else she owned, the shirt was smudged with oil paint—peaches, browns, ochers, blues. Matching smears marked her fingers and the bridge of her slim nose. "Working late again?" Val asked. "You getting enough sleep?"

Beth rolled her eyes. "Yes, Mother, I'm getting enough sleep. I've just got to finish Tommy Wilson's portrait. I promised Mr. Wilson I'd have it by Mother's Day, and I'm close to deadline."

"Well, don't push too hard while I'm gone." Val bit her lip, worrying once again whether she was doing the right thing in leaving Beth at home while she went to New York. Taping the interviews for Edward Ridgemont's memoirs would take a good three weeks. That was a long time to leave the kid alone.

Still, Beth was eighteen. She'd be going off to college soon. Too, Val had never met her new employer. Ridgemont looked clean on paper, but she wanted to get to know him before exposing Beth to his influence.

Frowning, Val dug her fingers into the muscles she could feel contracting into knots in the base of her neck. She'd been making decisions about her sister's welfare since their grandmother died seven years ago, but the process hadn't grown any easier. Not that Grandma had been all that involved with Beth's upbringing even before she died. The nearest bottle had always held far more fascination for her than her murdered son's children.

"Have Cowboy dreams ever gone bad before?" Beth asked.

She lifted a brow. "You changing the subject?"

"Yes. I'm not going to New York, Val. I've got that portrait and a portfolio to finish. So—Cowboy?"

"No." She looked down into the melting chocolate slivers swirling around her spoon. "God knows I've had plenty of nightmares about vampires, but he's always been the one saving me in them."

According to a slew of child psychologists, Val had created Cowboy to protect her from her parents' murderers—the killers who became fanged monsters in night terrors she'd been having since age twelve. Yet tonight he'd tried to feed on her himself. She wondered what buzzwords the shrinks would have used for that little twist.

Logically, Val knew there was no such things as vampires, any more than Cowboy himself existed. But logic didn't keep her hands from shaking at the thought of those sharp white teeth. "He. Is. Not. Real," she gritted, more to herself than her sister.

"Maybe not, but you've had him so long, he might as well be." Beth propped her chin on her fist and smiled slightly. "When I was little, I thought he *was* real, just from listening to you talk about those dreams."

"You weren't alone. I believed in him half the time myself." Sometimes she still did. Especially when she was impaled on that massive cock. Which definitely wasn't a thought she had any intention of sharing.

"I was so jealous." Beth shook her head. "I wanted Cowboy to visit my dreams too."

"You wouldn't have wanted him there tonight." Remembering the seductive tenderness of those big hands, she suppressed a feline smile. *Well, maybe at the beginning....*

Her sister's eyes narrowed. "Yeah, right. I see you fighting that grin."

"Let's just say his role in my dreams has..." The smile broke free, "...expanded over the years."

"A good eight inches, I'll bet."

"Beth!" She tried to look shocked, but a giggle spoiled the effect.

The guess was pretty damn close.

Cade stood with his face turned into the shower's hot, stinging spray. He couldn't seem to stop thinking about Valerie.

Her beauty dazzled him, of course—the delicate elegance of her features, the wild, curling Gypsy tumble of her red hair, the arousal shimmering in those gray eyes. Every time her full lips parted, carnal images spun through his mind.

But it wasn't her looks that had wrapped around his mind and held him fast. He'd known too many beautiful women over his long life for that. Of course, none of them had possessed Valerie's power—the psychic talent she didn't even realize she had, though he'd felt its strength even when she was a child. Still, Cade had known the dark side of such abilities too long to find them seductive.

No, it was the woman herself that made him willing to die to protect her. Her intelligence, her wit, her devotion to her sister. The courage she'd shown even as a twelve-year-old facing her parents' murderers. Courage that hadn't faltered even when she'd realized how close Cade was to killing her himself.

He turned to let the hot water blast his shoulders, remembering the horrific night seventeen years before when his desperate refusal to kill a child had collided with Val's desperate need to survive. For just an instant, their minds had…fused.

Which was impossible. Neither of them should have been able to penetrate the other's mental shields. Yet they had, and it saved them both. Without that connection, Cade doubted he could have found the strength to free her and her sister, then distract the killers until both children could escape.

Since then, Cade and Valerie had shared a link, if only in their dreams. When she'd begun having nightmares about the murders, her terror had reached out to him. He'd become Cowboy, slaying her dream vampires—including himself—and providing her with the male influence the death of her father had stripped away.

The dreams had stopped in her mid-teens. He'd thought, hoped, he'd never see her again, since every contact between them had the potential to draw his enemy's attention. She didn't need the risk.

But at twenty-two, she'd reached for Cade again. Her grandmother's death had left her to raise eleven-year-old Beth alone, and she'd wanted comfort. When she came into his dreams to get it, Cade discovered that the courageous, wounded child he'd known had grown into a sensual woman he couldn't resist.

Now, seven years later, there was something else she needed even more. Edward Ridgemont had reentered her life, and if he wasn't stopped, he'd destroy her. But if Cade played his hand well, she'd never even realize how close she'd come to death.

He shut off the water with a twist of his wrist and opened the shower door.

The ghost child waited for him, floating in the steam from his shower and the wafting scent of the peppermint candy she'd loved in life. Two enormous bows framed her head, binding her curling black hair into pigtails. The toes of her kid slippers floated six inches above the tile floor, and her white silk dress belled around thin, stocking-clad calves.

The gown had once been their mother's, cut down for Abigail after she'd outgrown all her own. When Cole had buried her in it in 1865, the dress had hung on a body wasted with yellow fever.

Damn you, Cade McKinnon. Abigail's thoughts drove into his mind, carried on a psychic wave of mingled jealousy and fear. Her ghostly body still looked like the thirteen-year-old she'd been, but her mind had long since left childhood behind. ***Valerie Chase is not worth dying for.***

Cade smiled slightly. "Oh yes, she is."

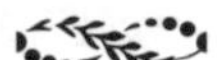

"I wish you wouldn't look like that," Beth said.

Resting her head on the couch's back, one hand steadying a mug of cocoa on her knee, Val opened one eye. "Like what?"

"So damn defeated." Beth sat curled next to her, legs drawn up, her face worried. She reminded Val of a brooding cat. "You don't do defeated. No matter how bad things get, you always come out slugging."

Val took a sip of the cocoa. "It's been a rough week."

Beth studied her with those dark, knowing eyes. The kid was entirely too damn smart for eighteen. "Did that conversation with Kim trigger this?"

"Didn't I ever teach you not to eavesdrop?"

"Yeah. Didn't take. Come on, what did Kim say?"

"She hung up on me." Leaning forward, Val put the mug down on the glass coffee table and ran a frustrated hand through her hair. The combination of the Cowboy dream and the week's events had left her wrung out and battered. "What the hell is going on? Damn it, I have a right to know why I was fired from a job I've held for ten years. What do they think I did?"

"And why are they keeping it such a deep, dark secret?" Beth wrapped paint-smeared fists in the hem of her long T-shirt and pulled it down as she drew her legs up under it. A frown scored the skin between her dark brows. "This whole thing is weird."

"Tell me about it." Bracing her elbows on her knees, Val fixed brooding eyes across the room on the painting of a rearing stallion Beth had done in the tenth grade. "One day I'm Gerry Price's fair-haired girl, the reporter who can do no wrong. The next, I walk into the office and everybody's looking at me like I French fried a puppy. Gerry fires me on the spot without telling me one damn thing other than I somehow betrayed the paper, journalism, and basic human decency. Yet nobody—not Gerry, not Kim, not even the guy who empties the trash—will tell me what the hell I'm supposed to have done. And now even Cowboy's sprouting fangs." Unable to sit still any longer, she stood and began to pace.

Beth watched her long, agitated strides. "I don't understand it either. You're good. Everybody knows it. And everybody knows you wouldn't do anything unethical."

Val stopped her pacing at the entertainment center to brace both arms against its oak cabinet. Sightlessly, she stared at one of Beth's clay figures, this one a dancing nymph. "You and that job were my whole life. How could they do this to me?"

"It's going to work out, Val. You've already got a new job. You'll be fine."

"Yeah, right. Writing some rich guy's memoirs. I'm a journalist, dammit, not a ghostwriter. I don't even know Ridgemont. Why did he pick me? I've never even written a book before."

Beth was silent a little too long.

Val glanced over her shoulder, then turned to stare. "Oh, I know that look. What are you thinking?"

"I hate to mention this under the circumstances," Beth said finally, "but don't you think there's something a little...off about that?"

"About what?" Her sister might be young, but over the years Val had discovered the kid's instincts were uncanny.

"I mean, you lose your job, and the very next day some rich guy calls up out of the blue and offers you big bucks for his memoirs—when you've never ghostwritten a word in your life. It's way too pat."

"So you think, what? Edward Ridgemont got me fired, and now he's offering me a job to lure me up to New York? Sounds like a romance novel." Val walked over to pick up her mug, summoning a smile as she lifted it to her lips. "Although if he turns out to be some brooding, handsome, sexually insatiable millionaire, I guess I'll just have to sacrifice myself for your well-being...."

"God, I hope not."

She lowered the mug untasted. "That sounded awfully fervent."

Beth bit her lip.

"Out with it."

"I got a call."

"What kind of call?" Something in her sister's tone made the hair rise on the back of her neck. "When?"

"Right after you went to bed. He asked to speak to you, and I told him you were asleep."

"Who was it?

Beth shrugged. "I don't know. I didn't recognize the voice. He said…I should try to convince you not to go to New York. That Ridgemont wasn't what he seemed."

Val thumped the mug back down on the coffee table. "Boy, somebody really is out to get me. First chance at a decent job I get, and he's trying to ruin that, too."

"What if he's right? Val, you don't know this Ridgemont. What if he's not what he seems?"

"I'm a reporter, dammit," she said, and began to pace again, her steps quick with simmering fury. "I check people out for a living. Ridgemont is clean. He's been a New York businessman for more than a decade, and he's got more money than God. There isn't even a whiff of rumor attached to his name."

"But…."

Val whirled on her. "I don't have a choice, Beth! You'll be starting the fall semester in a couple of months. Without that job, I can't pay your tuition."

"So?" Beth leaned forward and braced her hands on her knees, her young face taking on a determined scowl. "Look, I want to go to the art institute, but not bad enough for you to get mixed up with a crook."

"You're going to college, dammit!" She clenched her fists until her fingers went white. "You have talent, and you're going to get the training to make the best use of it you can. I don't care how many jerks try to scare me off, and I don't care what axe they have to grind. I'm not failing you."

There's got to be another way.

"There isn't." Staring into the mirror, Cade ran a razor over his jaw. Though he could see his own reflection, he couldn't see Abigail's as she floated behind him; unlike him, she was pure spirit. He'd always been amused by the legends that insisted vampires had no reflection. God knew there was nothing spiritual about them. "I even called. Val was asleep, so I tried to put the fear of God in Beth. Unfortunately, Val's not going to listen to her. She needs that job too much." Tilting his head, he stroked the razor down his cheekbone. "Which means Ridgemont has to be dead before she flies in tomorrow night."

So get to her first. If you made her a vampire, she'd be able to amplify your power enough to beat Ridgemont.

"Maybe." Cade ran the razor under the faucet's stream, washing away foam and the remnants of his beard shadow. "Or maybe he'd hack off my head and kill you both."

He'd be a little late in my case, considering I died a hundred and thirty-eight years ago.

He gave the ghost an annoyed look over his shoulder. "You know what I mean. And you know what he can do."

I'm willing to take the chance. Her little face hardened.

"I'm not." He turned back to the mirror and studied his own grim features. "Risking my life is one thing. Risking your soul is something else."

You're not risking your life, Cade. You're throwing it away.

"I can't think of a better cause."

If you Changed her....

"But I won't, and I'm going to make damn sure nobody else does either. We've done enough to that girl as it is." He took a towel off the black marble rack and wiped away the last traces of shaving cream as he turned toward the ghost.

She wore the same determined expression he remembered from his boyhood. Even at thirteen, Abigail could've taught stubborn to a field mule. ***The only thing you did was save her life. It was Ridgemont and Hirsch who did the killing. And they'd have killed her, too, if you hadn't gotten her out of there. The way I see it, she owes you.***

Cade shook his head as he walked past her into the bedroom. "If she does, I'm not collecting. She hates vampires, and I'm damned if I'm going to make her one. I want her to have a normal life. Kids. A husband." Never mind the fist that clutched his heart at the thought of Valerie with another man.

Abigail floated after him. ***Do you really think she'd want Cowboy to die for her?***

Striding to the closet, Cade pulled out one of the chauffeur's uniforms that hung in neat rows. He tossed it on his bed, then pulled out the starched white shirt that went with it. "Look, I know you don't like this, but I don't have a choice. Ridgemont's got to die, and since he has seven hundred years on me, there aren't a lot of ways I can kill him."

But….

"I'm sick of this, Abigail!" he exploded, slinging the hanger across the room. "I was that bastard's slave for one hundred and twenty years. I've finally broken his control, but I can't leave because he'd track me down, kill me, and destroy you. And God knows what he'd do to Valerie." Quickly, angrily, he jerked on his shirt. "Tonight he dies — even if I go with him."

Chapter Two

Cade stepped out into the mansion's opulent hallway and closed the door behind him. Thick plush carpet sank under his booted feet as he put on his chauffeur's cap and straightened his gray tunic with a jerk. Before he could turn, someone bumped him hard from behind.

Surprised, he pivoted just as a woman stumbled past. He glimpsed a white profile, dazed eyes, and a thin trickle of blood flowing from twin punctures in her throat. She faltered, sagged against the carved wainscoting, then pulled herself upright and started down the sweeping staircase that led to the mansion's lower level.

Dropping his eyes to watch her descend, Cade stiffened. Just below the hem of her short skirt, long red welts striped her shapely legs. She'd been beaten across the thighs with a riding crop. And he knew damn well who'd done it.

With a growl of fury, he looked up just as Gerhard Hirsch stepped out of his own suite across the hall.

Lifting an elegant hand, Hirsch smoothed the blond waves of his hair. There was a smear of blood at the corner of the German's wide mouth, and his gray eyes glittered with power from the aftermath of his feeding. Shooting the cuffs of his elegant gray suit, he started down the hall after the woman he'd abused. Even after sixty years, Hirsch still had the Master Race swagger of the Gestapo officer he'd been when Ridgemont Changed him.

Cade took one long stride to meet him and slammed his fist right into that perfect chin. The impact sent the German stumbling backward with a startled yelp. Cade snarled and followed, fists bunched.

Hirsch caught himself against the wall and threw up a forearm to protect his face. "What the hell is wrong with you?" he demanded, wiping blood from his split lip.

"I'm sick of watching you abuse every woman with the bad luck to cross your path." Rage lengthened Cade's corner teeth to fangs. He pushed closer as Hirsch straightened hastily and retreated a wary step. "How long has it been since I showed you what I can do with a bullwhip, Gerhard? Maybe a cut for every stripe you just gave that girl...."

Unease flickered in the German's eyes before he drew his muscled body to its full six-foot-six-inch height. "Try it, McKinnon," he spat. "It won't be that easy this time. I'm not a fledgling anymore."

"Maybe not, but you're not free either." Cade gave him a taunting smile. "I am."

Hirsch stiffened. He still lived in Ridgemont's thrall, unable to disobey any mental command his vampire sire gave him. "My freedom will come."

"You'll lick Ridgemont's boots for another century. Maybe two."

A low laugh rumbled from the other end of the hallway. Cade's muscles coiled in involuntary reaction to a sound he'd associated with suffering for more than a century.

"It's been sixty years, boys. Isn't it time you learned to get along?" Ridgemont strolled toward them. His power beat against Cade's psychic shields with an evil so intense it seemed to squirm. "I keep expecting to come in and find one of you has killed the other." He paused an artistic beat and smiled. "At least wait until I'm around to watch."

Ridgemont was four inches shorter than Cade, but his wool Armani suit was generously cut to accommodate the bull shoulders he'd built swinging a broadsword with Richard the Lionheart. His blunt, scarred face looked no more than thirty-five, but something in those eyes was older than the Eden snake.

He gave Cade a slow smile. "I'll be going out tonight. A…date with Elle. You will drive, of course, but perhaps you'd care to join us for the festivities?"

Cade remembered the last time he'd been forced to participate in one of the ancient's hunts. "Sorry, I don't find screams arousing."

"It's not the screams," Hirsch said. "It's the shamed moans afterward." His grin gleamed white and repellent against his sharply handsome face. "Enough power to gorge on."

"Some of us can get a reaction from a woman without resorting to torture," Cade told him. "Try making one of them come once in a while—if you can."

Hirsch's lips drew back from his teeth, but before he could retort, Ridgemont cut him off. "Ah, but wait until Valerie arrives. Now, that one will be truly delicious," he said, in that velvet rumble that made Cade's skin crawl. "You have no idea what it's like to take a woman who is one of us, my spawn. The pleasure…no mortal woman can match it. And the Change itself—that first, deep feeding, so rich with the taste of terror. Then the final voluptuous surrender as you force her mind…." The ancient sighed like a gourmet contemplating some particularly rare French delicacy. "It's a pity so few can survive the transformation. I've had only a handful of vampire lovers in eight hundred years."

"Too bad you couldn't resist the impulse to kill them all," Cade said, his face expressionless.

Ridgemont shrugged. "I have a low tolerance for female defiance. Still, Valerie should last at least a century. And she'll give me such power…Perhaps enough to bring even you to heel."

Cade didn't flinch; it was an empty threat. Even if his plan failed, the ancient would kill him for making the attempt.

His sire tilted his head, contemplating him in a way that made his muscles tense. "It's fortunate you resisted the urge to kill her, all those years ago."

It damn well hadn't been an urge. It had been a psychic compulsion Ridgemont himself had planted after starving Cade for two weeks. Then the ancient had cut Valerie until the smell of flowing blood had ripped away what little sanity he'd had left. "Yeah," Cade gritted. "Luckily, I'm stronger than you expected."

"Indeed," Ridgemont said, with a slight smile. "I must admit, I was impressed that you managed to resist the temptation. But I've always wondered, McKinnon…" He dropped his voice to a suggestive purr, "…just how close did you come to ripping out that soft little throat?"

Cade managed not to flinch.

"You look a little white around the lips, gunslinger," the ancient observed in the cool, cultured voice that had fooled so many into thinking he was civilized. He took a step closer until the lapels of his suit jacket brushed the front of Cade's chauffeur's uniform. "I've always wondered what would have happened if you'd lost that particular battle." One corner of his mouth kicked up in a cruel smile. "I suspect killing that child would have snapped you like a bird's wing. Then I could have made you do…anything."

"No." Cade stared coldly into his sire's eyes. "Because I'd have killed you for it."

"You wouldn't have lasted five minutes." Ridgemont grinned darkly. "But I'm sure you would have made it a very interesting five minutes."

He let his own cruel smile curl his mouth. "Maybe I'd have made it a little too interesting."

"Don't overestimate yourself, gunslinger." The ancient's power slammed against his mental shields like a fist. "You wouldn't be the first of my spawn I've killed for forgetting his place."

Cade stared into those reptilian eyes, refusing to yield to the brutal psychic power his enemy had built over most of a millennium. There was a certain cold pleasure in his ability to resist. Even five years ago, Ridgemont could have driven him to his knees.

No more. He was free now. It had taken him decades of struggle, but he was no longer a slave. The need boiled in him to strike out, to watch the bastard's blood fly under his fist, to get some of his own back for one hundred and twenty years of abuse. He fought the impulse down. What he had planned wasn't as satisfying, but it would have to do.

Ridgemont's cold eyes narrowed. "You should watch that stiff neck, gunslinger. I'd hate to have to break it for you." Yet oddly, there was a hint of something in his gaze that was less frustrated than…pleased? He turned away abruptly and headed for the stairs. "Come. I'm hungry, and my lovely meal is waiting."

This is it. Cade felt his muscles coil in anticipation. Involuntarily, his mind began a countdown of the last seconds of his life.

"Speaking of meals," Ridgemont said as the three of them descended the staircase to the sprawling ballroom, "you'll need to pick Valerie up tomorrow at La Guardia. She'll be on the midnight flight."

"Unless those Kith instincts warn her she's walking into a trap."

The ancient laughed, a short, nasty boom of sound. "If they do, she'll ignore them. I'm offering her a great deal of money to ghostwrite my memoirs. She'd be a fool to turn me down." He flashed his fangs. "Particularly after losing her job."

As Ridgemont, of course, had personally arranged. Last week the ancient had flown to Atlanta for a meeting with Valerie's publisher, supposedly to discuss investing in the newspaper. Instead, he'd psychically altered the man's memories. Now the entire staff of *The Atlanta Daily Independent* believed their star reporter had been caught making up a story. He'd also ordered that none of them tell her anything about it, ensuring she'd be unable to mount a defense against the trumped-up charges.

And since she'd never met her mysterious "benefactor," Val had no idea he was the same man who'd orchestrated her parents' murder seventeen years before. Cade meant to make sure she'd never find out.

The three vampires strode through Ridgemont's silent mansion. It was almost midnight; the servants and assistants who attended the ancient's business had gone home. To keep his heartbeat from betraying him to his sire's exceptional hearing, Cade concentrated on the decor—the original Rembrandt hanging on one wall, the Ming vase precisely positioned on the Chinese Chippendale table. All very beautiful, but he doubted the ancient noticed. Ridgemont was more interested in making a lavish display than anything else.

In the foyer, Cade strode ahead, boots clicking on the marble floor. He opened the door for his enemies with mocking subservience. They swept past him into the fragrant evening air. He locked up and followed them down the mansion's front steps to the limousine he'd left parked at the curb.

Ridgemont stopped beside the car and looked back at him. Knowing when he was being put in his place, Cade reached out and opened the limo's rear door, touching the bill of his chauffeur's cap in a taunting salute. Ignoring the gesture, the ancient ducked into the car.

Hirsch was already in the front passenger seat as Cade slid behind the wheel.

Looking into the rearview mirror, Cade met Ridgemont's cold gaze through the back seat partition. His heart pounded in long, slow beats. Time slowed to a crawl. He slid the key into the ignition.

But before he could turn it, the car was flooded with the sweet bite of peppermint. Abigail! She was trying to....

No! Ridgemont's telepathic command blasted through the car. *Hirsch! DON'T LET HIM START THE CAR!*

The German lunged forward as Cade started to twist the key. He let go of it just long enough to slam an elbow into Hirsch's face. His foe still managed to shatter the ignition housing with a blow of one big fist.

Oh, hell. Cade grabbed Hirsch by the collar and heaved him headfirst into the windshield. Safety glass exploded, showering them all with glittering fragments. Ignoring the German's curses, he flung open the door and lunged out to meet Ridgemont, who'd thrown himself from the limousine.

Cade ducked the ancient's first roundhouse and buried a fist in Ridgemont's belly with all his supernatural strength. The vampire retaliated with a backhand blow that sent stars shooting through his skull. "What did you do to the car, gunslinger?" Ridgemont snarled. "I saw my death when you put your hand on that key."

"A half pound of C-4 wired to the ignition." Cade spat blood into the grass and gave him a vicious grin, mentally cursing Abigail. Ridgemont wasn't precognitive; she must have sent the vision to him. "The cops wouldn't have found anything but a crater."

The ancient's blue eyes widened. "And you would have turned the switch." He coiled into a crouch. The right sleeves of both his suit and shirt had ripped, revealing thick muscle bunching underneath. "You'd have blown us all to hell."

"Oh, yeah," he snarled back as they began to circle. "Best place for us."

Ridgemont's fist shot toward his face. Cade threw up a forearm block, deflecting it the inch that saved his skull. Even the glancing blow was like being hit by a coal train. He went flying, tucking into a roll as he hit the ground. His momentum tumbled him a dozen yards before he got his feet under him again. Reeling upright, he shook his head to clear it. His ears were ringing. God, that bastard could punch.

When he looked up, Cade saw Hirsch charging toward him, blood streaming from the dozen cuts marring his too-handsome face. Ridgemont closed on him from the other direction, his speed inhuman. Cade took a deep breath and stepped to meet them both.

He blocked the first few punches and got in some of his own, but then Ridgemont landed a right to the jaw that damn near finished him. As he shook off a wave of blackness, Hirsch slammed his fist into his ribs. Something cracked and flared into agony. He ignored it, ramming a kick into Ridgemont's thigh. The vampire went down.

Before Cade could follow up, Hirsch was there, keeping him so busy with a flurry of punches, Ridgemont had time to get to his feet and wade in again.

Every time Cade blocked one of his opponents' blows, the other would streak a fist or a foot through his guard. He fought on, ignoring the impacts even as his body became one blazing mass of pain and blood slicked his skin from a dozen cuts.

Cade was going to die, and he knew it. He could take Hirsch, but he couldn't take Ridgemont. He'd lost too many fights with his sire to have any doubts on that score. And he certainly had no chance against them both. They'd kill him and go right on terrorizing anybody they chose. Including Valerie, who'd suffer for a hundred years—if Ridgemont let her live that long.

Snarling, Cade drove a fist into the ancient's smirking face. He had time for an instant's victory before his head detonated with a red starburst of pain as Hirsch's knuckles plowed into it. Staggering back, he blinked away blood.

Both vampires were grinning now, hunger hot in their eyes. They'd feed on him once they got him down. Then somebody would get a sword and hack off his head or cut out his heart, and he'd be finished.

He took a deep breath, smelling the stink of blood and sweat—and the cool, sweet scent of peppermint.

From the corner of one rapidly swelling eye, Cade glimpsed Abigail hovering nearby, watching the fight with panic on her translucent face. Realizing he'd spotted her, she pointed urgently toward the fence circling Ridgemont's property a hundred yards away. ***Run, Cade!***

I'm sick of running, he told her, mind to mind. *I'm done with this.*

If you die, who'll save Valerie?

Cade ducked a punch and swore under his breath. He wanted it over. He was sick of this game he could never win with an opponent he could never defeat. But dammit, Abigail was right. He couldn't allow Ridgemont to take Val.

Whirling, Cade sprinted toward the fence. It was fifteen feet tall and topped with foot-long spikes, but he gathered himself and leaped. Clearing it with a foot to spare, he hit the ground running. Blood rolled down his face and broken bones shifted and burned in his chest, but he didn't stop.

"Coward!" Hirsch started to leap after him.

"Let him go," Ridgemont growled, and the German felt his muscles freeze in the grip of his sire's will.

Unable to move, Hirsch rolled his eyes to stare at the ancient, so furious he forgot himself. "Are you mad? He almost killed us!"

Ridgemont grinned, licking blood from his split lip. "He did, didn't he?"

Suddenly freed, Hirsch stumbled forward, then regained his footing to whirl on his master. "Do you want to die?"

The ancient stretched his thickly muscled body and winced, putting a hand to his ribs. "I want a good fight. Terrorizing sheep holds no challenge." He sucked in a breath at a particularly nasty twinge. "Jesu, the gunslinger has a punch like a destrier's kick." Shaking his head, he looked over at Hirsch. "I'll kill him in my own time, Gerhard, but meanwhile he'll give me all the challenge I could want."

Three blocks from the mansion, Cade stumbled to a halt and reached out his mind, searching for the nearest taxi and drawing the driver to him.

When it arrived, the man almost drove by anyway, forcing Cade to send out another compulsion. Evidently his battered face and torn uniform didn't exactly fill the cabby with confidence.

The car rolled reluctantly to a stop. He dragged open the door and collapsed across the back seat, gasping as cracked ribs shot pain through his side. The cabdriver peered at him in the rearview mirror and asked in thickly accented English, "Hospital?"

"God, no. I'll heal—though I wouldn't turn down a little morphine in the meantime." Sucking in a breath at a particularly nasty twinge, he gritted out the Queens address of his current safe house.

By the time he got out of the cab, Cade's head was spinning. It took an effort to force his swollen, bloody fingers to pick the proper bills out of his wallet to pay the cabby. As he accepted them, the driver looked into his bruise-swollen face and winced. Glancing into the man's mind, Cade saw his own face and winced back. God, the bastards had outdone themselves this time.

Bloodied and exhausted, he turned to limp toward the aging two-story Victorian, noting that the garage doors were still down. With luck, nobody had made off with the Lexus while he was gone; he'd hate to have to acquire another car before the trip to the airport.

Climbing the three steps to the porch, Cade had to grit his teeth against the kettledrum throb in his head. He suspected he had a concussion to go with the busted ribs. That hunch was confirmed when it took him endless minutes of dizzy fumbling to get the door unlocked, punch the entry code into the burglar alarm, then lock the door and rearm the alarm. It was necessary, though. No matter how deep his healing sleep, if Ridgemont came to call, the alarm should jolt him awake in time to protect himself.

He hoped.

Limping for the stairs, Cade wrapped a bloody hand around the banister and began dragging himself toward the second floor bedroom. He knew he'd be lucky to make it there before he collapsed in his tracks.

He had never actually lived in the house, had rarely even spent the night. It was nothing more than his base of operations, a place to keep his weapons and money and organize his various campaigns. He slept, when he slept at all, at Ridgemont's mansion. He preferred having his enemies around him when he bedded down. At least that way he knew where they were.

Like the rest of the house, the bedroom was Spartan and clean, furnished with a double bed, a ladder-back cane chair, and a bureau. None of the furniture matched, but then, decorating hadn't exactly been a priority when he'd set up the safe house.

Wanting only to slip between the covers and heal for twelve hours straight, Cade staggered to the bed. A big gym bag was in his way, sitting in the middle of the bedspread. He picked it up and dumped it in the floor.

But as the bag thumped to the worn carpeting, an instinct for self-preservation worked its way through his haze of pain and exhaustion. Groaning, Cade gingerly lowered himself to one knee so he could unzip the bag and pull a sawed-off shotgun out of its thick nest of money.

Buffy the Vampire Slayer notwithstanding, a wooden stake wouldn't kill a vampire. It took decapitation or cutting out the heart, and the twelve-gauge could do either with one double-barreled blast. Not as cleanly as a sword, perhaps, but easier to use coming out of a dead sleep.

Still, it was a damn good thing the gun was already loaded. The spinning in his head was picking up speed, and he doubted he had the coordination to get shells into the thing now.

Cade slid the weapon just far enough under the bed that he wouldn't step on it if he got up to use the john, then fell across the mattress without bothering to undress. Concentrating hard, he dragged off his boots and hauled his leaden legs into the bed. As the room revolved like a merry-go-round, he squeezed his eyes shut.

And smelled peppermint. ***Are you angry with me?***

He didn't open his eyes. "Why did you do it, Abigail? You would have been safe from him. And with me finally dead, you'd have been free to go to God."

It wasn't worth it. Not if it meant watching you die.

"I had to watch *you* die, and you suffered a hell of a lot more than I would have."

Cade, I stayed for you. How could you think I'd allow you to kill yourself?

Put like that, she had a point. She'd been risking her soul for him for more than a century. He should have known she'd do anything to keep him alive. Even betray him.

Abigail was quiet so long he'd have thought she was gone, if not for the scent of peppermint. Finally she asked, ***Do you think they'll come after you tonight?***

That was a damn good question. With a groan, Cade reached out his mind for another scan. He didn't sense anything, which meant the two vampires were still outside his range. At least Ridgemont was; Hirsch had only been immortal for sixty years, and his power barely registered to psychic senses. Which was why Ridgemont wouldn't send him alone. Cade could kick Gerhard's ass, and they all knew it.

"I think they're probably back at the mansion," he said at last, and winced as his ribs protested. "Hopefully nursing a few broken bones of their own. And dawn's too close now. They won't bother coming after me tonight."

Though sunlight didn't actually cause vampires to burst into flames, the burns it inflicted were nasty. Neither Hirsch nor Ridgemont would want to spend time out in all that ultraviolet searching for him. And they'd definitely have to search. He'd concealed his ownership of the house with the hard-learned paranoia of a man who'd been a slave too long.

Just to be on the safe side, I'll keep watch, Abigail said. The scent of peppermint faded.

Cade sighed and shifted gingerly, trying to find a comfortable position. By the next evening, his vampire metabolism would have healed his injuries, but between them and the fight, he knew he'd be left dangerously drained. He'd have to find a woman and feed quickly tomorrow night if he meant to meet Valerie's plane before Ridgemont did.

As to exactly how he'd spirit his lover from under his sire's nose…

He'd cross that bridge when he got to it.

Chapter Three

January 15, 1985

He crouched in a red haze. Hunger. Everywhere. Pain burning his gut, gnawing, biting, coiled like a dragon, snarling and twisting and devouring itself. He no longer knew how long he'd been locked away. Why he'd been locked away.

Enemies. Hate. Death watching him with red dragon eyes, eating him alive from the inside.

A sound.

He lifted his head like a wolf. Stared at the reinforced steel door pockmarked with dents. Someone at the door. He inhaled. BLOOD! Enemy! He knew that smell. His mouth flooded with saliva. Strength flooded his weakened body.

Animal cunning stirred. No! Play dead. He ducked his head and curled tighter on his side on the cold cement floor. Smelled blood on his own hands from battering the door. Managed not to bite.

Creak of the warped door being forced open. "Jesus, Cade, it stinks in here!" German accent. Enemy. "And what the fuck have you done to the door?"

Scrape of shoes on concrete. He coiled tighter, the Dragon's flame searing his belly.

"Not so pretty now, are you, you bastard?" The voice sounded smug. "Guess that'll teach you to piss off Ridgemont, you stupid...."

He exploded off the floor, slammed into the prey, took him down, forced up his head. Dove for the throat. Bit.

BLOOD! BLOOD! BLOODbloodbloodbloodblood...

Didn't feel the massive fists battering his ribs, hear the screams, too lost in the delicious sensation of hot red life in his mouth, the Dragon humming in pleasure as it gorged.

ENEMY! He knew the scent, the footsteps. He bit deep, drew frantically, ignored the rib that cracked under a desperately vicious blow from the prey's fist.

"Get him off me!" Shriek of terror.

"Let him go, gunslinger." Awful power wrapped around his mind, but the Dragon was stronger. He snarled against the prey's throat and refused to obey.

Something massive struck him a stunning blow in the side of the head. His jaws unlocked. Felt himself rising, jerked away from the life giving flow of red. No! He twisted like a cat in the Enemy's grip, drove for the bull neck. Glimpsed startled fury on Ridgemont's face.

A fist knocked him into darkness.

Something soft, vibrating, under his head. He tried to move. He was bound. He snarled and began to struggle.

Stop it, gunslinger. The black, familiar power coiled around him tighter than the thick chains on his wrists. Locked his muscles, froze him.

"He's gone mad." The German's voice. Hoarse. Hurt him. Good.

"Two weeks of starvation will do that. You're lucky he didn't rip out your throat, you idiot. I warned you."

Looking up, Cade saw the backs of his enemies' heads. Car. They were in a car. He was bound in the back seat of a car.

The Dragon stirred and coiled and began to bite at his guts. He shuddered. Locked a whimper behind his teeth.

The car stopped. Ridgemont and Hirsch got out. He heard their voices retreat. Leaving him alone with the Dragon. It coiled and snapped. Red pain rolled over his head, submerged him in the cold, burning madness.

He'd lost track of how long he floated in insanity when the car door opened. A big hand grabbed his shoulder. Flipped him over. He wanted to struggle, but the Enemy's power kept him still.

Chains clicked and fell away. The Enemy seized his collar, hauled him out of the car. "Come on, gunslinger. You don't want to miss this. If you're good, I'll even give you someone."

Some tiny, sane fragment of his mind knew he'd kill any victim he was handed. It moaned a protest, but the rest of him was too wrapped in the Dragon's coils to care. Famished, mad, he staggered up a cement walkway, half-carried by the grip on his elbow.

Through the dragon's fogging breath, he heard screams coming from a big brick colonial just ahead. His own howl built in his throat, emerged as a strangled whimper.

Bad. This was bad.

The Enemy pushed him through a set of tall wooden doors. Just across the threshold, Cade almost stumbled across a male body lying unconscious on the floor. BLOOD! Instinctively, he started to dive for the new prey.

Stop!

The Enemy's will jerked him short like a wolf on a chain. He snarled and fought, but Ridgemont held him still long enough for something sane to realize that if he touched the mortal, he'd kill him. He fought for control…only to almost lose it again when he realized the shrieks he heard were coming from a woman Hirsch was raping on the couch. Her panic rolled over him, made the Dragon roar. He tried to lunge again, but the Enemy wrapped him in power. Frozen, tormented, he lost himself in the red fog, barely aware of the screams and pleas of his enemies' victims.

Gray eyes. ***Terror.*** *Mommy! Daddy!*

He jolted out of the Dragon's grip to see a little girl staring at them from the doorway.

Where was he? What the hellfire was going on?

Disoriented, Cade gazed around at the elegantly appointed living room. Hirsch had a naked woman down on the couch, feeding as he raped her. Ridgemont held a struggling, screaming man who battered at him even with the ancient's fangs buried in his throat.

The smell of blood almost cut Cade's legs from under him. The Hunger had never been so vicious in all his years as a vampire. He fumbled for an explanation. Ridgemont had been starving him. He didn't know how long. Days, weeks. He tried to remember why. Couldn't.

The child was watching, her face stricken and pale. She shouldn't see this. Instinctively, Cade fought Ridgemont's psychic hold, wanting to go to her, take her away from this.

His moment of sanity attracted his enemy's attention.

"Well," the ancient purred, thrusting his prey away with a backhanded slap that knocked the man cold. "If it isn't little Valerie Chase."

Gray eyes widened as the girl stepped back, but Ridgemont crossed the living room so fast, she had no time to run. She screamed as he snatched her thin forearm and dug the thumbnail of one hand into it. Blood welled. The child grabbed the cut and stared up at him in hurt bewilderment. He grinned down into her shocked eyes and let her go. "Run."

With a wail of terror, she obeyed.

Ridgemont turned to Cade, freed his locked muscles, and drove a new compulsion into his brain: "Kill her."

And the Dragon roared an explosion of flame that seared his sanity away.

Blood blood bloodbloodbloodblood!

Running. Chasing the prey. Stink of terror, delicious terror. Blood filling the air, hot sweet copper musk….

neednowfeedbitekillfeedfeedbloodscreambabyscreaming.

Baby screaming.... Baby?

Cade jolted back to sanity to find himself standing in a nursery facing a twelve-year-old girl who clutched a howling toddler. "Stay away!" the girl spat, her gray eyes huge as she pulled the baby protectively close.

He opened his mouth to tell her he'd never hurt a child...and scented the blood trickling down her arm. The Dragon lashed in his brain, backed by the ferocious weight of Ridgemont's command. He could almost taste her life, hot and sweet. Just what his aching, cramping body so desperately needed.

Staring at the red runnel snaking down her thin arm, Cade felt his empty stomach wrench with sickening horror. Normally he could control the amount he drank, but his sire had starved him too long and planted the compulsion to kill too deep. He was about to become a murderer.

No!

Determination, sick and desperate, stiffened his spine. He'd done things he wasn't proud of in three years of war, a decade as a Texas Ranger, one hundred and twenty years as a vampire. But he'd never harmed a child, and Cade was damned if he'd start today. He'd rather die himself.

If he could just reduce her fear somehow. Terror, like any strong emotion, made the Hunger worse.

He flung out his will to touch hers. "Sleep," Cade said, and was distantly surprised at the broken rasp of his own voice. "You're safe. Just go to sleep."

The child should have collapsed like a marionette with cut strings. Instead she met his gaze and sneered. "Do you think I'm stupid, mister? I heard him tell you to kill us." She backed up another step, hugging her sister, who had blessedly stopped screaming to cling like a frightened monkey. "But you'd better not do it, 'cause they'll put you in the electric chair."

Oh, God, she's Kith, Cade realized numbly. *On top of everything else, she's one of us.* If she hadn't been, she could never have resisted his command.

He drew in a breath, and her blood scent rolled over him again, maddening the Dragon. He felt his muscles coil to leap. Somehow he managed to drop to his knees. "Get out, dammit!" Cade gasped. "Get out before he makes me kill you! Now!" He could feel his strength failing as the Dragon coiled in his guts.

He lifted his head to meet her gaze, hot with fear and revulsion and the need to live.

Gray eyes. So wide. Burning with astonishing power. Reaching out to him. Pulling him in. Touching him. Knowing him. As he touched her, knew her. Felt her purity, her strength. Her power. Power that for an instant chained the Dragon until he could find his own strength.

You're not going to kill us. His mind reverberated like a bell with the strength of her will.

No, he said. It was a holy oath, sworn mind to mind, a vow that would bind him from then on. *I'll protect you.* From Ridgemont. From himself.

The child's eyes flicked past him toward the door. Ridgemont was in the living room, blocking her escape. Both of them knew she'd never get past him.

"That way." Cade pointed toward the nursery window behind her. "Climb out and run to your neighbor's. They'll protect you. I'll keep Ridgemont from following." Somehow.

She stared at him, those eyes so much wiser than a child's had any business being. "What about Mom and Dad?"

"I'll save them." He'd try. He'd probably fail, but he'd try.

She turned toward the window and reached for it with one hand, the baby still in her arms. He realized she'd never be able to raise it.

Grinding his teeth with the effort, Cade reached past her to grab the sash, though it brought him too close to her tempting throat. He jerked upward, and it lifted with a thunderous shriek of wood and reverberating glass.

He turned and caught the child by the shoulders—and damn near lost control as the scent of her blood flooded his head. The Dragon clawed at him, but he fought it off and jerked her into the air. Still clutching her baby sister, Valerie shrieked as he thrust them both out through the window. The instant her feet hit the ground, Cade snatched back his hands as though her skin burned his. "Run, dammit!"

And she did, never looking back. He watched her go, fighting the horrible instinct to chase her.

Instead he turned and ran toward the living room.

And let the Dragon have him.

Cade's eyes snapped open as he jerked upright, swallowing a bellow of rage. Rubbing his hands over his sweating face, he thanked God Valerie hadn't shared this particular dream.

He shuddered, still tasting the ghost memory of Ridgemont's blood. He'd been too late to save Valerie's parents, but he'd kept Hirsch and the ancient so busy trying to fight him off that the police had almost caught them all. For the first time, his sire had been utterly unable to control him. It took another twelve years to break Ridgemont's mental grip entirely, but that night the ancient had been forced to beat him unconscious before they could make their escape.

Shaking off the remnants of the nightmare, Cade looked down at his body. Despite the stink of dried blood, he could tell his injuries had healed. Unfortunately, the repairs had come at a cost, as they always did: they'd brought back the Hunger. Luckily it wasn't the roaring crimson dragon of his nightmare, just the usual pale rose need that could be satisfied by an hour in a woman's arms and a cupful of her blood.

As he rolled out of bed, he spotted his own reflection. His uniform hung on his bloody body in gray shreds. *Damn good thing I've got a spare in the closet.* Shower first, he decided, then dress.

Then hunt.

Jump Shots was a classic Brooklyn blue-collar bar with a TV set tuned to ESPN and autographed basketball jerseys tacked to the paneled walls. It wasn't the sort of place where the young and trendy went, but then, Cade wasn't interested in young and trendy.

Moving easily after the day's healing sleep, he slid a hip on a stool where he could watch the room in the long mirror behind the bar. Opening his consciousness to the crowd, he allowed their thoughts to flood his mind, borne on a tide of alcohol, anger or sex. But they weren't what he needed, so he brushed past them like a man walking through tall grass.

Then he sensed her.

Cade turned to focus on the woman with a predator's intensity. She sat alone in a shadowed corner, defeat weighing her shoulders into a leaden slump. Reaching into her mind, he learned she was Jean Riggs, a middle-aged school teacher whose husband had recently found someone two decades younger. Her need for companionship was almost as acute as his for blood. He rose from his stool with a confidence born of decades of seduction.

When Cade slid into the booth across from her, Jean looked up, startled. Taking in his face, her eyes widened in automatic alarm. He could see in her mind that she thought he was too young and too good-looking to be interested in her for any good reason.

Before she could obey her instinct to jump up and leave, he leaned forward. "You don't have to be afraid of me." He touched her mind and took away the fear.

And she smiled.

Val sat hunched in the uncomfortable airline seat, staring out the window at the lights jeweling the night-shrouded landscape below the 747's wing. Wispy clouds stole past like fleeing ghosts, glowing faintly in the milk-pale light of the full moon that rode the horizon.

Her eyes felt so scratchy with exhaustion, she let them close. After last night's restless dreams followed by a day spent packing for this trip, she felt drained. With a sigh, she slid into sleep.

And began to dream.

Cowboy was cheating on her.

He loomed over the strange woman, one of her plump thighs draped over his arm, a big hand gripping the bend of her other knee, holding her legs spread wide. The tight, hard muscles of his abdomen laced as he slowly pumped his thick shaft deep.

Bastard!

Valerie seethed in jealous rage as the woman tossed her head on the pillow, graying hair tangled around her face as she gasped in time to his rolling hips. He watched her, his expression absorbed and sensual, his eyes blazing crimson. She either didn't notice the demonic glow or was too lost in pleasure to care.

He rumbled something and shifted positions, moving over her, mantling her with his much bigger body. Muscle rippled up and down his broad back, flexing in the tight hemispheres of his butt with every thrust. She surged up against him until his curling chest hair teased the tips of her nipples. Her small, soft hands clawed at the tangled sheets. Eyes clenched shut, she keened softly, coming, pushing her head into the pillow, arching her throat.

His eyes glowed brighter and his sensuous lips parted to reveal canines that were an inch long. He bent his head toward the tight, thin skin over her pulse. Just above it, he paused. A slow, hot smile of anticipation spread over his handsome face.

Then he took her, sinking his fangs into her throat. She jerked against him with a gasp of shocked delight.

Horror stirred in Val's mind. He'd kill the poor woman! She struggled to wake, but the dream held her fast.

He circled his hips, screwing deep while he drank. The woman convulsed, screaming hoarsely, but not in pain.

In pleasure.

With a muffled growl, he rolled over with her, spreading her over his body. One strong hand locked in the soft, generous flesh of her bottom while the other fisted in her hair as if to prevent her escape. His jaw worked as he simultaneously surged upward, giving her such long, deep plunges that his big shaft almost slipped free with every driving thrust.

Suddenly the woman he held changed — grew younger, slimmer, the hair fisted in his hand taking on a rich autumnal copper.

Val recognized herself wrapped in Cowboy's vampire grip. Opening her eyes, she shuddered with helpless ecstasy as he fucked and fed on her.

She snapped awake with a gasp.

Wildly, she stared around the 747 at the passengers around her, some sleeping, some gazing, bored, out the plane's windows at the shimmering night.

A dream, Val thought, blinking hard as she scrubbed a shaking hand over her face. *It was only a dream.* She slumped back into her seat, then stiffened convulsively as the movement rasped hardened nipples against the lace of her bra. A flush burned her cheeks as she realized she was very wet.

"Oh, God, oh God, oh GOD!" Jean chanted as Cade drove his

cock upward into her plump, soft body. He could feel himself growing stronger as her orgasm fed him, the intensity of her emotion so sweet and hot it was maddening. Her pleasure kicked him into his own, and he growled out his own climax against her throat.

As it crested and began to recede, he was tempted to force her even higher. But he'd brought her to peak four times already, and to take any more would leave her dangerously weak. He drew his fangs from her throat and rolled onto his side, cradling her close.

For a moment Cade allowed himself to savor the sweet, rare peace, the pure animal satiety of his own body. Jean felt so deliciously warm, so deliciously female. He closed his eyes and wrapped himself in her scent, the softness of her skin, the taste of her musk lingering on his tongue.

Yet inside him, something felt … empty, as it always did after he fed. He knew why, of course.

His partner wasn't Val. They never were.

But maybe soon….

No. He pushed the temptation away. Even if he succeeded in rescuing his dream lover, he'd never allow himself to touch her. He didn't dare. He wasn't sure he could resist the urge to Change her, make her completely his.

Betray her trust.

Shaking off that depressing thought, Cade reached for Jean's mind and removed the memory of his bite. Glimpsing other mental wounds he hadn't inflicted, he prepared to repair those as well. He owed her for what she'd given him, and he paid his debts.

He could feel her bewilderment. Why had he chosen her, of all people? In her mind, she ticked off her own flaws—the fifteen extra pounds she'd never managed to lose, the strands of gray in her hair, the mouth that was too wide. He could have had a younger, more beautiful woman.

He could have told her that a younger, more beautiful woman

wouldn't have responded with the starved intensity she'd given him. Instead he kissed the top of her graying head and said softly, "You were amazing."

Jean laughed, the sound too close to a sob. "My ex-husband doesn't think so."

In her mind, he could see the hundred little cruelties Gary had inflicted as he'd worked himself into leaving her. Cade's grip tightened as he entertained the pleasant fantasy of hunting the man down and beating him bloody. "Why do you care what that bastard thinks? He didn't even have the sense to recognize the treasure he had in you."

She lifted skeptical hazel eyes to his, thinking he was being kind.

Cade met her gaze and used his power. "Don't let it eat at you anymore, Jean. Life's too short. There'll be another man, another love."

She lowered her lids. "But not you."

"No," he said. He liked her, liked her kindness and hidden sensuality. But she wasn't Val.

Since he couldn't say that, he gave her another simple truth instead. "I take too much." Though he never drank more than a pint of blood over the course of a night, he could kill or dangerously weaken his partners if he took them too many times. He never slept with anyone more than once. "You need a man who'll give. And you'll find him."

"Oh," she said in a small voice.

He caught her chin and brought her eyes to meet his. "You're a wonderful woman. *Believe in yourself.*"

Jean's mind seized Cade's telepathic suggestion and released her doubts. A brilliant smile spread across her face. She wrapped her arms around him, cuddling close. Slowly, gently, he stroked a hand through her hair, allowing himself to savor the moment's warmth. If he fought Ridgemont and lost, it might be the last he'd ever know.

Finally, with a regretful sigh, he urged her into sleep. He was due at the airport—and his duel for Valerie's life.

Val watched the lights of the runway speed upward to meet the plane, fighting the nervous jitter in her stomach. She was not, dammit, rushing toward her doom. And no matter what her overactive imagination insisted, Cowboy was not waiting down there to claim and betray her.

There is no such thing as vampires. And Cowboy's just a dream, she told herself firmly, forcing away the image of herself writhing astride his grinding hips with his fangs sunk deep in her throat.

Ridgemont had not come to meet Val's plane.

Grim, Cade scanned the airport lobby, but the ancient's dark mental signature was nowhere in evidence. It didn't make sense.

Frowning, he turned and studied Bobby Mason, who leaned against the information center flirting with the pretty girl who manned it. Mason was Ridgemont's backup driver, but according to Cade's mental scan, he didn't remember bringing either of the vampires with him. Of course, his memories could have been altered. Probably had been.

Ridgemont was no fool; he had to know kidnaping Val would be Cade's next move. And Mason damn well couldn't stop him from doing it. Which meant this was a trap.

Unfortunately, it seemed Cade had no choice except to walk into it.

He stepped up behind the chauffeur and murmured in his ear, "Hey, Bobby."

Mason straightened and jerked around. "What the fuck are you doing here?" he demanded, eyes widening in his square, pleasantly beefy face. He glanced back at the suddenly alert airport rep, then grabbed Cade's elbow and dragged him off to one side. Lowering his voice, he hissed, "You know how long it took the bomb squad to disarm that thing you left in the limo?"

Cade winced. He hadn't thought of that. "Anybody get hurt?"

"No, but where the hell did you get all that C-4?" His eyes flickered toward a Transit cop who watched them with post-9/11 paranoia. Cade looked at the man and mentally compelled him to believe he wasn't interested in the conversation. The cop glanced away, and Mason relaxed, though he dropped his voice even more. "That's military ordnance. They control that shit like nuclear material." He used to be in the Army.

Cade shrugged. "Took it off a terrorist. Figured it would be put to better use killing Ridgemont than blowing up a chunk of subway."

"Do I want to know what happened to the terrorist?"

"He gave a full confession to the Feds. I think he's awaiting trial." Cade met the mortal's hazel eyes. "Bobby, you need to take a walk. I'll give Ridgemont's guest a ride back to the house."

"Are you nuts?" Mason rocked back on his heels. "You left a half-pound resignation letter wired to the ignition, remember?"

"No, I didn't." He reached into the other man's mind and gently laid the force of his will across it.

"Oh." The chauffeur's face went blank as he instantly forgot the bomb. "Sure, Cade. Whatever you say." Turning, he wandered off.

With a sigh, Cade folded his arms and settled back against the wall to scan for Ridgemont and Hirsch. And wait.

When he heard the announcement that Val's flight had arrived, he straightened and moved toward the airport security station she'd pass through once she arrived.

His gut knotted. This could get nasty.

Chances were good she'd recognize him, either as Cowboy or the vampire who'd almost killed her seventeen years before. Of course, he'd been thin and half-starved back then, and she didn't believe Cowboy existed, so that might buy him a little time. But eventually it would hit her who he was.

And she wasn't going to be happy about it.

If she became hysterical in the airport, things would get dicey in a hurry. The latent psychic powers that made her a candidate for vampirism meant he'd be unable to influence her mind. If she started screaming, he'd have a hell of a time shutting her up before she attracted dangerous attention. Even he couldn't control a pack of pissed-off airport cops. That many minds would be impossible to manage.

He really needed to get lucky for once, Cade thought grimly, pulling his cap down over his eyes. Fortunately his black chauffeur's uniform was as far from his Texas Ranger's jeans and Stetson as it was possible to get. Maybe that would buy him just enough time.

Glancing beyond the security station, he saw a group of deplaning passengers headed his way—families towing weary children, business people draped like pack mules with laptop cases and carry-ons. As they poured past the security station, New York relatives met visiting family members with squeals and hugs.

Then he spotted a familiar, long-legged figure striding toward him. His throat tightened at the sweet symmetry of her face and the lush, tight curve of her breasts and hips.

Valerie.

She looked just as she always had in his dreams. Her face was a delicate oval set off by a pointed little chin and narrow nose, but her mouth was lush, with a hint of a wicked smile playing around its corners. She wore a summer weight cream suit that managed to look cooly professional even as it hugged her long legs. A silk blouse provided discreet coverage for round, pert breasts he knew from personal experience made a delightful handful. The blouse's mint green fabric contrasted against the dramatic tumble of auburn hair that frothed around her slim shoulders.

Valerie. There, in the flesh. Close enough to touch.

Cade's knees actually went weak.

"Okay," Val muttered, clutching her laptop bag as she scanned the milling crowd for somebody who looked like he was looking for her. Mr. Ridgemont's secretary had said she'd send a driver, though how Val was supposed to recognize him in this mob was anybody's guess. Maybe he'd have a sign with her name on it, like they did in the movies. "So where are you?" She lifted onto her toes, wondering if he'd be wearing one of those gray chauffeur outfits. The only man she'd seen in a uniform was that handsome cop....

"Ms. Chase?"

Val turned and looked straight into a broad chest covered in black linen. She blinked and adjusted her gaze upward—much further upward than she was used to. At five-foot-nine, she didn't have to look up at many men, especially when she was wearing heels.

It's the cop, she thought, taking in the billed black uniform hat he wore. Then she looked again and realized her mistake. It was a chauffeur's cap, tilted down over short black hair that looked as if it would have liked to curl if not for its ruthless cut.

"Ms. Chase, I'm Cade McKinnon," the man said, extending a big, gloved hand in greeting. His face was long and angular, with broad, jutting cheekbones, a deeply cleft chin, and a narrow nose. Despite those aggressively stern features, his mouth was intensely sensuous, with the kind of generous, mobile lips that could kiss and charm with equal skill.

Val shook off her reaction to his sculpted male beauty and opened her mouth to attempt a professional greeting. Just as she met his eyes.

Set just slightly aslant under black brows, their irises were a rich, dark chocolate. *God,* she thought, forgetting what she was about to say, *he's got the most beautiful eyes I've ever seen....* Entranced, she looked deeper.

Suffering. Ruthless determination. And hunger — devouring, threatening, somehow erotic.

She froze. It was Cowboy.

Chapter Four

It is not! she told herself firmly, trying to shake off the wild impression. Yet the jangle of her instincts refused to quiet. Unnerved, she took a step back so fast her ankle turned under her.

Before Val could fall, McKinnon caught her elbow and steadied her. Dark gaze lit with warm concern. "Hey, are you all right?"

God, he even sounded like Cowboy.

Shaken, she peered up into his face. His eyes were just eyes now—kind and ordinary. *I imagined that*, she told herself firmly. He was *not* Cowboy—Cowboy didn't exist. And she certainly hadn't touched the man's mind and found something alien. "Rough flight," she said aloud, as much to herself as him.

"Do you need to sit down?" He caught her other hand as though afraid she'd keel over. The black leather gloves he wore felt warm against her skin. He moved closer, and for a moment his heat and strength sizzled all up and down her body. Her nipples peaked.

She blushed hotly. "I'm fine." Shaking back her hair, Val straightened and pulled free of his light grip.

McKinnon studied her, frowning. "I'm Mr. Ridgemont's driver," he said at last. "He sent me to pick you up."

"It's a pleasure to meet you." Automatically, she held out her hand again and let him surround it in those long, leather-clad fingers.

He smiled, his teeth dazzling white—and perfectly ordinary. She grimaced at herself, realizing she'd half expected fangs. "Believe me, the pleasure's mine," McKinnon said, then neatly hooked her laptop bag off her shoulder and onto his own. "We'd better head to the baggage carousel for the rest of your luggage. We've got a long drive ahead of us, and I'd imagine you're tired."

Val nodded, trying to ignore the flicker of unease that slid through her at the thought of being alone in a car with him. He was not, dammit, Cowboy. It was just that he had dark hair, and any dark-haired man would remind her of her demon lover right now. As for that beautiful velvet voice of his … Surely Cowboy's hadn't been that deep, that resonant.

Unconsciously, her eyes scanned down his tall, well-muscled body. *Muscle rippled up and down his broad back, flexing in the tight hemispheres of his ass with every thrust….* She felt her face blaze in a blush.

Okay, so he was built like Cowboy. Maybe. Or maybe the shoulders of his black uniform jacket were padded. *Not judging by the strength in those hands….*

"Baggage pickup is this way," McKinnon said, in the sort of low male rumble that could spin seduction around even the most casual comments. He turned toward the carousel a short distance away, and Val followed, trying to convince her overactive imagination to settle down.

Despite her jumpy nerves, some feminine instinct purred approval of his long-legged stride and the easy swing of those powerful shoulders. He was just so damn big. She'd always had a weakness for big men.

Unable to resist another glance at the muscled length of his legs, she saw that his trousers were tucked into shining black boots that clicked as he walked. It occurred to her that there was something deliberately flamboyant about the chauffeur's uniform he wore—the black tunic with its gold buttons, the leather gloves, the riding boots when she'd bet money he never went anywhere near a horse. He looked like something out of a forties film noir, as if Gloria Swanson should be waiting in the car, wrapped in mink. It made her wonder about the kind of employer who'd choose such a rig for his driver in the twenty-first century.

Yet somehow McKinnon managed to carry the costume off without looking silly. He was one of those rare men who could have projected confidence and masculine charisma dressed in a clown suit. Val grinned, diverted, as she imagined a parade of women trailing hopefully behind a pair of big, floppy shoes.

McKinnon reached the baggage carousel and gave her a smile as she joined him. Yet his eyes weren't directed at her, or even down at the luggage circling on the conveyer belt. Instead, he scanned the surrounding crowd, his gaze flicking warily from face to face as he held his big body with a martial artist's loose-limbed readiness.

If that man is just a chauffeur, I'll eat my laptop, Val thought suddenly. *He's a bodyguard.*

The suit jacket of that black uniform was too well-cut to bulge, but she'd bet money he wore a shoulder holster under it when he wasn't picking somebody up at an airport.

What's more, she sensed he actively expected trouble. Was it just professional paranoia, or did he really expect someone to attack them here?

Val felt her own tension ease. The sense of danger she felt must be an unconscious reaction to his wariness. It had nothing to do with her vampire nightmare after all.

But what kind of enemies did Edward Ridgemont have, anyway?

Where the hell were Ridgemont and Hirsch?

Logically Cade knew he could expect to find his sire waiting out in the airport parking lot, ready to kick his ass again. Except he hadn't picked up even a ghost of Ridgemont's menacing psychic signature in any of his scans. The ancient wasn't here.

That left Hirsch, but Cade had beaten the German in every fair fight they'd ever had. Which meant this would not be a fair fight. Hirsch would ambush him. Probably with one of Ridgemont's twelve-gauge double-barreled shotguns that could blast his head right off his shoulders. Not the kind of weapon one ordinarily carried into La Guardia, but with a vampire's powers, anything was possible.

And yet.... Something about the idea of a shotgun ambush just didn't feel right. Ridgemont had talked about killing him too many times, with too much anticipation. He'd want to do the job himself. Yet he wasn't here.

So what the hell was going on?

As they watched the luggage slide past on the carousel, Val let her attention slip to McKinnon's face. Now that her overactive imagination had calmed down, she realized there was something in his brown eyes she recognized. Beautiful as they were, they were also a little flat with that particular resigned cynicism she knew from six years as a police-beat journalist.

She'd bet her last notebook Cade McKinnon was an ex-cop.

And not just any ex-cop, either. A man ended up with eyes like that by seeing life at its ugliest without being able to do a damn thing about it. And that meant homicide detective.

"How long has it been since you left law enforcement?"

McKinnon was scanning the crowd again. His gaze jerked to hers at the question, and she had the impression she'd startled him. Then he smiled slightly. "A very long time."

"N.Y.P.D.?"

"Texas Rangers."

Val stiffened. *Just like Cowboy* ... She pushed the thought away. *Don't be ridiculous.* Forcing herself to sound casual, she asked, "How'd you get involved in that?"

He shrugged. "The war was over, and I needed a job."

"Desert Storm?"

"Yeah." Silently, Cade cursed himself. He shouldn't have told her about the Rangers—he'd seen the flicker in her eyes as she associated that bit of information with Cowboy. He had to be more careful.

Unfortunately, there was something about her that demanded honesty, no matter what common sense told him. Hell, he'd damn near admitted he was talking about the Civil War. He'd barely bitten the words back in time.

"There," she said suddenly, looking past him to point at an expensive leather bag sliding by. "That one's mine."

Thank you, God. He bent over and scooped it up. They really had to get out of here before Ridgemont or Hirsch showed up.

By the time Cade grabbed her third and final bag, his skin was crawling. He led her toward the exit at a speed just short of a run, wanting only to get her as far away as possible.

As they stepped through the building's double doors, Cade hesitated, extending his vampire senses.

Still no sign of Ridgemont.

He took a deep breath, trying to pick up Hirsch's scent, but the smell of jet fuel and gasoline overwhelmed everything else.

"Mr. McKinnon?" Valerie looked up at him curiously.

He gave her a phony smile. "Just trying to remember where I parked the car. And call me Cade."

Muscles coiling in the back of his neck, he guided Valerie along the sidewalk toward the parking lot. He just wished he'd been able to find a spot a little closer to the building.

As they walked between the rows of parked cars, Val frowned, studying McKinnon intently.

The strap of her laptop was hooked over his broad shoulder, and he'd tucked one suitcase under his left arm while carrying the other in his left hand. Somehow he managed all three with such easy strength they might as well be empty cardboard boxes.

"I'm curious," she said. "Just who are you expecting to jump us?"

She thought she glimpsed startled guilt in McKinnon's eyes before his face went politely blank. "What? What are you talking about?"

Val nodded at his free hand, held loose and empty at his side. "You look like you're ready to draw down on somebody."

"Come on, Ms. Chase—you really don't think I carried a gun into a New York airport?" He gave her that charming grin she was beginning to suspect was a con.

"Did you?"

"Why would I do that?

Val lifted a brow at him. "You're Ridgemont's bodyguard, aren't you?"

McKinnon looked genuinely astonished, then barked out a laugh. "The exact opposite, actually."

She grinned. "I don't think so." When he lifted a brow, she explained, "The exact opposite of a bodyguard would be an assassin, right?"

All the humor fled his eyes as his warmly handsome face took on an executioner's chill. "Sounds that way, doesn't it?"

Val felt a shiver skate her spine as she remembered her last dream of Cowboy: his eyes glowing red as he buried his fangs in his victim's throat. "What do you mean?"

He shrugged his impressive shoulders and looked away. "Take my word for it, Edward Ridgemont does not need a bodyguard."

Her instincts began to clamor so loudly, she was tempted to tell him she'd catch a cab. Somehow she didn't want to see his reaction to that idea.

What the hell was going on?

They continued between the rows of cars until he pointed an electronic key fob at a black Lexus. The trunk lid popped open obediently, and he began stowing her luggage inside with that same quick, effortless strength she'd noticed before. There were more suitcases in there than just her own, and Val wondered if Ridgemont habitually kept his luggage packed in case he was called out of town.

Finally McKinnon closed the trunk and moved to open the front passenger door. She hesitated, her stomach jittery, her mouth dry. *Imagination,* she told herself. *Get in the car, you idiot.*

"Ms. Chase?" McKinnon turned to loom, his uniformed chest a solid wall of black.

Val licked her lips and stared up into his dark eyes. When she realized she was searching for a scarlet glow, she swore silently at herself and got into the Lexus, impatient with her own neuroses.

A nagging thought struck her as she settled into the butter soft leather seat. Didn't people who rode with chauffeurs normally sit in the back of the car?

Glancing behind her, she saw the back seat was full. A battered blue canvas gym bag sat on the seat, along with… Was that a sheathed sword? And the kite-shaped metal thing standing on the floorboard looked just like a shield. "Does Mr. Ridgemont collect medieval weaponry?"

McKinnon hadn't yet closed the door. As she watched, frowning, he crouched on the pavement beside her and took her right hand in his, reaching into a back pocket with the other. The glare of the parking lot security lights cast a harsh glow over the sharp planes of his face, making him look white and gaunt beneath the bill of his chauffeur's cap.

A seventeen-year-old memory rose in her mind.

He hunched on his knees on her bedroom floor, his black eyes burning, empty and feral. He was big, almost as big as the German who'd attacked Mama, but the bones of his face stood out as if he hadn't eaten in weeks. His clothing hung on his body, and he shook in racking quivers. In a voice that barely sounded human, he rasped, "Get out. Run before he makes me kill you."

He had fangs like a wolf.

She felt a weird plummeting sensation, as if the ground had suddenly dropped out from under her feet. "You're the third vampire. You're the one he sent to kill us. You were with them when they murdered my parents."

He flinched and tensed. As he lifted his head, the shadow of the cap's brim fell across his nose — just the way the Stetson's always had.

"Cowboy, you son of a bitch!" She drove her fist toward his elegant nose with every ounce of her strength.

Ah, hell.

It was worse even than Cade had expected. Controlling her flailing fists took no effort at all, of course, but then Valerie shoved one high heel against his crotch. Before she could grind the spike into anatomy every bit as vulnerable as any other man's, Cade dragged her out of the car. She howled and kicked as he wrestled her down onto the pavement.

"Calm down, Valerie!" he yelled over her curses as he worked to pin her wrists. "I'm not going to hurt you."

"Yeah, well, I'm going to hurt *you*, you gutless blood-sucking bastard!" She writhed like a maddened cat, all curves and fury and long, slim legs. "What the hell were you doing in my dreams? Pretending to be my friend! My lover! You were setting me up! Well, it's not gonna work!"

When she lunged for his lower lip with snapping teeth, he barely jerked back his head in time. "Dammit, Valerie," he snarled, baring the fangs that had descended when her foot had threatened his balls. "Stop that!"

She screamed back a string of curses that would have made a mule skinner blush.

Trapping both her wrists in one of his, Cade clamped a hand

over her mouth to muffle her furious shrieks. She dug her teeth into his palm and bit down hard. He jerked back, astonished at her gall. "Have you lost your mind? What's wrong with you?"

"What the hell did you expect?" she spat. "You spent the past seventeen years playing me for a fool! I was a child, you bastard! I trusted you!"

"And I helped you!"

She laughed, the sound short and ugly. "Helped yourself to my ass!"

"It was never like that!" Gritting his teeth, he gave her shoulders a ruthlessly controlled shake. "You're the one who reached out to me, Valerie! You wanted me to protect you from your monsters, and I did. Then you wanted a father figure, and I was. And later, when you wanted a lover…."

"…You fucked me," she snarled. She bucked under him, fighting to free her wrists from his grip, her knee driving up against his butt. Cade clamped his thighs around her legs, hooking her ankles with his feet to still her kicks. Dammit, surely she'd have to wind down sooner or later.

For the first time in his life, he was tempted to slap a woman, if only to shock her out of her blind frenzy. But as he looked into the crazed gray glitter of her eyes, Cade realized she wouldn't stop attacking him even if he did. She felt too betrayed.

With a frustrated growl, he let his full weight crush down on her. There wasn't much else he could do. He'd never lifted a hand to a woman in his life, and he'd certainly never hit Valerie. But he had to shut her up before someone heard her screams over the jet engine roar from the nearby runways.

Cowboy wrapped himself around her like a living straight jacket, heavy and hot. At first Val was too far gone in hysterical fury to be aware of him as anything other than a target for her fists and teeth.

But bucking against all that sheer strength and muscled weight was exhausting, and the massive chest pressing into hers made it hard to breathe. Her struggles weakened until she collapsed under him, panting in fury and exertion.

"You ready to talk now?" he gritted.

"What's there to say?" Dammit, vampires were supposed to feel cold and dead to the touch. Cowboy was all heat and brawn. "If you're going to rip out my throat, get it over with." Fear slid through her at the thought, only to be overwhelmed by another surge of rage. She couldn't believe he'd betrayed her like this.

Cowboy's sensual mouth flattened into a hard, tight line. "I've got no intention of hurting you, Valerie. Hell, I'm trying to save you. Again."

"Oh, yeah, you're a big hero, you lying son of a bitch. You said you'd save my parents, and you let them die!" Dammit, she should have seen this coming. Deep down, she'd always known Cowboy was real, no matter what logic insisted, just as she'd always known her parents had been murdered by vampires.

But finding out Cowboy was one of them—God, that hurt.

"I didn't 'let' them die, Valerie. I did fight for them. I was just too late." Tightening his grip on her wrists, he got to his feet, hauling her up effortlessly.

Val braced shaking legs under her and stared up into his handsome, implacable face. *There's no way to fight him*, she thought, bitter and terrified. *He's just too damn strong.*

Her parents had tried to fight too. It hadn't done them any good either.

Her father screamed and struggled as a short, muscular blond man dragged his head back by the hair and buried long white fangs in his throat. An even bigger man had Mom pinned on the living room couch. He'd ripped open her nightgown, and he was hurting her. She sobbed as he mocked her terror in a thick Ger-

man accent before leaning down to bite her neck. Blood spurted around his lips. He hummed in pleasure.

A gaunt, dark-haired man stood watching like a robot, his face blank and white.

The same man who held her now.

Something cold circled her arm, jolting Val out of the paralyzing grip of memory. She looked down to see Cowboy snapping one bracelet of a pair of handcuffs onto her right wrist. "What are you doing? Let go!" She tried to jerk back, but he'd already crowded her against the car and begun forcing her down into the seat.

"We've got to get out of here. We've wasted too much time as it is." He released her uncuffed wrist to thread the other bracelet through the door handle, then grabbed for her free hand again. She cocked her fist and aimed for that handsome nose.

The vampire jerked his head up, meeting her eyes with his lips drawn back from white fangs. "We don't have time for this. If you want to be something other than Edward Ridgemont's sex toy, stop fighting me."

Surprise penetrated her fury. "Ridgemont? What's he got to do with this?"

"Who do you think killed your father, Valerie?"

The leader knocked her father aside with a brutal swat. "Well, if it isn't little Valerie Chase." His accent was clipped and English.

Ridgemont had an English accent.

"That's right," the vampire said, snapping the handcuff closed. "He got you fired from your newspaper job and offered you all that money as a lure so he could get you to New York. Now that you're here, he means to rape you, Change you into a vampire, and rape you some more." He shot her a glittering look. "A fate I'll save you from—if you can resist the urge to screw up our escape!"

"Too late," growled a deep Germanic voice.

Cowboy spun. Something blurred out of the night at him. He

vanished like a leaf in a whirlwind.

Metal crunched and glass shattered. Val jerked in the direction of the sound and saw him roll across the hood of a car parked in the opposite row of spaces.

Brutal hands closed over hers. With a gasp, she snapped her head around. A man crouched at her feet, both her handcuffed wrists in his grip. Blond and GQ handsome, his face was as elegant as if someone had laid it out with a straight-edge, but his body was vintage Conan the Barbarian. "Hello, *Fraulein*." He wore a leather jacket and dark blue jeans that looked pressed and new. As he spoke, she glimpsed fangs in his mouth. "You've grown up to be quite the beauty. I do hope Ridgemont will share…."

Staring into the vampire's cold smile, Val recognized him. It had been seventeen years, but he hadn't aged at all. The cruel hands around her wrists were the same ones that had held her mother down as he raped her.

This can't be happening, a small voice wailed somewhere in her mind. *None of it. It's impossible. There is no such thing as vampires….*

But there was. Grandma had been wrong. They'd all been wrong.

A sudden vicious pain in her wrists snapped Val out of her shock. She looked down. The German was pulling her wrists in opposite directions, trying to break the handcuffs.

No!

Vampires or not, real or not, she wasn't going to let them take her. Neither of them.

Her paralysis shattered. Val drew in a breath and screamed with all the air in her lungs as she tried to throw herself back into the car. The handcuffs jerked her to a stop, ripping pain through her muscles.

Her panic gave way to rage again, cleansing and welcome. *God damn it, I'm not going to let them do this to me! I'm not going to let them kill me, too!* Val threw up both legs and kicked her captor savagely in the face. "Let go!"

"Bitch!" the vampire roared, releasing her wrists to knock aside her frenzied feet. He rose, drawing back a big fist as blood snaked from his nose.

A hand clamped into the leather collar of the German's jacket and snatched him off his feet as though he weighed no more than a child.

"That's one woman you're not going to hit," Cowboy snarled. With a twist of his powerful torso, he tossed the German skyward to sail thirty feet in the air, then watched him fall like a sack of cement.

The brutal impact should have broken bones, but the blond vampire bounced to his feet, one hand wiping blood from his nose. With the other he drew a huge knife sheathed at the small of his back. Its curving blade was fully as long as her arm.

"That's it, McKinnon, I'm going to cut out your heart." His chilly blue eyes glittered as he stalked her kidnapper. "And then I'm going to fuck her while I feed."

"Oh, come on, Gerhard." Cowboy drew the blade's twin from under his own jacket. "The only thing you're going to do is bleed, and you know it."

Val's heart lunged into her throat. The blond was three inches taller and outweighed him by a good fifty pounds. How was her leanly muscular Cowboy supposed to defeat that beefy monster?

And if he lost, she was dead.

Chapter Five

Val shoved the car door open and got out. The cuffs hooked around the doorhandle wouldn't let her straighten, but she barely noticed, too busy watching the vampires fight with her heart jamming her throat.

Enormous knives clashed together with the ring of steel. Leaping, feinting, the vampires circled in a muscular dance, fluid as wolves.

And just as inhuman.

Then Hirsch hacked for his opponent's head. Val flinched. Cowboy jerked clear of the blade only to snake back inside the German's guard. When he darted out again, the front of Hirsch's jacket hung in expensive leather shreds. Valerie exhaled in relief.

And instantly felt like a fool. *Idiot*, she told herself. *He betrayed you. It would serve him right to get gutted.*

"Ridgemont sent you after me all by yourself?" Cowboy gave Hirsch a taunting grin. "Either he's getting senile, or he wanted you to lose."

The German spat something vile and lunged.

Cowboy slipped aside like a bullfighter. His knife flicked out. Hirsch leaped back. A thin line of scarlet marked his throat, but he'd saved his jugular. Val cursed his reflexes.

He's my mother's murderer, she told herself. *Of course I want him dead.* The fact that he meant to kill Cowboy had nothing to do with it.

"Why didn't you bring a shotgun, Gerhard?" Her dream lover's gaze was as fixed and ferocious as a hunting tiger's. "You'd have had better luck."

"He wouldn't let me, or you'd be dead now. But then, he's always been soft on you." Hirsch's mouth twisted into a sneer. "Or should I say, hard *for* you. You must be a very talented cocksucker."

"Better not let Ridgemont hear you say that." Cowboy's grin held absolutely no humor. "He'd gut you—again. Besides, if anybody's hitting his knees, it's you. I'm not the one who's still in thrall."

This time Hirsch's slashing knife left a line of blood on his lean cheek.

Please, God, let Cowboy win.

She shook the thought off. Why the hell was she just standing here waiting to see who'd get her? There had to be something she could do to save herself.

Rising onto her toes, Val peered around the parking lot, scanning for headlights, a cop, a Good Samaritan. Anybody. But she saw nothing but rows of cars gleaming dully in the amber glow of the security lights. "Help!" she yelled, praying someone would hear her anyway. "Somebody help me!"

A jet roared by overhead, drowning her out. Fighting a sob, Val raised her voice, trying to make herself heard over the waves of sound. "Somebody please help! Dammit…."

The German glanced over at her and snarled. "Shut up, you stupid little bitch. If you bring the police down on us, I'll flog you bloody after I rip out their…." He broke off to suck in an agonized gasp.

Val jerked around. Cowboy stood nose to nose with Hirsch, one hand wrapped around his opponent's knife wrist. She couldn't see what he was doing with the other. "Your problem, Gerhard, is you never know when to shut up."

Cowboy released him with a shove. The German staggered backward and stumbled against the open door of the Lexus. It swung inward to pin Val.

As Hirsch fell past, she saw the black hilt of a Bowie knife protruding from his belly. When he hit the ground, he curled into a groaning knot of agony.

Boots rang on concrete. Val jerked her head up. Cowboy circled around the car to the driver's side, opened the rear door and reached in. When he straightened, he held a sheathed long sword in his hands.

He met her horrified stare with a cool, emotionless gaze. Drawing the sword, he tossed the sheathe into the back seat. "The stake thing is a myth."

Swallowing, Val looked down at Hirsch, realizing sickly that Cowboy was about to execute him.

"You play the hero with such flair, McKinnon," the German sneered from the pavement, blood snaking from his pale lips. He shot her a look seething with malice. "Don't imagine you're safe, girl. He'll pretend to be your knight in shining armor, but he'll rape you just as quickly as I would."

"I don't rape, Gerhard." He slammed the car door. "That's your perversion."

"You'll rape her." Hirsch rolled over and grabbed the knife, jerking it from his belly. Gasping, he lunged to his feet as Cowboy stalked him, sword raised and ready. Holding the Bowie knife in a shaking, bloody fist, the German backed away. "You need the power you'll get from her if you want to kill Ridgemont. And you want to kill Ridgemont even more than you want to be a hero."

"Not that much." Dark eyes studied him, deadly and intent. "Not that way."

"Ah," Hirsch's grin twisted. "You think to play Prince Charming, wooing the maiden fair." His eyes flicked to Val's face. "Are you going to let him seduce you, *Fraulein*? I wouldn't, if I were you. Not unless you want to spend the next century on the end of his leash, sucking his cock."

Val swallowed as her mind supplied the image with a coil of shameful heat.

"Are we going to do this with some dignity, or are you going to make me chase you down and butcher you like a boar hog?" Handsome and remorseless, Cowboy lifted the sword, looking more like a Renaissance archangel than a vampire.

And nothing at all like the noble Texas Ranger of her dreams.

"You're the one who'll die squealing," Hirsch spat. "Ridgemont will gut you and feed her your blood as he fucks her. Unless you do her first. I wonder if she's as tasty as her mother was?"

"You'll never know." He braced for the brutal horizontal slice that would take off the German's head. Val looked away.

"Police! Put it down!"

Cowboy whirled. So did Val, a grin spreading over her face as she saw the patrol car that had rolled up unnoticed in the midst of the fight. A New York Port Authority cop jumped out to aim his gun at him across its roof. The officer's cold eyes narrowed. "I said put the weapon down, sir!"

"What weapon?" Cowboy's gaze locked on his. "I don't have any weapon."

The cop blinked hard.

The scrape of faltering footsteps drew Val's attention just in time to see Hirsch staggering into the night.

"Dammit!" Cowboy half turned toward his fleeing enemy.

"Drop the sword, sir!" It was a roar now. "I will shoot!"

The vampire's handsome mouth twisted in a frustrated snarl. *"I said I don't have a weapon."*

The officer blinked hard, then looked at the gun he still held pointed. Swallowing, he straightened hastily and holstered it. "Sorry. I…I don't…."

"No weapon?" Val gaped. What the hell was Cowboy doing to him? "Are you nuts? There's a three-foot sword in his hand! Arrest him!"

"Shouldn't you radio in that you were mistaken?" Cowboy interrupted smoothly. "You don't want to look stupid."

"No. No, I don't." He reached for the handset clipped to his shoulder.

"Wait a minute! That man is abducting me!" Val tried fruitlessly to drag her handcuffed hands into view. "Look! He's got me chained to the door!"

The cop stopped and stared at her, his eyes confused. "What?"

"She's drunk, officer," Cowboy said in that deep voice he'd used to soothe her so many times. "I'll take care of her. You're needed elsewhere."

The man looked at him, his gaze clearing. "Yeah. I am."

"No!"

But the cop had already gotten into his car. As Val watched in horrified disbelief, he slammed the door and pulled off.

"No, please," she whispered, watching the patrol car's red tail lights recede. "Don't leave me here with him!" But the lights kept going, shrinking slowly into the darkness. Leaving her alone with the vampire.

Biting down on her lower lip, Val looked at him, fighting not to cry. "What did you do to him?"

"What I had to." Cowboy stared across the parking lot, scanning for Hirsch. "Damn it to hell and back, Gerhard got away."

"He won't get far," she said numbly. "Not with that gut wound."

He snorted. "The bastard will heal by morning."

Val heard the ring of his boots on the pavement and shrank back against the car as he walked over and pulled the door away from her body. Wide-eyed, she stared up into his starkly handsome face as he nodded to the Lexus' interior. "Get in."

Her heart was pounding so hard it ached. She sucked in a breath, preparing to scream her lungs out.

"Save it, Valerie." His dark eyes narrowed, his mouth pulling into a grim, cold line. "One, I'm not going to let anyone take you away from me, and two, if you annoy me enough, I've got a roll of duct tape in the trunk and no scruples at all about gagging you with it. Three, I'm in a very bad mood, and you do not want to test me."

She straightened. Damned if she'd cower. "I always knew you were a gentleman," she said with sugared acidity.

To her satisfaction, a flush mounted Cowboy's high cheekbones. He leaned down until he was close enough to kiss. She found herself focusing on the sensuous line of his mouth like a mouse staring at a cat. "As a matter of fact, I am a gentleman. I'm not going to kill you, and I'm not going to rape you. Those are two guarantees you will not get from Edward Ridgemont. Get in the car."

A line of sweat broke out over her upper lip at the velvet threat in his eyes. Her defiance collapsed. She sank into the seat and mechanically pulled her legs in. He shut the door.

As he walked around the Lexus to the driver's side, Valerie fought to recover her angry courage. By the time he opened the door, she'd managed it. "You expect me to believe I'm safe with you?"

"You should." He stripped off his leather gloves and tossed them into the back seat. When she glanced down at them in the dome light, she saw they gleamed wet and red with Hirsch's blood. "I'm not some movie vampire who drains people like a frat boy sucking down a Budweiser." Sliding behind the wheel, he closed the door and started the car. "I don't kill—at least, not that way."

"You almost killed me," she spat. "And I was twelve years old. Why should I believe I'm any safer now?"

"Ridgemont had spent weeks starving me." Cowboy threw the car into reverse and twisted his powerful torso as he looked over his shoulder to back from the space. She shrank a little closer to the door. "I was..." Something bleak flickered in his eyes. "Mad. Under normal circumstances, vampires need no more than a pint or so of blood a day." He braked the car and paused, staring out the windshield. "But if I'd lost control that night...Yes, I would have killed you." The look he turned on her was level, intense in its demand she believe. "But I didn't lose control. The Hunger was worse than it's ever been in my life, and Ridgemont had planted a compulsion to kill you. But I didn't. I didn't hurt you then, and I won't hurt you now. All I want is to protect you from that bastard."

For a long suspended moment, she stared into his eyes. She had the oddest sensation—as if she was falling. As if she could...touch his mind. *Impossible.* And yet... She felt some part of herself loosen. Relax.

Trust.

No!

Val jerked her gaze away from that too handsome, too familiar face. He'd betrayed her before, and he was betraying her now. "I don't believe you," she gritted. "You spent seventeen years lying to me, Cowboy. Pretending to be something you aren't—human."

He set his jaw, threw the car into gear with a violent gesture and drove through the parking lot. "I am human. I'm just not mortal."

"You're a vampire," she growled. "Undead."

"Oh, come on!" His eyes blazed at her, impatient, demanding she believe. "Quit thinking like a medieval peasant. I'm alive. I don't sleep in a coffin. I'm not afraid of crosses or garlic, and I cast a reflection. I've got a soul. I don't turn into bats or wolves or mist...."

"And you can make cops think you're unarmed when you've got a three-foot sword in your hand. Quit trying to snow me, Cowboy."

"My name is Cade McKinnon," he gritted.

"*But you never told me that.* Not once in seventeen years! In fact, you said for years you were nothing but a dream!"

"Because I never intended you to find out any different! I wanted to keep you out of all this. As far away from Ridgemont and Hirsch as I could."

"What do you care?" she demanded, furious. "Why did you come into my dreams, Cow… McKinnon?"

"You reached out to *me*, Valerie. You were a child and you were terrified. I killed your dream vampires for you so you could feel safe." He stared stonily out the windshield. The stark illumination from the passing security lights threw moving bands of light and shadow across the planes of his intensely masculine face. "I was afraid of what the trauma was doing to you. I was afraid it would break you. In retrospect, I should have known you were stronger than that."

Val curled her lip in disbelief. "*I* reached out to *you*?"

But as he started to reply, she glanced out the windshield. Her heart leaped in hope.

Just ahead, a parking attendant looked up in his booth. Balding, bored and double-chinned, he sat like a lump on his stool. Val thought she'd never seen anyone more lovely in her life.

He'd see the handcuffs! If she could just get his attention, he'd call the police. It might not do any good, but then again, this time she might get lucky.

She tensed, hoping McKinnon wouldn't realize the danger and do something to hide the cuffs. Instead, he drove calmly up to the booth, rolled down the window, and held out his ticket. The attendant took it from him and turned back toward his cash register.

Heart pounding, Val spread her wrists apart on either side of the armrest, trying to make the handcuffs more noticeable. She didn't dare call the man's attention directly. If McKinnon realized what she was trying to do, he'd use whatever magic he had on the cop to make him ignore what was happening. But if the attendant spotted the 'cuffs without giving her away….

As the man turned to give McKinnon his change, his eyes slid to Val's offered wrists and widened. His jaw dropped as his gaze darted back to the vampire's face.

"She likes kinky sex," McKinnon said, without a flicker of expression.

"Oh." The attendant slumped back into boredom. "Have a nice night."

The booth's arm slid up, and the vampire guided the car out into the night. "Among other things, I'm a telepath," he told her, his tone matter-of-fact. "People believe whatever the hell I make them believe."

Val stared at him. Well, that explained the cop.

Would he do the same thing to her? Would he turn those dark, hypnotic eyes on her and purr, "Strip for me"?

It was too easy to imagine obeying him like a sleepwalker, taking off every stitch until her body stood naked and vulnerable under that dark, hungry stare. Heat mounted Val's cheekbones as she remembered the way the vampire had felt holding her down during their struggle, his muscled weight covering her so completely. Would those big hands stroke and tease, or would he just order her to spread her thighs?

And then there was all those dreams, when Cowboy had made love to her with such heat and strength and sensuality, wickedly skillful, impossibly seductive.

His jaw worked as he fed, simultaneously surging upward in such long, deep plunges that his big shaft almost slipped free with every driving thrust....

She licked her lips and blurted, "Are you going to use your powers on me, too?"

The vampire glanced over at her. Whatever he saw made him inhale sharply like a wolf catching a scent. Something so knowing and amused slipped into his eyes, she wondered in horror if he'd somehow seen the erotic images in her mind. His mouth kicked up in a half-smile. "Why? Would you like me to?"

"What? No!" She shrank back in her seat.

Cade knew from her appalled expression she was afraid he'd somehow read her thoughts. He hadn't, of course — since she was Kith, he couldn't, at least not while she was awake. But he could still use his supernatural sense of smell, and there had been more than a hint of arousal in her scent just now.

For a moment he let himself imagine what it would be like to really touch her, taste her, just as he had in all those luscious dreams....

No, Cade told himself firmly. *Not now, not ever.* She was off-limits. Besides, they had to put several hundred miles between them and Ridgemont. There wasn't time for a seduction.

Unfortunately, his cock didn't care about logic. The image of Valerie spread and naked under him sent heat steaming through his veins. He cursed silently. All the situation needed to really go to hell was for her to catch a glimpse of the rock hard bulge growing behind his zipper.

The scent of Hirsch's blood didn't help. It splattered the front of his uniform, and he could still smell it on the gloves. With that dark, tempting aroma filling his head, it was all too easy to imagine biting slowly into Valerie's luscious throat as he rode her hard.

He had to ditch the blood-soaked clothing before he did something he'd regret. Spotting a trash can on the corner, Cade pulled over. Valerie tensed warily as he got out. "What are you doing?" she demanded. "Why are we stopping?"

"I've got to get rid of this damn tunic," he said as he started unbuttoning it. "Hirsch bled all over it, and the smell is driving me crazy."

Val watched wide-eyed as he stripped off the jacket. Beneath it he wore a white T-shirt that hugged every ridge, plane and hollow of his impressive chest. He opened the Lexus' rear door and got the gloves, then balled them inside the jacket. Striding to the trash can, he bent to stuff the gory bundle as deep as he could. The tight black trousers pulled snug across his muscled butt, and the riding boots gleamed in the light of the street lamp. Something hot and feminine clenched inside her. She gritted her teeth and fought the reaction. *He's a vampire, you idiot. And he's been lying to you for seventeen years.*

McKinnon returned to the car and got in. "To answer your question, no, I can't influence your mind the way I can other mortals," he told her, picking up the argument again as he started the engine. "If I could, we wouldn't have had that little wrestling match back there. And you wouldn't be in your current mess."

She studied him warily. "I don't understand."

For a moment he was silent, threading the car into the late-night airport traffic. "The fact that I can't influence your thoughts means you're Kith."

Val frowned. "Kiss?"

"Kith. As in 'Kith and Kin.' To vampires."

"What the hell are you talking about?"

"You have psychic abilities. And that makes you Kith."

What kind of game was he playing now? "That's bull, McKinnon. I've never read anybody's mind in my life."

"Yes, you have. And I know damn well you remember it." He paused to guide the Lexus around a stalled taxi. "Think back to that night when you were a kid. I was on my knees, trying not to kill you. You looked into my eyes…."

And felt the sickening sensation of falling into madness, into clawing pain, into a Hunger greater than anything she'd ever known. A Hunger only blood could satisfy.

She jerked her gaze away from him. "I imagined that." Her voice shook.

"No. You didn't."

Val looked down at her hands twisted in the cuffs and curled them into fists. "Why did you do that to me?"

"I didn't. You did. You reached into my mind. I still don't know how. Even a Kith mortal shouldn't be able to touch a vampire's mind—our mental shields are too strong. But you did it anyway." The vampire shrugged. "The nearest I can figure, we were both so desperate, our minds…fused."

Val wanted to deny it. But then she remembered…. "Did you have sex with a woman tonight? Gray in her hair? Late forties, early fifties?"

McKinnon shot her a startled look. It was all the answer she needed.

"Hell." She let her head fall against the side window.

"You saw that?"

"Dreamed it." Val bit back a laugh. He sounded mortified. "Why have I never noticed this before? I don't read minds. And I'd have known, because I get lied to for a living." Half the people she'd interviewed for the paper seemed to view the truth as something to control like nuclear waste.

"Most Kith never realize they have psychic abilities," McKinnon said. Glancing at him, she was amused to note he still wore an expression of profound discomfort. "We think it's because they develop mental shields as children to protect themselves from the thoughts of those around them. Even vampires can't touch a Kith's mind." He paused. "When I made love to that woman, it was because I needed to feed. I expected a fight with Ridgemont and Hirsch, and I…."

She slanted him an amused look. "You sound like a man trying to explain himself to his girlfriend, McKinnon. I don't care who you sleep with." But as she said the words, Val felt a twinge that made her frown.

Was she actually jealous of a vampire?

"Careful, you stupid son of a bitch!" Hirsch bit back a yelp as Bobby Mason helped him into the back of the limousine. He would have punished the mortal for his carelessness, but he didn't dare divert his attention from the gaping wound in his guts. It was taking all the power he had to keep from bleeding into unconsciousness. Summoning Mason telepathically had almost finished him.

McKinnon was as good with a knife as the redskins he used to fight.

Mason muttered an apology and helped him lie down in the back seat. Hirsch hissed and cursed the chauffeur, Ridgemont and McKinnon equally with each flare of ripping pain.

"I told the Old One," he snarled as Mason lifted his legs onto the seat. "I told him that American bastard was plotting against us. Any fool could see it. But no, Ridgemont did not believe me. And look where it got us. First McKinnon almost blew us up, and now..." He ground his teeth as an incautious breath sent agony searing through him. "...and now he's gutted me."

"Maybe if you didn't talk...."

"Shut up and drive!" Panting, Hirsch subsided a moment, one hand clamped hard against his seeping wound as Mason hurried around to the driver's side. "Ridgemont always favored the American. The stupidity of sending me against him armed only with that ridiculous pig sticker! Did he want me to lose? And now McKinnon will Change the little Chase bitch...."

Which meant that the next time they fought, Hirsch was a dead man.

He ground his teeth together at the thought of the American's revenge as Mason started the limo with a hasty roar. The car lurched forward. Hirsch strangled a scream. "Careful, damn you!"

"Sorry, Mr. Hirsch."

"No, you're not," the vampire snarled. "But you will be."

Mason's broad shoulders hunched.

Panting, Hirsch focused his attention on his butchered body. He knew he'd need Ridgemont's help to repair the wound enough to risk the healing sleep, or it would take him days longer to recover.

Fucking American.

McKinnon had been his bane even before Hirsch became a vampire, back in his days as a Gestapo major in Occupied France. Even as Hirsch hunted members of the French underground, McKinnon had helped them. Using his vampire powers, the American had been a major thorn in the Reich's side, killing German soldiers, disrupting communications, destroying equipment.

A little hobby Ridgemont encouraged in the name of keeping McKinnon's edge sharp.

Finally Hirsch received a tip that the Underground's mysterious superman worked for an Englishman. It wasn't hard to track him down from there. Taking a squad of German soldiers, Gerhard headed for Ridgemont's country chateau to arrest both foreigners as spies.

He'd just bullied his way past the maid when he looked up to see Ridgemont standing on the stairs, a thin, terrifying smile on his face. "Well now," the Old One had said. "Wouldn't you make an interesting addition to the family? A little sibling rivalry would do McKinnon a world of good...."

When Hirsch woke days later, his platoon was dead, and he himself was a vampire — and Ridgemont's slave.

And a slave he'd remained for the next 60 years. He—a son of the Master Race! It was galling.

If he could only get his hands on that little Kith bitch, Hirsch thought through a fog of pain. He'd Change her and use the power she'd bring him to rip out McKinnon's guts. Then he'd go after Ridgemont.

And he'd be free at last—with the girl as *his* slave.

"This Kith thing," Val asked. "Kith and kin to vampires? What the hell does that mean?" She frowned as an ugly thought occurred. "I'm not going to start growing fangs, am I?"

Cade gave her a dark smile. "Not without help."

"That kind of help I don't need."

"No." He focused his attention on the traffic again. "But you're basically right. You do have the potential to become a vampire."

The thought sent a shiver of revulsion through her. To drink blood, to view other people as prey….

Val shook the reaction off. This was not the time for blind emotion. She needed to understand what was going on if she wanted to find a way out of this mess. *Pretend this is just another interview.* "I gather most people can't Change, then."

"Nope."

"So—what? The whole 'three bites and you're a vamp' thing is a myth?"

"Basically. Nobody's sure, of course, but I suspect vampirism is actually an infection. A virus, maybe. It definitely changes the body—makes you faster, stronger, harder to kill. Some kind of cellular change must be taking place."

She eyed him suspiciously. "Viruses don't act like that, McKinnon. They hijack your cells to make more of themselves, not turn you into Superman with fangs."

"Maybe not, but you sure as hellfire get sick when you Change. Kith are the only ones who have even a chance of surviving the process—it kills everybody else. And given that the Change begins with a blood exchange, it does sound like a contagion."

"Or some kind of symbioses."

"Could be. I'm just an ignorant nineteenth century country boy, so what do I know?"

Interested despite herself, she studied his clean profile in the blue neon light of a passing bar. "Did you say 'nineteenth century'?

How old are you, anyway?"

He shrugged. "I haven't exactly been keeping track of the birthdays, but I was born in 1846. Guess that would make me…."

"One hundred and fifty-seven. You look about thirty."

"I was thirty-seven when Ridgemont Changed me. Stopped aging then." He grimaced. "At least where it shows."

"Were you really a Texas Ranger?" Her eyes narrowed as she remembered all the other things he'd told her. "Or did you lie about that, too?"

He submerged her in an icy stare. "You sure you really want to piss me off this bad—considering you're chained to the door?"

Val's first instinct was to back down, but then she curled a lip and stiffened her spine. She was damned if she'd grovel to anybody, vampire or not. "What are you going to do? Bite me?"

"Don't tempt me."

A chill rolled over her at the heat and hunger in his eyes. Maybe it was time to quit pushing her luck.

Chapter Six

Slowly, cursing every step, Hirsch hobbled into the mansion, one arm draped over Mason's shoulder.

In the formal dining room, Gerhard, Ridgemont's mental voice rumbled with psychic power he could feel all the way to the base of his skull. *I'm at supper.*

Hirsch ground his teeth against the pain as the chauffeur helped him through the mansion's endless halls to his waiting sire.

They found Ridgemont lounging amid the gleam of dark wood and polished silver, a stiletto in his hand and a bowl of lemon slices at his elbow. On the table before him rested an enormous silver platter. A nude woman knelt in its center on a carpet of roses. Her long, auburn hair was the exact same shade as Valerie's.

A length of rope bound the girl into a tight, usable package, looping around her back and knees so she was bent double, arms bound at her side. Looking closer, Hirsch saw the thorns on the rose stems dug into her bleeding shins and the tops of her feet. Three thin cuts marked the out-thrust bowls of her ass; Ridgemont was just getting started with his meal.

The smell of blood hit the back of Hirsch's throat, and his mouth began to water as the Hunger punched through the pain of his wound.

"Sit down, Gerhard, and report," Ridgemont said, drawing the point of his knife delicately across one of the girl's pale buttocks. She jerked with a strangled cry. The Old One leaned forward and ran his tongue over the slice. Her fear poured over Hirsch like a waterfall, and he drew it in greedily, feeling himself strengthen.

Ridgemont rarely killed his victims; he didn't like leaving corpses to draw unwelcome official attention. But even without actually taking her life, he knew how to terrorize a woman so thoroughly he could feast on her pain and panic.

As the girl whimpered and struggled fruitlessly in her bonds, Mason lowered Hirsch into one of the chairs. When Gerhard leaned back, he noticed the chauffeur's gaze flick to Ridgemont's victim, then quickly away. Mason's intense guilt at being unable to help her was as delicious as the girl's fear. Gerhard almost purred as he drew in the psychic energy from both victims and channeled it into his starving cells, repairing the damage McKinnon had done.

Licking the point of his knife, Ridgemont lifted a brow. "Hirsch?"

Prodded, Gerhard hastily began his report. He would have preferred to downplay the ease with which the American had beaten him, but he didn't dare. Ridgemont took a dim view of efforts to mislead him, and his sire's displeasure was something best avoided.

As Hirsch described his fight with McKinnon, Ridgemont licked lazily at the girl's wounds, then buried his face against her sex. She jerked in her bonds. Hirsch felt him give her a psychic push into arousal.

Ridgemont favored a complex blend of emotions when he fed, and he enjoyed creating a mix of pain, arousal, and fear in his victims like a chef preparing an exotic dish.

It all seemed unnecessarily complicated to Hirsch. He'd always found simply beating his women worked well enough. Their reactions provided a psychic charge that, along with blood, more than met his needs. Besides, he enjoyed the sheer sensual pleasure of laying on the whip.

Gerhard had always been a simple man.

When he finished his story, Ridgemont straightened away from the girl and lifted a golden brow. "Letting Valerie distract you was stupid, as I'm sure that gut wound amply demonstrates. You can't allow your attention to wander in any fight, particularly against McKinnon. He has too many advantages over you as it is."

"But he has none over you," Hirsch said, pain making him reckless. "Why didn't you go with me to claim her? By now, he'll have..."

"Done nothing." The Old One lazily traced a fingertip in the girl's blood. "The gunslinger is too gallant to rape her, and seducing her will take time. You still have a chance."

"I?" Hirsch stared at his sire. "Aren't you going to...?"

"He'd know I was coming."

"But you could take her away from him so easily."

"I could, but I have no intention of doing so." Ridgemont smiled that slow, chilling grin of his. "I'll make you a deal, Hirsch. If you recover the girl, you can have her."

Gerhard's eyes widened. Did the Old One mean it?

Excitement stirred beneath the pain — along with a wave of dark hunger at the thought of taking Valerie.

"If, God forbid, Ridgemont ever gets his hands on you, never challenge him the way you have me," McKinnon told Val abruptly, breaking the long, tense silence that had fallen as he drove. "He'd hurt you. Badly. And since he's planning to make you a vampire, he could do a lot of very painful damage without killing you."

"But why?" She bunched her fists in the cuffs. "I mean, why Change me? What does he get out of it?"

His eyes flicked for one searing moment to her breasts. "Why do you think?"

Her stomach twisted. "Oh. That."

"Yes. That. He's a sexual sadist, Valerie. And as a vampire, you'd be able to take damn near any damage he dished out and survive."

Suddenly it all made a dreadful kind of sense, particularly given something else McKinnon had told her, something she hadn't processed in the heat of the moment: *He lured you here.* "Ridgemont did the same thing to my editor that you did to the cop, didn't he? That's why I got fired. And then he ordered everybody not to tell me why!"

"Probably."

"That son of a bitch." Val let her head fall back on the headrest. "Now I understand." She shot him a look as another thought occurred to her. "Could you fix it?"

McKinnon shrugged. "Maybe. Depends on how strong the compulsion was. Ridgemont's a lot more powerful than I am."

Val hesitated, trying to decide whether to ask him to do it. God only knew what he'd want in return. "How long has he been planning this, anyway?" she asked instead. "Did he know I was Kith when he killed my parents?"

McKinnon tipped up a big shoulder in a half-shrug. "I've been trying to figure that one out for years. It doesn't make sense. If he'd known what you are before the attack, why did he tell me to kill you? Kith females are even more rare than the rest of us."

"But he knows I'm Kith now, right?" She gave him a suspicious glare. "How did he find out? Did you spill the beans, McKinnon?"

He shot her a dark look. "Not willingly."

"What'd he do—sprinkle you with holy water until you talked?" She felt like a bitch as soon as the words were out of her mouth. *For God's sake, Val, he's a vampire.* But some part of her still flinched at talking like that to Cowboy.

"Actually, he pried it from my mind," McKinnon gritted, visibly stung. "He acted as though he was surprised, but that doesn't mean a damn thing. He loves playing those kind of games." Frowning, he tapped his fingers restlessly on the steering wheel. "He had to have known you were Kith. If he hadn't, why did he go after your folks to begin with? That attack is the only time I've ever known Ridgemont to prey on an entire family. Lone women are his preferred game."

"Did you ever ask him?"

"Yeah, but he's not in the habit of explaining himself."

"Well, if he did find out right after the attack, why didn't he come after me then?"

He threw her a dark look. "Luckily, Ridgemont's not a pedophile. He was waiting for you to grow up."

"I'm twenty-nine, McKinnon. I've been grown for a while."

"I noticed."

She grunted. "You did more than notice."

"Actually," McKinnon said, ignoring the sarcasm, "I expected him to kidnap you when you turned twenty, but he didn't. Which is a good thing, since I hadn't broken his control yet, and I wouldn't have been able to help you."

"Why not?" She eyed his chiseled features suspiciously. "And why would you want to?"

Chocolate eyes turned from the traffic to meet hers. "You've suffered enough as it is. You lost your parents and your childhood because of us. I don't want to see you lose your chance at a normal life."

"Very noble. But Hirsch said you'd need the power you'd get from me if you want to kill Ridgemont. What did he mean?"

He steered the car around a creeping Toyota with blinkers flashing. "Ridgemont's been a vampire eight hundred years, which makes him incredibly powerful…."

"Eight hundred…years?" She sat back, imagining what it would be like to live that long, do what Ridgemont must have done. God, he'd make an incredible story …But he'd probably eat any reporter stupid enough to try to interview him. "I guess you really are immortal."

"Assuming no one kills me, yes," McKinnon said, his mouth taking on a dry curve. "Which becomes problematic in a fight with Ridgemont. I can hold my own against him for short periods, but in any extended battle I wouldn't stand a chance."

"But turning me would change that?"

"In theory. I'd be able to use your powers to amplify my own to match his, at least long enough to kill him."

"So are you going to do it?" Her heart began to pound. If he said yes....

"Are you willing?"

"No."

He shrugged. "Then I'm not."

"But you just said you wouldn't be able to beat him in a fight otherwise. What are you going to do if he tracks us down?"

"Don't worry about it," McKinnon said shortly. "I'll protect you."

"How?"

"I'll think of something."

She sat back against the seat and studied him. "So you're just helping me out of the goodness of your heart?"

His jaw firmed. "It's something I need to do."

"No, it's not. You could walk away right now."

"Look, regardless of the circumstances, I've known you for seventeen years. I don't want to see you become a slave."

"Then let me go. I can do my own running."

He snorted. "You'd be flat on your back under Ridgemont before daybreak. And believe me, you wouldn't like it there. He has very unpleasant tastes."

She snorted. "At the moment, it's your tastes that worry me."

Hirsch's heart began to pound at the thought of the power he was being offered so casually. If Ridgemont was serious, it would be the opportunity he'd always dreamed of—a chance to free himself of his sire's control and kill both his enemies.

There had to be a catch. "Why?"

"Perhaps I want to see which of you is worthy."

He knew Ridgemont assumed the winner would be McKinnon. But it wouldn't be. He was damned well going to prove the old bastard wrong.

Hirsch shifted unwarily in his chair. And gasped in agony as his distraction cost him control over his gut wound. Blood began to pour again. He grabbed for his belly, sending power surging into the torn flesh. The bleeding stopped, but he couldn't quite make the ruined vessels heal.

"Idiot." Ridgemont got up to cover his hand with a broad palm. Dark, ancient energy washed over his body. Instantly, damaged tissues began to knit.

"Sleep now, Hirsch," the Old One told him, straightening. "I'll have a nice, terrified little meal waiting when you awake."

The unholy amusement in that ancient gaze carried him into unconsciousness.

As the German slid under, Ridgemont looked deep into his mind, searching for a memory he could use.

There. The back of the Lexus. Hirsch had clearly seen the car's license tag.

Smiling darkly, Ridgemont decided it was time to have a word with somebody in law enforcement about keeping an eye out for the gunslinger's car.

He started to call for one of the servants to bring him a phone. But as he did, his eyes fell on Elle, still bound and bleeding on the table.

The gunslinger could wait an hour or two, he decided, and unzipped his slacks.

"What's your sister's phone number?"

Valerie stiffened and snapped her head around to stare at McKinnon. "Why?"

"You need to tell her to get to safety," he said. "With you in my hands, Ridgemont will try to kidnap her as a bargaining chip."

"What would he...?"

"Do with her? Any damn thing he wants. And knowing Ridgemont, that could be a very unpleasant list." It was better not to sugarcoat the danger; he wanted to make damn sure she sent Beth to safety. "You need to tell her to clean out your checking account and hop a train or a bus for anywhere, under an assumed name. I don't suppose she has a false ID?"

"Uh, no."

"Too bad. She won't be able to book a flight, then." Cade frowned, wishing he'd had time to arrange an escape for the girl himself. He'd had to put this whole thing together too damn fast after the car bomb attempt failed. "Tell her not to use credit cards or identification. Use cash for everything to avoid leaving a paper trail Ridgemont can track. And don't let her tell you where she's going, in case we get caught."

She gave him a searching look, lines of tension bracketing her mouth. "Could he force me to tell him where she is?"

"Once he Changes you, he could peel you like an onion."

"But the advance Ridgemont paid me to ghostwrite his memoirs is most of the money in our account. If she cleans it out and we both disappear, he could have us charged with fraud."

The idea of Edward Ridgemont running to the police made Cade grin. "He won't go to the cops. It would never occur to him, and even if it did, it would be a waste of time."

"What do you mean?" The handcuffs rattled against the armrest as she shifted nervously. Then the light dawned. "Oh, yeah. You'd just put the whammy on them."

"Exactly. What's the number?"

"Uncuff me and let me dial it."

"No. Valerie, we don't have time for this. What's the number?"

She recited it reluctantly. He punched the buttons, hit send, and waited for Beth to pick up. When a female voice came on the line, he extended the phone one-handed and placed it against his captive's face.

Obviously working to keep her tone calm and even, Val repeated the instructions he'd given her. As she spoke, Cade could feel the silken skin of her face brush against his knuckles. He found himself thinking about other parts of her he suspected would be equally soft. Like those full, pretty breasts that felt so sweetly tempting in his dreams….

Hastily, he diverted his mind from that line of thought and tried to concentrate on Beth's bewildered protests. Valerie and her lush little body were off-limits.

Val clung to her fraying patience with both hands as Beth pelted her with questions. "Look," she said at last, cutting her sister off, "I can't explain what's going on because I'm not sure I understand it either. But I do know that Ridgemont is the man who killed our parents, and now he's after us. Our only chance is to run like hell." At least, it was her sister's only chance. She strongly suspected she herself didn't have a prayer one way or another. But she couldn't tell Beth that.

She could hear the angry frustration in Beth's voice. "I can't believe this— either that he killed Mom and Dad or he's after us again. What's his angle?"

He wants to make me a vampire. But she couldn't say that. "I don't understand it either."

"Guess the man who called was right after all. Who told you this anyway?" Sudden urgency sharpened her tone. "Val, are you okay?"

"Yeah." *At the moment.* Val's gray eyes slid toward Cade's handsome, implacable face as he kept one eye on her and the other on the road. She realized he must have been the one who made that warning telephone call the night before she left for New York. "As to how I know—I heard it from a reliable source." *If you can call somebody who might decide to turn you into a vampire a "reliable source."*

"But …"

"Do you trust me?"

"Stupid question," Beth huffed.

"Then pack your stuff and get out, and don't tell anybody where you're going. Not anybody. Just go."

"Where can we meet?"

McKinnon shook his head, apparently having overheard. "It's not safe for her to be anywhere around us."

Val blew out a breath. "I'll let you know when we can get together. Take the beeper and I'll call." *If I can.* She hadn't told Beth she'd been abducted. The news would only frighten her, and her sister needed to concentrate on her own safety.

"But…."

"You don't have much time. He could be coming for you. Get out." She blinked hard as tears stung her eyes. "Baby, I love you. Remember that. I…."

McKinnon took the phone away and turned it off.

Val glared at him, knowing she might never get another chance to talk to Beth. "I wasn't finished."

"You'd told her enough."

"How will I know she's safe? "

"I'll let you call the beeper later."

Let you. She jerked her hands against the cuffs, but they only rattled smugly. There wasn't a damn thing she could do. She was at McKinnon's mercy. "Where are you taking me?"

"I've got a house in South Carolina," he said. "We'll be safe there for a while."

"We're driving all the way to South Carolina tonight?"

"We'll stop somewhere in a few hours."

"Why?" She glanced at the clock on the dashboard. One A.M. "Oh. It'll be dawn then. When the sun comes up, you do the human Bic thing." *If I'm lucky.*

"No, actually that's a myth, so if you're trying to figure out a way to get me into the sunlight, don't waste your time. Besides, you're a hell of a lot safer with me than Ridgemont and Hirsch."

She snorted. "That's not saying much. I'd be safer with Charles Manson than Ridgemont and Hirsch."

He grinned. "Now you're getting the idea."

They'd been driving in silence for almost a half hour when Cade scented peppermint. *Stay out of sight, Abigail. I've got a feeling one look at you on top of everything else would send her into screaming hysterics.*

She's mortal, Cade. She probably wouldn't be able to see me, Abigail said, but remained invisible anyway. ***Why did you tell her you don't plan to Change her?***

Because I don't.

Val looked over at him and frowned. "Do you smell peppermint?"

"It's the air freshener."

My, she is sensitive, the ghost said. ***She'll give you a lot of power.***

Cade sighed. Abigail's one-track mind could be maddening. *No, she won't. Were you listening at all just now? I am not going to Change her.*

You don't have a choice, Cade. Abigail's psychic broadcast was edged with fear and frustration. ***If you want to kill Ridgemont, you need the power she'll give you.***

I'll find another way.

How? You've been trying for years, and nothing's worked. That car bomb is the closest you've ever come….

He tightened his grip on the wheel. If Abigail hadn't interfered, Val wouldn't be in this mess right now. *I wouldn't bring up the car bomb, if I were you.*

But this is the opportunity you've been waiting for! I've never understood why you refused to go after Valerie once she grew up….

Look, I remember what it was like when Ridgemont turned me, Cade said. Thinking about that night still made his gut clench. And after what happened to Caro…. *Even if he hadn't been a psychotic son of a bitch, even if he'd left Caroline alone, I would have hated him just for the way he forced the Change on me. I will not do the same thing to Valerie. Period. It's not an option.*

So what happens when he tracks you down? And sooner or later, he will. She bulled on before he had a chance to answer. ***I'll tell you what'll happen—he'll butcher you like a suckling pig. And as for your precious Valerie, she'd think Caro got off lucky.***

He grimaced. Abigail was right, dammit, but he didn't care. There were some things he just couldn't do. *There's got to be a way of killing Ridgemont that doesn't include raping Valerie.*

Why don't you just explain it to her? She's not a stupid woman. If she realizes….

Dammit, Abigail, how many times do I have to say it? It's not an option. She's going to have a chance at a normal life.

No, she won't. In the end, it'll be you or it'll be Ridgemont, but it's going to be one of you. And you know it.

Not if I can help it.

Abigail's frustration rolled over him in thick waves. ***You're going to get yourself killed.***

Maybe. But I won't die a rapist.

No, just a fool. The smell of peppermint faded, leaving him alone in the car with his captive.

The Corrington Sleeper Motel in Corrington, Virginia was the first hotel in one hundred miles with a lit "Vacancy" sign. McKinnon drove into the lot and parked the Lexus in a space just beyond the lobby's line of sight.

Val watched as he got out and walked around to her side, her muscles coiled into knots. She bit her lip and looked up at him warily when he swung the door open, pulling her handcuffed wrists with it. The idea of getting a hotel room with a vampire— especially Cowboy….

Reading her expression, McKinnon sighed. "You'd be a lot safer inside with me than alone out here." Kneeling, he dug the key from the pocket of his uniform pants. Muscle flowed and rippled under his white T-shirt with the movement. "Hirsch ought to be sleeping off that knife wound, but he could have more endurance than I think. And Ridgemont…."

She winced. "Okay, you've convinced me."

He removed the cuffs and tucked them into a back pocket as Val rubbed at her chaffed wrists. With a courtesy that seemed automatic, he reached out to take her hand and help her from the car. She eyed him thoughtfully as she stood. If she had to depend on a vampire's protection, knowing he had a chivalric streak was decidedly comforting.

He took her elbow as they started across the parking lot. His dark eyes scanned the surrounding cars restlessly, searching for potential threats.

Val frowned. If Ridgemont did show up, McKinnon was going to end up dead. Her mind produced an involuntary image: those chocolate eyes blank and empty, that big body cold and still…. She shuddered.

Dammit, why did she care so much? He was a vampire. He'd

been lying to her for years. Why did she keep seeing him as Cowboy?

Part of the problem was that he still acted the part. Like telling her to warn Beth. Or back in the airport parking lot, when she'd tried to claw his eyes out and he hadn't used that vampire strength to knock her cold. Even seventeen years ago, when he'd fought both the Hunger and Ridgemont's compulsion to save her.

It'd be easy to resist the undead monster of her nightmares. It was much harder to say no to the handsome Texas Ranger of her dreams. Even if he did have fangs.

But she had to. If she let him win her over, she'd end up in his bed with those teeth in her throat before she knew what hit her.

And what really worried her was that thought wasn't nearly as appalling as it should have been.

Chapter Seven

Val was still glowering at her own errant libido when they stepped up to the cracked white counter to find the desk clerk engrossed in a portable television. The set was turned so that she couldn't see the screen, but judging from the gasps and moans in the soundtrack, she had a pretty good idea of the program content.

Good God, she realized, as blatantly sexual groans filled the lobby, *I'm about to get a motel room with a vampire. A cheap motel room.*

Another image from one of her dreams promptly flashed through her mind: *Cowboy loomed over the woman, one of her plump thighs draped over his arm, a big hand gripping the bend of her other knee, holding her legs spread wide. The tight, hard muscles of his abdomen lacing as he slowly pumped his thick shaft in and out....*

"Deeper, baby!" a female voice purred. "Pound your big cock into my tight little...."

"Turn that off," McKinnon snapped. "There's a lady present." His voice dropped to an irritated growl. "If there was another hotel with a vacancy in a hundred miles, I'd..."

Startled, Val looked over at him to see a tinge of red coloring his high cheekbones. He was blushing? The vampire was *blushing*?

The clerk's eyes widened and went blank as he fumbled to obey. Val grinned.

McKinnon caught sight of her smirk. "Well, it was disrespectful, watching that with you here," he said, looking defensive.

"And you wanted to protect my virgin ears? That's sweet,

McKinnon. That's really sweet."

Something dark and wicked sparked in his eyes. He leaned close to her ear and whispered, "I'd think you'd find my desire to protect your virgin *anything* a comfort. Under the circumstances." He looked up at the clerk. "We'd like a room."

Val blew out a hissing breath. *Note to self: don't tease McKinnon. He doesn't take it well.*

After McKinnon pulled the Lexus around to the motel wing where their room was located, Val got reluctantly out of the car.

Golden morning light poured over the parking lot and its motley collection of cars, most of them speckled with either primer or rust or both. A woman emerged from one of the rooms towing a pretty dark-haired child who knuckled sleep from her eyes. The mother nodded at Val and McKinnon with a Southerner's automatic courtesy.

Nodding back, Val said absently to McKinnon, "Looks like it's going to be a beautiful day."

"If you say so." He glowered up at the bright sky from behind the sunglasses he'd put on at daybreak. "I need to get the car unloaded. I smell barbecue, and I think it's me."

She looked over in alarm as he reached into the back seat and pulled out the sheathed long sword. "I thought you said the bursting-into-flames thing was a myth."

"It is. I don't burst into flames." He drew the weapon and popped the trunk as he walked around to get their bags. "I just turn a interesting shade of second degree burn."

"Ouch. Vampirism has its drawbacks, doesn't it?" Automatically, Val moved over to help.

"Yeah, though never getting old, sick, or bald doesn't exactly suck." He handed her one of the smaller bags and tucked two of the others under his left arm.

"Then again, there's Ridgemont."

He hefted the sword in his right hand and grimaced. "Put that way, old, sick, and bald doesn't sound that bad."

As they started toward their room, it occurred to Val that their teasing exchange was yet another sign of how dangerously at ease she'd become with him. And she couldn't afford that. He'd lied to her for too many years, concealing his vampire nature behind a mask of heroism. Maybe he was telling the truth now about his motives—but maybe he wasn't.

Yet her instincts still insisted she was safe. Could she trust those gut feelings, or were they just a conditioned response to a man who'd done far too good a job winning her trust?

Those instincts also told her something else, something she had no trouble believing: McKinnon wanted her. And that could mean trouble, because the man was too damn good at seduction.

While she contemplated the implications of that danger, McKinnon put down the bags outside the room and unlocked the door. He stepped back and gestured her inside. As she moved past him, the nape of her neck prickled with sensual awareness.

Yeah, she thought. *Way too good at seduction.*

Swallowing, she scanned the room as he shut the door. The decor was regulation cheap motel: blue carpet, drapes and bedspread, dark, pressed-wood furniture, a standard-issue ugly print hanging over the king-sized bed he'd insisted on.

The only bed in the room.

"Relax, Val. You look like you expect me to eat you," McKinnon said, looking far too handsome for her peace of mind as he put the suitcases down. The powerful muscles in his chest rippled under the thin T-shirt, and she unconsciously dropped her eyes to watch. When she glanced back up, he grinned wickedly. "I promise I won't even nibble—not without an invitation, anyway."

Val blew out an exasperated breath. "You need to make up

your mind, McKinnon."

He lifted a brow. "About?"

"One minute you're Dudley DoRight, the next you're the Big Bad Wolf. You need to pick a personality and stick to it, because you're giving me whiplash."

He laughed, a rich male rumble. Unnerved, she made for the bathroom beyond the bed.

"What are you doing?" McKinnon moved after her as she stepped inside.

"Some of us have to answer the call of nature." She batted the door closed, forcing him to retreat.

His voice floated through the thin wood. "I've been hearing the call of nature for hours, Valerie. I just don't think you want me to answer it."

"Aren't there some little pigs somewhere you should be terrorizing?" she muttered under her breath.

He heard her, of course. "Why should I settle for pork when I can have Red Riding Hood?" That seductive chuckle sounded again, teasing heat from parts of her that should know better.

"Stop that," Val whispered to her nipples. They stubbornly continued to thrust against the silk of her blouse. *Yep,* she thought glumly, plopping down on the commode, *I am definitely in trouble.*

McKinnon stared speculatively at the bathroom door, feeling every bit the wolf she'd called him. He tongued the tips of his fangs and tugged at his suddenly uncomfortable slacks. "The better to eat you with, my dear," he murmured.

Cut that out, he told himself severely.

Yet…making love to her didn't mean he had to change her. And there were definite advantages to seducing Valerie beyond the obvious physical delights. If they became the lovers in reality they'd been in dreams, he'd no longer have to worry about her making some stupid attempt at escape and running right into Ridgemont's waiting fangs.

And then there was the Hunger. He could go without feeding for quite some time, but eventually he'd weaken. He couldn't afford that, not with a fight with Ridgemont so likely.

Of course, he'd have to limit himself to a very small quantity of blood if he intended to make love to her repeatedly, but if her orgasms were intense enough, that would be sufficient. At least for the time being.

Except...having tasted Valerie, would he be able to let her go when this was over? He remembered all those dreams when he'd felt her move against him, silk and seduction. Damn. He couldn't risk it.

Which meant he had to use other means to ensure she didn't escape while he slept. She wouldn't like his methods, but he had no intention of giving her a chance to get herself killed.

Val dawdled in the bathroom finger-combing her hair. The longer she could put off crawling into bed with the Transylvania Kid, the better. She wasn't exactly confident in her ability to fend him off. She had to get away from him.

Maybe once he went to sleep. She'd wait for him to drift off, then grab his car keys and make for the parking lot. With any luck, she'd be in another state before he woke up. She could meet up with Beth and....

But was that really such a good idea? If Ridgemont caught them, they'd be defenseless. It was one thing to risk her own life, but she was damned if she'd expose her sister to that monster. And yet, leaving Beth to fend for herself wasn't a good idea either.

Too, the kid was due to start college in a couple of weeks. The Art Institute of Atlanta was prestigious and exclusive, and if Beth lost her slot in the fall, she might not be able to get in again.

On the other hand, Ridgemont would be able to find Beth there all too easily. If Val dropped out of sight, he'd kidnap her sister to force her back into the open. The thought of what he might do to Beth in the meantime made her blood run cold.

What the hell was she going to do?

First things first, Val decided. Get away from McKinnon, then go from there.

Staring at her reflection in the mirror, Val leaned her elbows on the counter and tried to come up with an escape plan. It all depended on how deeply McKinnon slept….

Suddenly she smelled the sugary bite of peppermint. Absently, Val looked around the bathroom, expecting to see a bowl of candy. She wouldn't mind a little comfort food right now….

Let him Change you, a childish voice whispered.

Stiffening in alarm, Val whirled. There was no one in the bathroom with her. Except…. The shower curtain was drawn across the tub. She reached for it. "Okay, kid, get out of there. Does your mother know…." She whipped back the plastic, but the tub was empty.

You'll die if you don't, Valerie, the piping voice said. ***It's the only chance you've got.***

The hair lifted on the back of her neck as Val stared around the bathroom. Empty.

She jerked open the door and stared out at McKinnon. "Did you hear something?"

He looked over his shoulder at her as he lay belly-down across the bed, the covers bunched in the floor. Both long arms stretched down between the headboard and the mattress, but she couldn't see what he was doing. "What?"

"Did you hear a little girl talking?"

He turned his head and went back to work. "No."

"Must have been my imagination." Under the circumstances, it was no wonder. She frowned at him as she stepped out of the bathroom, peeling off her wrinkled jacket to drop it over a chair. What was he doing now?

The thin fabric of his T-shirt and the position of his lifted arms made his back seem a mile wide. By contrast, his waist looked as narrow as a boy's, and his taut buns in those tight trousers reminded her of upturned cereal bowls. She wondered what he'd do if she bit him right on one of those deliciously muscled cheeks.

The idea is to stay out *of the vampire's bed, Val*, she reminded herself. Still, the thought was a little too tempting. To distract her clamoring libido, she asked, "McKinnon, what are you up to?"

"Making sure you don't do something stupid." He rose onto his hands and knees with a luscious muscular flex and backed off the bed, leaving a twisted length of sheet stretching out from under the headboard.

"What's that for?"

He pulled the handcuffs out of his pocket. "Well, I've got to tie the 'cuffs to something."

Val recoiled. "Forget it. I don't do bondage."

"Look, I've been smelling Hirsch's blood for about four hours now, and it's making me hungry. I need a shower, and I'm not going to risk you sneaking out the door while I take one."

She backed up, knowing she didn't dare let him cuff her; escape would be impossible. "What if I promise to be a good girl?"

"Sorry, you don't strike me as that trustworthy."

"Neither do you." Val whirled toward the door.

And went flying backward toward the bed as he caught her. She hit the mattress and bounced, but before she could even think about rolling off, McKinnon was on top of her.

Suddenly Val was covered in hard, hot male, his long fingers wrapped around one of her wrists. She tried to flail at him with her free hand, but the bracelet's cool metal had already snapped around her captured wrist. As the lock clicked, he caught her swinging fist and cuffed that wrist too. She cursed him breathlessly, bucking, but he ignored her struggles and calmly knotted the sheet around the short chain between the cuffs. Furious, Val arched against him…and was suddenly aware of a hard ridge mashing against her belly. It felt huge. She froze, eyes widening.

"Yeah, I've got a hard-on," he told her. As he spoke, she glimpsed the tips of his fangs. "That's why I'm taking the shower."

"May I suggest throwing in a few ice cubes?" she gritted.

"I might just do that." He rolled off her and turned toward the bathroom, bending to pick up the sword he'd propped against the chair as he walked by.

Val watched his broad back disappear through the door, then let her head drop to the pillow. As she blew out a breath, her stiff nipples rubbed against the lace of her bra. "Save a few cubes for me while you're at it," she muttered.

If you let him Change you, you could have him forever, the young voice whispered.

Val froze as icy fear instantly killed her arousal. "McKinnon!" she yelled, but water was already hissing through the pipes. She lifted her head and bellowed at the closed door, "McKinnon, dammit, use those vampire ears! I need you!" No answer. "Ah, hell." Disgusted, she turned her head away….

And looked right at a glowing little girl standing beside the night stand.

Val yelped and tried to roll off the bed, but the handcuffs jerked her up short. Kneeling with her arms twisted painfully, she stared at the child. "Who the hell are you?"

I'm Abigail McKinnon, the voice said, though the little girl's lips didn't move. ***Cade is my brother.***

McKinnon had said he was born in 1846. Any little sister of his would have to be….

"Oh, man," Val moaned. "First vampires, now ghosts. I'm trapped in a Halloween after-school special. All we need is

Frankenstein's monster and the Wolfman." She gave her hands a hard jerk, but the cuffs held fast.

The ghost blinked huge, dark eyes that looked a lot like Cade's. ***There is no such thing as Frankenstein's monster.***

"Does that mean there's a Wolfman?" Val asked with a flippancy born of raw nerves. "No, don't tell me—he's your other brother."

The little ghost's face hardened with bitterness. ***My other brother was shot down at Gettysburg. Pa tried to save him, but took a chunk of shrapnel in the chest and died for his pains. Cade is the only one left.*** Anger twisted that soft glowing mouth. ***And you're going to get him killed.***

Hoooo boy. "Look, I didn't ask Cade to get involved in my problems. I can take care of myself."

Abigail laughed silently. The mental sound of it was too grating and bitter to come from a child. ***You've never seen what Ridgemont does to women like you. If you have any sense, you'll beg Cade to make you a vampire. Now. While there's still time. It's the only way either of you has a chance in hell.***

No matter what she looked like, Val realized, the ghost was not a little girl. Not mentally, anyway. "But I don't want to become a vampire." Twisting her hands around, she fumbled surreptitiously for the knot tying the handcuffs to the sheet. She was damn well going to get loose and get out. She'd had enough of this. Count Cowboy and Ghost Brat could find somebody else to play with. "I don't want to become some evil thing that drinks blood."

My brother is not evil, girl. The ghost's lips peeled back from her small teeth. ***Don't confuse what the others are with him. Yes, Ridgemont and Hirsch are twisted and evil, but then, they always were. Cade is a good man whether he drinks blood or not. And he deserves to live.***

"So do I, damn it!" Val lifted her head to glower. "I just want a normal life. Ever since my folks were murdered, that's all I've ever wanted." Hoping to distract the ghost while she picked at the knot around the cuffs, she began to babble. "Two kids and a husband that loves me. And a dog. One of those big, fuzzy dogs." Damn, McKinnon had tied her tighter than a calf at a rodeo. "An Irish Setter, maybe. Setters are nice dogs. I had a friend who owned a Setter...."

Idiot. Abigail floated upward, her full shirt beginning to lift and whip around her as if in a rising invisible wind. ***You don't get a normal life. You're going to become a vampire.***

"No," Val whispered, a chill rolling over her at the utter certainty in the ghost's voice.

Yes. Either my brother will do it, and the two of you will kill Ridgemont together, or you'll refuse him and the monster will murder him and enslave you. Those black eyes started to glow with a cold, unearthly light as Abigail's hair streamed back from her head. Her heart-shaped face grew gaunt, the translucent skin darkening, sagging. Rotting.

A piece of the ghost's cheek plopped to the carpet to reveal gleaming bone. Her eyes bulged as her lids melted away, decaying lips blackening and shrinking from small white teeth. ***But I'll tell you this,*** the lipless mouth said, ***if you get my brother killed, I swear I will haunt you all your miserable, endless life.***

Jaw gaping in a silent scream, tattered bits of rotting flesh flapping around her skull, the ghost shot right at her.

Val shrieked with all the air in her lungs.

Cade was rinsing the last of the shampoo from his hair when he heard Valerie scream in utter terror. *Shit,* he thought. *Ridgemont!*

He dove from the shower, grabbed his sword off the narrow counter as he went by, and barreled through the door. Naked and dripping, he fell into guard, lifted the blade and scanned the room for his enemies.

But all he saw was Val, curled against the headboard in a quivering, hysterical knot. "Valerie!" He strode toward her, grabbed the twisted sheet that was still tied around the handcuffs, and ripped it in two with a yank so he could lift her off the bed. She hooked her handcuffed wrists over his head and clung to his neck, sobbing, her shaking body plastered against his. He slid a comforting arm around her waist, the other hand still holding the sword. "What happened? Did Ridgemont....?"

"No!" she gasped. "It was your sister!"

He blinked. Oh, hellfire. What had Abigail done now? "She can't hurt you, Val. She's a ghost."

"She *rotted*, dammit! She turned into a skull and she said if I got you killed, she'd haunt me! And then she...." Val broke off and sobbed. "God damn it, I feel like an idiot!"

Cade sighed and pulled her close, throwing the sword on the bed so he could hold her. "She didn't mean it. She's just protective."

Val drew back to shoot him a glare through glittering tears. "The hell she didn't mean it! You didn't see the look on her face. While it *rotted*. Jesus!" She burrowed against his neck again.

"Abigail!" Exasperated, he stared around the room for her. "You come apologize this minute."

"God, don't call her back...."

But the ghost had already appeared next to the television, her expression mulish. He was relieved to see she looked the same as always. ***I am not going to apologize,*** Abigail announced, glowering evilly at Val, who shrank back against his chest. ***Somebody has to make her see the risk you're running.***

That isn't your place. He clung to his fraying temper and tightened his grip on his shivering captive. *Tell her you're not going to haunt her.*

She bared her small, glowing teeth. ***No. Because if she gets you killed, I'm going to.***

Abigail....

With a flounce of lace and petticoats, she turned and flew right though the wall. Val jerked in his arms with a gasp.

He sighed. "I'm sorry."

She didn't answer, instead clinging to him as her shudders subsided. Her body felt deliciously soft and yielding against his. He stroked her narrow spine and crooned nonsense in her ear, trying to ignore his hardening cock. To hold her again, touch her, even under such circumstances…it was so damn sweet. So tempting. "You know, she's not really all that bad," he said at last, in part to distract himself from his own rising hunger.

"Oh, right." Val sniffed and wiped her eyes with one handcuffed wrist. "And the Headless Horseman was really a sweet guy. The whole decapitation thing was all a cruel misunderstanding…. Damn, McKinnon, you're wet." She pulled back from him and looked down. Her eyes widened. "And naked."

And she might as well be, he realized, heat washing through him as he got a good look himself.

A very good look.

When Val had burrowed against his dripping body, she'd soaked that pretty mint blouse right through. Now the wet, transparent fabric clung lovingly to her exquisite breasts. A cream lace bra cupped the full mounds, but one of the cups had drooped to reveal a shy pink nipple. He stared at it. And longed to flick the little point with his tongue until it was bold and red.

"Ummm." Blushing as furiously as only a redhead can, Val unhooked her arms from around his neck and eased away. "Don't you think you'd better dry…." Her eyes dropped to his lengthening erection. "Off!" The last word emerged as a squeak.

It suddenly occurred to him this might be a good time to try that seduction, if only to keep her too busy to run. He gave her his best wolfish smile—complete with fangs. "The better to eat you with, my dear."

If the Big Bad Wolf looked anything like McKinnon, it's no wonder Red Riding Hood ended up lunch, Val thought. *Though he sure as hell doesn't look like anybody's grandma.*

Not with that erection, anyway. She stared down at it, dry mouthed, feeling like a bird hypnotized by a snake. A very big snake.

It jutted out at her boldly, so broad she didn't think she could get her fingers all the way around the base, flushed dark with his arousal. The shaft was long and straight and beautiful, with thick blue veins snaking along its length, and a big, heart-shaped head. His balls nestled beneath it, cocooned in silken hair as they hung between his powerful thighs. Dazed, she let her eyes track up his body from that stunning shaft, realizing he was just as beautiful as he'd looked in all those erotic dreams. Six-feet-three inches of sculpted masculinity.

But this wasn't her dream hero. This was McKinnon, flesh and blood … and vampire.

Breath caught, Val looked into his eyes. There was hunger there, yes, burning and dark and thoroughly male. A hunger not for blood, but for sex. For her.

The nostrils of his straight nose flared as if drawing in her scent, and his tongue slipped out to wet his lower lip. Her gaze dropped helplessly to his mouth, remembering those burning dream kisses. Kisses she could now taste in reality if she just leaned forward….

His eyes narrowed and he stepped close again, so close her peaked nipples touched his damp skin. A bead of water slid from his wet hair and down his temple to trace a shining path along a high, arrogant cheekbone.

Heart pounding, Val watched his head dip until his mouth touched hers, just a silken brush at first, gently seductive. She knew she should step back, but desire rooted her feet to the floor. She heard a low of hunger and knew it was her own.

As if that helpless sound was the signal he'd been waiting for, McKinnon's arms slid around her, pulling her against his hard, powerful body. Helpless to do anything else, Val let her lips open. His tongue slipped in, gliding slickly. Unable to resist, she stroked her own against it. He deepened the kiss, his mouth growing more and more hungry against hers.

His skin felt cool from his shower, wet under her hands as she wrapped her arms around him to dig her nails into his shoulders. His body was all ridges and hollows, so hard and strong she had to draw back to gasp.

He suckled thirstily at the corner of her mouth, then tasted his way down her chin until her spinning head fell back so he could press a trail of burning kisses along the thin flesh of her neck. Val clung dizzily to him, whimpering at the intensity of it. His teeth scraped her skin, a tiny pain….

And she saw her mother, twisting in agony as Hirsch sank his fangs into her throat. Remembered the dream Cowboy feeding from the older woman as he fucked and used her.

That memory touched off one even more frightening: Cade's horrifying vampire Hunger seventeen years before. The Hunger that had scored nightmares into her brain like raking claws. A chill rolled over her, cutting through the erotic spell he'd woven so skillfully. Val jerked back, slapping her cuffed hands against his chest. "What are you doing?"

"Making love to you," he murmured, his eyes all velvet darkness as his muscled arms tightened.

Oh, God, she thought wildly. *What do I do if he won't stop?*

Chapter Eight

"No!" She tried to pull away, but he didn't let go. "You said you wouldn't make me!"

Cade stopped dead, looking down at her face a moment before squeezing his eyes shut, visibly fighting for control. She watched, tense. If he lost that battle….

McKinnon straightened his shoulders and stepped back, releasing her as his face assumed cool, expressionless lines. "And I meant it."

He pivoted like a soldier and walked into the bathroom. Val slumped, breathing hard from fear—and though she hated to admit it, lingering arousal.

He came out a moment later with a couple of towels. Handing her one, he draped the other over his shoulder and picked up his slacks, reaching into a pocket for the handcuff key. She held out her wrists.

"You can have the bathroom. Go change out of those wet things while I dress out here." He briskly unlocked the cuffs, his distant tone contrasting starkly with the lingering heat in his eyes.

Val nodded and walked on shaking legs to the suitcase he'd left on the bureau. As she bent, she saw his reflection in the mirror. He was staring at her bottom, his gaze simmering and feral. A shiver skated her spine.

McKinnon looked up and met her eyes in the mirror.

"I guess the vampires-cast-no-reflection bit is another myth," she said, trying for a less incendiary topic.

"So are a lot of the things you believe about us." A muscle

ticked in his square jaw. "I'm not a monster, Valerie. If I had been, I wouldn't have stopped just now."

He had a point. He had stopped—and if she was honest with herself, he could have seduced her out of her fear. He definitely could have forced her.

So maybe…maybe she really was safe.

Or not.

Val bent her head to dig through the suitcase with trembling hands. The moment she found a T-shirt and a pair of sweats, she escaped to the safety of the bathroom.

Clutching her clothes, she collapsed against the door, breathing hard. She saw the shower curtain hanging half across the tub and shuddered, the temptation to hide out dying when it occurred to her Abigail might put in another appearance.

She was dressed and back in the bedroom in less than a minute.

McKinnon had put on a pair of nylon jogging shorts that didn't do nearly enough to cover all that magnificent supernatural skin. Both muscled arms were lifted as he briskly toweled his hair dry. Val sat on the bed and tried not to watch the bunch and play of tempting brawn as he moved, but her rebellious eyes kept drifting in his direction.

When he finished and reached for the handcuffs he'd left lying on the bed, she stirred. "Please, McKinnon. Don't. I don't…." She stopped and swallowed. "Between one thing and…another, I'd really rather not be cuffed. I promise I won't try to escape."

He gave her a long, considering look and nodded slowly. "All right."

"Thank you." She let her shoulders slump in relief, then climbed quickly between the covers and flipped them up to her chin. Acutely aware that he stood by the bed watching her, Val curled up on her side facing the window. The lined curtains were thick, but she could still see the morning light filtering through. She stared at the golden glow, her eyes burning with exhaustion. *It's daylight,* she told herself. *I'm safe. McKinnon promised. He didn't handcuff me when he could have. He didn't force me when he could have. And he didn't seduce me. I'm safe.*

At least from him. If only she was so sure about all the other supernatural critters who had it in for her....

The bed gave as he climbed in behind her. A strong arm looped around her waist and pulled her back against his big body. His warmth enveloped her, and tense muscles loosened along her spine. He felt so damn familiar. Despite everything—despite his lies, despite her own traumatic memories, a part of her persisted in seeing him as Cowboy, her Texas Ranger hero.

Thinking how illogical it was to feel such a sense of safety in a vampire's arms, Val let her gritty eyes slip closed.

Officer Ken Bratton made his morning circuit through the Corrington Sleeper parking lot. Mostly it was a waste of time, but every once in a while he'd find a car listed on the day's hot sheet of stolen vehicles. Bad guys liked cheap hotels.

When he spotted the black Lexus in the line of ancient Toyotas and decrepit Fords, the car caught his eye because it was so thoroughly out of place. People who could afford vehicles like that didn't stay at the Sleeper.

Bratton scooped the day's Hot Sheet off the seat beside him. As he half-expected, he found the car's license tag number listed among the others cops were to watch out for. And the description matched—a black 2003 Lexus.

Then he frowned. The car wasn't listed as stolen, nor was he supposed to hold the driver for questioning. Instead, anybody who spotted the Lexus was directed to call dispatch, who was in turn ordered to notify the N.Y.P.D. Which was definitely strange, since they had no jurisdiction way out here in Virginia.

But orders were orders. Bratton picked up his radio handset and made the call.

Cade lay on his side with Val curled against his body. Each time he drew in a breath, her scent flooded his head, rich with the faint, heady perfume of lingering arousal. He tried to ignore it despite the marble-hard cock resting against her sweetly muscled bottom. The Hunger was awake and prowling, prodding him to roll her onto her back and finish the seduction he'd started.

Forget it, he told himself sternly. He'd sworn to leave her alone, and he damn well wouldn't violate her trust. Particularly considering it was astonishing that she'd trust him at all.

The fact that she slept so peacefully in his arms suddenly struck him as a rare gift. Lying there listening to her heartbeat, Cade slowly relaxed into a strange, fragile sense of peace. He knew reality would be back soon enough, but that only made him more determined to enjoy this moment. Savoring it, he drew her close against him, settled his erection against her backside, and felt the tension drain from his body.

Heat kissed Val's face. She heard a pop and crackle and smelled the autumn scent of wood smoke riding the wind. Dragging her eyes open, she saw a campfire a few feet away, licking at the darkness from a ring of uneven stones. Dazed, she lifted her head and looked around. Moonlight painted a landscape out of a John Ford movie—high cliffs clawing against the sky, sand, rocks and mesquite, all of it desolate and coldly beautiful.

A chuffing noise startled her. Val turned to see a huge white horse standing a few feet away, shimmering and ghostly in the moonlight. The animal studied her with eyes that reflected the campfire, glowing eerily green.

Across the fire from her, a man lay on a bedroll, his long legs crossed in a pair of Levi's, a white shirt straining over the powerful curves of his chest. The star of a Texas Ranger, handmade from a silver coin, gleamed against the darkness of his leather vest.

Then, with a dream's sudden illogic, the shirt was gone, leaving nothing but the vest covering his muscled torso. Val, submerged in sleep, silently approved.

He lifted a gloved hand and pushed up the brim of his white Stetson. His eyes, black in the firelight, studied her and began to burn with masculine arousal.

When Val looked down, she found that she was wearing a filmy modern negligee, lacy and thin as a whisper. Her nipples were tight pink points under the delicate fabric, and they ached, as if begging for Cowboy's mouth.

She shifted her legs as heat gathered between them. She was wearing a tiny pair of lace panties, but as she looked at them, they too disappeared, revealing auburn curls. Val jerked her eyes up, one hand shooting down to cover her vulnerable sex.

"You don't have to hide from me. Not here." He rolled off the bedroll and began to crawl toward her on his hands and knees, powerful muscle bunching in his biceps and shoulders as he moved. The brim of his hat cast his face into shadow, but she saw the glitter of his eyes, watching her from beneath it.

"This is dangerous," she told him.

"It's a dream, just like all the others. What can it hurt?"

"But I know you're real now. And you're a vampire. I shouldn't want you."

"But you do." He reared over her, the firelight outlining his broad shoulders in gold as he reached for her. "And it's safe here. We might fear ourselves when we're awake, but this is only a dream. Here I'm just Cowboy, and you're just Valerie. No vampires. No Kith. No complications."

He caught her face between his gloved hands. She took a deep breath and smelled warm leather and horse and man. His lips covered hers in gliding, silken temptation, and his tongue swirled into her mouth. He tasted of coffee and roasted meat—and Cowboy. Her sweet dream lover.

Val relaxed and let his weight bear her backward into the bedroll. Instead of wool and rough cotton, it felt like a thick cushion of silk against her spine.

"I never liked making love on the ground," Cowboy murmured against her lips. "It sounds more romantic than it is."

She felt him settle over her, his arms circling her in hard male strength, the rough fabric of his denim-clad hips pressing between her legs as his long fingers took possession of her breasts. The supple leather of his gloves felt delicious as he pinched and stroked her nipples. When he rolled his hips, hot moisture flooded into her sex like cream.

"God," he purred in her ear. "I love that smell."

He tilted back his Stetson and lowered his head. She stared at the crown of his hat and quivered at the sensation of his tongue painting pleasure over her nipple through the thin lace of her nightgown. Big gloved hands caressed and squeezed until she squirmed. His fingers swept down to the narrow indentation of her waist before stroking up the length of her thigh. The work-worn leather was warm, smooth against her skin.

Then he found the nest of damp curls between her legs. A leather-clad finger slid into her, and she writhed in voluptuous delight. When his teeth gently nibbled one erect nipple, the twin pleasures braided themselves together in her mind, each growing more lush in combination.

Suddenly the glove was gone, leaving his bare skin touching her. "Do you mind?" he whispered, lifting his head to look at her, his eyes shimmering in the shadow of his hat. "I wanted to feel you."

"No," she gasped. "No, I don't mind."

His thumb strummed her clit until rapture forced her to dig her nails into the tight ridges of his biceps to keep from screaming. His hard, flexing strength intoxicated her. She relaxed her desperate grip to brush her hands up the curving muscle of his arms to the contours of his powerful chest.

Two fingers thrust into her, eager and demanding. Val panted. Suddenly he pushed himself off her, but before she could murmur a protest, he moved down until his head was between her thighs.

His hands caught her legs and spread them wide. She felt the brim of his hat brush her skin just before his tongue began to lick, seeking out her most sensitive flesh and laving it with wet skill.

"God, Cowboy," she groaned, just as she had so many times before. As he nibbled and sucked, his hands found her breasts again, caressing with such delicate skill she could only toss her head in pleasure. But it wasn't enough. She wanted him. On top of her, in her. Now. She clawed at his bare shoulders. "Cowboy!"

He shoved himself upward, rising onto his knees. The jeans had disappeared, and he was naked except for the vest and the badge. His massive sex brushed against her thigh, a length of hot, steel-sheathed silk eager for her clamping heat.

She licked her lips. "Awake, I've never had anyone the size of you."

"Good," he growled, and then he was inside her. His strength took her breath. He felt endless as he entered, slick and thick and delicious. His hips rolled between her thighs as he began to thrust in driving lunges. She hooked her legs over his muscled rump, curled her arms around his broad back, and held on to his bucking body.

As she threw her head back in pleasure, Cowboy lifted his own, and the moonlight shone full in his face under his hat. His mouth was open and gasping in pleasure. His fangs gleamed, white and sharp.

He started to lower his head toward her throat...

Val's eyes snapped open. McKinnon lay on top of her, his massive body nestled between her thighs. His erection pressed against her sex, kept from entry only by her cotton sweats and his nylon shorts. For a moment she thought she was still dreaming, until she met his startled eyes in the daylight pouring in through the drawn curtains.

"First time I ever woke up from one of those dreams to find you actually here," he said, slipping his arms around her, drawing her even closer. His cock rubbed against her with the movement. "This has possibilities." Fangs gleamed in his roguish smile.

Val stared up at him. "You did that on purpose!" She shoved futilely at his massive shoulders.

McKinnon sat back on his haunches and let her scramble away. "Actually, I didn't. It just...happened."

"Well, it had better not happen again. Stay the hell out of my dreams!" she snapped, before it occurred to her the threat had no teeth at all. He could do any damn thing he wanted to her, and there was no way she could stop him.

"Hey, it wasn't intentional," he protested. "Besides, half the time you're the one coming into *my* dreams!"

He had a point, but she was damned if she'd admit it. "Whatever." Val rolled out of bed. "I'm going to go get a shower."

"You do that," he growled, his eyes flicking to the curtained windows, which were beginning to darken noticeably. "It's almost sunset anyway. We need to hit the road. I want to get out of here before Ridgemont comes calling."

Val snatched a change of clothes out of her suitcase and stormed into the bathroom, slamming the door behind her with a satisfying bang. "Jerk." She dragged off her shirt and shorts, then tossed them on top of the commode with her clean clothes before turning to give the shower tap a vicious twist. "Big, toothy, sexy jerk."

She started to turn the hot water off completely, but she wasn't that much a masochist. Setting the temp to lukewarm instead, she plunged under the needle spray and let it pound her over-sensitized body. Those damn dreams had always done this to her. And the effect was worse—infinitely worse—now that she knew Cowboy was real.

Her nipples were so swollen they felt like grapes. Slipping an exploring hand between her legs, she found she was as slick as whipped cream. So slick she couldn't resist stroking her own desperate flesh. Letting her head drop back, Val bit her lip and plunged her fingers deep as she remembered the way he looked, naked and dripping, his heavy cock tilted upward slightly with the force of his hunger.

It crossed her mind to hope Abigail was nowhere around. Then she forgot everything else. She was so hot it barely took a moment to bring herself to a hard, rolling climax.

When she was finished, she hurriedly soaped her tingling body, bitterly ashamed of herself. He was a vampire, dammit.

Yet nobody but him had ever touched her like that. Maybe that's why she'd never fallen in love with anyone else—no mere human male could compete with Cowboy. And now that she knew he was real, how the hell was she supposed to keep her hands to herself?

Val grabbed the hot water tap and turned it all the way off, biting back a scream as needles of ice-cold water pounded her overheated body.

The war axe was a work of art, intricately engraved across its foot-wide blade with scenes of battle, its thick oak handle carved with runes. Half-hypnotized, Hirsch drew his thumb along the edge and watched a runnel of blood roll down from the cut. He hefted the weapon in his hand, feeling the weight, the perfect balance. It could cut through a man's neck like a stick of butter.

Ridgemont had presented the weapon to him just before he'd left, with instructions to use it on the American.

The German closed his eyes, picturing the moment when he'd separate McKinnon from his head. The bastard's blood would gush like a fountain, and Hirsch would bathe in it. He could almost taste it on his tongue, the sting and bite of a vampire's life, so much sharper than the sweet copper of a woman's.

And once he'd fed from Ridgemont's precious gunslinger, there'd be Valerie Chase. Hirsch licked his lips and felt his cock swell.

A psychic flare of unease drew his attention to the man sitting across from him. Giovanni Casale was a skilled and merciless killer, a former mob hit man so renowned for the ice in his veins Ridgemont had been impressed enough to recruit him. Yet there was fear on his face as he looked at Hirsch now.

The German grinned in pleasure. He did so enjoy terrifying mortals.

"We'll be landing in five," the helicopter pilot said through his headset.

"Not too close to the motel," Hirsch cautioned into his microphone. "I don't want McKinnon to realize we're coming for him."

Ridgemont had gotten word of the fugitives' location at the ungodly hour of three in the afternoon. Hirsch hadn't appreciated being ordered from his cool bed and out into the stinging sunlight, but if the assault worked, it would be worth it.

Luckily both the limo and the helicopter's cockpit windows had been polarized to block ultraviolet, so the trip had been tolerable. Now night had fallen just in time, and Hirsch was more than ready to kill McKinnon and take the girl.

He wondered if the American had ignored his scruples and fed on his captive. It would be even sweeter if he had. How it would torture the American to die knowing what would happen to her at Hirsch's hands!

He couldn't wait to rape her. She had the kind of big tits and long-legged body he loved in his victims. Even better, he couldn't compel her like a normal female, so she'd fight the way she had back at the parking garage. The thought made his dick strain against his zipper. It had been decades since he'd had to hold a woman down. Sometimes he let them struggle, but that wasn't the same. The last time he'd enjoyed a genuine rape had been that French resistance fighter during the war. Screwing Valerie would be even better, especially if he did her while McKinnon was alive to watch.

Then he'd take her back to Ridgemont, along with the American's severed head.

Hirsch looked up and met Casale's uneasy black gaze. "While I take Cade, I want you to capture the girl. But don't hurt her." Hirsch smiled in hot anticipation. "I'll take care of that."

Valerie finally emerged from the bathroom just as Cade was considering going in after her. He'd already dressed, strapped on his gun, and packed the car with the sword and the rest of their gear.

"Took you long enough," he growled, trying to ignore the way her blue T-shirt and jeans showcased that mouth-watering figure. They'd better hit the road before he laid her back on that bed and finished what that damn dream had started.

Catching her by the elbow, he opened the door. "We've got a lot of ground to cover tonight, and we're not doing it dawdling here."

"What happens when we get where we're going?" Val asked as he guided her under the overhang toward the car.

"To start with, I'll…."

Cade, it's Hirsch!

Shit! He shoved Val behind him and drew his gun.

With a roar of triumph, the German plummeted down on him from the motel's overhanging roof. Something metallic flashed by his head. Hirsch's forearm hit his shoulder with a teeth-jarring jolt as they slammed into the pavement so hard the impact knocked the gun from his hand. Cade fisted both hands into Hirsch's shirt, kicked a foot into his belly, and sent him flying. Rolling to his feet, he silently cursed himself for letting the German take him off-guard.

"We'll see who gets butchered now, American," Hirsch snarled, leaping up with a foot-wide battle axe in his hand. That flash of reflection Cade had seen must have been the blade barely missing his head.

Oh, hell, the sword's in the back of the car! Cade scanned for the gun, didn't see it, and braced himself to fight barehanded.

The big German moved toward him on the balls of his feet, the axe glittering in the cold light of the street lamps. His smile was chilling. "This time I've got you, you sanctimonious prick."

"Not even in your dreams, Gerhard." But he wasn't as confident as he tried to sound. He'd underestimated Hirsch badly. If he didn't turn this around now, he was dead—and Val would pay for his bad judgement.

Val hit the ground on her belly, desperately searching for McKinnon's gun. She'd seen it slide under the Lexus. If she could find it, she was going to put a bullet in the German's brain. She was damned if she'd stand around wringing her hands like a Victorian virgin.

It was pitch black under the car, but as she plastered her face against the cold pavement, she could see the silhouette of the pistol on the ground. She stretched out a hand so far her shoulder joint protested. And just managed to touch the chill metal grip with her fingers.

Clawing at it, she worked the gun close enough to grab. The minute she got her fingers around it, she jumped to her feet and thumbed off the safety. A few months back she'd done some target shooting for a story, and her instructor had told her she was a natural shot. Now she'd find out whether he'd just been flattering her.

Val looked over at the two vampires just as Hirsch swung his axe at McKinnon's belly. He leaped back to avoid being cut in two, then lunged inside the reach of the axe and grabbed Hirsch's forearm. His momentum slammed him against the bigger vampire's chest, and the two surged against one another as they struggled for the weapon in an intimidating display of muscle and effort.

Val set her feet apart the way she'd been taught and raised the gun to take aim at the German's back. Her stomach pitched at the thought of shooting anybody, even such a monster, but she gritted her teeth and steadied her aim. She couldn't let him kill McKinnon.

"I wouldn't," a strange voice said.

Something cold pressed against the back of her neck. She knew without looking it was the muzzle of a gun.

"Drop it," the gunman ordered.

Damn, she thought, *Hirsch brought reinforcements.*

The good news was that it wasn't Ridgemont, judging by the lack of English accent. Which meant he was a flunky. And that meant she had a chance.

"I said drop it!" the man barked. "Or I'll blow your little red head right off."

Every trace of spit left Val's mouth, but she didn't put down the gun. "You won't shoot me."

He laughed, the sound so nasty she felt a chill crawl her spine. "A lot of dead people could tell you different."

"But Ridgemont didn't need them alive." Val began to turn, trying to ignore the icy pressure of the muzzle scraping against her head with the movement. "And he would be very, very unhappy if you killed me."

She almost thought better of her plan when she got a good look at the gunman. He wasn't a big man, but his navy blue windbreaker stretched over a barrel chest. His head was shaved smooth as a bowling ball, and he had a face like a hatchet, set with little eyes as cold and flat as black ice. Something in the way he looked at her suggested he considered murder on a par with brushing his teeth. She realized she was lucky he'd let her turn around without pulling the trigger.

Val took the biggest chance of her life and pointed McKinnon's gun at him. Amazingly, the weapon didn't shake in her hands. "I don't think you want to make Ridgemont unhappy." *He'd better not,* she thought grimily. *Or I'm dead.*

Those tiny black eyes flicked down to the weapon's nine-millimeter muzzle, then back to her face. "Thing is, letting you go would really piss him off. And I don't think you'll shoot me." The flunky's left hand swung up and around, grabbing for the gun.

Val fired.

He fell back with a howl. She watched him hit the ground, her ears ringing from the gun's rolling boom. Smoke curled around the gun in her hand, smelling like the Fourth of July.

"Bitch bitch BITCH!" The gunman writhed on the pavement, one hand clamping high on his shoulder. She'd realized at the last second that she couldn't kill him and aimed to wound. "You little whore." He lifted his head to look at her, his narrow, ugly face contorted in rage. "I'm going to shove that gun up your cunt and pull the trigger." Rabid black eyes locked on hers, he struggled to rise.

Oh, hell. She hadn't hurt him badly enough to stop him. And if Hirsch had put a compulsion on him.... Staring into that beefy, deadly face, Val realized the only way to stop the gunman was to blow his brains out—and she'd already learned she couldn't do that. Cursing herself, she whirled and fled.

"You'd better run, bitch!" She looked back to see him stagger to his feet.

Putting her head down, Val poured on the speed. If she could get away from this bastard, she wouldn't stop until she got to Beth.

Chapter Nine

When the gun fired, Cade glanced past Hirsch's shoulder just in time to see a man fall as smoke boiled from a gun in Val's hands. Cade recognized him: Giovani Casale, Ridgemont's pet assassin.

Panic flared in Hirsch's eyes as the German's thoughts blasted out like a shout: *That fool Casale has killed her.* Hirsch threw an instinctive glance over his shoulder toward the gunfire behind him.

Cade kicked him in the face so hard a mortal's head would have flown from his shoulders like a football off a tee. Hirsch went airborne, the axe whirling from his hand.

Jerking around, Cade saw Val running full out with the hitman at her heels. *Damn.* There was no time to finish Hirsch. He had to get to Val before Casale caught her or the police showed up. After that shot, it wouldn't be long before half the law enforcement in Corrington poured into the motel parking lot.

He shot Hirsch a look. The German lay on his back, out cold, his face a bloody ruin from the kick. Unfortunately, the damage was nowhere bad enough to kill a vampire. "We'll finish this later, you bastard," Cade muttered, and sprinted after his runaway captive.

He easily passed Casale, who staggered in Val's wake like something out of *The Night of the Living Dead*, firmly in the grip of one of Hirsch's compulsions. "Stop," Cade snapped at the gunman, driving the words home with a psychic blow of his own. "Go to sleep!" He paused just long enough to make sure the assassin dropped, then lengthened his stride.

Even at full vampire speed, he had to work to catch Valerie. God, that girl could run. "Val, it's okay!" he yelled. "Casale's down! Come back!"

She stopped in her tracks and whipped around, bringing the gun up to point it right at between his eyes. "Back. Off." She spat it, in two distinct words. "If you come any closer, I'll blow a hole in you."

Cade felt his jaw drop. Looking into her wide, desperate eyes, he knew she meant every word.

Wanting only to get away from them all, Val stared into McKinnon's handsome face. Her mind churned feverishly. A bullet wouldn't hurt him permanently, but it would slow him down. While he was recovering, she could make a run for it.

For a moment he looked stunned, as if unable to believe she'd actually consider shooting him. Unfortunately he was too much a warrior to let the threat throw him for long. "You can't kill a vampire that way," McKinnon told her, in the elaborately reasonable voice of someone trying to talk a crazy woman down from a ledge.

"I don't want to kill you," Val said, keeping the gun pointed between those velvety dark eyes. He looked so big and broad standing there in the light of the street lamp, the black T-shirt that hugged that gorgeous chest tucked into worn jeans that made his legs look a mile long. She dragged her attention away from his raw male beauty and steadied her aim. "I just want you to leave me alone. I've got to get to Beth."

"That'd only put her in more danger, Val, even if you made it." He took a slow pace toward her, his gaze focusing past the Smith & Wesson's muzzle to meet hers. "And you wouldn't. Ridgemont would have you before sunrise. I'm the only chance you've got."

"But you said you're not a match for him, not without Changing me. If I stay with you, the only thing that happens is you get killed and I become Ridgemont's slave." And she couldn't stand the thought of McKinnon dying. "Or you Change me and I end up a vampire. I don't like either alternative."

"There are other ways to kill Ridgemont than taking him on hand-to-hand. Don't underestimate me." McKinnon took a step closer. Val backed up another pace. "Come on, Valerie," he coaxed in that deep, patient voice. "We don't have time for this, the police are on the way. I can hear the sirens."

She licked her dry lips. "Good. They can bust me. I'd be safer in jail."

"Not if Ridgemont bails you out." Dark-lashed eyes stared into hers, intent and demanding. Val watched his eyes narrow and knew she couldn't look into them while she shot him. She dropped her aim to a point midway between his broad pecs and shut her eyes.

Just as her finger tightened on the trigger, she felt a rush of wind and movement. McKinnon's hand clamped down over hers, jerking the gun up as his other arm snaked around her waist. Before she could even open her eyes, he pulled the weapon out of her hand as easily as a man taking a toy from a toddler.

Astonished, she stared up into his grim face. "How did you do that so fast?" He'd been standing ten feet away.

"I'm a vampire," McKinnon snapped, tucking the gun into his empty shoulder holster as he hauled her around and dragged her back toward the car. Stumbling after his long strides, she heard sirens wailing their way steadily closer. "And you're lucky I'm not Ridgemont, because he would have made you eat that gun. Only an idiot shuts his eyes when he shoots somebody."

Stung, she glared at his stony profile. "Sorry. The next time I blow a hole in you, I'll make sure to watch."

"See that you do." Muscles in his strong jaw worked as he lengthened his stride. The sirens were getting louder. "And what the hell's wrong with you, anyway? I thought we'd been through this. Without me, you don't have a prayer."

She opened her mouth to answer, but before she could say anything, a patrol car bounced into the parking lot, blue lights spinning, sirens howling. Several others screamed down the street.

"Oh, hell." He pulled her into a run.

"What?"

"There are too many cops. We've got to get out of here."

"What? Why not put a psychic whammy on them?"

"I can't compel more than one person at a time. And it sounds like half the force is on the way. If they get here, we're screwed." As they reached the Lexus, he pulled open the driver's door and pushed her inside. She scrambled across the gear shift and fell into the passenger seat.

"Hey!" A burly cop got out of his patrol car and bore down on him. "Sir, I need to talk to you. Now."

Cade looked up and caught him with a stare. "We didn't have anything to do with it."

The man broke stride, confusion clouding his eyes. "But there's a body on the…."

"No, there isn't." He slid behind the wheel and started the engine. The cop stared at them blankly as Cade backed the Lexus out of its space and shot toward the back exit.

Glancing into the rearview mirror, he saw another cop get out of a second car and stalk toward the first, gesturing. Cade winced, knowing he'd just gotten his victim a reprimand at the very least. Unfortunately he didn't have time to worry about that. There was a good chance they'd gotten a plate number, in which case every cop in town would soon be looking for him and Valerie.

He hit the gas, turned off the headlights, and took off with all the speed and razored reflexes only a vampire could manage.

As Cade punched it, Val fumbled automatically for her seatbelt and clicked it home. This had not been her finest hour. She felt sick to her stomach—the aftereffects of an adrenalin jag mixed with despair. But it wasn't the cops or even Ridgemont she was most worried about.

It was spending more time with McKinnon—and getting seduced.

Sandra Kent frowned down at her patient's battered face, barely registering the beep of the monitors ranged around him. An ambulance crew had just brought him in to the E.R.

Dr. Bryson had taken one look and told her to prep the man for surgery. She suspected it was a pointless effort. They were going to lose this patient; there was no way he could survive head injuries like the ones he'd sustained.

He had been hit with what must have been a ball peen hammer. His jaw was broken, his nose splintered and facial bones shattered, but more important was the skull fracture to the back of his head. With the blows it had taken, his bruised brain was already swelling inside the cage of his skull. Soon the growing pressure would kill him.

But they had to try.

With a sigh of resignation, Sandra reached up to check the flow from the unit of blood hanging over his head. She caught a dim glimmer of blue and looked down. Amazingly, the man's eyes were open, though she could have sworn they'd been swollen shut a moment ago. He smiled up at her through cracked and bloody lips.

Sandra stared in astonishment. How could he grin with his jaw wrecked? Looking closer, she saw the swelling seemed to have gone down. Delicately she reached out to touch the man's shattered face. And gasped.

Half an hour ago, bone had shifted under her fingers when she'd touched him. Now it felt whole. Which was utterly impossible. She'd seen the X-ray films. Those bones had been splintered like glass.

A bruised, scrapped hand snapped around her wrist so hard she gasped in pain. "*Fraulein*," the patient said, his voice so distorted by his mangled jaw she could barely understand him, "get me out of here. And then we'll…play."

It wasn't the first time Sandra had dealt with a patient who was out of his head. She opened her mouth to gently tell him he wasn't going anywhere except surgery. But as she did, she met those cold blue eyes.

And found she couldn't say anything at all.

Eluding the police kept Cade's mind firmly occupied for most of an hour as he wove through the darkened streets of Corrington. Spotting a man on the side of the road fixing a flat, Cade stopped long enough to influence him into switching license plates, then made sure he wouldn't remember anything about it.

To further confuse things, Cade stopped just long enough to repeat the process, once at a house where the lights were on, again in a convenience store parking lot. The plate change should muddy the waters nicely as far as the police were concerned, though it wouldn't stop Ridgemont.

Now that Cade stopped to think, it was obvious Hirsch had gotten the tag number at the airport. The ancient had then used law enforcement to track them down, something Cade damn well should have foreseen. Brooding, he glanced at Val's impassive profile. He must have been distracted.

Well, using the tags to trail them wouldn't be as easy this time, though Ridgemont could still do it. Cade knew the ancient would interrogate the owners as each switched plate was found, then get the new tag number and find that one in turn. Eventually he'd track Cade and Valerie down, but it would be a long process. Long enough, hopefully, to give Cade time to set a trap for him.

Unfortunately, at the moment Cade had no idea what form that trap would take. And he'd damn well better get it figured out in a hurry. Going up against Edward Ridgemont without a well-constructed strategy was a good way to get your head handed to you. Literally.

Cade looked over at Valerie as the lights of a passing car painted the clean line of her nose and stubborn little chin. She'd rested her forehead against the side window, eyes closed. For the first time, he found himself questioning his determination not to Change her. Was he being honorable—or just squeamish?

There was a certain ruthless logic that demanded he head for the closest hotel and get it over with. The Change would cost her any chance of a normal life and she'd hate him afterward, but it would still be better than her fate if Ridgemont caught him unprepared. Cade knew that better than anyone, having watched helplessly as his sire raped far too many women.

But even with Cade as her sire, the Change would still be terrifying for her. Of course, unlike Ridgemont, he had no intention of having sex with her during the process. It wasn't necessary, and he doubted he'd be able to perform even if it was. The idea of forcing Valerie was just too repellent. But he'd have to feed repeatedly, and she'd find the experience nightmarish.

No. Forget it. He'd have to come up with some other way to kill the ancient. Maybe another bomb.

I could seduce her.... The thought stole into his mind. She had responded eagerly enough to his kisses back at the motel. Not to mention those incredibly erotic dreams.... He blew out a breath and studied her again. He could tell by her breathing that she'd fallen asleep. Probably exhausted by the trauma of shooting Casale. And damn near Cade too, come to think of it.

He ground his teeth. It was ridiculous to feel hurt that she'd almost put a bullet in him. She was a captive, for God's sake—of course she'd try anything to escape. It wasn't as if she really could've killed him. But if she'd been the vampire and he, the mortal, he knew he damned well wouldn't have been able to point a gun at her.

To look at her, you'd never think she'd even be capable of it. Her face looked so lovely framed by that auburn mane, like a sleeping Renaissance angel. Her long eyelashes fanned against porcelain cheeks, her eyes flicking back and forth behind her closed lids. Wondering what she was dreaming, Cade automatically reached out his mind to touch hers, forgetting for a moment he wouldn't be able to make contact. Instead he found her mind opened to him, her Kith shields down in sleep.

His psychic probe touched a vivid dream image—Cade himself, looking like the hero of a cowboy flick on the back of a big white stallion, holding Val perched on the saddle in front of him.

Cade grinned. She was naked. It was one of those nude-in-public nightmares everybody had. *But my, oh, my,* he thought wickedly, *the possibilities!*

Of course, the gentleman his mother had raised would never have invaded Val's privacy as she slept. The vampire he'd become saw it as a unique opportunity to seduce a woman who was more than half-willing anyway. And the man… remembered she'd damn near put a bullet in him.

Cade took the first exit he came to. For this, he needed to pull over.

Val squirmed in the saddle, but the hard-muscled arms around her waist didn't loosen. She desperately needed to put on some clothes, but Cade wouldn't let her down. Mortified, she wanted to scream. She couldn't imagine how he'd gotten her on the back of a horse buck naked.

Suddenly the dream took on a vivid clarity that surprised her sleeping mind. She could feel the leather of the saddle between her bare thighs and the warmth of the powerful arms around her. A night breeze blew across her breasts, and her nipples hardened at the cool, delicate sensation.

"What'd you do, darlin'?" Cade purred. His breath teased the sensitive whorls of her ear. "What nasty crime did you commit to get arrested by a Texas Ranger?"

"What?" She pushed at the arm that held her, but it didn't budge. "I haven't done anything."

"You're shackled, sweetheart," he rumbled, his chest vibrating against her head. She looked down and saw that her hands were chained in front of her. "You must have done something. Steal a horse? Rob a bank?" He lifted a gloved hand and closed his fingers around one bare breast with exquisite tenderness. "Maybe you're a soiled dove, and the ladies of the town decided to drum you out for tempting their menfolk into sin." Leather-clad fingers teased and rolled the tight, hard point of her nipple. His drawl lengthened. "You're certainly tempting me."

"Cade, stop that!" She squirmed. And froze, eyes widening, when her bottom rubbed against the thick bulge of his erection.

"And now you're out here in the middle of nowhere with a ranger who's having a hard time remembering he's supposed to be the good guy." Lazily, he trailed his fingers down her belly to slide between her tight, damp folds. Rough leather brushed her erect clit. His voice deepened and dropped. "Then again, considering how wicked you are, maybe it's my duty to dish out a little frontier justice."

He lifted the reins and stroked the supple straps against first one breast, then the other.

Obeying the pressure on its bit, the stallion began to dance under them. Black hooves left the ground in a partial rear that threw Val back onto Cade's lap. His thick erection, covered in the coarse fabric of his jeans, rubbed between her bare cheeks.

"I think I might enjoy disciplining you," he rumbled, and scraped the reins over one nipple again. Obediently, the horse hopped forward on its back legs, jarring her against his cock. His cupping fingers rasped over her clit, the wicked swirl of pleasure making her writhe. Cade laughed in her ear, the sound wolfish. "Would you like to do a little hard time, Valerie?"

"Stop it," she told him. "You're supposed to be the guy in the white hat, remember?"

With a tug on the reins, he brought the horse to all fours again, then grabbed his Stetson and shoved it into her hands.

"I'm not wearing my hat now," Cade said in her ear, his tone a velvet threat. Lowering his head, he pressed his mouth to the side of her throat. "Now I'm a vampire."

Slowly, taking his time, he sank his fangs into her skin. She arched in erotic shock at the burning penetration. "Oh!" The sound emerged as a tormented little whimper.

But after that one sharp sting of pain, it didn't hurt. She could feel his lips moving on her neck as he drank from her in long swallows, rumbling in pleasure. His mouth was warm and soft and arousing as his hands stroked her body. An orgasm gathered low in her stomach like a building storm, only to hover there, not quite breaking. Unable to stand any more, she moaned, "God, Cade, please!"

Still feeding, he growled a feral sound and cupped his long fingers over her sex, pulling her against his jeans-covered cock as he rolled his hips as if driving hard into her. She twisted desperately, trying to get that last little stimulation she needed to come, but it eluded her. She cried out in frustration.

Just before she lost her mind, he released her throat and licked up the straining cord to her ear. His breath gusting on the delicate flesh made her gasp in desperate arousal as he whispered, "See? It doesn't hurt. Wake up, and I'll show you...."

Hard as the broadsword in the back seat, Cade slipped out of Val's dream just as she jolted awake. He watched as she lifted trembling fingers to the side of her throat, searching for the marks of his fangs. They weren't there, of course. He hadn't bitten her.

Not that he hadn't been tempted.

"That was interesting," he drawled, grinning. Any minute now, she'd sear his ears with one of those inventive curses of hers, maybe even try to punch him in the nose again. He suspected he deserved it.

She looked over at him. Her eyes were dazed, unfocused. "You dreamed with me again?" Licking her lips, she glanced around as if trying to get her bearings. "Where are we?"

"I pulled off the road." Her sleep-drugged confusion sent a shaft of guilt through him. When she woke completely, she'd really let him have it. "Except it wasn't an accident this time. When you sleep, your mental shields drop, so I was able to enter your mind." And it had been one of the hottest experiences he'd ever had in his life.

She blinked, looking stunned and vulnerable. "You did that? You made me dream that?"

He winced, the guilt intensifying. "Well, the basic idea was yours, but I helped it along some."

Actually, the whole thing had gotten out of control. He'd meant to tease her with a dream bite, not practically fuck her in the saddle.

Val's eyes slid away from his, blinking hard. As he watched in growing alarm, embarrassment and betrayed hurt flooded her face. She fumbled for the door handle and opened it.

"Val, what are you…."

Ignoring him, she got out. He'd pulled well off the road into a little grassy clearing, and now she started across it in the moonlight, her shoulders stiff.

Oh, hell, Cade thought, his stomach dropping as he shoved his own door open. *I really did hurt her.*

Val trudged mechanically across the grass, her body still flaming almost as hot as her mortified embarrassment.

Cade had reached into her mind. He'd seen how much she wanted him, used that knowledge to plunge her into this helpless arousal. He knew how to get her now. Could take her any time he wanted. She wouldn't have expected it of him.

He's a vampire, moron, Val told herself savagely. *To him, you're a blood supply and pussy in one convenient, easy-to-use package. A two-for-one combo.* And she kept seeing him as her noble Cowboy. How stupid could she be?

The really galling part was how brutally she still ached for him. In the face of that clawing hunger, all the reasons to stay away from him no longer seemed like enough—not the fear of his vampirism, not even her own instinct for self-preservation.

Why should she deny herself, she wondered bitterly. It wasn't as if she had a prayer of survival anyway. Why not grab what fleeting moments of pleasure she could, considering the precipice she teetered on?

Before she could take another agitated step, Cade's strong fingers caught her shoulders, dragged her to a halt, and turned her around.

Val glared up at him. Even after what he'd done, the sight of him made her body vibrate like a tuning fork—and she was sure he knew it. She waited for him to push her down into the grass.

But instead of triumph, she saw guilt in his eyes. "Val, I'm sorry. I didn't mean to hurt you."

She rocked back on her heels, studying him. Part of her wanted desperately to believe his apology, but she remembered the mocking vampire seducer from her dreams a little too well. She wondered which was an act—Good Guy Cowboy or the Big Bad Wolf.

Did he even know?

"Why should you be sorry?" Val demanded, and was pleased

at how bitter she sounded. Bitter was much better than hurt. "I'm not a vampire or a ghost. I'm just a mortal. You screw mortals over all the time—make us believe whatever you want, *do* whatever you want. You're the lord of everything with a pulse."

That stung him. She saw anger flare in his eyes mixed with a wince of recognition, and her battered spirit celebrated that small victory.

Cade opened his mouth, then closed it again and visibly reined back on his anger. "All right, I deserved that. I told you I wasn't going to rape you, and then I turned around and did just that, mentally if not physically. But whatever you believe, I don't make a habit of acting like a blackguard."

"The modern term," she told him with a weary sneer, "is 'asshole.'"

Instead of being offended, he laughed in relief. "I knew you'd get around to scorching my ears sooner or later." Tapping his elegant nose, Cade lowered his head. "Okay, go for it. Hit me. Right here."

She lifted her brows. "Hit you?"

He grinned. It was a devastating grin, handsome and boyish and wry, and she'd bet money he knew exactly how much punch it packed. Fangs weren't his most devastating weapon by any means. "You've wanted to slug me since I snapped on the cuffs. Here's your chance. I won't stop you. See if you can break it." He shut his eyes and braced himself as if she could actually do some damage.

Val stared up at him, amused despite herself. His thick eyelashes fanned against his high cheekbones, and his tempting mouth was quirked in a half-smile. The moonlight silvered his broad shoulders and silken hair with cool white light. She considered the pleasant fantasy of knocking him on his tightly muscled ass.

Instead she did what she'd been aching to do for hours. Wrapping both arms around his neck, she went up on her toes and took his mouth.

Cade's eyes snapped open as soft breasts pressed against his chest and even softer lips sealed over his. His body instantly burst into flame at the silken intensity of her kiss.

When he moaned, her tongue swept into his mouth, agile and slick and impossibly tempting. He drew back just far enough to murmur, "I thought you wanted to break my nose."

"It'd only heal," she growled against his lips. "Right now, there's something I want a lot more."

"And what would that be?" Cade asked with a wicked grin.

She slid a hand between their bodies and cupped him boldly. He sucked in a breath as long fingers stroked and squeezed flesh that leaped at her touch. "Actually, vampire, I'd like to drain *you*." Those fingers measured him as heat poured into his balls. "Though from the feel of things, that could be a lengthy project."

"And getting lengthier all the time." He lifted her chin to search her eyes. He could feel the points of his fangs against his lips as he spoke. "Are you sure about this, Val?"

"Yes," she said softly, huskily. "I want you, Cade. I've wanted you for years. Make love to me."

Breathing in, he could scent her arousal, thick and tempting, confirming just how much she meant that. "Yes." With a soft growl of need, he swept her into his arms and turned to retrace his steps in long strides.

She giggled and clutched his shoulders. "Where are we going?"

"The car." He looked down into her eyes and watched the way they shone in the moonlight like something precious. "I don't want to make love to you with rocks digging into my butt."

Val toyed with a lock of his hair. "That does sound distracting."

"And I don't want to be distracted." He reached the car and walked around behind it, still carrying her. Gently, he put her down on the trunk and leaned her back against the rear windshield.

Cade straightened to pulled his shirt off, then balled it up and tucked it behind her head as a pillow. She looked up at him, heat and a reluctant trust in her eyes. Catching the hem of her own T-shirt, she pulled it up and over her head to reveal full breasts cupped in lace. The sweet, high mounds seemed to beg for his hands, his mouth. A pulse beat hard in her long throat.

The sight of her offering herself made the Hunger leap. He throttled back on his searing need, determined not to betray her. He'd give her what she wanted—and only what she wanted—if it killed him.

Chapter Ten

What am I doing? one last sane voice screamed in the back of Val's brain as Cade reached for the fly of her jeans. Watching his long fingers unzip her pants, she ignored it.

All that mattered was this moment—and making love to Cade.

He paused and looked up at her. The Hunger made his eyes burn with a wolfish light that would have frightened her if she hadn't also sensed his iron restraint. "If I start to take more than you want to give," he said, in a low, determined rasp, "tell me. I swear to you I'll stop." The points of his fangs showed as he spoke, yet she believed him.

When he reached for her waistband to pull off her jeans, his big hands shook. As he stripped them down, she remembered her dream of the woman he'd taken. His hands had been rock steady then. Did the faint tremble she saw now mean this meant that much more to him, or was she guilty of wishful thinking?

He straightened with her jeans dangling from one hand, staring at her with dark, ravenous eyes. She swallowed, abruptly conscious she wore nothing but a bra and a tiny pair of panties. The metal of the Lexus' trunk felt cold against her naked legs.

He looked so damn big standing there, the muscled contours of his chest silvered in moonlight. Hunger turned his handsome face hard, feral. He dropped her jeans and reached for her. She went into his arms with a moan he muffled with his mouth. His tongue slipped between her lips in a slow, seductive stroke as one strong hand caught the front of her bra and tugged it up, baring her nipples. Long fingers curled around her breast, hot and tender.

She closed her eyes and whimpered against his lips. His tongue circled hers.

Building heat drove her to wrap her legs around his waist and hook her heels against his muscled ass. She dragged her mouth from his as he took possession of one pink nipple, squeezing gently, rhythmically.

"You feel so..." She stopped to moan as his fingers slid up her thigh in a gliding caress, "...good."

"You feel like silk," he whispered back. The cool glass of the windshield against her back was a stark contrast to the wet heat of his suckling mouth closing over one nipple. Each pull sent pleasure blooming delicately along her nerves. A velvet tongue-stroke over a tight rose point made her arch against him. She gasped and felt her bra dig into the tops of her breasts.

Cade feasted on her beautifully sensitive nipples as her slim body twisted against his, smooth and warm. Her scent flooded his head with the rich, salty smell of aroused woman, and her heartbeat thundered a driving beat that sent the Hunger spiraling. The energy of her building pleasure gathered around them like a narcotic cloud.

Seduced, he reached for her panties, hungry to bring her to that first, delicious climax. When he felt the thin, silken fabric under his fingers, he barely resisted the urge to rip it away. As he pushed it down her thighs, his thumb brushed the crotch. It was wet. Goaded, he growled against her breast and pulled back just long enough to jerk the panties completely off.

She blinked up at him, sprawled deliciously across the Lexus' black metal skin, light against dark, warmth against cool. Her nipples were hard and pink and wet from his mouth, her long legs bent and spread. His eyes locked on the fluffy auburn triangle between her thighs. His mouth flooded with saliva. Moving between her thighs, he buried his face against her.

The first stab of Cade's tongue almost shot Val off the car. Instinctively she grabbed for his biceps and dug in her nails as he licked and sucked with ruthless skill. The sheer hot pleasure made her writhe. He reached up her body to knead her breasts, stroking and squeezing while he feasted. She curled a knee over his shoulder and dug her heel hard against his back. Cade flicked his tongue back and forth across her clit until she writhed. The slick glass of the window felt deliciously cool against her hot, sweaty back.

Still thumbing her nipple with one hand, he reached between her thighs with the other. A single big finger slid into the wet, thick cream that filled her sex just as his tongue gave her clit the perfect stroke.

Light exploded behind her eyes. Her spine arched like a bow. "God, Cade!"

He lifted his eyes to watch her come and slid another finger into her. Head thrown back, pink-tipped breasts arching as her full, rosy lips opened on a gasp, she looked like a ravished angel. The energy of her climax poured over him, and he shuddered at the power flooding his mind. His fangs ached and his cock throbbed with the need to bury themselves in her. He fought down the Hunger and gave her another long, delicious lick.

Dazed, she looked down her body at him to see those black eyes watching her over the curls of her sex. She was surprised they didn't glow. Then his hands moved, one twisting her nipple, the other driving three fingers into her tight flesh as his tongue danced over her clit. Her fading climax jack-hammered back to full force.

When he finally released her, she sprawled on the car, dazed and weak from the rippling multiple orgasms he'd wrung from her. She barely stirred when his hands caught one hip to gently turn her over, draping her belly down across the trunk. "Cade?"

His zipper whispered. Instantly, her sated senses snapped alert.

Twisting her head around, she watched him free his thick cock from his briefs. His eyes burned, narrow and hot as he stepped up to her wet, spread sex. Reading the question in her gaze, he said, "If I took you missionary, I don't trust myself not to drink from you."

She remembered how his fangs had felt sinking into her in the dream. Though some traumatized part of her recoiled in terror, the rest felt the rise of a dark excitement. "You can…." She gasped as the thick, rounded crown of his cock brushed her folds. "…You can have me that way if you want."

His eyes met hers and flared with hunger. "Oh, I want." Her slick flesh flowered open as he pushed inside. He felt so thick and hard, she wondered for a wild moment if she could take him. "But I think I'll save it for next time." She gasped as he came on and on. The possessive heat in his gaze as he watched her face made her shudder. "When I'm hungrier."

Val moaned. "I'm not sure I'd survive if you get any hungrier than this."

He smiled slightly, feral and male. "You have done a pretty good job of…." His cock slid in the last inch. "…whetting my appetite."

"Oh, God."

He stopped, buried in her up to the balls, such a massive, invading presence that her pleasure balanced on the edge of pain. "You're so tight," he breathed in her ear as he bent over her.

"It's been…" She sucked in a breath as he pulled out a millimeter at a time. "It's been a long time since I made love." She smiled slightly. "Anywhere but in a dream, that is."

"Was it worth the wait?" More of that satin organ slid out, only to press slowly deep again.

"God, yes." The trunk was just high enough that her feet didn't quite touch the ground. She clung to the slick surface. The car rocked under Cade's weight as he braced one knee on the bumper and rolled his hips. She whimpered at the feel of his shaft stuffing her so thoroughly.

Turning her head, she looked up at him over her shoulder. He loomed over her, his shoulders blocking the stars, his gaze intent on her face as he ground into her slick cunt. She rolled her hips up for him, meeting his thrusts. The pleasure built, twisting along her spine until she writhed.

He lowered his head as his lips parted, showing fangs that gleamed in his open mouth. Val quivered and bit her lip. His breath blew warm against her throat. She twisted her head back in invitation. Cade started to bite, then jerked his head back. "Not this time." He swallowed. "Later."

He rammed his cock so deep she screamed at the ruthless pleasure. The car rocked on its tires as his powerful body surged and ground against her ass. Each thrust of that big shaft drove another jolt of pleasure up her spine. "Cade!" She gripped the edges of the trunk with both hands, holding on helplessly as the rising orgasm battered her senses in time to his goring strokes. At last her climax crashed over her in a molten wave. She screamed.

The energy of her orgasm burst like fireworks in Cade's mind, driving the Hunger into a sustained shriek. He could almost taste the blood thundering in the pulse beating so hard in her slim throat. He fought the need, determined that this time, the first time, he'd take her as a man rather than a vampire.

Her slick, clasping flesh pulsed hard around his cock. Fiery pleasure rolled up from his balls and down his shaft. He drove himself into her as far as he could reach and threw back his head. And drowned in ecstacy.

Her senses battered, Val lay still under Cade's steamy masculine weight. *God,* she thought, *I just had sex with a vampire. And it was incredible.*

Almost purring, she closed her eyes as she listened to his breathing deepen and settle. She supposed she should do an angst-propelled tailspin into guilt right about now, but she felt too damn good. Weightless and floating, she lay still and let her muscles twitch.

Cade draped over her body, a blanket of sated masculinity. When he finally started to seem heavy, she tried to move, only to wince as her skin stuck sweatily to the car's metal surface.

Feeling something move deep within her body, she paused. His cock was still inside her. Soft now, yes, but the connection between them remained. "God, Cade," she said, and swallowed to clear the rasp. Her throat was sore. She suspected it was from screaming. "That was…." She couldn't think of a word that did it justice.

"Yeah." He sounded a little rusty too. "You okay?"

She chuckled. "'Okay' doesn't even come close."

"Are you sure?" He drew away, his cock slipping from her. She felt a twinge of regret. "I was a little rough at the end. And you were pretty…vocal."

Val smiled at the concern she could hear in his voice. "Don't worry, those were screams of pleasure." She lifted her head and groaned, abused muscles protesting. "Ouch. So much for the fabled Lexus luxury ride."

"I think they only promise that if you're *inside* the car." His strong hands helped her turn over, and she winced as her sweaty skin pulled away from the trunk.

Val opened her mouth for another quip, then forgot what she was about to say as his eyes met hers. Despite the stunning passion they'd just shared, she felt her heartbeat speed again at the tenderness in his.

Cade leaned in for a slow, thorough kiss, his mouth moving gently as his big hands cupped her face. Pleasure curled through her, sweet and lazy now rather than hard and driving. When he drew back, he rested his forehead on hers for a moment. "Thank you for trusting me."

She licked her lips, tasting him. Tasting them both. Something in her heart turned over as she looked into dark eyes as warm as melted chocolate. *How could I do anything else?* She bit the words back, suddenly afraid of what they meant.

He straightened, clearing his throat as he looked around. "What did I do with your clothes?"

They spent the next few moments getting dressed. Despite herself, Val felt the warm romantic glow beginning to dissipate as sanity took hold.

What the hell had she been thinking? If she wasn't careful, she was going to end up with a whole new set of dental work.

Frowning, she tugged on her T-shirt. Her stomach rumbled loudly. Cade looked over at her and grinned. "I see I'm not the only one who's hungry. There's a Waffle House up the frontage road. Want to go for it?"

"I could do with a big stack of waffles." Which sounded like a much safer topic than dwelling on the taste of his mouth and the feel of his body surging against hers.

And the warmth that bloomed in her whenever she looked into his eyes.

Cade sat in the restaurant booth and watched Valerie demolish a plate of waffles. As late as it was, there was nobody in the 24/7 diner except a weary cook and a drunk dozing over his coffee.

"How did you end up with Ridgemont to begin with?" Val demanded between mouthfuls. "I mean, considering how you loathe him."

"Didn't have much choice." Cade took a sip of coffee. His vampire metabolism could handle food, as long as it was in small enough quantities. "Ridgemont made me a vampire. Until I broke his control five years ago, that gave him power over me. He couldn't manipulate my mind the way you can a mortal's, but he could control my body, my hunger. He could lock my muscles so that I couldn't move, or compel me to obey his commands no matter how repellent I found them." He met her eyes steadily. "Like when he told me to kill you."

"But before you Changed, you were Kith, right?" Frowning, she swirled a forkful of waffle in her maple syrup. "If you survived the process, you must be. I thought you said Kith are immune to psychic influence."

"And I am. No other vampire could force me to obey, no matter how powerful he was. But during the Change, Ridgemont forged a deep link with my mind. Without it, I'd have slipped into a coma and died. And he maintained that link until five years ago, when I gained the strength to break it." He gazed into his coffee cup for a long, grim moment before he continued. "He's so damn powerful, it took me a hundred and fifteen years to free myself. I've been free five years now."

She frowned. "But you only just left? Why did you stay with him?"

Cade shrugged. "You and Abigail make very good hostages."

"Why? I mean, I understand what he could do to me, but Abigail's already dead."

"She's also pure psychic energy." He took another sip to wash the taste out of his mouth. "And we feed on more than blood."

Her eyes widened in horror. "You mean...he could *eat* her?"

"Given his power, yeah. Wouldn't be possible for a younger vampire, which is why she's safe from Gerhard. Even for Ridgemont, it wouldn't be easy—she'd fight, probably give him a serious psychic burn. But he could do it. And he's held that threat over my head for twelve decades."

"Bastard."

"That's about the size of it."

Staring into his brooding face, Val felt a deep, welling anger as she realized how he must have suffered. "How did you survive?"

"Ridgemont didn't give me much choice," he said, shrugging. "And I found ways to distract myself. He travels a lot, and wherever we were, there was usually something that needed doing. We were in France for a while during World War II, so I fought in the Resistance." His expression lightened in a sudden grin that was remarkably boyish. "We've been in New York for the past ten years, so I've been making life miserable for drug dealers, terrorists and assorted other lowlifes…."

"Yeah?" She studied him with interest. "Where were you on 9/11?"

The humor faded from his eyes. "In Paris with Ridgemont. Checking out the fashions."

She winced. "You can't be everywhere, Cade."

"No. But I damn well wish I'd been there."

"Sounds like you've done your part. I have a feeling the dip in the New York crime rate has your fingerprints on it."

"Not entirely, but I've had my moments. Plus the dealers have money, which has come in damn handy fighting Ridgemont. The Lexus belonged to this…."

"Wait a minute." She put down her fork to stare at him. "You *rob* drug dealers?"

"Cops seize their assets too, if I recall." He lifted a brow and took another sip of coffee.

"But they're cops!"

"And I compel the bastards I catch to confess to the police, give up their drug-dealing buddies, and turn over a new leaf, none of which the cops could have done on their own."

He had a point. Especially since without him, the dealers, their drugs, and their money would have otherwise remained on the street, doing God knew how much damage. And since with his abilities, he really could make criminals go straight, it was probably worth whatever money he took. Still…. "It's a slippery slope, McKinnon."

He snorted. "My life is a slippery slope, Val."

As they drove down I-95, Cade listened absently as Val chatted with Beth on her cell phone. Having beeped her sister, she was engrossed in reassuring herself Beth was all right. When he glanced over at her, he found himself enthralled by the movement of her full lips. And was surprised to feel as much tenderness as lust. *Damn,* he realized suddenly. *I'm falling in love with her.*

The idea carried a slow, sweet bloom of warmth and a sense of inevitability, as though it was something he was meant to do. Hell, maybe he'd been falling for her for the past seven years, since they'd started sharing those heated, erotic dreams.

He tried to remember the last time he'd been in love—and realized it had been more than a century. Not since Ridgemont's victimization of Caroline Johnson had taught him any woman he cared about became an instant hostage in the ancient's sadistic eyes. Not that he could spend more than a single night with his lovers anyway without running the risk of taking too much blood.

He had no illusions that his relationship with Valerie would be any more enduring. Eventually he'd have to give her up, as he'd had to give up Caro, as he'd had to give up all the women since. Even if Val decided to become a vampire—a very remote possibility—he doubted he'd survive the inevitable battle with his sire. The best he could do was make sure he took the ancient with him.

But one way or another, he was damn well going to make sure she survived. It wouldn't be so bad to die if he knew she lived on, free at last of Ridgemont.

They were heading down the interstate again when Val smelled peppermint. She jerked sideways against the car door as Abigail leaned between the front seats. A glowing, translucent finger pointed at an exit up ahead. ***There's a motel sign up that way,*** the ghost said. ***Shouldn't you stop?***

"No," Cade said shortly. "I want to make it back to the house by dawn."

The ghost frowned. ***Are you sure you ought to wait? The process will take days as it is, and you don't know how long it will take Ridgemont to find you. I think you should get started now.***

Val looked warily from Abigail's glowing profile to Cade's. "What process? What's she talking about?"

"We've already been through this, Abigail," he said, his jaw tightening. "I told you, I'm not Changing her."

Val drew back. "God, no."

Shimmering eyes shifted to hers. ***Why not? You made love to him.***

"You were watching?" Outraged, she glared.

The ghost gave her chin a haughty tilt. ***Of course not. But I sensed it Beyond.***

"Beyond where?"

Abigail shrugged. ***The place Beyond***.

"It's like an alternate dimension that exists alongside this one," Cade told Val. "All kinds of psychic energy manifest there." To Abigail he added, "What happened between us has nothing to do with…."

Ignoring him, the ghost turned to stare at Val, her expression icy with condemnation. ***Are you a whore?***

Val stiffened. "You just stepped over the line, Ghost Brat. I…."

His life is in danger, mortal, Abigail snapped. ***He could die. Nobody but a whore would take him into her bed and not do everything she could to help him***.

"That's dirty pool." Stung, she tried to ignore the nagging feeling that the ghost had a point. "You've got no right to send me on a guilt trip just because I don't want to lose my humanity."

Cade stands to lose more than that if you refuse, because Ridgemont will kill him. The ghost's eyes narrowed. ***Perhaps you need to see a demonstration.***

"Abigail…." Cade growled.

Ignoring him, the ghost leaned forward until her face was inches from Val's. ***You may be able to shield your mind from* them *when you're awake, but you can't keep me out. Look and see what I've seen.***

Involuntarily, Val looked into the little ghost's black eyes—and felt herself begin to fall, plummeting soundlessly into….

Light!

Val blinked hard, blinded. Shaking her head to clear it, she looked around to find herself standing in the middle of an arena. The walls were a good fifteen feet high under a vaulting ceiling, and the floor was thickly covered in sawdust.

The ring of blade on blade drew her eyes to the center of the huge space, where two medieval knights hacked at each other with swords.

She blinked, confused. Had she somehow traveled back in time?

Then she realized the fighters weren't really knights; the armor they wore was something other than simple steel. Looking closer, she saw the taller of the two men was Cade, his handsome face cold and set with concentration behind the bars of his faceplate. His opponent…. Val felt a chill shudder through her. She knew those blunt, brutal features. It was the blond man who'd ordered Cade to kill her.

Ridgemont.

They came together in a blur of raw, inhuman power. Blades slashed and stabbed, blocked by parries or lifted shields, steel clanging and scraping as if from blows of a blacksmith's hammer.

It was nothing like the fights with Hirsch, bad as those had been. These attacks were harder, faster, even more brutal, though the two vampires moved like dancers in their massive armor.

But what frightened Val most was the look on Cade's face. Instead of the confidence he'd displayed against Hirsch, there was a sheen of sweat on his upper lip, and his jaw was tight with effort. Yet the master vampire was smiling, cruel enjoyment shining in his pale eyes.

Ridgemont swung his sword like Babe Ruth swatting a home run. Cade barely managed to block the blow. Even so, the impact slammed his shield into his chest, driving a hoarse grunt from his throat. He stumbled backward and almost went down, then dug in his heels and caught himself. Visibly summoning his strength, he launched a ferocious attack of his own, his face twisted in a grimace of exertion.

But Ridgemont swatted his blade away with mocking ease.

They've been fighting for an hour, Abigail whispered. ***Cade can match Ridgemont for short periods, but eventually the old monster wears him down.***

Val blinked, astonished he'd maintained this level of grueling combat for so long.

Suddenly it was over. Ridgemont lunged forward, driving his sword toward Cade's belly like a spear. Desperately, Cade tried to parry the strike. His sword broke against the oncoming blade. It smashed through the armor like an eggshell and speared into his body so hard it lifted him off his feet.

Val cried out. Abigail filled her vision with Cade's face, his eyes wide with the shock of the blow, his mouth twisted in a silent howl of agony.

Ridgemont grabbed his shoulder, easily holding him off the ground. Slowly, deliberately, the vampire twisted the blade. Cade dropped his sword and shield to clutch futilely at his torturer's wrist. Blood bubbled between his lips. His face paled as he visibly fought not to scream.

"Your guard dropped a bit at the end," Ridgemont told him, his tone as cool and clinical as a surgeon's. He dipped the blade to let his victim's feet touch the ground again. Panting in agony, Cade met his gaze with a hot glare.

Ridgemont grinned, planted a foot against Cade's crotch, and kicked him off the sword. Staggering, he fell hard with a wheezing gasp of pain.

His sire lifted the gory sword as if to behead him. Panting and unarmed, Cade curled his bloody lips in a sneer. The sword arced down. Val screamed.

The point buried itself in the sawdust an inch from his throat.

"I do hope you'll give me a better fight than this when the time comes, gunslinger," Ridgemont taunted. "Otherwise it will be somewhat…anticlimactic after one hundred and twenty years." The master vampire turned and swaggered away. "All right, Hirsch, it's your turn…."

"Shit!" Nauseated and gasping, Val fell against the car door as the vision released its grip on her mind.

Cade stared at Abigail in chilly displeasure. "I don't appreciate that."

The ghost shrugged. ***She needs to know what you're facing.***

Swallowing convulsively, Val looked at him. "God, Cade… How often did he do that to you?"

He looked away and focused his attention on the traffic. "It wasn't as bad as it looked, obviously. I did survive."

Only because he's a vampire, Abigail said. ***A human would have died rather quickly. And considering how he suffered while that particular injury healed, he probably would have preferred death.***

"Yeah, well, I didn't die," he told her roughly. "I never do."

You mean you never have. Yet. Abigail turned her demanding gaze on Valerie. ***Now will you let him Change you?***

"Abigail, go Beyond," Cade said. "Now. You've done enough."

But….

"Now, Abigail."

With an outraged little huff, she flew up through the roof of the car. Val, stunned and sick, barely noticed.

Chapter Eleven

The image of Cade's chocolate eyes glazing in agony ripped at her. Val shuddered. "Changing me would keep him from doing that to you again?"

"No," he said.

She blinked at him. "But I thought you said...."

"It would make the odds more equal, but that's all. He could still defeat me in battle. There's no guarantee."

She balled her fists in her lap. "But if you don't Change me, and you fight him again...."

"I'll probably lose," he admitted.

"Don't fight him."

Cade laughed shortly. "I wish it were that simple. Unfortunately, Ridgemont has a way of forcing the issue."

Val's thoughts churned as she struggled to come up with an alternative. "But does it have to be swords? Isn't there some other way to kill him?"

"Oh, yeah. Anything that takes the head off or destroys the heart would work. A shotgun blast might do it, though with Ridgemont you never can tell. I tried a car bomb a few days ago, but Abigail warned him and he escaped...."

She stared at him. "Why on earth did she do that?"

"I was in the car at the time." He shrugged.

"You were going to blow yourself up?" The chill in her heart grew even colder. Cade could have died before she had the chance to know he was real, touch him, kiss him....

"I wanted to take him out before you arrived."

He was willing to give his life to protect me, she thought. That dream image of him as her cowboy hero was a lot closer to the truth than she'd realized.

How could she refuse to do anything that would help him? And yet.... Becoming a vampire meant giving up her humanity, turning her back on any chance she'd ever had for a normal life. She'd never be able to go back.

But could she live with herself if she let Cade die without doing everything in her power to save him?

She swallowed and looked away, feeling her gut clench at the brutal conflict. She couldn't have turned her back on anybody, much less the man who had sacrificed so much to save her. Her heart began to pound. "Cade...."

"No."

She blinked. "No?"

He faced her. "I'm not letting you make that decision out of pity for me. If I Change you, you won't have children. You'd never again work at the job you love. You'd never marry—at least, not a mortal. Everything your life has been up until now will be over...."

"Which will be equally true if Ridgemont gets me," she told him. "If you make me immortal...."

"The point is, you won't *be* immortal." A muscle ticked in his jaw. "You won't age and you won't get sick, but you can still die. And if I fight Ridgemont and lose, he'll kill you in the most humiliating, sadistic way he can. I'm not putting you...."

"Wait a minute," she interrupted. "You said you'd Change me if I were willing. Why the sudden turnaround?"

I realized I love you, Cade thought. He bit back the words. "I've reassessed the situation, and I've decided the risk is unacceptable," he told her shortly. "I'll come up with something else."

She frowned at him. "Like what?"

Cade shrugged. "I don't know. An ambush, maybe. Something."

She shook her head. "Cade…."

"Val, drop it."

"Quit being a pigheaded jerk, McKinnon," she snapped. "This is my life too. I have a right to a say in…."

"Who the hell do you think you are, Buffy the Vampire Slayer?" he growled. "Until three days ago, you didn't believe any of us even existed. You have no idea what will work against us and what won't, so I suggest you just shut the hell up and let me think."

Stung, she snapped her teeth closed.

Cade greeted her icy silence with a mental sigh of relief. He'd take pissed over pitying any day.

You're an idiot, do you know that? Abigail said.

Shut up.

Frowning at the dotted line blurring past the Lexus as it sped down I-95, he focused on trying to come up with a solution to the problem of killing Ridgemont. And tried to ignore the feeling his sister was right.

Cade's house sprawled across its wooded three-acre lot, long and low, vaguely Spanish in design, with white stuccoed walls that shimmered rose in the early morning light. The lights were on behind stained glass windows that spilled color out onto the dewy grass. As the Lexus rolled up the drive, a robin took off and flew into the trees.

"Damn." Val gazed at the elegant arched doorway and the play of bright color in the windows. "I'm impressed."

Cade slanted her a grin as he reached past her to get a garage door opener out of the glove compartment. "Thanks. Invested some of the drug money I seized, and it paid off."

"In this market?" She lifted a brow and snorted. "You must have magic powers."

His grinned widened. "No, before the crash. This house is

several years old." Cade pulled the car into the garage next to a blue Windstar minivan.

Wondering where it came from, Val studied it. It was packed with boxes, all labeled in black magic marker. One of them read "Camille's clothes." Who the heck was Camille, and why did Cade have her clothing?

Before she could ask, a door opened at the other side of the garage. A slim black woman stepped out of the house, a broad smile spreading across her round, pretty face. She was dressed in jeans and a T-shirt with a college logo on the front. "Hey, Mr. McKinnon. You made good time."

"Hello, Camille." Cade got out of the car and went to shake her hand, then tilted his head as he studied her. "You look relaxed, considering the pressure I've put you under. Sorry about that."

"What pressure? Any stress I was ever under, you got rid of. Starting with Cleave, the bastard." Warm brown eyes watched Val get out of the car. "This your lady friend?"

Val came around the hood to shake the woman's delicate hand. "Hi. Valerie Chase."

"This is Camille Robbins," Cade told her. "She and her three children have been keeping an eye on the house for me."

"You mean we've been living here rent free," Camille corrected dryly as she led the way into the house and down a short entrance hall into a huge kitchen. "Which is something I'm going to do something about as soon as I graduate."

While Cade told her he had no intention of accepting her money, Val looked around at the kitchen's gleaming white appliances, butcher block counter tops and red ceramic tile floor. Copper pots hung over a central island, and herbs grew in pots on the window sill. Organized, efficient, with an underlying love of simple beauty, it looked like Cade.

Finally Camille gave up the fight to convince her benefactor to accept rent. "Look, I'm sure you're tired. I've bent your ear long enough, and I've got to get to get the kids to school."

"Yeah. Have a good day, Camille."

"Sleep well." She stopped short. "Oh, I've got the master bedroom ready for you. Through the living room, down the hall, only door on the left."

As Camille padded out, Val turned to Cade. "You didn't have to send them away. They could have stayed here."

"And get caught in the crossfire between me and Ridgemont?"

"Oh. Didn't think of that." She hesitated. "We could have gone to a hotel."

"Endangering the guests and staff instead? Not likely. No, this was the best way." He turned back toward the garage. "I'll go unload the car, then I'll show you around."

"I'll help." She followed him.

Camille walked back into the kitchen. She could hear McKinnon arguing with his lady friend out in the garage about whether she was going to carry her own bags. Smiling slightly, Camille reached for the phone. McKinnon had been a lifesaver for her and her kids. Literally. She had no doubt she'd be dead now without the help he'd given her. If Cleave hadn't killed her, the drugs eventually would have.

When the man answered the phone, she identified herself and said, "He's here."

"Good. Forget you spoke to me."

Camille hung up, then frowned, unable to remember what she'd come into the kitchen to do. Why was she just standing here? She had to get the kids to school. "Jena! Lashonda! Antwon, let's go!"

Hirsch tucked away his cell phone into his jacket with a smile of satisfaction. When he'd found the letter from Camille Robbins on

McKinnon's desk months before, he hadn't mentioned it to anyone. He's just followed a hunch and flown to South Carolina, where to his delighted surprise, he found the woman and her children living in a house McKinnon had built. He'd promptly put her under a compulsion to keep him informed any time the American came to visit. That bit of foresight had just paid off handsomely.

Now he needed to have a word with Ridgemont. When he went after McKinnon this time, he intended to have reinforcements.

"I think I've got an idea about how to kill Ridgemont, but it's going to be tricky," Cade told Val as they carried their bags into the master bedroom. "I need to get to work on it if I'm going to pull it off before he finds us."

"What about just giving him both barrels with a shotgun? You said that would work."

"On an ordinary vampire, yes." He shook his head as he stacked the bags he carried on the bed. "But with Ridgemont, I'd have to get close enough to use it, and he'd know I was there. I need to be outside his psychic range, but inside the range of whatever weapon I use. Which limits my options considerably, because Ridgemont's got a hell of a range. About the only thing that would do the trick is a Stinger missile."

Val stopped in her tracks to gape at him. "Are you serious?" But she could tell by his grim expression he was. "Where the hell do you plan to get one of those?"

Cade shrugged. "Planted a compulsion in this Army general I met a couple of years ago. He'll give me anything I want, up to and including a Stinger." Frowning, he rubbed the muscles at the base of his neck. "Trouble is, the Army would find out about it and hang him out to dry, so I've hesitated to use him. Unfortunately, I'm backed into a corner now."

She put her laptop case on the bureau and turned to look at

him. "You can't ruin the man's career, Cade."

"I'll come up with a way to protect him. I just need to give him a call and figure out what to do."

Folding her arms, she settled a shoulder against one wall. "You know, if you Changed me, none of that would be necessary."

Cade gave her a cool stare. "Only by putting you at risk of a lot worse. Nobody's career is worth your life."

Val blinked and straightened in surprise at the blunt refusal. Before she could wonder whether he actually meant it, he said, "I'm headed across the hall to use the phone. If you need anything, help yourself. Everything I have is yours."

"Okaaay." Blowing out a breath, she turned to take in the room around her. She needed rest and a clear head if she wanted to make sense of this.

She'd unpack, then grab a shower and hit the bed. Maybe this whole situation would be a lot more understandable after she got some sleep.

The carpet gave lushly under her feet. A soft pearl gray, it felt as thick and soft as foam. The furniture was massive and dark, with a huge mirrored bureau, an armoire, and a bed the size of an aircraft carrier. Two burgundy armchairs stood in a little grouping at the other end of the enormous room.

The whole effect would have been severe if it hadn't been for the two huge stained glass windows that took up most of one wall, gorgeous landscapes of waterfalls and forests. In each image, wolves prowled, wild and dark. Such windows weren't cheap; considering the house had more stained glass than most churches, the expense must have been staggering.

But then, given Cade's vulnerability to sunlight, the investment was probably worth it. The rich colors would cut out most of the harmful rays and allow him to enjoy the light without worry. She was just wandering over to take a closer look when the air suddenly filled with the scent of peppermint.

Val sighed. Suspecting she'd never be able to eat another candy cane as long as she lived, she turned to look at Abigail. "If you want to bitch at me about becoming a vampire, don't. I'm willing. Cade is the one you need to talk to."

The ghost twisted her translucent hands together. ***I'm not here to harangue you. I just...I'm worried about Cade.***

Well, that was understandable. For something to do with her own hands, Val walked over to the suitcases piled on the bed and snapped the locks open on one of them. "I'm worried, too."

Looking up, she jerked. Abigail's face was inches from hers as the ghost floated above the bed, gazing closely into her eyes. ***I think you are. And I need your help, because I'm afraid Cade is going to get himself killed.***

Swallowing, Val pulled a shirt out of the suitcase and turned to hang it up in the closet. The ghost might be in a mellow mood, but she felt spooked anyway. "If it's any comfort, the Stinger idea does sound as though it would work."

Yes, it does. But if it fails, Ridgemont will kill him. Unless Cade Changes you to get the strength he needs to fight.

"But he refuses to do that." She opened the closet door and reached in to get a hanger.

And have you wondered why? It's more than his fear of getting you killed, though that's certainly a factor.

Frowning, Val slid the shirt onto the hanger. "A pretty damn big factor, judging from the look in his eyes a few minutes ago."

Of course. He is in love with you, after all.

The ghost's matter-of-fact confirmation of her suspicions took Val's breath away. She stared at Abigail in suspended astonishment.

No. The little ghost was wrong, or trying to play her. Or something.

But that's not his only concern, Abigail went on, as if the world hadn't just tilted on its axis. ***Have you asked yourself what***

would happen if Cade makes you a vampire and you both succeed in killing Ridgemont?

"You mean other than me dancing on the bastard's grave?"

I'll join you. We'll have a hoedown. But what comes next?

Val shrugged and reached into the closet to pull out a handful of hangers. "We all live happily ever after, I guess." *Could* Cade be in love with her? God, what a seductive thought…

Which, considering you'd both be vampires, could be a very long time. Would you stay with Cade?

"Stay?" On her way back to the bed with the hangers, Val looked at the ghost, frowning.

As his lover. Or even his wife. The two of you, united for centuries.

Cade. Hers. With no fear of Ridgemont or Hirsch. Hers to touch and taste. Decades of his wickedly skillful hands drawing pleasure from her body as his big cock surged and thrust deep. The idea was darkly tempting. "I…don't know. He hasn't asked me to stay." She lifted her chin. "And I'm not in love with him." She couldn't be.

Aren't you?

Val looked away. "No."

Abigail smiled. ***The point is, Cade believes you wouldn't even consider staying. He thinks you would reject him.***

"What? Why?"

Because Caroline Johnson did.

"Who the hell is Caroline Johnson?"

The only woman, other than you, he ever loved.

Val waited in suspended fascination, but instead of continuing in that vein, the ghost floated to the stained glass window and looked out, as if she could see beyond the glowing colors. Maybe she could.

The land this house sits on was once part of our family plantation, did you know that? That's why Cade bought it to begin

with. Before the war, you could see the cotton nodding in the wind, a huge expanse of it, like a field of snow. Cade spent hours out there with Pa, learning how to tend it, how to make it grow. Yet after the War, he left without a backward glance.

Val frowned, wondering where Abigail was going with this. "There probably wasn't much left, not if it was like other plantations in this part of the country."

True, but there was more to it than that. Mostly he just wanted to forget. He was only sixteen when he enlisted. He was nineteen when the war was over, but those three years had left decades worth of scars. She went silent for a long moment, as though remembering. Finally she continued, ***He blamed himself for the deaths of Pa and our brother. Maybe still does. Thought he should have been able to save them, though I don't know how.*** The ghost smiled a slight, bitter smile. ***Cade always did have a talent for guilt. Pa taught him responsibility a little too well.***

Something in Val pulled into an aching knot at the idea of McKinnon carrying such a burden at such a young age. "You know, I never thought what his life was like before Ridgemont." She shook her head. "I'd hoped it was…happy."

It wasn't. Cade got home just in time to watch me succumb to yellow fever. Ma had already died from it. I don't know how he avoided being infected himself, particularly given that he buried me with his own hands. Her expression was sad, brooding. ***All the servants, all the slaves, they were gone.***

Well, you can hardly blame them, Val thought. She didn't say the words, knowing Abigail wouldn't see it that way.

With no field hands and no money, he couldn't bring in a crop. He stayed on the next year only because he was so weak and starved he needed to build up his strength. But as soon as he could, he lit out, heading west. He drifted for several years, working as a field hand or helping lay railroad line, until eventu-

ally he reached Texas and decided to become a Texas Ranger.

"What about you? Where were you all this time?"

Abigail turned to look at her, light from the window streaming through her translucent body. ***After I…died, I remained. Almost everyone does, at least a day or two. And I saw this.***

Suddenly her eyes seized Val's like a trap snapping closed. Everything spun, and…

She was looking down at Cade as if she floated in the air just over his head. But it was a Cade who was too young, too thin, bony wrists protruding from the too-short sleeves of a ragged gray uniform as he knelt on a raw mound of dirt. A wooden cross made from two pieces of board stood at the head of the mound. It was, Val realized, Abigail's grave.

He wasn't crying—his face was too desolate for that, his gaze blasted and empty like the windows of a house that had been pounded by artillery.

Suddenly she remembered a laughing young boy's face, dark eyes dancing with merriment, long fingers digging into her ribs while she shrieked, "Cade! Cade, stop!"

Abigail's memory. Sharing it, Val felt her heart ache.

But then her eyes shifted upward, and her heart skipped a beat. Just above his head, something roiled—a blackness, half-seen, radiating a sense of horror so intense the hair rose on the back of her neck.

"What the hell is that?" Val said.

Cade's future, Abigail's ghostly voice replied in her mind.

"Evil," Val whispered. "Suffering."

I didn't know what it was, but I knew it waited for him. And I knew it would be worse than everything else he'd endured.

Suddenly a bright gold light spilled over Abigail's grave, but Cade didn't look up. It was as though he didn't see it. Yet Val sensed…something coming from that light. An emotion—a patience, a kindness so infinite it brought tears to her eyes.

The presence spoke to Abigail, its voice a gentle thunder imbued with a texture she could feel on her skin, a taste that filled her mouth, exquisite and alien and indescribable. But though she could feel the sound reverberating in her chest, she couldn't understand the words.

Abigail could. ***I can't just go!*** the ghost's voice protested. ***I can't leave him like this! Can't I help him?***

The being replied in a long, rolling rumble. It was frustrating, Val thought, like hearing half of a phone conversation. Yet somehow she wasn't sure she wanted to hear what the golden presence said.

But I could help him?

Now the rumble sounded like affirmation and warning, all at once.

I don't care. I'll do whatever I have to. I can't let it have him.

WRENCH!!

Val sat on Cade's bed, her head swimming as she stared at the ghost floating before the stained glass window. She swallowed. "Was that...God?"

Abigail shrugged. ***I don't really know, but I don't think so. I believe it was an angel.***

"You gave up your chance to go with it so you could stay with him?"

The ghost smiled. ***I couldn't do anything else. Could you, after seeing what waited for him?***

"No." Val frowned, reassessing her mental image of Abigail. She'd thought the ghost a cold little bitch, but now she realized how much love and loyalty lay beneath that ruthless willingness to do anything for her brother. "How did he react to having you suddenly appear?"

Oh, he didn't know I was there until Ridgemont Changed him. As a mortal, he didn't have your power. Another eighteen

years would pass before he saw me.

"You followed him for eighteen years without ever talking to him at all?"

Valerie, I'm dead. It's not as if I had anything better to do.

"Good point. What happened then?" Suddenly she wanted to know more, craved to know more.

As I said, he wandered. Images flashed through her mind: Cade, slumped in the saddle of a tired horse, a five-o'-clock shadow darkening his jaw as he rode beside a herd of weary cattle. Cade, shirtless in the sun, swinging a pick. Cade driving a mule team, his eyes patient and bored.

SHIFT. Looking like the cowboy hero of Valerie's dreams, he rode hard on a galloping horse, his eyes narrow and hot with determination. A badge glinted on his broad chest. ***Until he joined the Rangers. It gave him a sense of purpose again, the feeling he was doing something to help those who needed it.***

SHIFT. Another man, a badge pinned to his chest, standing at Cade's side as the two fired their guns at three men running from a bank. Two of the bandits went down, but the third snapped off a shot, hitting the other Ranger. With a shout, Cade blew away the killer, then dropped to his knees beside his fallen comrade.

"Take care of her, McKinnon," the dying Ranger gasped, "Don't let my Caroline starve."

Then came Caro.

SHIFT. Cade stood with both arms wrapped around a woman as she sobbed, an expression of pity on his face—pity, and an uncomfortable awareness mixed with guilt.

SHIFT. Sitting at her kitchen table, he watched her laugh at something he'd said. Masculine hunger glowed in his dark eyes as he looked at her.

SHIFT. Cade kissed Caroline, drinking in her mouth. Val felt a surprising stab of jealousy she knew was all her own.

I knew it wasn't going to work, the ghost said. ***She wasn't like you. There was a weakness in her that was no match for what waited for him. And I was right.***

SHIFT. Cade and Caroline stood on the porch, his mouth moving over hers with gentle, wooing skill.

Suddenly a man shouted something, and Cade's head snapped up.

The other man strode toward him, dirty, beefy face twisted with rage as he went for his gun. Cade's hand blurred toward the Colt on his hip. He was just a fraction faster. Smoke billowed from his pistol, and the man went down, his own weapon firing wild.

Caroline stared at the fallen gunman, her eyes widening with horror. Cade looked down at her and froze as he read the revulsion in her gaze.

"But the guy was going to kill him!" Val said, outraged. "He was just defending himself!"

Yes, and she'd already lost one husband. She couldn't stand to lose another, particularly when she'd come so close to getting shot herself in the process. She broke it off with him that night.

SHIFT. Cade wearily climbed a set of narrow stairs. Defeat rounded his broad shoulders, and there was pain in his eyes. ***He went back to his hotel, thinking it couldn't get any worse.***

As Val watched him climb, she sensed something waiting for him at the head of the stairs. Something dark. Something evil.

"Oh, God," Val whispered. "Ridgemont."

Chapter Twelve

The Abigail of the ghost's memories screamed a warning Cade couldn't hear as he walked down the hall to his room. Val's stomach twisted. She didn't want to see any more, but she held her tongue. If he'd had to endure it, she had to see it.

Cade! Stop! the ghost cried again. ***Please, stop! Please!***

He broke step, frowning. For a moment Val thought he'd actually heard Abigail's psychic cries, but then a feminine whimper of pain sounded, and she realized it was that sound that brought his head up.

Cade turned as if trying to determine the origin of that tiny, hopeless noise. A deep male voice growled something menacing from behind the door to his left. He turned and looked at it, eyes narrowing, broad shoulders tensing.

Oh, God, Val thought. *It's a woman, and he's going to try to go to the rescue. And Ridgemont's on the other side of that door.*

Another muffled sound, unmistakably a scream, cut off in the middle by a hard slap.

Cade drew his gun and rammed his booted foot into the door. It flew open with a thunderous bang. He strode into the room, gun at the ready. "Hands up!"

Ridgemont looked up as he leaned over a woman lying on the bed. He was fully dressed, while she was naked and hog-tied. Her bare breasts were smeared with blood from a pair of puncture wounds set just above one nipple. Her desperate gaze met Cade's over her gag, wide with terror, silently begging for help.

Cade flicked a shocked glance at her brutalized body, then

turned to level his gun at Ridgemont with a snarl. "What the hell is going on here?"

The vampire wiped a smear of red from the corner of his mouth. "Get out."

Cade brought the gun up to point it right between those thick blond brows. "I don't think the lady's willing. Step away or take a bullet."

Ridgemont tried to compel him, Abigail explained. ***But he was Kith, and that was before their link. So it didn't work. And that's when the evil bastard realized what Cade was.***

Surprised interest flickered in chilly blue eyes. "Well, well. And who would you be?"

"I'm a Texas Ranger, mister, that's all the hell you need to know. And I'm not in the habit of giving an order twice. Step away from the lady."

"As you wish." Ridgemont moved back, still grinning. Cade started toward him, sliding his free hand into his back pocket as if reaching for something to use in restraining the other man.

Before he even completed the step, the vampire's massive fist slammed into his jaw with such blinding speed he had no time to react. Val gasped in horror as Cade hit the wall behind him with a crash, then slid down to collapse on the floor in a boneless heap.

Ridgemont rocked back on his heels, studying his victim. A slow smile curved his lips.

The ghost moaned, ***Oh, no. Oh, Cade….***

SHIFT. Cade sat slumped unconscious in a straight-backed chair, his wrists bound behind its back, his ankles tied to its legs. He lifted his head with a groan of pain, lids slitting open before promptly squeezing shut again.

"It's been three hundred years since I've found anyone like you," Ridgemont said.

Cade's eyes snapped open.

The vampire sat on the bed with his back propped against

the headboard, his long legs crossed at the ankle in black wool breeches, a black vest stretching across his massive chest. "My last spawn died a century ago," he said. "A leader is nothing without followers, and I have been a leader all my life. I've missed it."

"A century?" Cade's eyes flickered.

He thinks he's dealing with a madman, Val realized.

"But just any follower won't do," Ridgemont continued, watching his face closely. "I prefer my men have a certain … steel. And judging by the way you broke down that door, I think you'll do nicely. All in all, I'm pleased."

"I wouldn't be, if I were you." Cade jerked his bound hands with all his strength. The ropes didn't even creak. "Because when I get loose, I'm going to beat you bloody."

Ridgemont laughed. "I'm almost tempted to untie you and let you try. Unfortunately, you wouldn't be much of a challenge in your current state. Cheer up, though. That's going to change." He swung his legs off the bed and stood. "And so are you."

Cade stared at the vampire with rage blazing in his eyes. "You'd better kill me now, you son of a bitch. Because if you don't, I'm going to gut you like a Comanche."

The vampire eyed Cade with clinical interest as he prowled around behind his chair. "I wonder how long it will take me to make you scream." He bent suddenly until his lips were level with his captive's ear. "My name," he said, "is Sir Edward Ridgemont."

"Tell it to the undertaker, you…." Cade's defiance turned to astonished shock as he saw the fangs gleaming between Ridgemont's parted lips. "What the hell?"

The vampire grinned. "I'm afraid this is one time you really shouldn't have ridden to the rescue, my gallant friend." He wrapped a big fist in his captive's hair and dragged his head to one side.

The cords in Cade's neck strained as he fought Ridgemont's strength. "Fuck you!"

"If you were a woman, I'd do just that." He licked his lips and lowered his head. "But I can't have everything." Taking his time, he buried his teeth in Cade's muscled neck, biting so deep and brutally his victim hissed in pain.

Softly, Abigail began to sob.

The image shifted again, melting rapidly from scene to scene as Ridgemont bit Cade again and again.

It took the ancient two days to drain and infect him.

SHIFT. Ridgemont dragged a knife across his own thick wrist, then forced the wound against his captive's lips until Cade had to drink the blood or drown.

SHIFT. Cade sat barely conscious in the chair, his eyes slitted open as the vampire raped a sobbing woman on the bed. ***Two day of horror and helplessness.***

SHIFT. ***Until finally he slipped into the coma of the Change***. Held in his seat only by his bonds, Cade slumped, head lolling, eyes closed. Ridgemont leaned close, his expression fierce, his eyes almost glowing. ***I think he fought to die then. I prayed he would, because we both know what would happen to him if he lived. But Ridgemont was too strong and dragged him back.***

SHIFT. ***That's when he finally realized what had been done to him.*** Cade's face twisted in revulsion as he spat two teeth on the floor and looked up, revealing the fangs that had replaced them.

SHIFT. A woman struggled in Ridgemont's arms as he forcibly bent her across Cade's lap, one fist clenched in her hair to hold her head back. Cade stared at her in shame and desperate need before he squeezed his eyes shut, leaned forward and sank his fangs into her throat.

But simply Changing him wasn't enough. Ridgemont had to prove that he owned Cade, and he wanted to do it in a way that would drive the lesson home. So he kidnaped Caroline.

SHIFT. The elder vampire strolled into the room leading the

widow, one big hand wrapped around her elbow. Her expression was blank, as though she was firmly in Ridgemont's power. Cade, lying asleep on the bed, jolted awake. Seeing her, his eyes widened with hopeless horror as his face went pale.

Ridgemont gave him a malicious grin. "She won't say no this time, gunslinger."

Cade rolled off the bed and backed away. Shirtless, his Levi's riding low on his hips, he looked big and impressive, four inches taller than the elder vampire. The look in his eyes revealed the helplessness he felt. "Let her go home, Ridgemont. Her kids need her."

The ancient grinned, clearly enjoying himself. "Oh, she'll go home. Eventually." He turned to Caroline. "Show him that pretty body, my dear. He's wanted to see it for months."

Her eyes empty as a sleepwalker's, the widow lifted her hands and began unbuttoning the high neckline of her severe blue gown. Ridgemont barely spared her a glance, far more interested in the panic in Cade's eyes. "There's more to feeding than blood, gunslinger. And there's nothing like sex to get the victim going— especially if you mix in a little fear."

As Caroline dragged the gown down her hips, her eyes suddenly flooded with horrified awareness. But it didn't stop her from mechanically stepping out of the circle of the gown, or reaching for the tapes of her petticoats.

"Taste that, McKinnon," Ridgemont said softly. "Fear. It's sweet, isn't it?"

As she slowly undressed, revealing a petite, delicately rounded body, Cade lowered his head and bared his teeth. The cords of his neck stood out rigidly against the rise of need. "No."

"Yes." Ridgemont stepped up behind Caro and reached around her waist to begin unlacing her corset. "Strip, gunslinger. We'll do her together."

The horror in Cade's eyes deepened as his hands went to the

buttons of his Levi's. His face contorted with effort as he fought the compulsion, but his fingers obeyed anyway. "God damn you."

The ancient laughed and cupped her breasts in both hands. "You may as well stop fighting it, McKinnon. You just don't have the power to keep my mind from overriding yours." Lazily he tugged her nipples. "She's got pretty tits, doesn't she? So full and white." Ridgemont lowered his head and said into her ear, "Think of it, Caroline. Two cocks, two sets of fangs. It's going to hurt—and I'm going to make you like it."

The widow's gaze flew to Cade's and silently begged. His expression hardened with determination even as he slid his jeans down his long, muscled legs. "Did you like it, Ridgemont?"

"Like what?" the ancient asked as he squeezed and fondled Caroline's breasts.

His voice was low and deadly. "Did you like it when the Saracens took their turn on you, back when you were mortal?"

Ridgemont's big hands stilled, his mouth going slack with shock.

"While you were so busy invading my mind during the Change, I got a look at yours." Naked, Cade stepped up to him and looked down into his eyes with a taunting smile. "Your precious Lionheart hesitated too long about ransoming you when you were captured by the Saracens during that Crusade. And they got a little bored. It's been eight hundred years, but no matter how many women you rape, you can't forget what it was like being on the other end of the cock."

The ancient shoved Caroline aside with a roar of raw fury. She fell, then scrambled to her feet and lunged for her clothes, not even glancing around as Ridgemont strode across the room and drove his fist into Cade's face. He crashed into the wall, but she didn't look back as she balled up her things and ran naked out the door.

"She left him like that?" Val demanded. "Bitch."

Ridgemont was so furious he released her mind, just as Cade

had intended. She knew she wouldn't get another chance—and Caroline's first priority was always Caroline. Besides, to her mind, Cade had become just as big a monster.

As Cade went reeling from another pile driver punch, Ridgemont drew up short, visibly working to bring himself back under control.

Licking the blood from his split lip, Cade stood, though he had to brace his back against the wall to do it. He grinned viciously, a demonic light in his dark eyes. "Oh, come on, Eddie—be honest with yourself. You liked it all those centuries ago. In fact, you don't really want me to fuck Caroline—you want me to fuck you."

With a bellow of berserker rage, the elder vampire whirled and grabbed a sheathed long sword lying on a pile of luggage. He drew the weapon with a hiss of steel. And spun, the sword gripped in both hands as he slashed viciously at his tormentor. Cade didn't even flinch.

The blade stopped a fraction of an inch from his neck. Breathing hard, Ridgemont glared at him. "No. You're not going to escape me that easily, McKinnon. You're going to live, you bastard, and curse every day you breathe."

He threw the weapon aside with a clatter. "But first you're going to learn your place if I have to beat it into you." He buried his fist in Cade's belly so hard he lifted the bigger man's feet off the ground.

WRENCH.

Val collapsed on the bed, shaking and sick. The image of Cade watching that blade come at his face was seared into her mind.

She shivered and swallowed. "God. Oh, God. I can't let Ridgemont do that to him again." She stopped as the realization hit her like a freight train. "Oh, sweet God."

What? Abigail demanded, worried at her tone of stunned realization.

"I've got to get him to Change me." She'd offered before, but she'd been secretly relieved when he turned her down. Now she knew she had to persuade him no matter what. Even if it meant giving up her humanity.

But how? He's already refused once.

Only one way came to mind. Val straightened her shoulders. "Abigail, go Beyond."

What? the ghost demanded, startled. ***But….***

"We don't need an audience. Go Beyond, and don't come back until we call you."

Abigail's bewilderment gave way to a knowing gleam. ***Oh. You're going to seduce him.***

"Not with a thirteen-year-old audience. Get lost."

I'm actually a hundred and fifty, but I won't quibble. Giving a satisfied nod, the ghost vanished into the ceiling.

"And no peeking!" Val called after her.

Don't be insulting.

Val grinned at the ghost's indignant tone, then sobered, her eyes narrowing. There wasn't much time. Cade would be back soon, and she had to be ready for him.

Moving quickly to one of the suitcases lying on the bed, she flipped it open and began a survey, looking for lingerie. She knew the only chance she had of pulling this off was to get Cade so hot his impressive cock started doing the thinking for him.

But as she dug through the bag, she realized she hadn't packed a damn thing that was suitably slinky. This was supposed to have been a business trip, after all; seducing vampires had never been part of the itinerary. *Damn.*

On the other hand, if the idea was to hit his hormones so hard and fast his brain didn't have time to engage, maybe she'd be better off in nothing but a smile. He might be an immortal creature of the night, but he was still a man—and nothing was guaranteed to switch off the male brain like finding a naked woman in his bed.

A shower. What she needed was a shower. And this time she was leaving out the ice cubes.

Half an hour later, Val climbed into bed clean and naked, her hair artfully tumbled, her face made up just enough not to look made up at all. Her belly turned slow, nervous flips as she settled back against the pillows she'd piled against the headboard. *What the hell am I doing?* she wondered wildly. *If he Changes me, I can never go back. I'll be giving up children and long morning walks on the beach and my journalism career. What will Beth think? I'll never eat another piece of chocolate. I'll have to drink blood. This is nuts!*

Then she remembered the stark, hot wonder on Cade's face as he entered her, the raw pleasure in his eyes as he climaxed.

Oh, hell, Val thought. *Chocolate makes me break out anyway.*

She had to put aside her doubts. Cade always knew when she was aroused, which meant he'd also know when she wasn't. She'd better be genuinely hot when he walked through the bedroom door. And there was only one way to make sure of that.

But what if he caught her?

On the other hand, that would probably help.

Heart pounding, Val pushed the covers down, thought better of it and got up to arrange them neatly out of the way. She fluffed and restacked the pillows into an artistic mound, then crawled back onto the bed to settle against them.

Biting her lip, she slid one hesitant hand between her thighs and pinched a nipple with the other. *Hot. Think hot. Think Cade screwing my brains out on the trunk of the car.* She pushed away all thoughts of embarrassment, Ridgemont, vampirism—even Beth and the murder of her parents—and concentrated fiercely on the muscled contours of Cade McKinnon's big body.

The image was so potent it didn't take long for her sex to grow slick under her stroking fingers. When the door swung open, she was just hitting her second climax.

Val jerked her hands away and snapped upright as Cade stopped dead in the doorway, his eyes widening. Her face went so hot, she knew she was blushing cherry red. *Dammit, I'm supposed to be seducing him, not jumping like a virgin*, she thought, thoroughly annoyed with herself even in her embarrassment. *Shake it off, Val!*

Cade blinked and swallowed, raising the breakfast tray he held in both hands. "I, uh…thought you might be hungry."

"Uh, yeah." She considered jumping up to wash her hands, then thought better of it. *Seduction, seduction….* "A little something before bed would be good."

Val thought she heard him murmur, "Just what I was thinking."

Cade walked over to the night table and put down the tray. His gaze was definitely beginning to heat. She rose to her knees to examine the tray, less because she was hungry than out of an acute awareness of her own nudity. She'd never done anything like this in her life. *I've only known him two days!* babbled a little voice in the back of her head. She told it to shut up.

"Strawberries," Val said, surveying the deft arrangement of food. In the middle of the dewy red pile was a bowl of something dark brown. "And…chocolate?" She grinned up at him, realizing he'd planned a seduction of his own. "You read my mind." She scooped up one of the berries and dunked it in the melted sweet.

Cade watched as she slowly sank her white teeth into the fruit's firm, red flesh. When he swallowed, he could taste her arousal in the air. His cock lengthened behind his zipper.

She picked up another strawberry and swirled it in the chocolate. Meeting his intent gaze, she grinned wickedly and touched the dripping fruit to one hard nipple. Cade inhaled sharply as chocolate rolled onto the delicate pink tip.

Eyes heavy-lidded, Val stroked the berry over her flesh, painting it in sweet, dark rivulets. "I was wondering," she purred. "Do vampires like chocolate on their…food?"

"Let's find out." He tipped her backwards onto the mound of pillows and swooped down to lick the hard, chocolate-covered peak. It tasted deliciously of candy and Val. With a greedy moan, he suckled it until she whimpered.

When the little point was clean and pink and desperately hard, Cade looked up and met her eyes. "Yep. Vampires definitely have a sweet tooth."

As she groaned at the bad pun, he reached over to the tray, picked up a strawberry and plunged it into the bowl. With a dark grin, he presented the chocolate-coated berry to the pouting lips of her sex and spread the wet flesh with his free hand.

"Hey!" Val straightened, but before she could scoot away, he slid the fruit into her tight channel. He groaned at the feeling of her around his fingers. She was incredibly wet and tight. "That's cold!" she protested with a laugh as she grabbed his wrist.

"Actually, I was thinking it's hot." He slipped the berry a little deeper. "And very, very tempting." Going to his knees beside the bed, he buried his face against her sex and began to nibble at the fruit.

Val grabbed his head with both hands and arched into the pillow, squirming deliciously as he took tiny, delicate bites of the berry, stopping frequently to tease her wet flesh. "I didn't think…" She stopped to gasp. "…vampires could eat."

"Oh, we can eat." He pulled the last bite of the fruit from her cunt. "We can also lick, suck and bite."

She moaned. "Oh, yeah. And you're really, really good at it… Cade! Ohhhhhhhh, God!"

With a low growl, he buried his face against her sex and sucked the hard nubbin of her clit into his mouth. In seconds, he brought her to a voluptuous, shuddering climax. As she collapsed into the pillows, limp, he rose to his feet and began unbuttoning his shirt with quick, impatient hands.

He wanted *in* her. And the Hunger was howling now, brought to full intensity by the sight and smell of Val's arousal. This time he'd give into it and take her. The thought of penetrating her with his fangs and cock made him as hard as an I-beam inside his jeans. Cade stripped off the shirt and threw it across the room, then reached for his fly.

Val opened her eyes to watch him strip with a kind of dazed anticipation. "Yeah, I'd give up tanning beds for this." As he shoved the jeans down his thighs, she said suddenly. "Change me, Cade."

He froze in the act of kicking out of his pants. There was a wicked temptation in that thought. To have her, keep her. Forever.

But it wouldn't be fair to Val. She was hot now, entranced by sex and need, not thinking about everything she'd be giving up. And she could end up getting killed in the fight between him and Ridgemont. "We'll talk about this later."

"But we'd be together," she protested. "And I hate the idea of you being helpless against him again."

The minute the words were out of her mouth, Val winced—and winced again when Cade stiffened. His gaze narrowed and sharpened on her face. "My sister has been showing her psychic home movies again, I gather," he said in a low, hard voice.

Damn it, Val. You've stepped in it now, she thought.

"What nasty little incident did she unfold before your wondering eyes?" His dark gaze was distinctly hostile now. She looked away from his too-discerning stare and swallowed. Cade swore viciously. "Caroline."

"He almost killed you," Val said miserably. "And she just left you there."

"He almost killed me a lot of times." Cade's sensuous mouth

twisted into a chilling smile. "So is this pity sex?"

"No! I just think we should…do it. Change me."

"So you decided to seduce me into it, is that right?" His voice sounded low and silken, but something about it made her eyes widen in alarm. "Oh, I get it. That's why you had those fingers buried in your tight little body when I walked in. You figured you'd overwhelm my hapless male mind with the smell of wet pussy."

"No, I…."

Suddenly strong hands clamped around her waist. She yelped in shock as he jerked her off the bed like a man snatching up an errant toddler. He straightened, holding her easily in the air with her feet dangling. Wide-eyed, she scanned his hard, angry face, acutely aware of the sheer muscled width of his chest.

"So you think you're going to save helpless little me from Ridgemont by nobly sacrificing yourself. Well, maybe you'd better rethink that, sweetheart. Because from where I'm standing, the only one who's helpless here is you."

She swallowed. "You're being a jerk, Cade."

"And what are you going to do about it?" He tilted her against his chest and shifted his hands until he could cup her thighs in his palms. Despite her instinctive resistance, he spread her legs easily and dragged her body against his. The firm, velvet crown of his cock brushed her sex. He smiled slowly into her eyes, taunting and nasty. "Like I said, you're helpless."

She gritted her teeth. "You've made your point. Ridgemont can eat your face with my blessings. Put me down!"

Cade smirked, slipping one hand around to support her bottom as he lifted the other to gently cup her breast. "But I don't want to." Delicately, he stroked his thumb over her nipple. Despite her outrage, she felt a curl of heat. He lifted her easily until he could nuzzle under her chin, licking the soft, thin flesh just above her pulse. "I'm … hungry." He lowered her slightly until the head of his massive length pressed against her folds. She squirmed in reluctant arousal. "And you'd make a delicious feast."

Val bit her lip. "Cade…."

"Maybe I will Change you after all," he growled, releasing her breast to reach under her body. She felt his cock dig harder against her as he aimed it, seeking the tight opening of her sex. "What man wouldn't want his own personal love slave? Want to be at my mercy, Valerie?"

He found her channel and gave a shallow half-thrust, just barely entering. Saliva flooded her mouth at the wicked pleasure of the sensation. She closed her eyes. "You're getting deep into jerk territory, Cade."

"I'm about to get deep into your territory, Val." He lowered her, slowly impaling her on the big shaft. He groaned in pleasure as she shivered, her slick, gloving flesh yielding to his width. "There's a lot to be said for being your master," he said hoarsely. "I could make you do anything I want, any time I want it."

She closed her eyes. "You wouldn't…" She caught her breath as he penetrated another inch. "…You wouldn't hurt me."

"Hell, no," he said roughly, abandoning the pretense of threatening seducer. "That's the last thing on my mind." Groaning, he shifted her in his arms. "I've got to get a better angle. Hold on, sweetheart."

Val curled both legs around his waist, keeping him seated as he lowered her back onto the bed. Immediately, he began thrusting in long, heavy lunges that tore a strangled scream from her throat. She squeezed her eyes closed as the massive shaft advanced and retreated, each plunge setting off a burst of light behind her eyes. "God, Cade, doesn't that thing get in the way when you walk?"

He chuckled in her ear. "No, darlin', I can honestly say that has never been a problem."

As he looked down at her, his head spinning from the brutal

glory of her creamy heat, she threw back her head and arched her back. The movement threw the long stems of her hard nipples and the sweet curve of her throat into relief. "I'm coming!"

The Hunger drowned him in fire. "Let me drink from you."

She bit down on her lower lip, the delicate lines of her face so sensual in her pleasure he wanted to weep, wanted to roar, wanted to come. "God, Cade, yes! Do it!"

With a moan, Cade lowered his head and sank his fangs deep into the delicate satin skin of her throat. She cried out in pleasure as her blood poured into his mouth, tasting of life and distilled sex. Her orgasm exploded in his skull as her Kith mental shields dropped. He groaned as he drank, savoring each intoxicating mouthful. And came in long, fiery jerks of his cock. Still drinking.

Despite all the women he'd had over a century and more as a vampire, it had never been so utterly hot. He knew without doubt it was because he loved her.

He only wished he knew what the hell to do now.

Chapter Thirteen

Cade! Abigail's psychic shout stabbed into his brain as he lay curled against Val. ***You've got company!***

He rolled out of bed before he was even fully awake, lunging for the sword and shield he'd left propped beside the bed. After Hirsch's attack at the motel, he'd made sure his weapons were always close at hand.

Throwing his mind out in a quick scan, he frowned. Ridgemont was nowhere around. "Who is it?" he demanded, putting down his weapons to grab a pair of jeans and shove his legs into them.

Val lifted her head in alarm. "What? What's happening?"

Ridgemont's sent a hit squad. Abigail flashed them images of men, at least thirty of them, all with Mac-10 automatic weapons. They'd broken into teams— one to disable the security system, one to search the house, another to surround it and block escape. A smaller squad was creeping up the hallway even now.

Hell, Abigail, it would have been nice to have a little warning before they were in the damn house! Cade lunged toward the door. There was no time to get the guns out of the closet. He'd have to make do with his sword.

I was Beyond! I didn't sense them until now.

Dammit. Where's Hirsch?

Not here.

Judging from the sunlight pouring through the stained glass windows, it was afternoon. *Probably didn't want a tan.* "Get behind the bed and hit the floor," he instructed Val. "There's going to be gunfire."

He jerked open the bedroom door and lunged. His sword speared into the chest of the man who was about to force his way in. The merc howled in agony as Cade picked him up on his blade like a cocktail sausage and thrust him into his mates, who instinctively grabbed him with startled shouts.

This bunch had come into his house to kidnap his woman. Their lives were bought and paid for.

Pivoting, he slammed his shield into the face of the nearest mercenary as the man lunged for him. Blood sprayed. The gunman toppled, dead before he hit the ground. Cade jumped between the three remaining invaders, snarling into their terrified faces with bared fangs.

In this situation, the mercs' numbers actually worked against them. They couldn't shoot those high-powered weapons without risking that the bullets would punch right through Cade and into their own allies.

So for thirty crucial seconds, they held their fire. The closest man lashed out with a rifle butt, but Cade was quicker. His fist shattered the mercenary's skull. Blood and gore splattered his face as the weapon hit the wall and fell to the floor with a clatter. It went off, firing a volley of bullets as mercenaries dove aside.

"Fuck!" somebody screamed. Cade's shield jolted and rang in his hand as one of the three surviving mercs panicked and fired his Mac-10 into it. The shield had been designed for vampire combat, and its space-age alloy surface didn't even dent. But the merc adjusted his aim and fired again, and this time the bullet ripped into Cade's thigh. He snarled in rage, swinging his sword as he whirled. The weapon bit deep. The invader screamed and toppled.

But before Cade could finish off the last two men, the rest of the team thundered into the hallway from the opposite direction. "Shit!" one of them gasped as they took in the carnage.

Cade brought up his shield and bared his teeth at them from

behind it. Doing a silent count, he felt his heart sink. There was at least eight of them. There was no way he could take them all before they blasted him to hell and gone. And if they put enough bullets in his chest to destroy his heart, immortal or not, he was dead.

Cringing at the sound of screams and gunfire from the hallway, Val crawled on her hands and knees toward the closet. She was damned if she was going to cower under the bed while Cade fought for their lives.

As she hoped, she found Cade's athletic bag sitting in the floor next to his tall leather boots. She thought she'd spotted a sawed-off shotgun in the bag the last time he'd opened it….

When she opened the zipper, Val sighed in relief. There was the shotgun, short, black and deadly in its nest of money. She grabbed it. Spotting a nine millimeter half-buried in the cash, she scooped that out too, made sure the safety was on, and stuffed it down the front of her jeans. The shotgun cradled in both arms like a deadly infant, she got to her feet and scuttled toward the door, bent double to avoid any random bullets from the hall.

As her heart pounded in hard, sickening lunges, Val peered around the doorframe, praying none of the mercs would shoot her by mistake while she shot them on purpose.

Bare-chested and blood-splattered, Cade stood surrounded by a mob of black-clad men, pivoting and lunging as he chopped his sword into the invaders like Conan the Barbarian in a really bad mood. Several bodies lay at his feet, none of them moving. Arcs of blood flew in the air with each slash, splashing the white walls. Huge, spreading pools of crimson soaked the cream carpet.

We're going to have a hell of a time cleaning that up, Val thought, with the illogic of shock.

"Fall back!" somebody bellowed. "We need some fucking room!"

She ducked behind the doorframe and flattened her back against the bedroom wall, her shaking hands clenched around the shotgun. If she opened fire, she could hit Cade. But if she didn't.... Cautiously, she looked around the corner again.

The men surrounding Cade tried to back off, three going one way, two going the other. He pounced on the pair, bringing his sword across in a hard, diagonal slash that took both men down.

Behind him, one of the retreating trio spun and lifted his Mac-10.

The three mercs were standing so close together, she thought their bodies would protect Cade if she fired. Without allowing herself to think about what she was doing, Val leaped into the hallway. She met the startled eyes of one of the squad as he stood less than a foot away. Then she opened up with both barrels.

And realized she'd miscalculated. Two of the gunmen were too close for the blast to spread very far, and the pellets punched into them both. A sickening rain of blood arced across Val's face, blinding her as a man shrieked in agony.

But she'd missed the third man.

A Mac-10 went off in a rolling, thunderous volley as the third merc opened fire on Cade. With an agonized yell of her own, Val scrubbed a hand desperately across her face, trying to wipe away the blinding, sticky blood. The smell made her stomach heave. Blinking hard, she managed to clear her vision just enough to see the two she'd shot were down.

So was Cade.

Throwing aside the now-useless shotgun, she jumped over the bodies of the dead men and ducked around the assassin who'd shot her lover. The merc snapped his gun around to blast her, then held his fire at the last moment. Val couldn't have cared less.

Cade lay sprawled face down across one of the fallen mercenaries. The submachine gun had punched a line of bleeding, ugly holes diagonally across his back. Heart in her throat, she grabbed him by one brawny shoulder and managed to turn him over.

"God, Cade..." she moaned.

The exit wounds in the front of his chest were even bigger than the entry wounds. His black eyes stared past her, and for a moment she thought he was dead. Then she felt the muzzle of a gun nudge the back of her skull.

Bad guys seem to like doing that, she thought numbly.

"Okay, bitch," said the merc who'd shot Cade, "hands up before I...."

Cade spat blood and gasped. "You. Freeze."

Licking her lips, Val dared a glance over her shoulder. For a moment all she could see was the muzzle of the submachine gun yawning like the pit of hell. Then she managed to focus beyond it at the mercenary who held it. He was staring down at them, his eyes wide and panicked, his hands still holding the gun pointed at the spot where her head had been. She jerked back from him, but he didn't move. With a sigh of relief, Val realized Cade must have used his power to lock every muscle in the merc's body.

Staring into the man's beefy face, she felt her lips peel back from her teeth. This bastard had shot Cade in the back. Her hand went to the grip of the pistol in her waistband and jerked it free. She leveled it right between his wide hazel eyes.

"Better not, bitch."

At the strange male voice, Val whipped around. "Oh, hell," she whispered. A fresh crowd of mercenaries stood in the hallway behind her. Reinforcements.

One of them aimed his gun toward Cade. "Surrender, or we'll see if the vampire can heal a missing head."

Acid invading her mouth, Val threw down her gun and raised her hands. The mercenaries padded down the hallway, guns leveled and ready. Their leader grabbed her wrist and hauled her roughly to her feet. She gasped as a shaft of pain stabbed up her arm from the force of his grip.

A low growl rumbled, and Val looked down. Despite the bloody holes in his chest, Cade snarled up at the mercenary, fangs bared, such threat in his eyes that the big man stepped quickly back, dragging Val with him.

"Look, buddy, don't push it," the merc told Cade, aiming his weapon between those hot brown eyes. The guy was damn near as big as Hirsch, Val saw, with a head full of iron gray hair that stood up in untidy, sweaty spikes. Despite his size, his beady blue eyes were nervous as he looked down into Cade's savage face. "Mr. Hirsch wants to do you personal, but if you try me, we'll put so many bullets in you you'll clank when you walk."

She wondered why Cade didn't compel him to let them both go, then realized that even if the leader had tried to give that order, the others wouldn't have obeyed. Especially if they'd been warned about vampire powers.

When Cade only lay there and panted, his black eyes feral, the merc commander nodded in satisfaction. "Smart choice, vamp. Now, you just stay there and bleed." Hauling her with him, he backed down the hall, waving to his men to accompany them.

A growl rumbling in his throat, Cade lifted his head to watch them go. For an instant his eyes met Val's, and she saw the agony in them.

Before she could respond, the merc leader stopped in his tracks, jerking her to a halt. Looking up at him, Val noticed the spiral cord of an earpiece looping into his collar. He must be wearing a radio.

The commander glanced around at his men and made a quick chopping gesture with his free hand. The whole pack whirled and marched down the hall. As they dragged Val with them, she stared over her shoulder at Cade. Bloody and helpless though he was, his hot black eyes sent her a fierce message she could almost hear: *I will save you.*

"Get a move on." The merc gave her wrist a jerk that almost pulled her arm out of its socket. "We don't have time for longing looks, bitch."

"What about the wounded, sir?" a tall black mercenary asked.

"If we hang around here trying to move 'em all, we'll be ass-deep in law before we're finished," the leader grunted. "Let the cops take care of 'em. They won't talk."

Hope stirred faintly in Val. Apparently the police were on their way, no doubt alerted by some neighbor who'd heard World War III going on next door.

And that meant Cade was safe. The cops would make sure he got a blood transfusion. Considering his vampire recuperative powers, by tomorrow night he'd have healed his injuries. Unfortunately, the officers would also have questions he wouldn't be able to answer.

It was obvious the mercenaries had broken in, and as a homeowner attacked in his own house, Cade wouldn't be charged with killing them. But the police could and probably would detain him for hours questioning him about the details. He might be able to magic his way out of custody if he could get hold of a commanding officer he could compel, but if a group ganged up on him, he wouldn't be able to quash the investigation.

In any case, Val knew he wouldn't be able to mount a rescue until tomorrow night at the earliest. The thought of what would happen to her in the hours until then made her feel sick and cold.

Dammit, she should have tried to persuade Cade to Change her earlier.

On the other hand, at least if he came after her tomorrow, there'd be no time for Ridgemont to finish the process either. But what if the monster killed him during the rescue attempt?

It might be better if Cade didn't come after her. If he died, they'd have no hope at all. But if he waited long enough, she'd eventually be able to free herself from Ridgemont's control. It might take a century or so, but she'd manage sooner or later. Then they could figure out a way to kill Ridgemont. She could withstand a century of abuse if she knew she had Cade waiting at the end of it.

Unfortunately, Val knew him a little too well to believe he'd just leave her in Ridgemont's hands. He'd have to attempt a rescue, even knowing he couldn't possibly win. And if Cade died, she might as well die herself. In fact, judging by the images Abigail had shown her, she'd probably long for death before Ridgemont got through with her.

And what about her sister? Would Ridgemont leave her alone once he had Val, or would he come after Beth too?

Had she lost everyone she cared about?

As Val's thoughts churned in despair, the mercenaries hustled her outside to a huge white moving van parked at the mouth of the garage. They'd backed the truck in so closely the men could enter and leave without the neighbors realizing they were carrying enough firepower to invade Mexico. Craning her neck as the men filed on board, she saw the truck's back gate was lowered, revealing the bench seats, communications equipment and weapons racks that filled it.

Val's captor pushed her down on one of the benches and sat down beside her as the rest of the men settled in. Sunk in misery, she barely noticed when they closed the gate and the van lurched down the curving driveway.

Closing her eyes, she fought tears, knowing that even as they drove away, Cade lay helpless in his own blood.

Pain blazed through Cade's chest in throbbing waves. He gritted his teeth and ignored it. A bullet had nicked his aorta, and he had to focus all his power on holding the wound closed and healing the damaged tissue before he passed out from blood loss. And he'd damn well better get it done as fast as possible.

Every minute healing took him was another minute Val was at her captors' non-existent mercy.

The other bullets had damaged both lungs, his stomach and intestines. Cade had been able to keep himself from bleeding out internally, but that was the best he could do until he could get to a secure location and concentrate on putting himself back together. Of course, his body would eventually heal the damage on its own, but that would take much longer and put him out of the action for days Val couldn't afford.

As if that wasn't bad enough, Cade could hear the distant wail of sirens. Fortunately, the house was so far out in the country, it would take sheriff's deputies another few minutes to arrive on the scene. With any luck, he'd have just enough time to get into hiding.

Which meant he'd need the help of his would-be murderer. The mercenary still stood there in the hallway like an abandoned android, paralyzed by Cade's last compulsion. His buddies had left him behind with the dead and wounded.

Gathering his strength, Cade looked up at his captive. He had a stone killer's hard, square features, but oddly, his hair was carrot red, and freckles speckled the bridge of his nose. Despite the Opie Taylor coloring, he was a big bruiser, easily six-foot six, with the thick, powerful musculature of a body builder.

Just what Cade needed to get him the hell out of the house before the law arrived. *Help me up,* he ordered silently, diverting enough power to make sure the man obeyed.

Eyes wide with terror, the mercenary knelt and looped Cade's arm over his own shoulders, then wrapped a brawny arm around his waist and heaved him to his feet. Agony detonated in Cade's chest in waves of alternating heat and cold. Wheezing, he tightened his grip around the merc's thick shoulders. *My sword and shield.* Blood surged against the psychic bandage he'd created. *Get 'em.*

As obedient as a robot, the merc bent and picked up the sword. Cade clutched his shoulders to keep from falling on his face. The man handed the weapon over. Somehow he managed to force his weak fingers to close around the hilt. Collecting the shield, the mercenary straightened.

The hallway spun around Cade, and he only barely managed to fight back a wave of blackness. *Let's go.* He wrapped his slick, bloody fingers more securely around his weapon.

The mercenary—whose name was Hank, Cade saw from his thoughts—obediently helped him stumble through the house. Each step set off rolling reverberations of pain, and he had to use every last erg of his power to keep blood from flooding his chest cavity from the wounds that riddled him.

It was a damn good thing Val had let him take her. Without the blood and energy she'd given him, he'd never have been able to hold himself together like this.

When they stepped outside into the morning sunlight, Cade gasped in pain. As weak as he was, it was like walking into a furnace. He could feel his skin beginning to burn.

The woods. Hurry. The shade would give him at least a little protection.

Rebellion stirred in Hank's mind; he wanted to drop his erstwhile victim and run. Cade hastily diverted just enough power to bring him back into line, then telekinetically plugged the wounds that instantly began to bleed again.

One arm clamped around Cade's waist, the other thrust through the straps of his shield, the mercenary reluctantly dragged him toward the woods. Cade let Hank do all the work while he concentrated on controlling the big man and preventing himself from bleeding out. Sweat poured down his face, both from effort and the sunlight that pounded on his unprotected head, but he scarcely noticed.

When they reached the trees, Cade was only distantly aware of their cooling shade. The police were minutes away, and he wanted to get far enough into the woods that they wouldn't find him until he was healed enough to fend them off. Mentally prodding Hank onward, he gritted his teeth against the pain as the big mercenary lengthened his stride.

When the mercenaries' van stopped up in front of the small brick ranch-style house ten minutes from Cade's home, Val was astonished. She'd expected to be loaded onto an airplane for the flight to New York.

Instead the leader hustled her out of the van and through a carport entrance. She vaguely noticed a small kitchen with olive green appliances and dark paneling before he shoved her through a doorway into a tiny den.

As Val regained her balance, she got a good look at what waited for her and felt her heart twist in pity. Two young women, neither more than twenty, sat on a couch that looked as if it had come from a thrift store. Both girls had deep puncture wounds in their throats. Dressed for spring in shorts and tank tops that bared a constellation of bruises, they wore identical expressions of dazed suffering. Neither flinched when the mercenary dragged Val over and forced her down on the couch beside them.

Val winced at their blank, shocked stares and hunched poses. When she murmured a sympathetic greeting, they didn't respond, too dispirited—or too dazed—to care.

Glancing around, she spotted a college chemistry textbook on the battered coffee table and a backpack lying on a flowered armchair. They must be students at the community college, renting this house for the semester. Now their bodies and their home had been commandeered by vampires. Imagining Beth in their shoes,

Val shuddered. Somehow she had to keep Ridgemont and Hirsch from getting their hands on her sister.

She studied the nearest girl's bruised, blank face, wondering if there was something she could do to help the pair in the meantime. Then she grimaced. From what Cade had said, they'd probably be released eventually, though much the worse for wear. She herself was unlikely to be that lucky. Yet to do nothing....

Footsteps in the hall.

Val jerked her head up just as Gerhard Hirsch walked in, grinning and smug. "Hello, *fraul....*" He broke off in mid-word. Fury twisted his features.

Val cringed as he strode toward her, moving with that oddly weightless grace that was the mark of vampire strength. "You whore," he spat, grabbing her by one arm. "You've been fucking him! You've got his mark on your neck!"

Hirsch drew back his hand for a slap. Val threw up both arms to shield her head, but instead he transferred his grip to her hair and hauled her brutally off the sofa. She bit back a scream, damned if she'd give the bastard the satisfaction.

The German shoved his face against hers. She hunched her shoulders in revulsion as he drew in a deep breath, inhaling her scent.

When Hirsch pulled back, the fury had faded from his eyes. "His stink is all over you, but he hasn't begun Changing you." Slowly, tauntingly, he grinned. "Saving yourself for me, *Fraulein*?"

Finally Cade judged that they'd gone far enough into the trees. The deputies would have to separate to search the woods; anyone who might stumble over them this far out would probably be a lone man he could telepathically send somewhere else.

He looked at the mercenary and sent a mental command: *Put me down.* Hank obediently lowered him into a pile of leaves. Pain seared him as his body shifted position, but he gritted his teeth until he was finally prone. Blessedly still at last, Cade closed his eyes and panted for breath.

His skin was already stinging with a sunburn; it was mild enough now, but it wouldn't be in a few hours. Luckily he'd spotted a tarp used to cover a swimming pool at one of the neighbor's homes. He sent Hank an image of the sheet of plastic draped over a fence. *Go get it.*

The big man set off at a jog, the compulsion planted so deeply he couldn't have disobeyed if his life had depended on it. While he waited for the mercenary to carry out his orders, Cade stared blankly at the painfully blue sky and fought to keep himself from bleeding to death.

Finally he heard the rapid thud of running combat boots. Hank skidded to a stop, looming over him like Frankenstein's monster. Without wasting his breath on speech, Cade mentally instructed the merc to tent the tarp over his body. The big man got to work, draping the thick rubber sheet across a tree limb over his head and anchoring the corners with stones.

When he was done, Cade ordered Hank to crawl into the tent with him. Then, so lightheaded with pain he could barely focus, he looked up at the man and whispered, "Freeze."

Instantly Hank's body locked into place, eyes focused straight ahead, his face settling into expressionless lines that were belied by the stark panic he felt at finding himself helpless. Cade could have calmed his fear, but right now he needed the son of a bitch scared out of his wits. All that emotion made a good power source.

Safe now, Cade allowed himself to slide into a half trance as he spread a web of psychic energy over his injuries. It was a new experience for him; he'd never before used his powers to accelerate the healing process. Ordinarily he'd just go to sleep and let any wounds take care of themselves, but he didn't have time for that now. He had to recover as quickly as possible, no matter how much energy he had to burn to do it.

One by one, he found the bullets and directed his power at each, forcing them out along the entrance wounds they'd torn in his flesh. Sweat broke out on his face with the effort, and his head began to pound.

It was just as well a vampire's telekinesis only worked inside his body. Considering how hard it was to move a tiny piece of lead, he could imagine the effort it would take to budge anything larger.

Finally the last bullet oozed from his chest, leaving a snail trail of blood. With a relieved grunt, Cade urged his body to begin healing, knitting the torn flesh, repairing the injured organs until he no longer had to work so hard to block the bleeding.

As the hours passed, he lost all track of time, rousing from his trance only long enough to use his powers on any deputies who wandered too close.

Again and again, Cade's mind drifted to Val. Where was she? Was she in the hands of Ridgemont or Hirsch by now, and if she was, what were they doing to her?

The raw panic triggered by that thought forced him to drive it from his mind. He had to save his own life before he could save hers. *I'll get to her in time,* Cade told himself.

He had to.

Chapter Fourteen

Val fought Hirsch's pitiless grip as he dragged her into one of the house's tiny back bedrooms, but she might as well have saved her strength. The German easily forced her down on the twin bed and straddled her hips, pinning her with his weight as he jerked a piece of thin cord from a back pocket. Val aimed a punch for his nose, but he grabbed her fist before it could land and began lashing her wrist to one of the bedposts. She darted her head forward and clamped her teeth down on his muscular forearm.

He damned well wasn't going to rape her without a fight.

"Stop that, you little bitch!" Light detonated behind her eyes. Val went limp, stunned by a slap she hadn't even seen coming. Over the ringing in her ears she heard him growl, "You're going to start learning your place right now, slut."

Sucking in a gasp, she smelled his scent. Calvin Klein and something not human. She felt her arms and legs being spread, ankles and remaining wrist tied. *Fight!* Val mentally screamed at herself, but her dazed body refused to cooperate. Something grabbed the front of her shirt and jerked, lifting her half off the bed. Fabric tore. *Oh, God,* she thought as her head spun, *he's ripping off my clothes.*

Suddenly Calvin Klein became peppermint, and something shattered directly over Val's head. A rain of small objects pattered against her face. Opening her eyes, she saw fragments of porcelain hit the mattress beside her head.

Hirsch swore. "What? What the hell is…?" Then he snarled, "Abigail!"

Abigail? Val thought. *What's she doing here?* She opened her eyes just in time to see a college textbook sail across the bedroom to slam into the German's head.

The vampire flinched and leaped off her, looking wildly around the room. "Abigail, you little bitch, this is none of your affair!"

She's Cade's, Gerhard. Leave her alone.

Abigail floated in one corner of the room like something out of a horror movie, her hair streaming around a half-rotted face, her eyes yellow and bulging. Judging from the German's wild stare, Hirsch found her as thoroughly unnerving as Val had when the ghost had played the same trick on her.

Abigail, what are you doing? Val thought, still confused from Gerhard's slap.

I'm trying to save you, child. Be still.

I take back everything I ever said about you.

"She's mine now!" Hirsch blustered, backing up a pace. "As for Cade, he won't even have a dick—or a head—by the time I'm through with him."

Assuming Ridgemont lets you live long enough to fight him. Your master is not going to like this, Gerhard.

He bared his teeth. "That won't matter after I've Changed her."

"At the moment, Gerhard, that looks doubtful."

Hirsch spun. A short, muscular man stood leaning against the doorframe, his powerful arms folded, desert robes draping his brawny body in yards of flowing white cotton. The face framed by his Arab headdress wasn't handsome; his nose looked as though it had been broken a few times, and there was a thin, white scar over one cheekbone.

Something about those features snapped Val's mind sharply into focus. *Oh, God*, she thought, going cold as she recognized him from Abigail's visions and her own tormenting childhood memories. *It's Ridgemont.*

Even the ghost recoiled as the master vampire strolled into the room. He flicked Abigail a dismissive glance. "Get you gone, spirit, or I'll drink you down like a virgin's blood."

Abigail seemed to expand in size as she floated toward him, her face darkening and rotting even more until Val felt her stomach twist in revulsion. ***Keep your hands off her!***

One of Ridgemont's huge hands flashed out and closed, impossibly, right around the ghost's thin neck. Terror twisted Abigail's little face as she tried to jerk away, but he held her fast. He gave her a slow, mocking smile. "I'd think by now you'd know your place, child. Which could easily be across my trencher with an apple in your mouth."

How the hell is he doing that? Val wondered in shock.

The ghost stopped struggling and met his eyes with defiance, her rotted features blurring back to their normal contours. ***Do it, then. I'm sick of being used as a stick to beat Cade with.***

His grin revealed a horrifying length of fang. "Perhaps I will, at that. My plans are at endgame now—you're no further use. And you'd be delicious. So much power…."

Oh, God, Val realized. *He's going to absorb her.* And her destruction would kill Cade. "No! Abigail, go Beyond!"

He won't let me. The ghost stared at Ridgemont, hopeless defiance on her face. ***He's holding me here.***

He must be exerting some kind of psychic energy, Val realized. *If I could distract him….* "Let her go. I'll do whatever you want."

Ridgemont lifted a brow and looked toward her. "Intriguing offer. And rash. Are you sure you want to…?"

The ghost seemed to dissolve like mist between his fingers, only to reform right over the bed. *What are you doing?* Val thought, staring up at her furiously. *Go Beyond before he eats you!*

Cade is on the way, the ghost told her, voice weakening. ***Hang on. Don't push him, Valerie. I want to help, but he's hurt me.***

I'm losing my grip on this plane.

Just go! Val thought, though part of her cringed at the idea of being left alone with Ridgemont.

Abigail bit her lip, looking torn. She didn't so much fly away this time as vanish like smoke.

Watching the last wisps disappear, Val thought, *Damn, I never thought I'd be sorry to see you go.*

When she looked around, she found Ridgemont staring at her, an expression of profound amusement on his face. She wondered what the hell he found so funny.

Before she could ask, Hirsch demanded, "What are you doing here? You said you'd let me handle it." He stepped in front of the bed as if to block his sire's view of her.

"I did," Ridgemont said coldly. "But you didn't. You sent in an army of armed mortals while you stayed safe in this little hovel and amused yourself with the two children in the other room." He lifted a brow. "The idea was to prove your worth in combat with the gunslinger."

"He tried that. Twice." Val curled her lip at the German's back. "Cade kicked his butt both times."

She heard a noise like a slap and started in surprise. Ridgemont was suddenly standing beside Hirsch, who was now facing her. The master vampire's hand was locked around the German's forearm, keeping his fist from striking her. They'd both moved so fast she hadn't even seen the exchange.

"You haven't won the right to beat her, Gerhard," Ridgemont told him, his tone so matter-of-fact Val felt a chill.

"You swore she'd be mine if I could get her away from him," Hirsch gritted. "You didn't specify how."

"You're stupid, but not that stupid." As casually as a man tossing aside a ball of paper, Ridgemont threw him into the wall. The whole house shook with the impact. "You knew exactly what I intended."

Hirsch jerked himself away from the indentation his body had made in the plasterboard and coiled into a snarling crouch. "You've always favored the American over me. There's something unnatural about it."

"Oh, it's entirely natural," Ridgemont said, lifting an insulting brow. "The gunslinger is a warrior with a sense of honor. You're a fool ruled by your fangs and dick."

Hirsch opened his mouth to spit a retort, but before he could speak he crashed to his knees as if someone had kicked his feet out from under him.

As the German fought to rise, the master vampire slowly walked around behind him. "Do you think I'm such a fool I don't know the one who gets the girl will challenge me?" One hand blurred out, fisting in Hirsch's blond hair and jerking his head back until Ridgemont could peer down into his rolling eyes. "That's exactly what I intend, you ignorant peasant. But you have to prove yourself worthy of her. I'll not see her wasted on someone I'll kill in ten minutes."

"Do you think me a fool?" the German spat. "Even if I gut your pet, you'll keep her for yourself—and I'll remain in your thrall for another century."

Ridgemont's icy eyes narrowed. His free hand clamped around Hirsch's throat, grip tightening until his captive gagged. "Do you question my honor?"

The German licked his lips. His gaze slid away. "No."

"Perhaps you're not such a fool after all." He released Hirsch and stepped back with a wintery smile. "Go. Find him. Prove you're entitled to my gift."

Hirsch looked at the closed curtains. "But it's daylight!"

"If you want her so desperately, a little sunburn is not going to stop you. I can assure you, it hasn't stopped the gunslinger."

The German's mouth tightened as he rose to his feet. He turned toward the door, then looked back at Ridgemont. "It's early yet. He'll still be healing. May I feed before I go out to hunt him?"

"I assume you refer to the two captives in the next room," Ridgemont said, a note of warning in his voice.

Hirsch's eyes flicked to Val's naked body and lingered in a way that sent a chill up her spine. "Of course," he said, his smile nasty. "There'll be time enough for her once McKinnon's dead."

"An hour, no more." The German disappeared from the doorway so fast it looked as though he'd vanished into thin air. "Puppy," Ridgemont muttered.

Val opened her mouth to protest his handing the two girls over to Hirsch, but before she could say a word, he turned and lifted a brow at her. "It seems we have a little time alone."

It occurred to her Hirsch's victims might have the better end of the deal.

"What time is it?" Cade licked his cracked, swollen lips.

Hank's hazel eyes darted in fear, but his voice was flat when he spoke. "Three fifteen."

Cade cursed silently. It had taken him hours to heal his injuries—hours Val couldn't afford.

Where was she? And what were they doing with her?

God, he was weak. He managed to roll over and push himself onto his hands and knees. For a moment he knelt there, his head hanging, his arms and thighs trembling so violently they could barely hold him up. His mouth felt dry, his tongue felt swollen. Gathering the last of his strength, he pushed slowly to his feet, clawing at the tarp until it fell away. The sunlight of late afternoon stabbed through the trees and into his eyes, but he ignored it.

He needed to feed. Now. Fortunately, there was a ready source of blood waiting.

Cade looked down at Hank, who still sat on the ground, helplessly paralyzed. Glancing into the mercenary's mind, he could sense the pain of stiffened joints, the numbness from sitting motionless for so long—and Hank's utter terror at the sight of his vampire victim on his feet, his chest whole and unwounded despite the dried blood crusting his skin.

Why isn't the bastard dead? the merc mentally gibbered. *I shot him six times!*

"But not in the right place." Cade felt an unpleasant smile stretch across his lips. Leaning down, he reached out and lifted the big man's square chin, forcing him to meet his gaze. "Scared, Hank?" The mercenary stared at him, unable to speak. He lifted part of the compulsion. "Answer me. Are you afraid?"

"Yeah," Hank croaked.

"Good," he whispered, his voice silken and menacing. "So is the woman I love. And you're going to help me save her." He bared his fangs. "In a way."

Ridgemont sat down on the edge of the bed. Val swallowed, acutely aware of her nakedness, of the bruise she could feel rising on her face from Hirsch's slap. He reached toward her. She flinched back instinctively, but his big, blunt fingers simply brushed her throat. "I see my spawn have been entertaining themselves."

Val realized he referred to Cade's bite as well as Hirsch's heavy hand. "Some attentions were more welcome than others."

He chuckled. "I'll wager so." His eyes drifted back down her naked body, and she drew in a breath at the cruel interest she saw in them. He rose, and Val instinctively shrank into the mattress. "Your heart is thumping like a rabbit's," Ridgemont observed, one corner of his wide mouth lifting in a malicious half-smile. "That's a very erotic sound to a vampire. You'd be wise to calm yourself."

She licked her dry lips and choked out, "I'll keep that in mind."

"See that you do." He bent down to pick something up off

the floor. When he straightened, he held a limp, brown bundle. She flinched. But then he shook it out, she realized he held the bedspread Hirsch had stripped from the mattress before tying her down. With a neat snap, he flipped it over her.

Ridgemont met her eyes and shrugged. "I find I could do without the temptation. I suspect that after having you, I'd find it difficult to give you back."

He picked up a ladder-back chair that sat in the corner, put it down beside the bed and sat down. Stretching out his muscled legs, he crossed his ankles and said casually, "Though I could easily persuade myself that abusing you for a while would drive Cade into a very satisfying frenzy."

Val licked her dry lips and dared a question. "So why keep Hirsch from beating me?"

"The bastard pissed me off with his cheating," he said with a shrug. "If he'd had the guts to go along on the raid, he could have flogged you with my blessing. One look at your welts would have been all the incentive Cade needed to rip out his heart and eat it."

She blinked in surprise. "Hirsch is right. You do favor Cade."

"Well, of course. The German is all very well for a drinking companion, but I'd snap him like a twig in a fight, even with the power you'd give him. If I'm going to sacrifice the pleasure of your company, I'd rather it be to some good purpose." His eyes lingered regretfully on the rise of her breasts under the blanket. "I'll have to kill you when it's over, of course."

Val had actually begun to relax. At his words, her whole body jerked into a knot. "Of course," she said faintly.

"Without the bond from transforming you, you'd be impossible to control," Ridgemont explained. "Though I'll probably fuck you a few times before you die."

Just like my mother. Dammit, she would not let the bastard see how much that thought terrified her. Stiffening her spine, Val forced herself to meet his eyes. "That's assuming Cade doesn't kill you first. And I think you're going to find him harder to defeat than you expect."

Ridgemont shrugged. "Actually, I'm not at all sure I can beat the gunslinger once he Changes you. Which is the whole point. True, I'll still have more power, but he's cunning enough to find a way to defeat me anyway." An odd expression crossed his face. Almost...pride? "Even without you, he almost killed me last week. A bomb isn't quite what I'd had in mind, but I was pleased by his willingness to eliminate me in any way he could."

"Pleased? You were *pleased?*" She stared at him, so startled she forgot to be diplomatic. "What kind of lunatic are you?"

"No lunatic at all." He smiled slightly. "Just a knight stranded in the wrong century. Though being a twenty-first century female, I suppose that's something you'll never understand."

"Uh, huh." She eyed him. "Why don't you enlighten me?"

He glanced lazily out the window. "Since I don't hear a fight going on outside, I might as well." Leaning backward with the air of a man settling in to tell a particularly entertaining story, he laced his hands behind his head. His thick biceps bulged under his sleeves. "When I was a member of Prince Richard's retinue...."

"Was this before or after the Saracens captured you?"

Ridgemont went as still as a snake, his eyes flattening with reptilian menace. "McKinnon mentioned that, did he?"

Oh, God, Val realized, staring at the murderous fury in the vampire's gaze, *I'm about to get my throat ripped out.* She swallowed and sent up a quick, silent prayer. "Actually, it was the ghost. Abigail."

Ridgemont relaxed, curling his lip. "That little brat is something of a pest." He shrugged. "But she's been a useful hostage since Cade won his freedom. Otherwise he'd have left years ago, and that didn't suit my plans."

"He is rather … fond of her." Val carefully unclenched her fists. She'd diverted him from killing her — at least for the moment. "You were saying?"

Ridgemont eyed her for a long moment, his gaze flattening until her heart started pounding again. The moment stretched out, vibrating with agonizing tension as she began to sweat.

Then he smiled ever so slightly and snapped the tension like a guitar string. "When we were young men, back before Richard became king, we traveled the tourney circuit." Ignoring Val's involuntary sigh of relief, he settled back in his seat once more. "Earned quite a nice living taking other knights hostage. God, I loved those days." His expression softened, becoming almost dreamy. "You have no idea what it's like to have a war-horse between your thighs and a sword in your hand, going to meet another knight in combat. In the next few seconds, you will live or die, depending on your strength, skill and luck. Every sense is so acute, it seems the world has edges, like shards of glass." Slowly the warm glow faded from his eyes. "I have lived eight hundred years, fucked and tormented more women than I can even begin to count, tempted the Inquisition and the Nazis, but I have never felt that way since. There are no more knights, and I am old and powerful. And bored. But Cade … given enough power, he would be a most satisfactory opponent."

Val stared at him as the light slowly dawned. "You're an adrenaline junkie. And you think he could give you the perfect fix."

Satisfied, he smiled slightly. "Now you begin to understand."

"So everything you've done to him…."

"… Has been toward that end," he agreed. "That's why I took him when he charged in to save that silly girl more than a century ago, and it's why I've spent all these years goading him." His gaze intensified on her as if waiting for her reaction. "And it's why I killed your parents."

Stunned, she stared at him. "What?"

"Just any Kith female couldn't have provided him with what he needs to match me," Ridgemont said. "I had to find someone with a great deal of latent power. And you fit the bill perfectly, so much so it was obvious even when you were a child."

"You *did* know I was Kith!"

"Oh, yes." He grinned at her. "I saw you in an Atlanta shopping mall one night. You were walking hand in hand with your father, and I could see the power blazing off you. So much potential.... And in those days, you looked a bit like Abigail. Same coltish child build. You were perfect."

Her stomach twisted with sick guilt. *Mom...Dad...* "For what? I still don't...."

"At the time, Cade was still under my control, and had been for more than a century," Ridgemont explained. "I was getting impatient, and I wanted to give him the incentive he needed to start breaking my grip."

"Why didn't you just let him go?" *God,* she thought, staring into his calm, reasonable eyes, *he really is a monster.*

The vampire shook his head. "It's rather like building physical muscle. You gain strength by working against another force. Cade had to break my grip himself or it would mean nothing." Rising to his feet, he began to pace, gesturing as he spoke. "Knowing how he is about his sister, I decided the thing to do was set him up to kill a child. I knew he'd do anything to avoid that."

"But what if he'd failed?"

He shrugged. "No harm done."

"Except to me! I'd have been dead!"

Ridgemont lifted a blond brow at her. "I would advise you to wipe that condemning expression off your face if you want to live long enough to fuck the gunslinger again."

Too furious to care what he did to her, she sneered. "You won't kill me—it'd take too long to find another Kith female with as much power as I have."

He stared at her, such anger rolling across his eyes that a shaft of fear pierced her outrage.

Then he threw back his head and laughed. "Oh, you're perfect for him. I doubt you'll outlive him by half an hour before you goad me into butchering you, but I suppose I can't have everything."

She glowered. "I really want to watch him kill you."

"Somehow I doubt you'll enjoy that fight as much as you think."

Val curled her lip. "We'll see."

"Yes. We will. Where was I? Oh yes. It was really simple good luck that I found you. If we hadn't been living in Atlanta at the time…." He shrugged. "Then when I saw you, realized how much power you have, that was when the whole plan burst upon me. It was perfect. He would save you from himself, get free in a decade or so, gather his strength…. And then I'd put you in his path again."

He planned the whole thing, Val thought, stunned. *Every move, from the beginning, just like a chess game.* "And it worked."

He grinned smugly. "One of the best long-range scenarios I've ever put together."

"But why murder my parents? You didn't have to involve them."

"Being Kith is a genetic trait. Your father had it. If I'd let him live, it was entirely possible he would have packed you up and taken you off, leaving me unable to find you again."

Her father had been like her? She blinked, stunned. "But what about my mother?"

"I'd intended to let her go." He shrugged. "But Hirsch got carried away. Luckily your grandmother was sufficiently compliant for my purposes."

"My grandmother?" She stared at him blankly. "What does she have to do with this?"

He gave her that chillingly pleasant smile again. "Why, I used her to keep track of you for years."

"Grandma was a spy for you?" She'd known the woman was a drunk, but….

"I didn't give her much choice. She had a trace of psychic power herself, so it took a little work, but it was worth it." He folded his massive arms and aimed a contemplative look toward the window. "I think she actually became aware of what I was doing at times. Not that it did any of you any good, of course…."

Suddenly Val realized she might be looking at the reason for her grandmother's drinking problem. "Is there any aspect of my life you haven't ruined?"

He contemplated the question, then grinned. "Probably not."

Cade swore violently, staring at the little brick ranch as he crouched in the concealment of a field across the street. Judging from the dark power he could almost see swirling around the house, Ridgemont was inside.

When the hell had he showed up? Cade had scanned Hank's memories half an hour ago—punching through the mental blocks Hirsch had set up hadn't been hard—but the merc did not remember Ridgemont being present then.

He should have known taking Val back wouldn't be that easy.

To make matters worse, the vampires had already been busy, judging from the barely conscious thoughts of two female victims inside the house. Scanning them, Cade saw that Hirsch had just finished amusing himself.

The girls also remembered seeing Val, though he couldn't sense her presence directly because of her Kith shields. Then he touched another memory in their minds, one that made his gut clench: they'd heard her scream. Dammit, if only he'd been half an hour earlier.

Unfortunately, getting here had been a bitch. He'd picked the location of Hirsch's temporary lair from Hank's mind easily enough, but transportation had presented a problem. His house was still swarming with cops processing the crime scene and trying to figure out where all the dead bodies had come from. There was no way Cade could get to the Lexus, so he'd had to make other arrangements.

After telepathically summoning a deputy to find Hank—Cade had reluctantly decided to leave the merc alive, since he didn't kill helpless men—he slipped off to a neighbor's house and asked to borrow the man's car. The neighbor did not, of course, refuse.

Hirsch, out of either arrogance or impatience, had chosen a lair a short distance away, so it hadn't taken Cade long to drive the route Hank remembered. He'd left the car parked the next street over and slipped across to reconnoiter.

The results didn't thrill him. The surviving mercenaries were on guard outside, though anybody looking at them would think they were having an outdoor cookout. They'd traded the Rambo gear for shorts and unbuttoned shirts, some with T-shirts underneath, some bare-chested. Doing a quick scan to find out who was armed, Cade discovered all the shirts hid shoulder holsters, and there were enough automatic weapons hidden in easy reach to make an arms dealer jealous.

The whole homicidal gang milled around a barbecue grill, laughing and joking as they drained cans of beer from a cooler. But though they looked like college students enjoying a kegger, Cade's vampire hearing picked out snatches of conversation about South America and the Middle East. Hirsch's boys were talking shop.

He could probably battle his way past them, of course, but what would Hirsch and Ridgemont do to Val in the meantime? For that matter, what were they doing to her now?

Chapter Fifteen

Cade cursed silently to himself. He didn't like the odds, but it didn't look as if he had much choice. He couldn't leave her there with them. Yet a frontal assault would be suicide.

Just as he was trying to come up with a plan, a familiar figure stepped out of the house. Even swathed in desert robes likes something out of the *Arabian Nights*, those bull shoulders were instantly recognizable.

Ridgemont.

The ancient dragged Val by one wrist. A blanket draped her slim shoulders, but from the long, bare flash of her legs as she moved, Cade could tell she was naked underneath it. She looked furious but otherwise unhurt.

Cade's sense of relief was so overwhelming he had to close his eyes for an instant. *She's alive!* God, he hadn't realized how terrified he really was until he saw her. He wanted to hold her so badly, he ached.

He opened his eyes just in time to see a second man shoulder through the door, dressed in white from head to toe. If Ridgemont looked like a desert sheik, he could have been an escapee from a ninja movie—except for the war axe and shield he carried. *Hirsch*, Cade realized, recognizing the axe.

The German wore a white fabric mask that completely covered his face, except for a pair of black goggles designed to protect his eyes from the sun.

Then Cade felt the weight of Ridgemont's mental touch. *I thought I sensed you out here, gunslinger. We're going for a ride.*

Care to follow?

Cade rocked back on his heels, wondering what the ancient had up his sleeve. Ridgemont rarely went out in the sunlight; at his great age, he was more vulnerable to it than Cade or Hirsch. *Where, exactly, are we going?*

I'm told there's a very pleasant meadow up the road, screened nicely by trees. Good spot for a duel.

We wouldn't want to be interrupted by any inconvenient cops, Cade agreed.

I think that's unlikely in any case, Ridgemont told him. *I understand every law enforcement officer in ten miles is still cleaning up the mess at your house.*

Just for curiosity's sake, will I be fighting both of you?

Actually, no, the ancient said. *I plan to sit this one out. I'm going to let you two decide who gets to keep her.*

Incredulous, Cade attempted a deeper scan. To his amazement, Ridgemont allowed it. What's more, he saw his sire meant what he said. He intended for Cade and Hirsch to duel, and he did not plan to interfere even if Cade won. He meant to hand Val over to the victor one way or another. And once she'd been Changed, he'd duel the winner.

It'll be me, you bastard, Cade snarled mentally.

I'll be highly disappointed if it isn't. Come along, gunslinger.

Rising from his nest of weeds, Cade ran back toward his car as Val and the vampires got into the limo. He looked back over his shoulder just in time to see the car roll to a halt in the driveway. Wary of a double-cross, he stopped to watch.

Ridgemont leaned out the window. With Cade's vampire hearing, it was easy to pick up the conversation. "You're all dismissed. Send me an invoice."

One of the mercs snorted. "It's going to be one hell of a bill, considering how many of my men you got killed." But none of them tried to prevent the car from leaving as it continued down the drive, proving they were more intelligent than he'd thought.

Cade turned and raced on. As he ran, he became sharply aware of the suffocating heat of the ferocious, pounding sunlight. And that, he knew, was going to be a problem.

He'd commandeered Hank's long sleeved shirt, boots and gloves to wear with the jeans he'd gone to battle in. To protect his face, he'd hacked up a piece of the tarp to make a hooded mask, cutting broad slits for the eyes and mouth. Hank had a pair of sunglasses stashed in a pocket, and he'd put those on as well. Though the whole rig provided some protection from the sun, he knew it wouldn't be enough if he was forced to fight for very long. Hirsch would ironically have the advantage for once. At his age, he had a greater tolerance for daylight than either of his elders.

Reaching the wooded lot where he'd left his neighbor's Toyota, Cade pulled the door open and got in as the limo passed. He started the car and followed, pulling out between two trees and hitting the gas as he turned out onto the street.

He knew taking Hirsch wouldn't be easy this time. He'd had to spend a hell of a lot of energy healing his wounds, and even feeding from Hank hadn't brought him to full strength. Hirsch, on the other hand, hadn't done any fighting at all. And judging from what Cade had seen in the girls' minds, the German had practically gorged on them half an hour before.

All in all, this duel would be far more equal than he liked, especially with Val's life on the line. Yet if he succeeded, Ridgemont would give her back. She'd be safe… if Cade could win the coming duel with the ancient.

Suddenly some of Ridgemont's more inexplicable actions began to make a bizarre kind of sense. The ancient loved a fight. In fact, he'd often said he never truly felt alive unless he was in imminent danger of dying. It had always been a source of frustration to him that he couldn't find a proper opponent. Which begged the question: just how long had he been planning this, anyway?

Cade?

"Abigail?" he said, frowning at the limo's bumper. Her mental voice sounded much fainter than it usually did. "What happened to you? You don't sound like yourself."

Ridgemont absorbed some of my energy. And I wore myself out playing poltergeist to divert Hirsch. He was beating Val.

"Are you all right?" Cade tightened his grip on the wheel. "How badly was she hurt?"

I will… survive. As for Val, she suffered a few bruises before Ridgemont put a stop to the beating.

Whatever the ancient's motives, Cade was grateful for them. "Thanks for trying to help, Abigail."

I only wish I could do more, but I've got to go Beyond. I've used too much power fighting them, I've got to rest…. Her voice faded completely until even the smell of peppermint was gone. Cade sent up a quick prayer for her well-being, hoping He was still accepting messages from former Texas Rangers turned vampire.

Just ahead, the limo turned down a dirt road and bumped its way along it in a cloud of dust. Cade followed warily, his psychic senses on full alert, searching for any movement, any thought, that was out of the ordinary.

They rounded a bend in the dirt road, snaking around a stand of pines. Beyond the trees stood a wide, oval grassy area bordered on one side by a narrow creek. Nearby, a massive oak with broad, leafy branches spread a generous blanket of shade. It looked a lot like somebody's private picnic spot. Cade noticed with approval that the grass had been recently cut, which would leave the footing clear.

Hirsch parked the limo comfortably near the oak. Cade pulled in behind him, cautiously leaving a little distance between the two cars. Ridgemont got out, then reached back into the car to pull Val from the back seat. She came easily enough, though there was a glower on her face that said she'd dearly like to put up a fight. Stiffly, she allowed the vampire to tow her over to the tree and position her under one of its thick limbs.

Cade picked up his sword and shield and slid from the car to watch warily. Looking up, her eyes met his. Her face flooded with a tangle of joy, relief and anxiety. She took a half-step toward him, but Ridgemont jerked her back. Reaching into the sleeve of his robes, he pulled out a length of thin rope and flipped it over an overhead limb.

Lips tightening, Cade strode toward them. Before he could interfere, Ridgemont pulled Val's bound wrists over her head. As her arms raised, the concealing blanket fell away, leaving her naked.

"Now wait just a damn minute," Cade snarled, breaking into a run. Hirsch stepped into his path, his shield raised, axe ready in his hand.

"Just making sure everyone has his eyes on the prize," the ancient said calmly, tying the rope around the cord binding her wrists. Val glared at him, color flooding her cheeks. *Probably dying to spit in his eye*, Cade thought.

Feeling murderous, he scanned her body, checking for injuries. The only bite he could see was the one he'd put there himself, but there were bruises mottling her pale skin he knew hadn't been there last night.

Cade wheeled on Hirsch with a snarled obscenity. The German barely jerked his shield up in time to block the downward stroke of his long sword. Over the ring of steel, he heard Ridgemont laugh. "Now that's what I like to see."

Aching arms bound over her head, Val watched numbly as the fight began. There was a sense of unreality about the whole thing—two men, one dressed all in black, the other all in white, hacking away at one another with medieval weapons so fast it was hard to see exactly what was happening. The hatred between the two was almost tactile, like a thick, cold fog. Though their faces couldn't be seen under the masks they wore, rage burned under the surface of every move they made.

"Ah, very nice combination, Hirsch," Ridgemont murmured, as the white figure swung his axe, then abruptly reversed the heavy weapon's stroke midway in a move no human could have matched. Cade leaped back just in time to keep the blade from lodging in his chest. "Hirsch caught him that time."

"What?" Val asked, alarmed, as Cade brought his sword up and over in a smashing blow the German barely blocked. "Did Cade get hurt?"

"Slash across the chest," Ridgemont told her. "With weapons like these, a misstep can get you cut in half."

She glanced over at the vampire in horror. There was an absorbed enthusiasm in his tone that reminded her bizarrely of one of her old boyfriends explaining a football play.

"They're looking very good today," Ridgemont continued in that sports fan voice. "You have no idea how difficult it was to teach gunpowder warriors to fight like knights. Took years. But they've gotten quite good."

Hirsch made another blurring attack with his axe. Cade ducked back, then snaked forward and thrust his sword straight for the vampire's ribs. The German batted the blade away with his shield and reversed his stroke. Cade retreated again.

A chill stealing over her, Val realized he seemed slower than the other times he'd fought Hirsch, his timing a fraction off.

"They're more evenly matched today," Ridgemont said, confirming her suspicions. "Normally Cade has the advantage of strength and experience—I've been working with him for more than a century, after all—but healing his injuries has cut deeply into his reserves. He's not hitting as hard as he usually does, and his parries are slower."

Her stomach knotted with anxiety. She wanted to yell at Cade to stop, to go home and forget her and Ridgemont and Hirsch. She'd rather be left at their dubious mercy than watch him die.

Suddenly Cade lunged with a howl, spinning his sword in a hard, overhead attack that sent Hirsch scuttling back.

"On the other hand," Ridgemont added as her heart gave a little cheer, "he's really pissed off."

God, where was his speed? Cade wondered in desperation. If he wasn't damn careful, he was going to lose this fight, and Val would pay the price. *Don't think about that,* he told himself savagely, catching an axe blow on his shield. If he let himself imagine what Hirsch would do to her, the distraction could be fatal.

He tried desperately to settle into the familiar rhythms of combat, but it was harder than it had ever been before. His arms and legs seemed weighted with lead, and his blade felt awkward in his hands, as though poorly balanced. He couldn't seem to get his full strength behind it.

Damn it, he'd been doing this for years; he should be able to beat Hirsch in his sleep. No matter where they'd gone in their travels, Ridgemont had always forced Cade to drill with sword and shield, axe and armor, until he'd become more familiar with them than he'd been with his Colt's Peacemaker. After Ridgemont had forcibly recruited Hirsch, Cade had beaten the German with monotonous regularity.

But the bastard had drilled endlessly to make up for his lack of experience, and as the years passed, he'd become harder to defeat. Now his greater size and longer reach was beginning to tip the scales in his favor, especially since Cade's power had been sapped by his injuries.

And the sun wasn't helping, either. Cade was conscious of the brutal heat of its radiation burning through his clothing. Even if he avoided major injury, he'd have to go into a healing sleep just to take care of the burns he was suffering. Worse, the light was sapping his strength.

Adding to his misery, he'd lost his borrowed sunglasses a moment ago, and now his eyes were stinging from a combination of glare and sweat. Hirsch didn't have that problem, with those thick polarized goggles.

Quit whining and focus, you bastard, he told himself savagely. *You're going to let the prick win.*

Gathering his energy, Cade concentrated on pouring it down his arm and into his sword. The next time the weapon struck Hirsch's shield, it rang with more conviction. *Better,* he thought grimly.

"I'm going to kill you," the German hissed in a low, poisonous voice. It was the first time either of them had spoken since the fight began. "I'm going to bathe in the blood from the stump of your neck, and then I'm going to your woman with your blood on my hands, and I'm going to …"

As he started describing what he'd do with the blood, Hirsch lunged, spinning the axe. Cade pivoted away, swinging his long sword in a long, flat arc. But as he turned, the afternoon sunlight drove into his eyes like a spike. Blinding glare exploded in his skull.

Instinctively Cade jerked his head aside to save his vampire vision, missed his swing…

And realized he was wide open, his sword too far in its stroke to reverse. Hirsch's axe stroke was going to cleave his head open. By sheer instinct, Cade swung his shield with every ounce of supernatural strength, aiming blindly for the spot where his opponent's head should be.

He heard a choked-off scream, felt the sharp metal edge of the shield bite into flesh, grate against bone. Jerk free. Something hot and wet sprayed his face. A massive weight struck his shoulder, slammed him to the ground.

"Cade!" Val screamed.

He lay on his side, fighting to breathe. His chest felt paralyzed. He knew he couldn't actually suffocate, but his instincts screamed anyway.

At last he sucked in a breath and his lungs began to work again. Still blinded, he tried to turn his head and couldn't. The movement was blocked by something metallic. Oddly, he felt no pain, only a spreading sensation of cold. It took him several dazed minutes to realize what had happened.

Hirsch's axe was buried in his shoulder.

Cade reached up and groped blindly until he found the handle. He jerked. Something grated against bone. Hot liquid gushed down his side. Smelling copper in the air, he knew he was bleeding. *Damn it, not again.* Wearily, he gathered his power and blocked the spurt of blood as he threw the axe aside.

Cade's vision began to clear just in time to see Val running toward him, naked and desperate. "Get back!" he called hoarsely. "Hirsch ..."

"...Is no longer in the picture." Ridgemont sauntered up as Val fell on her knees beside him and began frantically examining his gushing shoulder. "You decapitated him with your shield. Very nice. Unfortunately, your performance was otherwise pitiful. I hope you'll do better when we meet, or it will be a very short fight."

"Oh," Cade grunted, glaring at his enemy, "you'll get your fight. And it'll be the last thing you get."

Val had no interest in their posturing. "I need something to staunch the bleeding," She turned and held out a hand to Ridgemont. "Give me that head cloth thing you're wearing."

The master vampire put a protective hand to it. “Not likely. Besides, he’s already bringing the bleeding under control. You’ll do him more good by giving him your throat and letting him feed as he pleases.” To Cade he added, “I have been in the sunlight quite long enough on your account. I’ll be in touch.”

“So will I, you bastard,” Cade grunted.

“Not for a week or so, I’ll wager,” Ridgemont said, subjecting Val’s naked body to a leering appraisal. “Have fun, gunslinger. I rather envy you the next few days.”

“Better him than you,” Val told him.

The ancient eyed her. “I’ll get my turn soon enough.” He turned and looked over his shoulder at Hirsch’s gory corpse with a grunt of disgust. “I suppose I’d better get rid of the remains. You’re not up to it, and if I don’t take care of it now, they’ll find him and do an autopsy. The next thing you know, someone would be publishing a paper in a journal somewhere. And I do not care to be outted by my own spawn.”

Grumbling, he stomped toward the fallen vampire.

As Ridgemont dealt with Hirsch’s body, Val hastily turned her attention to Cade. It could too easily have been him being removed for disposal. “You scared the hell out of me,” she told him fiercely.

“I scared the hell out of myself,” he said. “Help me up. I need to get out of the sun.”

As she knelt to slide an arm around his shoulder, one bare breast brushed something wet and sticky. Glancing down, she saw the entire side of his body was slick and red. Her stomach heaved. “Jesus.”

“It’s not as bad as it looks,” he grunted, tightening an arm around her shoulders with bruising strength.

“If it was, you’d be dead,” she told him grimly, struggling to pull him to his feet. The smell of blood was so strong she wanted to gag. As Ridgemont's car stared with a roar and pulled away, Cade swayed against her. She tightened her grip, wincing at his grunt of pain. "You okay?"

"Just get me to the car," he gritted.

Remembering the master vampire's advice, Val studied Cade's hooded face as they hobbled toward the Toyota he'd arrived in. "Do you need to bite me now?"

He looked down at her, his dark eyes startled behind his mask. The skin visible through the eyeholes was burned bright red. "Uh, not at the moment."

"Ridgemont said…."

"I'm sure he did, but the blood by itself wouldn't do me much good without strong emotion to give it a charge. I'm not up to making love, and unlike some people I could name, I've got no interest in terrifying you." He gave her a strained smile. "But if you'll give me a rain check…."

Her smile was equally strained. "You must feel bad, if you're refusing sex."

He laughed in a pained bark. "Don't worry, I heal fast. Particularly with that kind of incentive."

When they reached the car, she opened the door for him. He eased carefully into the passenger seat with a hiss of pain. As Cade settled back, he pointedly scanned her nude body. "Don't you think you'd better go get the blanket? There's probably a law against driving naked in this state."

"Are you kidding? This is South Carolina. There's a law against *being* naked." He grunted a laugh as she closed the door. Thankful for the trees that screened her from the road, she turned and hurried off to retrieve her fallen quit.

Despite the searing pain in his shoulder, Cade watched her go. Her slim nudity seemed to glow in the fiery light of the setting sun. He'd almost lost her today.

The pain in that thought broke his mental grip on his wound. It instantly began to gush. Hastily Cade tightened the web of power and cut off the blood flow, but the guilt was still sharp. If Hirsch had won, she'd have been victim to the German's sexual sadism until he killed her or she escaped. How many decades would she have suffered?

And her future was even darker if Ridgemont killed Cade in the coming duel. Even if Cade tried to send her away, the ancient would track her down, if only to punish them both for trying to disrupt his plans.

Abigail had been right all along. Cade had to Change her. At least as a vampire, Val would have some chance of fighting back. And without the mental link formed during the Change, Ridgemont would lack most of the means to torture her.

But he'd still kill her if Cade didn't get him first. And considering how difficult it had been taking on the much weaker Hirsch, how the hell was he supposed to do that?

Val found her blanket lying under the oak and snatched it up. Twisting and tucking it around herself to make a toga, she trotted back to the car despite the littering acorns that seemed intent on digging into her feet.

As she slid behind the wheel, she looked over at Cade to give him a reassuring smile. Sitting painfully erect in his seat with both eyes closed, he didn't seem aware of her. He still wore his protective hood. She eyed the sunset through the windshield and wondered if it was dark enough to remove the cloth. She wanted a good look at him.

He opened one eye an exhausted slit. "We're going to have to go to a hotel. The house is swarming with police, and I'm not up to dealing with them."

Val tucked a wandering fold of makeshift toga back into place. "Uh, Cade, how are we supposed to get a room? I'm not exactly presentable, and you look like you lost a fight to the death—which you damn near did. To top it off, I seem to have left my wallet in my other blanket."

Cade sighed and pulled off his mask. She flinched at the band of brightly burned skin around his eyes. The rest of his face was pink, as if the sun had punched right through the fabric. Scrubbing a shaking hand through his sweat-slick hair, he let his head drop back against the headrest. "That is a very good question." His eyes fell on a cell phone lying on the dashboard of the car. "Luckily, I've got a good answer." With a groan of pain, he reached forward to pick it up, then used his thumb to punch in numbers.

"Where did that come from?" Val asked.

"My neighbor must have left it in the car before he let me borrow it," he told her as he listened to the phone ring.

At last a familiar voice said, "Hello."

"Camille? This is Cade. I was wondering if you'd mind helping me out a little...."

Forty-five minutes later, Camille Robbins pulled into the clearing to give Val a wad of money and a K-Mart bag containing a change of clothing for herself and Cade.

"We'll pay you back as soon as we get things straightened out with the police," Val told her.

"Don't worry about it," Camille told her absently, peering at Cade, who sat slumped and motionless, his hair standing up in sweaty spikes. The darkness in the car kept the blood from showing, but something about his silhouette suggested he was in pain. "Looks like you've got more than enough to worry about as it is. He doesn't look too good. Shouldn't you take him to a doctor?"

"No doctors," he said, without opening his eyes.

Camille met Val's worried gaze with a snort of disgust. "Men."

She grinned reluctantly. "Yeah, that's about the size of it."

Dressed in the white shorts and T-shirt Camille had brought, Val waited for the hotel desk clerk to hand her the room keys. Tapping her fingers impatiently on the counter, she remembered the last time she'd checked into a hotel with Cade. Then, she'd been terrified he'd make her a vampire.

Now she knew he had no choice.

Five minutes later, she helped Cade limp into their room, trying not to stagger under his weight as he leaned against her. His breathing sounded ragged with pain. "You do realize what we have to do now?" she asked, partly to give him something else to think about as she struggled to help him lower his weight to the mattress without jarring his wounds.

"Yeah," he said shortly. She could tell he wasn't happy about it, but was as painfully aware as she was that they had no choice. His face looked paler than the pillow his head sank into. "Later." Seconds later, he was deep in the healing sleep.

Val badly wanted to pull off his shirt and look at the wound, but she didn't want to jostle him. Instead, she curled up on the room's other bed with her eyes wide open, far too wired to sleep. When Cade woke, he'd be hungry again. They'd make love—and start the process of Changing her.

Staring at the strong, masculine lines of his face, the muscled contours of the powerful arm he'd flung outside the covers, Val had to admit that the prospect of spending forever with him wasn't exactly a hardship. If only they had forever.

If only they had a week.

Once Cade Changed her, he'd go after Ridgemont like Ahab after his whale until either his sire was dead—or he was. Yet—what if they did succeed in killing Ridgemont? She realized that prospect frightened her almost as much as the first alternative.

She'd be a vampire.

Val had seen enough of the Hunger's power to worry about her own ability to control it. As heroic and iron-willed as Cade was, it had almost forced him to kill a child. What would it do to her?

And what would her vampirism mean for their relationship? The passion between them was hot now, but what would happen once that fire burned itself out? Too, as her sire, he'd own her. Being the kind of man he was, he'd never misuse that power. But would his affection turn to contempt once she belonged to him? She didn't think she could endure looking into those dark eyes and seeing nothing there but indifference…

Val caught her breath as she suddenly realized why that thought hurt so viciously. She was in love with Cade McKinnon.

Chapter Sixteen

The idea seemed so inevitable, so natural, as if she always had been in love with him. And maybe she had, if only as Cowboy. On some level, she'd always adored her dream Texas Ranger, first with a child's affection, then with a woman's passion. Discovering he was both real and a vampire had shaken that love, but it hadn't destroyed it. That's why she'd always been so torn, why she'd instinctively wanted to trust him even when logic insisted she shouldn't.

God, suddenly she needed to talk to Beth. Studying Cade's haggard face, Val decided he was so deeply in his healing sleep that she'd be unlikely to wake him. She reached for the bedside phone and punched in the number for her sister's beeper.

The phone rang almost immediately, and Val pounced on it, wanting to make sure it didn't wake Cade. "Beth?"

"Val?" Her sister sounded so relieved she felt instantly guilty she hadn't called earlier. "Thank God! I was getting worried. Is everything all right?"

"Yeah," she lied automatically, "everything's fine."

"It doesn't sound fine," Beth said, with that unerring talent she had for reading her sister's emotions. "You sound depressed."

The next time you talk to me, I may not be human. "I'm just missing you. It's been...a rough three days."

"Well, I've been making the most of our impromptu vacation." Her tone sounded so jaunty it was obvious she was trying to cheer Val up. "Lying on the beach, getting a gorgeous tan..."

Val made a strangled sound halfway between a laugh and a

sob. *There's something I won't be doing again....* "Don't tell me where you are."

"You are so paranoid. Anyway, the guys here are to die for ...."

She looked over at Cade, sprawled in all his blood-smeared glory across the next bed. "They ain't bad here, either."

"Oh, yeah?" Val could almost picture Beth's ears pricking like a cat's.

"Oh, yeah."

"So, who is he and how did you meet him?"

"If I told you, you'd never believe me," she muttered.

"What...? I didn't catch that."

"I've fallen in love."

"Get out!" Beth's voice spiraled into a delighted shriek. "When can I meet him?"

"I don't know." *I don't even know if I'll even see you again.* "Things are ... complicated right now. Dangerous."

"Okay, now you're being so damned mysterious you're starting to get on my nerves—not to mention scaring the hell out of me. What's going on?"

Val ached to pour out the whole story, but if she did, Beth would be on the next plane to South Carolina. And smack dab in Ridgemont's bull's-eye with the rest of them. "Like I said, it's too complicated to go into right now."

"Val...." Beth's tone held a note of warning.

"Oh, here comes Cade with our margaritas," she interrupted brightly. "And I think he's in the mood for love. Gotta go."

There was a long, cool pause. "I am so not buying this."

Val sighed. "You always were way too smart for me. Look, I can't go into it. I just can't. But it's extremely important for you to be careful. Don't use your credit card. Don't leave a trail. This guy we're dealing with isn't somebody to play around with."

Beth hesitated. "Don't worry, Val. I'll be careful."

"I love you." Her voice broke, and she took a deep breath to steady it. "You know that, right? I couldn't ask for a better…."

"I'll remind you of that next time I filch your favorite sweater." Beth sounded a little watery herself. "Listen, you be careful, you hear? Don't let your stud and his huge margarita distract you too much."

"Don't worry. I've got it all in hand."

"I'll just bet you do, big sister. I love you."

It was all Val could do to get out another "Goodbye, I love you," without bursting into tears. Slowly she hung up the phone and stared, biting her lip, at Cade's sleeping profile.

Beth hung up the pay phone. Remembering her sister's warning against leaving a trail, she frowned guiltily. When she'd gotten Val's beep, she'd scrabbled for her cell phone only to discover it was dead. Worse, there was no money in her purse. She'd been so determined she wouldn't miss the call, she'd dug out her calling card.

She shrugged. Well, once shouldn't hurt.

Cade's sword flashed sparks of reflection as he hacked at his white-clad opponent. The two men moved like cats, the setting sun giving their weapons a blood-red sheen.

But as they circled each other, the treacherous light hit him full in the face. And he missed his stroke again. This time he had no time to swing his shield. His opponent was too fast, the axe moving in a blurring, glittering arc.

Cade's head spun from his shoulders.

Val screamed, feeling her heart tear open in her chest. Ridgemont turned and grinned at her over his bloody axe.

Her eyes flew open as she sat up with a jerk, staring wildly into the darkness. The room was pitch black—it was still the middle of the night. Sweating, panting, she fumbled desperately for the bedside lamp until she managed to turn it on.

Cade lay in the opposite bed, whole, the last of the pain gone from his face. His shoulder was completely healed, though blood still crusted his clothing.With a little whimper of relief, Val crept out of her own bed and curled up against his side, ignoring the lingering smell of blood. Resting her head against his chest, she listened to the reassuring thump of his heartbeat.

It was a long time before she slept again.

Cade awoke, and Val was there. Draped across his chest, weighing hardly more than a cat, her body soft and warm in sleep. The scent of her kicked the Hunger into a full, roaring blaze. He ached to roll over with her and bury his cock in her sex and his fangs in her throat. Clenching his teeth, he fought the need until his willpower was steady enough to risk putting his hands on her.

But when he wrapped his hands around her arms and started to lift her body off his, the soft, silken texture of her skin sent the Hunger into a sustained howl: *Take her takeher takeherTAKEHER!* His head started to lower toward her pulsing jugular.

Moving fast, Cade slipped out from under her and fled toward the bathroom, not daring to look back.

Val snapped awake as the door closed behind him. *Oh, God,* she thought. *It's time.*

Time to give up being Human with a capital "H." Time to start becoming something else, something that drank blood and stayed out of the sunlight—and loved Cade McKinnon, who would own her in a way no human could really own another.

No, not "own." "Possess." Possess in the Exorcist "oh-my-God-he's-in-my-head" sense, and possess in the thoroughly carnal, dominant male sense.

I can't do this, Val thought wildly. Rolling off the bed, she snatched the car keys off the nightstand table. And stopped in her tracks. "Oh, hell."

She couldn't leave him. He needed her. Needed her blood, needed to Change her. Needed *her.* If she ran out on him, Ridgemont would kill him. And Val herself, too, once the ancient hunted her down, but that was really beside the point.

Shoulders slumping, she turned and looked toward the bathroom.

Abigail stood beside the bed, watching her with solemn eyes. Val jumped with a shriek and fell back against the bed. "Don't do that!" Gasping for breath, she inhaled the strong, sharp bite of peppermint.

Thank you, the ghost said.

"For what? Almost dropping dead with a heart attack?" She clutched at her chest and waited for the panic-stricken pounding to slow.

For loving him enough to sacrifice so much. I know it's not easy for you. The rest of us didn't have a choice in what we've become. You're doing it voluntarily.

"More or less," Val muttered. Eyeing the ghost, she added, "Thank you for distracting Hirsch, by the way. If you hadn't stepped in, he'd have raped me."

Abigail shrugged. ***Ridgemont would have stopped him. He was furious at Hirsch's cheating.***

"Maybe. Unless it suited his purposes to allow it."

The ghost grimaced. ***Good point.***

"When you defied Ridgemont...." She hesitated. "Did he...was he really about to...eat you?"

Yes. He's been threatening to absorb me for years, just to keep Cade in line. Her voice dropped to a low, fierce hiss. ***And I hated being used as a club to beat my brother with.***

"God."

They stared at one another for a long, uncomfortable moment. Finally, unable to stand the silence, Val blurted, "I'm afraid I'm going to hurt somebody."

You won't. You're not the kind to kill for lust. And Cade will help you maintain control.

"He'll know everything." *Know how much I love him.*

Yes.

Val laughed, the sound a little wild. "I'm terrified."

You don't have to be, the ghost said, her mental voice calm and certain. ***He loves you. He'll protect you.***

"Oh, I know he'll protect me. Knowing Cade, that's a given. But love me? I don't think so."

Val, the thought of you has driven him for seventeen years. Otherwise, he'd have killed himself in some stupid, suicidal attempt on Ridgemont the minute he escaped his control, if only to protect me.

"Guilt isn't the same thing as love, Abigail. And I don't want guilt from him."

It's not guilt anymore. It hasn't been in years. Not since you became a woman and bonded with him in the dreams. The little ghost studied her with that un-childlike gaze. ***And I think it's time I go Beyond so you can find that out for yourself.*** She turned and walked into the wall.

Val looked toward the bathroom door. Squared her shoulders. And began to undress, her heart banging like a kettledrum as she pulled off her shorts and T-shirt and folded them with shaking hands. She stacked them neatly on the bureau, then rocked back on her heels and stared at them. *Well, I'm out of excuses to stall.*

Biting her lip, she walked to the bathroom on legs that felt as weak as a newborn colt's. The air felt chill on her naked skin, and she shivered as she reached for the knob. Pushing the door open, Val hesitated, listening to the water beating the porcelain tiles. She could see his silhouette moving behind the shower's thin plastic curtain. Taking a deep breath, she stepped across the tiny room and pushed the curtain aside.

Cade's head snapped up and around like a wild animal's, his dark eyes meeting hers. They seemed to burn with such hunger she felt her heart leap into her throat. "Hi," she croaked, and tried a weak smile.

"Hi." But he didn't smile back. Instead his eyes dropped to her nudity with blatant possessiveness. Val sucked in a breath. She'd never had a man look at her that way. Not even him.

There was the Hunger, of course. She'd expected that, knowing what healing that shoulder wound would do to him. But the expression in his eyes was even darker and more ancient than vampire lust, more thoroughly male, more fiercely triumphant. As if he'd...won her. As if she was his.

Val could only stand there, immobilized by the sheer predatory intensity of his stare. He'd been in the middle of shampooing his hair, and now the lather rolled down the seal-slick strands, gliding over the strong cords of his throat and along the broad muscled planes and ridges of his chest. Half-hypnotized, she unconsciously tracked the flow of foam down the bas-relief shapes of his abdomen to the thick, hungry jut of his cock.

"You're getting water all over the bathroom floor," he rumbled at last. His nostrils flared. His hungry gaze flicked from her nipples to the delta of soft hair between her thighs, then up to her eyes. "Why don't you get in and close the shower curtain."

She nodded jerkily and started to step into the tub. But before she could even complete the motion, big hands closed around her upper arms, picked her up effortlessly, and plastered her against the wet, hard length of his body. His mouth came down over hers, sealing in her gasp of surprise. The shower pounded over their heads in a hot spray.

Her senses were suddenly full of him: his size, his heat, his strength. His tongue glided smoothly between her lips, tasting and stroking, seducing her into yielding even more. Long fingers fisted into her hair, holding her still as he fed on her mouth. His free hand gliding down the curve of her spine, discovered her bottom. Curled possessively into the taut flesh, lifting her to fit her body against his. As her feet left the tub floor, she made a startled little sound and caught at his shoulders instinctively. Wrapping her legs around his narrow male hips, she gasped at the feeling of his massive cock against her soft belly. He rumbled in pure, dark satisfaction. Turning with her, he pressed her back against the cool, wet tile of the shower wall and braced her there with his body, setting his hands free to possess and explore.

"I love your nipples," he said against her mouth as he plucked and stroked one of them. "Such sweet, pink little tips." Beneath her rump, the long fingers of his other hand slid into the cleft of her thighs, gliding between soft lips that were rapidly growing damp as she lost her nervousness in desire. She could feel his thick shaft pressing against her all the way to the navel. Soon he'd thrust it into her.... She caught her breath and closed her eyes, imagining the searing delight of that moment. Something began to melt and trickle deep in her sex.

"Yeah, that's it," he growled, and bit gently at her lower lip. "Cream for me, sweetheart. Drench my fingers. Get ready for me, because I'm going to fuck you deep and hard."

Those crude, blunt words would have been a turnoff coming from any other man, but from Cade it was the pure, unvarnished truth. She shuddered. "God, you make me so...."

"Yeah," he growled in her ear over the hiss of the shower, driving his fingers into the slick opening of her sex. "You're mine, darlin'. I'm going to take you. I'm going to take your blood, and I'm going to take your cunt, and I'm going to make you drink from me. And then I'll be in your mind and you'll be in mine, and you'll belong to me. Jesus, I've loved you so long...."

Love? Her heart leaped. His tone was so hot and sure, she had no doubt he meant it, but how much of that emotion was born of guilt and his driving sense of duty?

He lifted her in his arms, then brought her down and impaled her on his big shaft with a ruthless twist of his hips. She threw back her head and cried out in shock. The shower spray pounded against her face in a warm needle spray. Clinging helplessly to him, she gasped in pleasure as he began to thrust, bracing one hand against the tile as he rolled his hips, driving deep inside her. He felt thicker than anything she'd ever known, even bigger than he'd seemed before. She wanted to howl in pleasure.

"Mine," Cade growled in her ear. "Say you're mine."

Her feminist training rebelled, but something much deeper, much older knew it was the truth. "Yours," she gasped. "I'm yours."

"And I'm yours." He deepened his strokes until he was pounding into her in a rolling masculine storm of lust. Gasping in pleasure, she could only tighten the grip of her thighs and cling to his wet, hard body.

"He's never gonna touch you," he whispered savagely, his grip tightening on her hips as he ground deep. "I'm going to kill the son of a bitch. I swear to you, I'll protect you."

"I know," she gasped, even as her awareness began to splinter with the first deep pulses of her orgasm.

"I love you," Cade said, and lowered his head to her pulse. She felt the tiny pain as the tips of his fangs pressed into her flesh. She waited for the bite, but it didn't come.

And she needed it. "Cade, take me!"

"Do you love me?" he demanded against her skin.

"God, yes!"

"Yes!" His teeth sank into her skin as he drove his cock all the way in, stuffing her almost brutally. She convulsed in stunned ecstasy, kicked over the edge of pleasure by the ruthless double penetration of his fangs and shaft. The orgasm burned like a wave of fire crashing over her head, and she twisted against him, screaming as she came. She felt his cock pulse and shoot inside her, heard his deep groan against her throat.

When it was finally over, she hung limp in his arms, sated and boneless, aware of his mouth working as he fed in deep swallows. Her head was spinning, and she wasn't sure if it was from blood loss or raw pleasure. She tilted back her face into the shower spray, hoping the warm, stinging water would clear her head.

Finally, still buried in her, he eased back slightly. As she watched with a vague, floating kind of interest, he lifted one hand and dug his thumbnail into the skin over his chest, raking a thin cut that instantly began to bleed. He caught the back of her head and pulled her face to the tiny wound. "Drink," he said hoarsely. "Taste me."

Dreamily, she obeyed, licking at the blood.

"More," Cade ordered. "Suck it."

With a muffled, giddy giggle, she obeyed. His blood had a strange taste, fiery and intoxicating, more like cognac than the prosaic salty copper she knew from childhood paper cuts.

He had gone soft inside her, but as she drank, she felt him harden again. Slowly, carefully, Cade began to thrust. Clinging helplessly, she swallowed his blood as pleasure bloomed lazily under his gentle strokes.

"Mine," he whispered again.

When she became aware of herself again, she was wrapped in his arms, feeling as empty and limp as a wrung-out rag. "Damn," she croaked. "If we're supposed to do that all week, I'm not sure I'll survive."

"Neither am I," he groaned, easing his limp sex out of her and letting her feet touch the tub floor. There were several inches of water around her ankles. "But God, what a way to go."

Her knees gave, but he steadied her with a hand on her elbow. "I drank your blood," Val said in a small voice, clutching his shoulders. "And I liked it." She already felt alien to herself. She'd never had such an erotic experience in her life.

"I'm glad." He lifted a hand and slowly stroked her wet hair. She shivered. Frowning, Cade reached out a hand to shut off the shower taps. "We'd better get you dried off."

He lifted her out of the tub as if she weighed no more than a two-year-old, then stepped out himself and snagged a towel with a long, brawny arm. She met his gaze miserably as he began to dry her skin with brisk strokes. "Cade, I'm scared."

"I know, baby. So am I."

She licked her dry lips. "Did you mean what you said, about loving me?"

"Yes." His gaze met hers steadily. "I've always loved you."

She smiled, slow and brilliant, believing him. The knowledge was just there, bone-deep and total, as if she'd absorbed it with the taste of his blood.

Uncertainty flickered in his eyes. "Did *you* mean it?"

Her smile widened. "Yes."

With a groan of pleasure, he scooped her into his arms and carried her to the bed.

Val woke to the gentle sensation of Cade's hands drifting over her skin. She moaned and stretched, then clung to him as her head went into a long, lazy spin. "Oh!"

Cade stopped stroking to hug her comfortingly. She relaxed against him, savoring the warmth of his enveloping strength. He felt so big, so solid, so male. It was hard to believe anything could ever threaten him.

"When we made love that last time, I touched your thoughts," he said softly, his chest rumbling under her ear. "I felt your fear. It's natural, but you're stronger than you think."

"Am I? The Hunger…."

"Isn't normally anything like what you touched in my mind when you were a child."

"I realize that, but what if somebody starves me the way Ridgemont did you? What if…."

"One, I would never place you under a compulsion to kill anybody, and two, even if someone did starve you, you could handle it. You're one of the strongest people I've ever met." He smiled slightly, combing his fingers through her hair. "Even as a child, you were so damn brave…."

Val snorted. "I was scared out of my mind."

"Darlin', you had a starving vampire at your heels, programed to kill. Any reasonable human would have run like hell, but you went to rescue the baby first."

"Well, yeah," she said. "I couldn't abandon Beth."

"Actually, you could have." He coiled a lock of her hair around a big finger. "Most people would have."

"Not most people, Cade," Val protested. "Not leave a baby with vampires."

"I wouldn't be so sure about that. You could have reasoned you'd be leading me to her, that if you just ran, we might not find her."

"Oh." She frowned, thinking about it. "You know, when you put it that way, it was kind of stupid."

"No, because we would have found her anyway. I doubt Beth would have been in danger even from Ridgemont and Hirsch—they have no interest in any female under the age of puberty—but you had no way of knowing that. So going after her was pretty damn heroic."

She gave him such a skeptical look he had to grin. "Are you trying to get me into bed again, McKinnon?"

"If you'll notice, we're already *in* bed. And no, I'm not just flattering you. I was two feet taller and more than a hundred pounds heavier, and I have fangs. But you just looked at me with such defiant courage in those big gray eyes, I knew you'd grow up to be a hell of a woman. And I was right."

"Because of you. Your guidance made all the difference when I was a kid, particularly given that my grandmother was too drunk most of the time to notice what I was into. I remember one time when I was thirteen. I was letting my grades go to hell—didn't care about them, didn't care about anything. And you showed up in that dream and raked me over the coals!" She laughed. "I straightened up. Didn't give a damn about what Grandma thought, but I couldn't stand to disappoint my hero. And I didn't even think you were real!"

"Don't be too hard on your grandmother. Ninety percent of her problems were caused by Ridgemont's grip on her mind. I think she drank because she knew what he made her do was wrong."

"Yeah, I realized that after Ridgemont talked about influencing her." She let her head rest against his shoulder and let her fingers play over his chest hair. "Her life was so damn tragic. Her son dead, her mind invaded and subverted. And on some level, she knew it."

They lay together for a long moment, lost in their respective thoughts. "The year you turned seventeen, he had your grandmother send him your picture. You'd stopped dreaming of me by then, and I hadn't seen you in a long time. I was shocked by how you looked in that skimpy little cheerleader costume. The things he said—I punched him in the mouth." Cade smiled, the dark pleasure of that well-deserved blow lighting his eyes. "I must have caught him by surprise. He paralyzed me and gave me the kind of beating I hadn't had in years, but it was worth it."

Val winced, remembering too well the other times she'd seen Ridgemont abuse Cade in Abigail's memories. "You know, he told me he planned that. It was all deliberate, designed to drive you into breaking the compulsion. He may have told you he was punishing you for something else, but that was an excuse. It was all about throwing us together." She stopped as a thought struck her. "In his own perverted way, the creep was matchmaking." She shuddered.

"Ridgemont always was the master of the long range plan." Shrugging, he drifted his fingers in circles over her bare shoulders. "And he had me pegged, as much as I hate to admit it. I worked my ass off breaking his control and building my strength so I could save you. I'd have done it anyway, but not with the same kind of single-minded obsession." He met her eyes again and tilted his head, submerging her in the warm darkness of his stare. "You were a hell of an inspiration, even when the only contact between us was those dreams. Intelligent. Beautiful. Stubborn." His sensuous mouth curled into a smile. "You made me fall in love with you."

"You, on the other hand, are heroic, handsome, sexy, and disgustingly noble."

Cade quirked a brow. "'Disgustingly?"

"Seems to fit, given your obsessive drive toward self-sacrifice."

"Do I detect a note of implied criticism?"

"It's more than a note, and it's more than implied." Val looked him in the eye, determined to return his honesty with her own. "I love you, but you scare the hell out of me. I get the impression you're not just willing to sacrifice yourself to get Ridgemont—you'd prefer it that way. It's like, that's the only thing that will erase whatever he did to your honor."

Cade stiffened, the easy smile fading from his mouth. "You don't know what you're talking about. I have no intention of killing myself."

"See that you don't." She looked him in the eye. "Because I'm not putting myself through all this so I can watch you die."

Chapter Seventeen

Dressed again, they walked across the parking lot to the motel diner, where Cade made her order a big breakfast and bullied her into eating it despite her lack of appetite. She didn't have to be encouraged to drink, however. Her throat was so parched, she kept the waitress busy filling her glass every couple of minutes.

As the woman topped it off one more time, she looked up at Val. "You okay, honey? You sure are pale."

"Yeah, I'm…" She broke off, distracted by a slow, deep pounding. "Somebody needs to turn his boom box down."

"What?" The waitress gave her a strange look as Cade glanced up sharply.

Val blinked and braced against the table as the room seemed to dip and spin. "I'll never understand why kids feel the need to serenade the neighborhood with their car stereos. You'd think…"

"May I have a refill?" Cade interrupted, holding up his coffee cup.

"Sure, hon. Let me get my pot." Giving her a last worried glance, the waitress hurried off.

"What's her problem?"

Cade leaned across the table and lowered his voice. "That wasn't a boom box, Val. That was her heart."

"What?"

"That drumming. It's her heartbeat."

"Get out."

He shook his head. "I hear it, too."

A chill rolled over her. "But why do *I* hear it?"

"I think you know the answer to that." He met her eyes in a long, steady stare.

Val swallowed. *The Change has started.* "Yeah. I guess I do." Now that she stopped to listen, she could hear another beat—slow, deep, steady. Somehow she knew it was Cade's. "Isn't it distracting?"

He shrugged. "After a while, you quit noticing it. It's like the air conditioner or the refrigerator. Background noise."

She started to ask another question, but shut her mouth as the waitress returned to fill Cade's cup. The woman gave her a sidelong glance. *High as a kite.*

"I am not!" Val said, indignant.

"Why don't you bring us our check," Cade said as the waitress's eyes widened. She nodded jerkily and retreated.

"Don't answer questions people don't ask," he hissed.

"She thinks I'm on drugs!"

He drew in a breath as if searching for patience. "Under the circumstances, that's probably understandable. You're not exactly yourself."

Val bit back the hot words that gathered on her tongue and frowned. He had a point. She definitely felt a little muzzy, as though she'd had one glass of wine too many.

She didn't ask if it was going to get worse. She knew it would.

After returning to their room, they made love again.

When they finished drinking from each other, Val draped herself over Cade's chest and shut her eyes, trying to ignore the rapid revolutions the room was making around her.

It didn't take her long to lose her grip on consciousness.

Cade's injured arm wasn't hurting anymore, and blood streamed down it from forearm to knuckles, pouring into the saw-

dust. Looking down, he watched the sword slide from his nerveless fingers. A scan with his vampire senses told him Ridgemont had hit something vital.

He was bleeding out.

Seeing Ridgemont about to leap for him, Cade managed to scoop up his opponent's fallen shield with his left hand. But he couldn't bring it up fast enough to block, and Ridgemont's sword chopped into his breastplate. Something cracked. He hit the ground on his back and skidded in the sawdust.

Desperately, he struggled to regain his feet, but his legs buckled under him and the lights of the arena spun around his head. Cade fell back, then fought to rise again. And failed. He'd lost too much blood.

Numbly, he watched Ridgemont circle him, limping, his sword dangling in one hand. Blood smeared the side of the master vampire's ribs; he too, was badly hurt.

But not badly enough.

Cade had always known it would come to this. The son of a bitch was just too powerful. He was going to die, and it was no more than he deserved.

Ridgemont grinned into his eyes. "You gave me a good fight, gunslinger. Hurt me, even. Rather badly. But it's not enough to save you." He tilted his head to one side and raised his sword. "I think perhaps I'll cut out your heart and keep it to remember you by."

Val jolted upright in bed and looked around wildly. Cade lay next to her, his eyes closed. For one panicked moment she thought he was dead. Then she saw the steady rise and fall of his chest and fell back against her pillow with a gasp of relief.

A dream. It had only been a dream.

No it wasn't, insisted a small voice in the back of her head.

She frowned uneasily at the ceiling. What if the dream had been another one of her clairvoyant visions?

It couldn't be.

And yet…somehow she suspected with a chill of horror that it was exactly that. She'd seen Cade's future. Ridgemont was going to kill him. Unless she did something to prevent it.

Val stared at his sleeping profile and knew she couldn't let him die. She had to help him kill the ancient first. And the best way to do that was to complete the Change as quickly as possible.

Sitting up, Val threw the cover off them both and looked down at him. His cock lay soft and curled in its nest of thick hair. "Now that," she muttered, "won't do at all."

Cade woke to the mind-blowing sensation of a hot female mouth engulfing his cock. He groaned and stiffened, his back arching with shock at the sheer, searing intensity of his pleasure. Opening his eyes, he saw Val crouching over him, her pretty little ass in the air, her mouth wrapped around his shaft. Instinctively, he tunneled both hands in the thick red silk of her hair. "God!"

The long fingers of one hand rolled his balls tenderly as her mouth sucked with such raw power he thought the top of his head would blow off. He twisted helplessly in the sheets, for once totally in a woman's power. Just as his cock reached its full, straining length, she lifted her head. He gasped. "No, don't stop!"

"Oh, I have no intention of stopping," she growled, sounding more determined than seductive. She sat up, straddled his hips, grabbed his shaft in one hand, aimed it, and impaled herself in one breathtaking swoop.

"Jesus!" He arched his spine, instinctively driving to his full length.

"Yes!" she said through clenched teeth. "That's it!" Ruthlessly, she ground down on him, taking him deep and fast and hard, circling her hips as she rode him so his cock seemed to screw into her slick, tight depths. He grabbed her hips and held on as she plunged and bucked. She leaned back, arching her spine as she grabbed her ankles and forced herself up and down. She felt so incredibly wet and clamping he knew he had only seconds before he shot her full of his come.

Suddenly she leaned forward over him, still fucking him hard. A cool droplet of her sweat struck his face. "Give me your blood," she gritted. "That son of a bitch is not going to kill you!"

In no mood to argue, he lifted his own wrist to his mouth and raked his fangs across it. Blood welled. He lifted the shallow wound to her mouth. She grabbed his forearm, pressed her lips against it, and drank, still grinding down on his cock.

The combined sensation of her mouth on his skin and her sex pulsing around his cock sent heat corkscrewing down his spine. He could feel the orgasm boiling deep in his balls, getting ready to detonate.

She dragged her mouth from his wrist and screamed. Her sex clenched on his cock as she came. "I love you!" Val gasped. "God, I love you! And I'm not going to let you die!"

"And…I…love…you!" he panted back, pounding into her with all his strength. Her mouth sealed over the small wound again as he ground his head into the pillow and let himself come. And come. And come.

And come.

She woke the next day with a pounding headache. Every joint and muscle ached, and her mouth felt dust dry. Before she could even croak out a request, Cade rolled out of bed and went into the bathroom, returning with a glass of water and a plastic pitcher. She drank it greedily, and he filled another one for her. As she downed that, he put a hand to her forehead. His skin felt deliciously cool.

She lifted dazed eyes to his, managed a whisper. "Fever?"

"You're burning up. I'm going to go get you something to replenish your electrolytes. I won't be long."

"Ice," she said. "Get some ice."

He nodded.

Reading her need for mindless distraction, Cade turned on the motel room's television for her and handed her the remote, then dressed and strode out carrying the room's small plastic ice bucket. Five minutes later, he was back. He filled the pitcher with water and ice cubes, then handed her a glass and left her numbly channel surfing while he made for the nearest convenience store.

The thirst was worse than anything she'd ever known—so maddening it seemed to reduce her to the level of an animal. Cade did everything he could to soothe it, feeding her sports drinks and ice chips and his blood, but it still wasn't enough.

To make matters worse, every muscle and bone in her body ached brutally. He tried to reach into her mind to control it, but he couldn't get through her Kith shields. The hours wore past as she tossed in her bed, growing weaker, her strength draining with such speed it frightened her. She was dying, and she knew it.

Finally he reached for her mind again—and this time found weakness had eroded her barriers enough to allow contact. *I think I can help you now,* Cade told her mentally, breaking through her terror. *Do you want me to get rid of the pain?*

She nodded eagerly. He laid a large, cool hand on her forehead and slid into her mind more easily than he ever had before. He felt both familiar and alien, and she tried to pull away in fear at the depth of the connection. She found she couldn't. But before her panic could grow, the pain began to drain away, sliding out of her joints and muscles like boiling water. The awful, racking chill of the fever ebbed, until for the first time in hours she was actually comfortable.

Instantly, she slid into sleep.

Cade maintained his connection with her, controlling her pain as she slept. He could feel the Change accelerating, the cells of her body taking on new structures and functions. Becoming vampire. Had it not been for his psychic help, the transition would have been agonizing.

As the hours went on, the sleep deepened into a coma, and he had to work hard to maintain his link to her deepest mind. Val didn't want him there. In unconsciousness, her mind reacted with ferocity to his invasion, fighting to drive him out, to rid itself of his profoundly alien presence. Without even knowing what she was doing, she instinctively turned her own nascent psychic power against him, hammering against his consciousness with bolts of pain.

Cade knew if he released her to defend himself, she'd slip beyond his grip and die. So he endured, refusing to let her go, remaining deep in her mind. Keeping her alive.

Ridgemont, you bastard, he thought, teeth gritted as his skin seemed to blaze with the pain she inflicted, *you never mentioned this part.*

He thought he heard a ghostly laugh.

In self-defense, Cade wove the connections between them stronger, deeper, building a net of power through Val's mind until at last he could force her to stop torturing him. She subsided against his psychic grip, but he could feel her subconscious mind raging at his invasion.

Gently he purred reassurance to her, telling her he loved her, that she was safe with him, that he'd never misuse the power he was gaining. Until at last her fury faded, replaced by trust.

When Val began to relax, he caught a flash of recent memory. Something about Ridgemont.... Frowning, he looked closer and saw the dream in her memory. "So that's why you practically raped me," Cade murmured. She'd thought the dream would come true, and she'd tried to prevent it in her own mind-blowing way.

Not that he minded.

Contemplating the dream, he narrowed his eyes. It took place in the arena at Ridgemont's mansion, which he knew Val had never seen. But the events the vision described hadn't happened—yet. Maybe she was right. Maybe it was a precognitive dream.

Val had thought she could stop the vision from coming true, but Cade wasn't sure it worked like that. Then again, Ridgemont hadn't actually killed him in the dream either; it ended before the ancient swung his sword.

He frowned. He'd always known his chances of defeating his sire weren't good, even with Val's help. And judging by the ancient's injuries in the dream, it looked like she had indeed been giving him that help. Cade had never been able to inflict that kind of damage on his own. But if the dream was precognitive, it seemed he was fated to lose his fight with Ridgemont. Which meant that somehow, he had to make sure Val survived the fight without ending up at the monster's mercy.

Unfortunately, he had no idea how to do that.

It took Cade another full day to teach Val's human brain how to run her vampire body. Finally he decided she was past the danger point, her heart and lungs working in their new rhythm. As the coma became a natural sleep, he let himself surface.

When he became aware again, he was lying sprawled against the headboard of the bed, his chin against his chest, one hand resting on her forehead as she curled next to him. Slowly, painfully, Cade sat up, wincing as his stiff neck protested the change in position. Rolling his head on his shoulders, he stretched his aching muscles. It felt strange to be in his own body again, separate and alone. There was a sense of relief, but at the same time, he found himself missing her.

She lay next to him, looking so still and pale his heart clenched in his chest. Then his vampire hearing picked up the slow, steady bang of her heartbeat, the sigh of her breath, and he relaxed.

Frowning, he studied her. There were dark shadows under her eyes, and her skin looked drawn tight over her high cheekbones. Her auburn hair spread out over her pillow, damp with sweat. Her eyes flicked back and forth beneath her lids. She'd regain consciousness soon.

He'd better hurry. He had burned a lot of power guiding her through the change, and now he needed to find enough blood to feed both himself and her. As he rolled out of bed and went in search of his clothes, he felt the Hunger stir. But it felt… different. He stopped in his tracks, frowning as he analyzed it, trying to determine what had changed.

Instead of the familiar driving erotic need he knew so well, there was only a deep thirst. He had to have blood, but that was all. Ridgemont had mentioned this once—that the link between male and female vampires satisfied the sexual component of the Hunger.

Good thing, too. Cade doubted seriously he could have tolerated watching Val seduce some handsome stud. Feeling oddly light, he buttoned his jeans, stomped into his boots and strode from the motel room.

Out on the motel breezeway, Cade stopped to inhale the evening air with a sigh of pleasure. The sky was a deep indigo blue, with the brilliant reds of sunset painting the horizon. He wondered absently how many days it had been since the Change had begun.

Looking toward the road, he saw a short, bearded man walking past. "Hey, buddy!" The man stopped and looked over at him—and was caught. The Hunger stirred and flexed. Cade said softly, "Come here a minute."

Val woke to a raging thirst, worse than anything she'd ever known even in this interminable illness. Her mouth was so dry, her tongue felt like a piece of cracked and swollen leather. With a groan, she turned over and fumbled for the water pitcher beside the bed, but only succeeded in knocking it over. Nothing spilled; it was empty.

Moaning in frustration, she tried to roll out of bed, but her arms and legs felt like inert hunks of wood. She whimpered at the rise of helplessness.

Big hands closed around her shoulders, lifted her until a strong male body could settle behind her back. Her head lolled, but fingers gently caught her chin and lifted it. A blessedly cool glass pressed against her lips, tilted. The scent of water filled her nose. Desperately she began to gulp at the life-giving liquid, welcoming even the wet chill as some of it dribbled down her chest. She drained the glass and managed to croak, "More!"

"Sure, darlin'," Cade's deep baritone said, his chest rumbling under her back, his breath puffing against her ear. "Just wait a second."

She opened her eyes and watched with desperate intensity as he filled the glass from a plastic pitcher. As he brought the tumbler to her lips, the rim knocked against one of her incisors. It gave. She lifted a hand and weakly pushed the glass back as she probed the tooth with her tongue. It came out in her mouth.

Horrified, Val straightened and doubled over to spit the bloody incisor into her palm. With the movement of her mouth, another tooth came loose, and she spit that out as well. "Oh, God, Cade, what's happening to my teeth?" she moaned.

He reached around her with a tissue and scooped them out of her palm. "Don't panic. It's just your incisors."

"Oh, great. Now I'll look like a hillbil…" But as she inhaled, the scent of him flooded her nostrils. Hunger hit her so hard, she gasped as her belly cramped. A sharp pain stabbed her upper jaw, and she grabbed her face, crying out as the sensation intensified to agony. Blood from her cut gums flooded her mouth. She shuddered at the taste. But not with disgust.

"That," Cade told her dryly, "would be your fangs."

Val looked at him wildly. "Fangs?" She winced at the way the word sounded when it emerged. "Oh, God, now I'm lisping. I sound like an eight-year-old."

He grinned at her. "You have to get used to talking with them."

"Oh, yeah." She smiled a sudden memory. "I did that when I first got braces. I…"

But as Val looked at him, leaning on one elbow beside her, she forgot what she was going to say. He was shirtless and barefoot, dressed in nothing more than a pair of jeans. The play of muscles in his chest and arms instantly entranced her. He smiled down at her, a tender smile that lit his handsome face and chocolate eyes. His scent filled her head, male and strong and distinctly Cade.

She wanted him. Now. She wanted to taste his skin and breathe his scent, she wanted to feel him surging into her in those long, ruthless thrusts of his.

As Cade met her eyes, his smile faded, replaced by desire—and a knowing expression. He lay back on the bed and opened his arms. "Here."

She went to him eagerly, draping herself over the hard arch of his chest, loving the way he felt. His hand came up to the back of her head. But instead of guiding her mouth to his, he pressed her to his throat, tilting back his head to allow her access. She tried to pull away. But then she heard a sighing roar that reminded her of the sea, rising and falling over a strong, steady bass thump. Intrigued, she turned her head and pressed her ear closer.

"You're hearing the blood in my veins," he told her softly. "And my heartbeat."

His hand tightened on her head, directing her mouth against his skin. His scent flooded her skull, impossibly tempting. Her stomach cramped. Val moaned in a blend of horror and excitement.

She wanted his blood.

She'd tasted Cade's blood before, of course—but not like this. Not from biting and drinking from him like a vampire. Yet the Hunger was so insistent, she knew she had no choice.

"Follow the sound," Cade whispered.

Despite the ravenous need twisting her belly, Val drew back. "I don't want to hurt you. What if I bite too hard?"

"You won't. Besides, even if you did, I could heal it." His hand urged her closer again until her lips brushed his strong throat. The sigh of his blood seemed to call her.

Closing her eyes, she opened her mouth and tried to put her teeth against him. But her fangs were longer than the teeth she was used to, and she had to widen her jaws further until she could press the points into his skin.

Two tantalizing drops slid into her mouth, but that was all. Frustrated, she drew harder.

She heard a deep rumble under her mouth as Cade chuckled, then his hand tightened on her head, moving it to shift her teeth fractionally. Blood poured into her mouth. "You have to widen the punctures, or your fangs plug 'em," he told her.

She barely absorbed the information, too entranced by the alien flavor spilling over her tongue. She'd tasted his blood before, of course, but it was even better now—hot, spicy, intoxicating. She drank greedily, wanting more.

Cade moaned and stiffened under her. The link snapped into place between them with such intensity her eyes widened. She felt the sudden lust that swamped him at her touch, her mouth on his skin. An echoing desire blazed through her. He reached down and unzipped his jeans with one hand as he reached under the hem of her shirt with the other. Grabbed the waistband of her panties. And ripped them away.

Cade rolled her under him without breaking her hold on his throat and settled between her thighs. Smoothly, he thrust into her. She was so ready for him he slid inside like a knife into clotted cream. She threw her legs across his narrow rump and hooked her ankles together, then held on as he began to drive, moving with long, hungry strokes that matched the starving pull of her mouth on his throat.

He groaned as she hummed against his skin, her head spinning with the shared pleasure of his touch, his size, her own slick, tight grip. They came at the same instant, fused in a hot explosion that detonated in her skull like a bomb.

When it was over, she gently released her grip on his throat as he slowly slid out of her. "Yeah," he croaked. "I could do that for another three hundred years."

Remembering the dream, she just hoped he'd have the chance.

Val had thought her senses were acute before, but now each sensation was so much more powerful, even the most mundane act became a sensual assault. Colors were brighter, more vivid, smells stronger, sounds louder. When they took a shower together, every touch of Cade's hands as he lathered her head with shampoo felt more deeply erotic than ever.

They made love again, but she held off on drinking from him; she saw from his thoughts he'd need to go out hunting as it was.

"Besides," Cade told her as he got up to dress, "I need to get things straightened out with the cops so we can go home."

"That's not going to be easy," Val warned him, speaking from years of experience as a police beat reporter. "They're going to want to know why it took you so long to check in. It's pretty damn obvious those mercenaries broke into the house planning to kill somebody, so you probably won't be charged. But I'd be prepared for some tough questions if I were you."

"I am," Cade told her, tugging on his shirt. "I'll even have the answers."

"As soon as you can think some up."

"Well, I can't exactly tell the truth, can I?" He grinned and sauntered toward the door.

"Bring me a change of clothes when you come back," she told him as he stepped outside. "I'm definitely ready to part company with these shorts."

Cade looked over his shoulder and gave her a wicked smile. "In that case, I'll hurry."

As the door closed behind him, Val chuckled. And grimaced at the smell of old sweat. "Okay, that's it," she grumbled under her breath. "I don't care if he does bring me a change of clothes, this outfit is getting washed. I can't stand to be in the same area code with it."

Val was ankle deep in water, wringing out her shorts in the tub when she looked up to see Abigail's head sticking through the shower curtain. She jumped—and yelped as her head smacked into the ceiling. Coming down hard, she slipped and fell on her backside with a splash that sent water arcing across the bathroom.

"Dammit, Abigail!" Lying in the tub, she glared up at the ghost and rubbed her aching head. "Don't do that!"

The ghost's glowing little face looked suffused, as if she was fighting a laugh. ***I gather you got through the Change. You must have leaped three feet straight up.***

"Apparently," Val grumbled, as she sat up and started to clamber out of the tub. Her behind protested, and she rubbed it, eying the ghost resentfully. "Though I'd rather have learned about that particular talent some other way."

Abigail sobered. ***Unfortunately, you have a great many other difficult lessons ahead of you. Cade's going to have to teach you how to amplify his power, and that won't be easy.***

She lifted a brow. "You mean it's not automatic?

No. It took Ridgemont more than a week to teach him the skills. It will be even harder for you, since you've never done any fighting at all.

Reminded of her vision of Cade's loss to Ridgemont, Val frowned uneasily. "Abigail, I had a…dream. It…."

The ghost frowned, picking the memory out of her mind. ***That's the arena at Ridgemont's mansion.***

"He's got his own arena?"

Abigail shrugged. ***It's where he taught Hirsch and Cade swordplay.***

"So that part of the dream is real," Val said. "Damn. I was hoping it was just a nightmare. Could it be a memory of something that's already happened?" Reading the answer in the ghost's worried eyes, she winced. "I was afraid of that. What the hell are we going to do?"

Make sure it doesn't come true.

Chapter Eighteen

When an hour passed and Cade still had not returned, Val felt exhaustion begin to weigh at her. Her body was still adjusting to the Change; like a newborn baby, it needed to sleep. Leaving her clothes drying over the shower rod, she wrapped herself in a sheet and curled up naked on the bed.

Val woke to a burning sensation. Opening her eyes, she discovered her hand was lying in a shaft of morning sunlight. She frowned at it muzzily. The skin of her fingers felt hot, swollen—as if she'd been lying out on the beach too long. But….

"Oh, hell!" She jumped back so fast her vampire muscles propelled her halfway across the room to bang against the wall. Catching herself barely in time to keep from falling on her face, Val scurried around the bed toward the window and gingerly flicked the curtains closed. "It's a good thing the bursting into flame things is a myth," she grumbled under her breath, "or I'd be one long cigarette ash by now."

This vampire business was going to take some getting used to.

She padded naked into the bathroom to check her clothes. They were wrinkled and slightly damp, but she knew her body heat would dry them. She dressed, grimacing at the feeling of clammy fabric against her skin.

Her stomach rumbled. Suddenly she was ravenously hungry. An image flicked through her mind—Cade, sprawled gloriously naked under her, tilting his head back…. Her nipples peaked, and her fangs slid to their full length in her mouth.

Frowning, she reached for one of the toothbrushes Cade had

bought from a vending machine. "Usually when I'm this hungry, I fantasize about Egg McMuffins, not Stud McMuffins," she grumbled to herself. There was something more than a little unnerving about this new Hunger and the way it combined the need for sex and blood.

Squirting toothpaste onto the brush, she lifted it and peeled her lips back from her teeth—and stopped short at the sight of the two neat fangs. They were sharp, white, and an inch long. "Oh, God," she murmured. "I really am a vampire. What the hell have I done?"

Gazing hypnotized into her own mouth, she didn't even hear the knock. She finally jolted from her trance at the sound of the motel room's door swinging open as a cheery voice called, "Housekeeping!"

God knew the room needed it; Cade had hung out the "Do Not Disturb" sign days ago during her illness. "Come in!" she called back, and closed her mouth to hide the fangs.

Val walked into the bedroom as the maid bustled in with a stack of towels in her arms. The scent of shampoo and soap came with her, as intense as if she'd just stepped out of the shower. And something else, dark and musky—the woman's own natural scent.

Val drew in an instinctive breath, never having smelled anything like it. And gasped as the scent of blood flooded her mouth and nose. It didn't smell like Cade's. It was a little blander, a little less fiery somehow. Yet there was something so rich and tempting about it, it made her fangs ache.

She froze in the bathroom doorway, unable to move, paralyzed by the sudden intensity of her need. Walking toward the bathroom, the woman almost ran into her. Startled, the maid looked up and met her gaze. "Is there something...."

And Val could feel her thoughts. Her name was Mary Sanders, and she was working to support her two kids while she went to night school to obtain her nursing degree. She was worried about George Billingham, her live-in boyfriend, who'd fallen off the wagon again. Just yesterday he'd slapped her for not having dinner ready, though she'd worked all day while he'd stayed home watching talk shows and polishing off a bottle of vodka.

"You ought to get rid of that bastard," Val told her. "He's going to put you in the hospital again."

Mary's eyes lost their focus. "Okay," she murmured.

And she'll do it, Val realized in amazement, watching the compulsion close over the woman's mind. *I influenced her. Just then, without even intending to. No wonder Cade uses his power so much. It's instinctive.*

What a terrifying talent. She stared down into the smaller woman's blank face, wondering wildly if she'd done the right thing. Yeah, Mary obviously needed to get rid of George, but what if he hurt her when she told him to get out? And what right did Val have to make that decision one way or another?

Maybe she needed to go looking for George, too....

And maybe you should tell her to tip up her chin, the Hunger whispered suddenly.

Val's eyes widened. *It would be so easy*, the Hunger's dark, soft voice continued. *You don't need much. It won't hurt her, and you can make sure she won't remember.*

"What's going on?" Cade asked from the open motel room door.

She jumped guiltily as he walked in, dressed in his familiar black jeans and black T-shirt. His acute chocolate eyes flicked from her to the maid's blank face. "Oh, hell," he muttered. She felt him touch Mary's thoughts, watched him wince at what he saw there.

"I didn't mean to!" Val burst out, twisting her hands together.

"I know, but you've got to be careful." He sent a wave of psychic energy to erase the accidental compulsion from Mary's mind.

"Even as young as you are, you've got a lot of power. You could do real damage without meaning to." To the maid he added, "Why don't you come back later. I've already checked out, so you can clean up after we're gone."

Mary nodded mechanically and left with the slow, dreamy steps of a sleepwalker.

"But what about George?" Val asked. "He's going to hurt her sooner or later. Badly."

Cade's handsome mouth took on a grim line. "No, he's not. I'm going to have a word with him this evening about the proper treatment of women."

"Can I watch?" She grinned. "In fact, can I slap him around a little?"

He shot her a look and shook his head with a short laugh. "No, you may not, you bloodthirsty little wench."

"Literally," Val muttered with a grimace, remembering how close she'd come to biting the maid.

"Goes with the territory," Cade told her, shrugging. "In the meantime, let's go. I've squared things with the police and brought in a crew to clean up the house. I want to get home."

She flexed her sunburned hand. "But it's daylight."

"I returned the neighbor's car and got the Lexus. The windows are polarized, so if we don't hang out in the parking lot, you won't even get a tan." He pulled the door open and gestured her out.

Cautiously, Val stepped outside, wincing as the morning sunlight instantly assaulted her eyes. Hearing the Lexus' locks click open, she ran toward the car, intent on getting out of the murderous glare. Cade strode ahead to pull the passenger door open for her, and she slid inside gratefully as he went around to the driver's side. "So once we get home, what then?"

"Then," he said grimly, "we get to work."

Val sent him a searching look. "The psychic amplification thing?"

"Yeah." He shot her a sudden, wicked smile. "But that we'll have to do outside, which means we'll have to wait for sunset. In the meantime, we really need to paint the upstairs hallway. I scrubbed down the walls, but there are stains you wouldn't believe."

They did indeed spend most of the day working around the house, repainting the hallway while an installation crew put down new carpet. After her experience with the maid, Val went out of her way to avoid them.

But once night fell and the crew went home, it was time to get to work on a more urgent project.

"We have to learn to amplify each other's energies," Cade told her, as they stepped out into the darkness of the back yard. "Even combined, we don't have the power to take Ridgemont.... "

"What?" She stared at him, outraged. "I thought that was the whole point of this!"

"Will you give me a minute? I meant that if we just put our power together, it's not enough. But if we bounce it back and forth between us, we can intensify it."

Val thought about it, then shook her head. "I don't understand."

"Look, have you ever heard a microphone feedback squeal—that shrill, high pitched sound you hear sometimes when somebody's trying to give a speech?"

"I'm a reporter, remember?" She grimaced, remembering countless meetings, assemblies and speeches. "Any time I'd cover any public gathering, somebody's mic would feed back at least once and deafen everybody in the room."

"Yeah. Well, what happens is the mic is so close to the amplifiers, it picks up its own sound from them, then feeds that sound to the amps, which feed it back to the mic, and on and on. It happens so fast you instantly get a blast of noise."

She shaped her mouth into an O of understanding. "And we've got to do the same thing."

"But quicker. Unfortunately, I've only practiced this a couple of times, and that was in 1872, when Ridgemont made me learn how to do it for him. But he was so damn powerful we never had to actually practice it in combat, and I'm not sure how it's going to work."

Val eyed him grimly. "That sounds encouraging."

"Yeah, well, it's the only game in town. Touch my thoughts."

Like this?

Right. Now deeper, like we do when we make love. Try to feel what I'm feeling.

Val stepped in close, focusing on his dark eyes, the planes and angles of his face, the long, straight blade of his nose and the full curve of his mouth. *You know, you're kind of cute.*

Concentrate. The thought boiled with impatience. *We need to get this. Try to look through my eyes.*

She killed her smile and looked at him harder, fighting to slip into his mind. In the background, she could hear the murmur of his thoughts, the tension, the worry. A image of Ridgemont's fist shooting toward her face flashed through her mind, followed by searing pain that burst in her skull like a bomb. Startled, she stepped back.

"Dammit, you almost had it."

"Was that your memory?"

"Yeah. There are probably a lot of them like that. Ridgemont made a hobby of beating the hell out of me." He sighed. "Look, maybe we're going about this all wrong."

Cade's big hands closed on her shoulders. *Concentrate on this.* The next thing she knew, she was plastered against him as he kissed her. The embrace started out hard and businesslike, but then he gentled it until his lips were moving softly over hers, seducing, caressing.

The warm velvet of his lips felt different to her new senses as they brushed and stroked, the familiar sensations grown startling and intense. His tongue slipped into her mouth to swirl a sweet dance around hers. She felt his Hunger grow.

Cade's tense body relaxed against her, and she sank into him, savoring the long, hot strength of his body. Just as he felt her, slim and soft against him. His mind caught hers, drawing her closer in an embrace that matched the one their bodies shared.

See how you feel to me, he thought. *So good.*

She got a startling image of her own body, naked and languorous, nipples hard and legs spread. She flushed in embarrassment, but at the same time she felt his hungry approval as he thought, *You're so beautiful.*

Now you're playing with me, she told him. *That looks like something out of a centerfold.*

You're telling me! The male satisfaction in his mental voice made her giggle. He kissed her again, hungrily, his mouth moving on hers in delicious lust.

She reached for a memory of him, rock hard and hungry, his black eyes gleaming. *You're not so bad yourself, cowboy.*

The image startled him as much as his memory had her. *I think you're idealizing me.*

Uh-uh. She began kissing her way up his jaw toward his right ear. *You're the sexiest man I've ever met.*

He pulled her closer, his arms closing tight around her as his mind drew hers deeper. Nibbling his earlobe, she felt the delicate sensation of teeth on her own ear, though she knew his mouth was nowhere near it. The sensation stopped her dead, and the gentle nibbling ceased.

It's a mental echo, he told her. *Closer. You've almost got it.* She nibbled again, concentrating on the ghostly sensation until it intensified.

With a jolt, she found herself suddenly standing in a different position, looking down at a slim shoulder. A weight fell against her. Her arms supported something limp and heavy. She turned her head and saw a woman's profile, eyes closed, mouth slightly open, apparently out cold with her auburn head resting on Cade's shoulder.

Where the hell did she come from?

It's you, Val, Cade told her. *You did it. You're in my body.*

Her eyes snapped open. Straightening with a jerk, Val looked up at Cade a little wildly.

"Damn," he said. "We lost it."

She pulled away from him, blinking. "What the hell happened?"

"We fused." He reached out to brace her as she staggered. "Your consciousness was inside me."

The hair rose on the back of her neck. "What about *my* body?"

Reading her fear, he shot her a look. "Do you think I'd let you do anything that would hurt you?"

She sighed. "No. So what happened?"

"When our minds fused, you passed out. Your autonomic nervous system continues to function, though, operating your heart and lungs and everything else. It's like a deep sleep—well, more than that. A doctor examining you would probably think you were in a coma."

"My mind left my body?" She didn't like the sound of that.

He shook his head. "No, but the link is so deep it seems to. As soon as we separate, you regain consciousness."

"This is scaring the hell out of me, Cade."

Cade scrubbed a hand over his face. "Yeah. It should. Unfortunately it's the only way we have a chance in hell of killing Ridgemont."

"But what if we can't?" She swallowed, remembering that terrifying dream. "What if we lose?"

"I'll get killed." Cade shrugged. "Fortunately, if I die when we're fused, it won't kill you—it'll just throw your consciousness back into your body."

She glowered and fisted her hands on her hips. "To a very short life as Ridgemont's sex toy. Not that I'd care, with you dead."

"Do you want to back off from this?"

"He wouldn't let us even if I did." Val smiled tightly. "Besides, it doesn't take telepathy to know you've never run from a fight in your life."

He looked down at her, his dark eyes solemn. "I'd run from this one to keep you alive."

"Yeah, well, the only way to do that is kick Ridgemont's undead butt." She sighed. "What are we supposed to do now?"

"Try it again." Cade stepped against her and slid his arms around her waist. "At least this particular method has its charms." Smiling, he lowered his head and took her mouth with his. She reached for him, with her arms and her mind.

And became one with him.

The next thing Val knew, she was looking down at her own unconscious face. "This is just too creepy." The words came out in Cade's deep voice.

"Don't do that," he said, swinging her body easily into his arms. She was startled at how light she felt. "Look, don't try to do anything at first, okay? Just watch ..." He stumbled and caught himself. "Or you'll trip me. My muscles can only obey one set of commands at a time. And you're not used to running a body this size."

I hope the neighbors aren't watching, or they'll think you're talking to yourself, she told him, switching to mental communication.

It's so dark, they can't see a damn thing back here. And a good thing, too. He carried her inside and laid her down on the living room couch. As he straightened, he looked down at the slim, pale woman on the couch.

"That does not look like me," Val said.

"It's really disconcerting to hear my voice saying somebody else's sentences."

Sorry. Do I really look like that? I'm…small.

You're used to seeing yourself from close up in the mirror, Val. Different perspective. Besides, I'm six inches taller than you are. Compared to me, you are small.

Should I get a boob job?

An image flashed through his mind of her round, bare breast just before his mouth closed around her nipple. *No. You're perfect.*

That wasn't a comment, I was just thinking. You know, sometimes thoughts just flash through your mind that you don't want to share with the world.

I'll remind you of that the next time some really stacked blonde walks by.

Wickedly, she pictured a pig with fangs and a vampire cape.

Yeah, well, you seem to have developed a taste for bacon, darlin', so you're just gonna have to live with it. Let's get to work.

As he headed back outside, she wondered how close she had to be for the link to work.

I'm not sure, Cade replied. *We could experiment and see. I think it depends on how strong we are.*

We'd better find out. I'd hate for us to get out of range in the middle of the fight.

Good point. He frowned as he stepped out onto the yard. Val was instantly distracted by the sensation of cool grass under his feet and the rich, floral scent of spring in the air. *Pay attention,* he told her. *We're going to start with a series of* katas.

She was unfamiliar with the word, but she knew its meaning from his memories: martial arts routines designed to drill skills until they became automatic. *Why does somebody who can bench press a Buick need to study karate?*

When you're planning to fight an eight hundred year-old immortal, you study any damn thing you can. Cade slid into the drill, his body moving fluidly as he threw punches and kicks at imaginary opponents.

He'd begun practicing the various martial arts in the 1970s, so now he no longer had to think about what he was doing. For Val it was profoundly disconcerting, looking out of his eyes to see a long, thickly muscled arm or leg piston out instead of the slimmer, shorter one her mind insisted should be there.

And the sheer animal speed and power of his body was amazing. Feeling him move, experiencing the intense concentration and discipline he'd worked to build over the decades—it all touched off a slow, hot burn of arousal in Val. She wanted to savor that hard, delicious strength sliding into her, taking her....

He stopped in his tracks. *Val, if you don't cut that out, I'm going to have to go back inside and ride that delicious little body of yours, whether you're in it or not.* There was a sensation of heat and heaviness in his groin she suddenly realized was a rock-hard erection.

Oh, she said, mortified. *I'm sorry!*

No, you're not. And I'm not either. But we really need to get this down before we play.

Trying to distract herself, Val focused on watching everything around them as he went back to his *katas*. But that only reinforced her disorientation, since Cade's vampire senses were even more acute than her own. The night was full of a constant rustle and scuttle she'd never heard before, and the air was redolent with smells she couldn't even identify. Even the trees and grass looked strange, each leaf and stem visible in the darkness.

Yet to Cade, it was all familiar. He knew that crack and rustle was a cat slipping over the grass behind them, recognized that the sharp, musky smell meant a possum had waddled through three or four hours earlier.

Three or four hours? You can smell something that went by three or four hours ago at this distance?

Well, yeah. There was an undercurrent of *Can't anyone?* to the thought. It had been so long since Cade had looked at the world through mortal senses that he no longer remembered what it was like.

Suddenly Val had the dizzying sensation that she was becoming not human. And it would only become worse as the years went on. Opening her eyes, she looked up at the living room ceiling, back in her own body again.

Val?

Give me a minute, dammit. She sat up on the couch, staring down at her hands as she laced her fingers together tightly. She'd never noticed how delicate and thin they were compared to Cade's huge paws. Even her own body felt like a stranger.

"Val, we have to do this."

She looked up to see him standing in the doorway. And felt the punch of vertigo. For the first time in her life, she knew what it really felt like to be somebody else. "I can never go back to what I was," Val said softly. "I'm losing myself."

"No, Val. You're not. You're stronger than you think," Cade said, then laughed softly. "Hell, you're the strongest person I know. As time goes on, you'll find yourself settling into your new body. It won't seem so strange then."

He walked over to the couch, sat down beside her, and picked up one of her hands to hold it comfortingly. She curled her fingers into his and leaned against his muscled shoulder. She could feel him reining in his impatience, his drive to master this new skill so he could reach the goal he'd been working toward for the past one hundred and twenty years.

Killing Ridgemont was more than an obsession to him, she realized, understanding him in a whole new way now that she'd *been* him. For Cade, slaying the ancient was a holy calling. His comment about running from the fight with his enemy revealed how much he truly loved her.

"What if we can't do it?" Val asked softly, the memory of the dream tormenting her. "What if *I* can't do it? I don't want to get you killed."

Cade opened his mouth, then shut it and sighed. "I started to give you a rah-rah 'buck up' speech, but you know I'm not any more certain of pulling this off than you are. I just know we aren't going to get a damn thing sitting on this couch. C'mere."

He didn't mean physically. She gritted her teeth and launched herself. Watched while he caught her body before it could hit the floor. Cade arranged her limp form on the couch again, then walked back outside to start another kata. *You're going to have to start doing it with me,* he told her. *The idea is to amplify each other, so we have to work together.*

He pivoted. She tried to move with him, but halfway into the turn his left leg locked. They hit the ground with a jarring thud.

"Dammit, Val, my… " he began, at the same time she said, "I'm sorry!" His mouth froze open, his throat locked, and a deep grating sound came from his chest. She quit trying to talk, and Cade exploded, "…muscles can only obey one set of commands at a time!"

Look, I've never done this before! What do you expect?

His anger collapsed. *Ah, hell. I know this is difficult. We're just going to have to learn to get synchronized.*

What if they did that fighting Ridgemont?

We won't, he told her, reading her fear. *Once we drill long enough, it will become second nature.*

How much time is that going to take, Cade?

I have no idea.

We'd better get started, then.

Chapter Nineteen

They worked for hours, spinning and turning—and often falling on Cade's face—until the sweat ran off his body and bruises mottled his skin. Gradually he began to move more smoothly as she learned the trick of merging so deeply with him she was no longer even aware of herself.

Finally he stopped. *I think that's enough. We'll work on the strength amplification tomorrow night.*

With a sigh, Val let go and opened her eyes to stare at the living room ceiling. The aches and exhaustion that had been building for hours were suddenly gone. In their place was a long, deep throb in her skull, a vicious headache that seemed to have appeared from nowhere.

The French doors opened and Cade limped in. His dark hair stood straight up, and his knee was bleeding from a nasty scrape. She scooted over for him as he threw himself on the couch. Knowing what he'd been wanting for the past hour, she got up and went to the kitchen to scoop a beer out of the refrigerator.

"I think I got the better end of this deal," she told him, popping the top as she handed it to him. "We work your ass off, and I'm completely rested." She felt another nasty throb. "Except for a killer headache."

He downed the beer in one long, rippling swallow. Crunching the can in his hand, he said, "Wait 'til we fight Ridgemont."

She winced.

Despite her relative lack of injuries, Val found herself feeling so battered she decided a shower was in order. But when she walked into the master bathroom, her eyes fell on the enormous garden tub that sprawled next to one of those gorgeous stained glass windows. Around the tub stood bayberry candles in crystal bowls, and in one corner sat a bottle of peach-scented bubble bath. Evidently Camille had left them behind.

Acting on impulse, Val stripped, ran a tub of deliciously hot water, poured in a generous quantity of bubble bath, and lit the candles. With a sigh of sheer, voluptuous pleasure, she sank into the water and leaned back, closing her eyes. The pop and hiss of tiny bubbles filled her vampire senses as the silken flow of water caressed her skin. *God,* she thought, *I needed this.*

She relaxed into the heat and scent, letting herself half-float as her headache drained away. Until Cade's velvety voice purred, "Mmmm. A naked redhead and bubbles."

Val opened one eye. He stood in the doorway, a delicate champagne flute in each big hand, wearing nothing but a wicked smile. She felt a sweet, hot tingle just looking at him. "A naked vampire and champagne," she said, watching him stroll into the room. "I didn't think we drank…wine."

"We drink all kinds of things," he told her, handing her both glasses. "If you'll allow me to join you, I'll demonstrate."

"Come on in, if you don't mind smelling like peaches." She sat up and scooted forward to let him get into the tub behind her. Cade slipped in and settled into the water, which sloshed alarmingly near the tub rim. Val settled back against his hard chest with a sigh of pure delight, then handed him one of the flutes.

He tilted the glass up for a sip, the relaxed under her. "God, I needed this."

"Just what I was thinking."

"Sorry about the slave driver bit. I'm a little wired when it comes to Ridgemont."

She twisted her head around to look up into his face with a wicked smile. "You think?"

"Smartass."

"In any case...." Val stopped to drink a sweet, bubbling mouthful of the champagne, "I don't want to hear the 'R' word any more tonight. I just want to sit here in the candlelight and bubbles and be hedonistic."

He put down his glass on the floor beside the tub and reached around to gently brush his thumbs over her soft nipples. Instantly, they peaked and began to blush. "Is this what you had in mind?"

She let her head drop back against his shoulder. "You read my mind."

"Oh, yeah. And when I did, I found out what a bad, bad girl you are." Slowly, lazily, he stroked and tugged the little pink tips until they were stiff and rosy.

They weren't the only things, either. Val could feel him hardening against her back. She bit her lip and moaned.

"You know, I really like bad, bad girls. Especially when they have such pretty breasts," he rumbled in her ear.

She stroked his hard, strong thighs under the water, enjoying the delicate currents that swirled around her fingers. "You're pretty bad yourself, Cowboy."

"Let's see just how bad I can be."

Murmuring dark, hungry words, they curled together, stroking and touching, listening to the pop of soap bubbles, inhaling the scent of sex and peaches. "I love you," Cade said suddenly in a low, hard voice. "No matter what else happens, never forget that."

"And I love you," she murmured back. "Loving you, knowing you—it's worth the risk. It's worth it all. Even knowing we'll have to fight...."

"Don't say that bastard's name," he growled, rolling her beneath him. Water sloshed. Bubbles popping around her shoulders, she smiled hotly up at him. "There's no room in this tub for anybody but us."

He slid into her, a long, hot stroke into her ready cream that tore an erotic gasp from her lips.

Dark eyes focusing down into hers, Cade began to surge against her in slow, driving thrusts that sent the bath water sloshing over the rim of the tub. Dazzled, she watched him, memorizing the strong lines of his face in the glow of the candlelight.

Still filling her hard, he leaned down and took her mouth in a kiss that tasted of champagne, sex—and desperation. In minutes, he spilled her burning over the edge into a long, rolling climax and followed her down, blazing.

We're going to break every bone in your hand, Val told him the next night.

Not if we do it right. Carefully, Cade positioned the safe door against the massive oak. He'd picked out the foot-thick chunk of solid steel at a scrap yard earlier in the day, paid the owner and told him they'd be back for it later, after they got a crew together to transport it. The crew actually consisted of himself and Val, though they were careful not to let anyone see them pick up the door when they returned that evening; it weighed close to a ton. They'd had to borrow a neighbor's pickup truck to transport it, and the vehicle had sunk on its wheels when they'd loaded the door onto it.

Val was still a little shaken at how easy it had been to lift the damn thing.

By myself, I could dent a door like this, but not much more, Cade told her as he took up a martial-arts horse stance in front of the thick steel panel. *Ridgemont could put his fist through it. We have to be able to do the same.*

She winced and thought longingly of her own body, lying unconscious on the couch. *This is going to hurt.*

Pain is good for you.

No, it's not. That's why they call it pain. Normal people avoid it.

Look, we've mastered moving together. Now we have to learn how to amplify my strength, and that's a lot trickier. Besides, if we do this right, it's not really my fist that touches the metal, it's the force we generate together.

You're beginning to sound like a Kung-fu *rerun, Grasshopper.*

Cade sighed. *Just watch.*

He gathered himself. His fist pistoned out and back so fast a mortal wouldn't have been able to see it at all. When she looked at the door, there was a large dent in its scarred metal surface.

I didn't even feel you hit it.

That's because I didn't.

And in his mind, she saw that his fist had acted as the carrier for the wave of telekinetic force he'd sent shooting toward the target. What she had to do was pick up that force and amplify it, then shoot it back to him.

Understand?

Maybe. Let's try it.

This time as he gathered his power, she tried to help build the energy. His fist flashed out, but the dent was no bigger than the first one.

Timing's off.

You hit it too fast. I didn't have time to amplify it.

We have to do this fast, Val. Ridgemont is not going to be fighting me in slow motion.

Over and over again, they practiced, pounding on the door until Cade's body ached and sweat trailed itching paths down his ribs. The dents gradually grew deeper, but not deep enough.

"You're holding back!" he told her. "You've got to give it everything you've got, or this isn't gonna work."

"I am *not* holding back!" Val snarled, barely even noticing the deep growl of Cade's voice.

"Do you remember that damn dream, Val? Do you want it to come true? Put your back into it!"

Furious, she rammed her fist at the door, not knowing or caring that it was Cade's fist, barely aware when he picked up the energy and slammed it back at her, or that she returned it like a tennis volley, all at the speed of thought.

There was a thunderous boom and the shriek and grate of metal.

Stunned, Val stared at Cade's arm. It was buried to the elbow in a ragged hole in the steel. "The door isn't that deep. Where's the rest of your arm?"

"I think it's in the tree."

"What the fuck are you doing?" a strange male voice demanded. "Do you know what time it is?"

Startled, they looked up to find an irate potbellied man dressed in slippers and robe standing in the yard a few feet away. "It's three o'clock in the goddamn morning," the man snarled. "What the hell are you doing pounding on sheet metal with a ball peen hammer at three o'clock in the goddamn morn… " His eyes fell on the thick door gleaming in the light of the full moon, Cade's arm buried in it to the elbow.

He paled and began backing up. "Uh…Sorry to bother you. I think I'll just go…ah…take a sleeping pill."

They watched him hurry away. *Shouldn't you hypnotize him or something?*

By morning, he'll have convinced himself he dreamed the whole thing. Besides, I seem to be stuck.

With that skill mastered, they spent the next several nights drilling with sword and shield. Each night, after they finished attacking imaginary opponents in the moonlight, Cade would take her out to stalk real drug dealers and thieves so she could perfect the use of her powers.

They'd just pulled into the driveway after one of those excursions when Val heard the phone ringing inside the house. She expected the caller to give up before she got in to answer it, but it went right on shrilling.

Something about that loud, demanding chirp dug spurs of anxiety into her skin. She raced inside and jerked the phone out of its cradle, Cade at her heels. "Hello?"

"Val?" It was Beth's voice, sounding watery and strained.

The bottom dropped out of her stomach. "What's wrong?"

"I screwed up, Val."

"What? Baby, what do you…"

Ridgemont's voice came on the line. "Hello, darling. Let me talk to Cade."

A wave of cold rolled up from her belly and across her face. "What have you done to her, you son of a bitch?"

"Nothing, yet. But that's going to change if I don't hear the gunslinger's voice on the line in the next…."

Cade gently pulled the phone from her stiff fingers. "Okay, I'm here."

"Having fun, McKinnon?" With Val's enhanced hearing, she had no trouble making out Ridgemont's voice.

"Until now. What are you doing to Val's sister?"

"As I said, nothing so far. But I'm been giving it a great deal of thought. You do know Valerie isn't the only Chase sister who's Kith?"

Oh, God. *Beth is Kith?* Val stared at the phone, staggered. *And Ridgemont's captive?*

"Why?" she managed, her voice choked. "Why did he drag her into this? I thought the whole idea of turning me was to give you a fighting chance. If he Changes her…"

"I've no intention of doing any such thing—yet," Ridgemont said, apparently having overheard her comment. "But it occurred to me that having had you, the gunslinger might decide not to put you at risk by fighting me. Now I've given you both a little incentive."

"We were coming!" Val snarled at the phone. "You didn't need to… "

"She's really quite lovely, you know. I'm not sure how long I can resist the temptation. You'd be well advised to be on the next flight up here."

Cade's face set like stone. "We'll be there."

"Of course." There was a smile in his voice. "That heroic streak makes you rather predictable, McKinnon. You really should do something about it."

The phone clicked as he hung up.

"How did he find her?" Val whispered, panic and rage beginning to rise. "How the *hell* did he find her? Did we give her away somehow? I know he didn't get it from me; I didn't know where she was."

"It doesn't matter," Cade said, walking over to the phone book sitting on the kitchen counter. "We've got to deal with it one way or another. Go pack us a bag while I book the flight."

Without another word, she raced for the stairs and took them three at a time. She charged into their bedroom to snatch open the closet door, grab Cade's shoulder bag and one of her own, and throw both of them on the bed. Hurriedly, she crossed to the bureau to dig out a change of underwear and a pair of jeans for each of them.

Judging by her own experience, she knew Ridgemont hadn't had time to change Beth, but there'd been plenty of time for his other hobbies. She shuddered, remembering images she'd seen in

Cade's mind of the ancient's treatment of women.

Then she stiffened at another memory, this one her own: Ridgemont smiling down at her naked body after the mercenaries had taken her. *"I could easily persuade myself that abusing you for a while would drive Cade into a very satisfying display of rage."*

Oh, God.

When Cade stepped into the bedroom, she was crying stormily and stuffing clothes into an overnight bag until it bulged so full they'd never be able to zip it.

His heart twisting at the grief and rage he could feel radiating from her, Cade walked over and gently pried the pair of jeans from her hands. "That's enough, darlin'. We only need one change of clothing as it is. Why don't you sit down and let me finish this?"

She fell onto the bed and buried her face in her hands, her slim shoulders shaking. "God, Cade, I can't fail her, too!"

He paused in the act of pulling a sweatshirt from the overstuffed bag as he picked up the torrent of guilt swirling in her mind. "You haven't failed anybody, Val."

"Yes, I did." Her tone was so flat and defeated, he had to look deeper. She was remembering her mother, naked and struggling while Hirsch raped her as Ridgemont fed on her father.

He sighed and sat down on the bed, slipping an arm around her shoulders. "Val, knowing what you do about us now, what do you think you could have done? You were a lone twelve-year-old girl, and we were vampires. And even at that, you still managed to save your sister."

She lifted her head with a snap and glared at him from red, swollen eyes. "But I haven't saved her this time, have I? We let the son of a bitch get her."

"But he's not going to keep her. We will get her away from him, I swear to you."

"But what's he done to her in the meantime, Cade? And what if we lose? He'll kill us, but she's not going to be that lucky. I don't want her to live in the kind of hell you did for the next hundred years." She took a deep, hitching breath. "Or until he kills her."

Cade reached out and took her chin in his hand so her eyes met his. "Then I guess that means we just won't lose. Will we?"

She stared back at him, and he let her read his determination and the desperation that mirrored her own. Her chin firmed. "No. We aren't going to lose."

They got lucky on booking the flight to New York. Val huddled next to MacKinnon, one hand clasped in his, taking comfort in the sensation of his warm, long fingers. Despite her new nature, she found that terror affected her the way it always had—with roiling nausea. Her vampire senses didn't help, assaulting her with a bewildering variety of smells: plastic, cologne, sweat, blood, jet fuel. She knew she would have lost it at least once if not for the waves of calm her lover broadcast at her, helping settle her stomach with a thought.

Far back in her mind, a small voice kept gibbering, *We're not ready for this. I need more practice. What if I screw up? What if I trip him again and get him killed? And what about the dream? What if it comes true?*

You're not going to get me killed, Cade thought back. *Look, I've fought Ridgemont before....*

And lost.

Because I didn't have you. The bastard has been drilling me for decades, getting me ready for this day. I know how he thinks, I know how he fights. We can defeat him.

The problem with sharing minds, she told him, *is it's damn hard to give the other person a pep talk when she knows you've got the same doubts.*

Yeah, well, we both need to push them aside. Doubt can kill us. We are going to do this. We are going to succeed. Concentrate on that.

She clamped her hands around his. And struggled to forget her fear.

As they flew toward New York, dawn was breaking. Val watched in dread as the sky lightened from black to deep indigo and realized she'd never see a sunrise the same way again.

She might never see a sunrise again, period.

At that thought, she put aside her dread of what the sun might do to her vampire body and concentrated on the slow bloom of light across the sky. Purple shaded into rose, lightened into pink, then intensified into salmon before blazing into hot burning orange as a slice of the sun slid over the horizon. The light stabbed into her eyes so hard she winced in pain and had to turn away. Had it always been like that, she wondered, eyes watering, or was it her new senses that let her see the glory?

"Some of both," Cade murmured in her ear. "Plus, when you're getting ready for a fight, everything's more intense, more real. I guess that's why Ridgemont does this. He's lived so damn long, just about the only time he really feels alive is when he knows he could die."

She snorted a strangled laugh. "I guess it's some comfort he's got that much faith in our ability to give him a run."

As they landed, Val's nerves coiled tighter and tighter. Yet when she touched Cade's mind, she found only a cool steadiness. The only fear he felt was for her.

She saw a flash of something—Ridgemont with a bullwhip in his hand, a memory of pain so intense it made her gasp. Twisting to look in a mirror and seeing Cade's broad back slicked in blood, flesh torn in a dozen places. Sickened, she whispered, "Why?"

"Because he could." There was hate in Cade's eyes. "And I couldn't stop him."

My sister is in the hands of that.

"Not for long," he growled.

"I guess we need to rent a car," Val said to Cade, as they walked into the airport lobby.

"Yeah, I …"

"Hey, Cade!"

They turned to see a massively built man in a copy of Cade's old chauffeur's uniform. Val saw from his thoughts that his name was Bobby Mason, Ridgemont's backup driver. "Boss sent me to pick you up," he said.

Cade looked at Val and shrugged.

Is it really safe?

Yeah, he told her. *Ridgemont wants a straight-up fight. For once, he isn't going to play games.* His eyes flickered. *Not with me, anyway.*

They both knew Beth might not have been so lucky. Val's stomach gave another violent wrench, and she took a deep breath to calm it.

"So what the hell's going on, Cade?" Mason asked after relieving Val of her carry-on. "Hirsch has disappeared, and the boss won't say where he went. Not that I miss the sonofabitch. And the boss has this girl locked up …"

"Has he hurt her?" Val demanded.

The big chauffeur froze, his mouth open. She saw a pinwheel of memories in his mind—*Beth, pale and frightened as Mason escorted her to her room, Ridgemont grinning...*

Let him go, Val. You're using too much force.

She started at Cade's mental command, and Mason jolted, staring down at her with a sick, glassy look in his eyes. She caught a ghost of a thought, just as she'd plucked his name from his mind: *I've got to quit this job …*

She felt a sudden wave of shame. "I'm sorry."

"Don't worry about it," the big man mumbled. The thought, *Another fucking vampire,* zipped through his mind and was immediately stifled. His eyes snapped guiltily to hers, and he flinched.

She could see it all in his memory. Having worked for Ridgemont for two years, he'd been backhanded more than once for a careless thought. His jaw had been broken twice and his skull fractured by those offhand slaps, but he'd discovered he just couldn't duck fast enough. Yet whenever he opened his mouth to quit, Ridgemont would look at him and freeze the words on his tongue. He'd thought about just slipping away, but somehow he couldn't do it.

Ridgemont's got him under a compulsion, Val thought.

Yeah. And it's time I do something about that. Cade dropped his bag on the floor, then stooped to reach inside it. Pulling out a couple of stacks of cash—and ignoring the startled stares of passersby—he handed them to Mason. "There's your pay, plus enough to keep you and your family while you find another job."

Mason shot him an agonized look. "I can't."

Cade stood and started to reach into his mind, but Val stopped him with a hand on his shoulder. "Let me." At his lifted brow, she shrugged. "I think I owe him."

He nodded. Biting her lip, she looked into Mason's desperate blue eyes and searched for the alien command that held him. She found it easily enough, but instantly realized she didn't know what to do with it.

Smooth it away, Cade told her.

Nodding, she concentrated, gently erasing the compulsion, working hard to press it out of his thoughts without hurting the mind beneath. Until, at last, it was gone. Val took a deep breath in relief. "You're free."

A broad grin spread across his face as he realized it was true. "God, lady, thank you!" Mason fumbled in his pocket, pulled out a set of keys and slapped them into Cade's hand. "Here's the keys to Ridgemont's cars. Tell him he can kiss my ass." He hesitated, looking Cade in the eye. "You're the only one of them that ain't a fuckin' monster."

Cade nodded. "Just so you know, Hirsch is dead. And I'm going to kill Ridgemont."

The big man whistled softly. "You sure that's a good idea?" An image flashed through his mind—Cade on his knees, blood pouring from his mouth and nose, right arm broken and cradled against his side.

Cade looked at Val. "I've got a secret weapon."

Mason glanced at her skeptically, then smoothed his expression into an easy smile. "Sure." He hesitated, guilt shooting through him. Val could see he hated letting Cade go against Ridgemont with nothing but a woman for backup. "I wish I could help you, buddy."

"Yeah, well, we both know why you can't. Go get yourself a new life, Bobby. And in case I screw it up, make it far from here."

The big man stuffed the cash in his pockets and thought of his wife and three-year-old son. He turned and walked away through the crowd with a stride just short of a run.

Val watched him go. *It's a scary power we've got, Cade.*

Yeah. I'd have freed him long before now, but I knew Ridgemont wouldn't have allowed it.

She thought of Beth, and fear slid through her veins like a river of ice. *If that's the way that bastard treats his own help, what's he been doing to my sister?*

I don't know, but we'd better get over there and find out.

Chapter Twenty

The drive to the mansion took more than an hour through the afternoon New York traffic. Luckily, the limo's polarized windows kept out the worst of the light, or Val knew they'd have been fried by time they got there.

As it was, she had entirely too much time to brood. It was all she could do to keep her mind off the image of Cade bleeding and broken she'd seen in all too many memories—his, Abigail's, even Mason's.

Cade himself said nothing, though when she tried to touch his mind, she saw he was busy planning, remembering past fights and trying to work out strategies to counter the ancient's favorite moves.

Without him to distract her, Val felt her fear intensifying. She rolled her shoulders, trying to fight it off. This was necessary. They had to confront Ridgemont if they were going to save Beth. Yet in the back of her mind, a small voice hissed, *Evil. Run.*

Dammit, no. She clenched her fists and gritted her teeth. She was not a coward. She would not leave her sister at that thing's mercy. He had to be stopped for everybody's sake.

But by the time they pulled up at a set of wrought iron gates set in a massive stone wall, Val's heart was pounding so hard it was all she could do to breathe. She watched, swallowing, as Cade glared up at the camera mounted on a pole jutting from the fence. "I'm here to see Ridgemont."

There was a pause. Cade looked over at her in the silence. Despite his grim expression, he sent her a wave of warmth and love that made her fear recede. *I love you, Val. No matter what happens, remember that.*

But even as he comforted her, she could sense the guilt in his mind, the regret at taking her into danger. *Ridgemont set us on this road*, Val reminded him, trying to shield her fear from him. *We're just playing the hand we were dealt. Anyway, I love you, too. And we're both walking out of this thing alive.*

She caught a shadow of doubt before he quickly hid it.

We are going to make it, Cade.

Yeah.

The gates swung open. As they drove through them, a small voice in Val's mind whispered, *Behind you. There's something behind you.* She fought it, trying to concentrate on Cade's grim, handsome profile. But every instinct she had was screaming that clawed hands were reaching over the seat for her face. Until, unable to take anymore, she whipped around and stared wildly over the back seat.

Nothing there.

Shamefaced, she looked over at Cade, who was looking at her sympathetically. She gave him a sickly smile. "I'm a little...jumpy."

"It's not you. You're picking up Ridgemont's power field."

"What? You mean this sense of...." She hesitated to say "evil." "... this feeling is real?"

"Yeah." He pulled over and parked the car.

At the end of a curving walkway in front of them was a huge mansion that looked like something out of an English comedy of manners. It should have looked cheerful in the morning sunlight, sprawling, built of sturdy red brick, covered in ivy, surrounded by perfectly maintained beds of flowers. Yet staring out at it, Val shuddered at the sense of darkness it radiated. "Damn. It's got its own psychic soundtrack."

He nodded and opened the car door. "The first time I saw *Psycho*, I thought, 'I know that music. Follows Ridgemont wherever he goes.'"

"And you lived with that for a hundred and twenty years?" Wrinkling her nose, she got out of the car. "How did you keep from going nuts?"

Cade took her elbow and started up the walk. "You can get used to damn near anything."

"Wait." Val licked her dry lips and stared at the door, fighting to ignore the voice that hissed, *Run.* "Are you just going to go knock? Shouldn't we try to sneak in or something?"

Cade shot her a glance of barely contained impatience. "You don't sneak up on somebody with that much power, Val. He feels us just as clearly as we feel him."

She blinked. "Damn, I hope we don't feel anything like that."

Cade's lips twitched. "I let slip a thought about the *Psycho* comparison once. He said he hears the theme from *Mr. Rogers Neighborhood* when I'm around. I was deeply offended."

Val grinned. "He was pulling your chain. I think it's more like *The Good, the Bad and the Ugly*."

Then the front door opened and evil rolled out in a dark wave. Val whirled to face it as her heart leaped into her throat. Ridgemont grinned at them, then winced up at the blue sky. "Miserable day out. Why don't you come in out of the sun?"

The light was beating down on top of her head, but Val instantly decided she preferred third degree burns to getting any closer to him.

Then Cade lifted a brow at her, and she gritted her teeth. She was not a coward, dammit. But stepping through that door was the hardest thing she'd ever done. Her instincts shrieking a warning, Val made herself saunter past Ridgemont as he stepped back to let them in.

He looked so damn normal with those scarred, battered features and the beefy shoulders that put her in mind of an aging jock. But each time she glanced away, her instincts insisted she'd look back to see rotting flesh. She'd met him before, when Hirsch had captured her. She couldn't understand why she hadn't sensed it then. *Why do I keep wishing for a cross?* Val thought to Cade.

"Wouldn't do you any good," Ridgemont said, with a slow, mocking stretch of the lips.

"If you broadcast, he's going to pick it up," Cade told her, then slanted a look at Ridgemont. "Let's get this done."

The vampire nodded and turned. "I've got the arena ready."

Arena? she thought with a new flare of fear. *Oh, God. They fought in an arena in my dream.*

They followed the ancient, Val grateful not to have him walking behind her. The thought of her sister in his power made her shudder. "Where's Beth?" she demanded.

Ridgemont shot her a white smile that made her flesh crawl. "Waiting for us."

How the hell are we supposed to kill that, Val wondered, trying to keep the thought from surfacing far enough to be read. Despair threatened to swamp her. She shook it off. Despite the dream, Cade believed they had the strength together. That was enough.

It had to be.

As they walked through the house, she was vaguely aware of an impression of wealth and taste—fine paintings, rich carpeting, antique furniture. If not for the sense of suffocating evil, she might have been impressed.

They started down a corridor. Ridgemont nodded toward a set of stairs and told her, "Up that way is the gallery where you'll find your sister."

Automatically, Val started toward the stairs, then stopped in mid-step and looked back at Cade. "What about you?"

"I'll be in the arena," he said. "You'll be able to see me."

Close enough to link when he needed her, she realized, reading the reassurance in his eyes. She nodded and started up the stairs two at a time.

The doorway opened out into a balcony overlooking a huge, round room. Val stepped through warily, her eyes immediately flying to a familiar figure sitting straight and still in a chair. Beth's head snapped around, brown eyes widening with terror until she recognized her sister. "Valerie!" Automatically, she started to get up, only to sink back down. She was handcuffed to the arms of the chair.

"God, baby!" Val rushed over to her and stooped to give her a fierce, hard hug.

"Are you...Ouch! You're squishing me!"

Val remembered her new strength and let go hastily. Swallowing her anxiety, she scanned her sister's face, taking in the pale, tight features, the long, white neck revealed by the scooped neckline of her knit shirt. *No obvious bites.* She sighed in relief.

"Are you okay?" Beth asked, looking her over just as hard.

For a moment, Val almost put a guilty hand to her own throat, then remembered the evidence of Cade's fangs had healed. "I'm fine. Has he hurt you?"

"No, not yet." Beth's soft mouth drew into a grim line. "But I could tell he's been thinking about it."

Val stared grimly down at the steel bracelets locking each of her thin wrists to a chair arm. "We've got to get you out of these cuffs."

Beth frowned down at them. "One of his flunkies has the keys."

"Yeah, well, I don't have time to find him." Val caught a handcuff bracelet in one hand as she braced the other against the arm of the chair. She could do this. She could.

She yanked.

Beth gasped. The thick handcuff chain snapped like a five-dollar necklace. With a grunt of satisfaction, Val grabbed Beth's other arm and broke the chain that held it as well. Grinning, she looked down at her sister's eyes. And saw fear.

Beth shrank back in her chair, gray eyes widening until the whites were visible. "He said McKinnon would make you one of them. He did, didn't he?" The blood drained from her face until it looked as though she'd pass out. "You're a vampire." She spoke the last words in a soft, despairing whisper.

Val's heart contracted in a hard, hopeless ball and lodged in her throat. Oh, hell. "It was the only way to stop Ridgemont," she said, knowing her sister would never understand.

Beth scrambled to her feet and backed away, grief and fear on her face. "What… what are you going to do to me?"

She reached out, then dropped her hand as Beth recoiled. "You don't really think I'm going to hurt you?" Hurt bloomed in her chest.

"Are you?"

"It's not like the movies, Beth! We're not killers."

Beth thrust her chin at Ridgemont, who was watching from the arena below. "He is."

"That's because he's a sociopathic sonofabitch."

"Thank you!" the ancient called mockingly from the arena.

She ignored him. "Cade and I are different. We're still human. We're just changed. It's a virus or something."

Beth shook her head. "Viruses don't give you fangs, Val."

I've got to get her out of here, Val thought. *So just go with this.* Looking into the fear and pain in those beloved gray eyes, Val forced her shoulders to straighten. "Okay, you win, I'm a monster. Get out. You're free. Go."

Her sister shot a look of raw hate over the balcony railing at the ancient, who watched them from below. "*He's* not going to let me leave."

"Ridgemont doesn't give a damn about you," Val said, knowing it was true. "He just used you to make sure we didn't back out." She glanced down at the ancient. "Isn't that right, bloodsucker?"

He grinned, arms crossed, obviously hugely entertained. He now wore something that looked like the armor she'd seen in her vision. So did Cade, who stood nearby. "Oh, yes. In fact..." He glanced at a slim black man who was working with a tangle of equipment at his feet. "Miller?"

The man looked up at him. "Yes, sir?"

The ancient nodded toward the balcony. "Escort that young lady out of the house and call her a cab. I'm done with her."

"Yes, sir." He slipped out the door.

Beth looked at Val, tears flooding her huge gray eyes. She said nothing. Val couldn't think of a single word. Finally Miller stuck his head in the balcony doorway and said, "Miss?"

She looked from him to Val and hesitated, obviously torn.

"You remember one thing," Val said in a low, shaking voice. "No matter what happens, I love you. I'm still human and I still love you, and I'll love you until I die."

Beth stared. "You think he's going to kill you."

"I'm already dead, remember?"

Gray eyes looked into hers for a long, suspended moment. Then Beth drew herself up to her full height. "I'm not leaving you. No matter what you are."

Val cursed silently. "I don't want you here. It's not safe." What if they lost and Ridgemont decided to celebrate afterward?

"I don't care." Her face took on that mulish expression Val knew too well from living with her for eighteen years. "You're still my sister, no matter what else you are."

If Beth refused to go and Ridgemont took her, the whole thing would be pointless. Cade could easily die for nothing. Helpless rage boiled up in Val, triggering a rise of the Hunger. Cursing the bad timing, she started to suppress it, then changed her mind and let it come. Fangs erupted into her mouth. Deliberately, she opened her jaws and bared them, pulling her lips back into a snarl she made as monstrous and terrifying as she could. "LEAVE, Beth!"

Her sister's eyes widened in horror as she stumbled back a pace in shock. Val hissed like a movie vampire. With a strangled scream, Beth whirled and ran past Miller. Her feet thumped on the carpeted stairs as she descended them two at a time. It was all Val could do not to collapse in the chair and sob.

Slow, mocking applause filled the air. "I haven't seen a show this good since I watched the Bard play Hamlet," Ridgemont called mockingly.

A loud crack sounded.

Staggering, the ancient turned, lifting a hand to his bleeding mouth as he stared at Cade. "Why, gunslinger—a sucker punch. I'm surprised at you."

Cade replied with a roll of inventive obscenity, at least half of it in a language Val didn't even understand.

Ridgemont grinned at him. "I didn't even think you knew those words."

"You broadened my horizons, you son of a whore. Let's quit fucking around and finish this." Cade snarled. He looked up at Val, his eyes flat and dark. "Come on, sweetheart."

Shaking off her grief, she moved to the chair, ignoring the handcuffs still hooked to the arms. She sat down and leaned back, closed her eyes and let her body go limp. And went to him.

He enveloped her in all the warmth and sympathy he couldn't show in front of their enemy. *Baby, I'm sorry.*

She thinks I'm a monster.

She's wrong.

Is she? She remembered the look in Mason's eyes, the taste of blood in her mouth.

Look at him and tell me we're anything like that.

Ridgemont watched them with dark amusement while one of his assistants buckled something onto his forearm. He looked smaller through Cade's eyes, but the sensation of age, power and evil swirling around him felt even stronger. *How are we supposed to kill that?* Val demanded, appalled.

Yeah, he's a formidable bastard.

"Lift your arm, Cade," one of the men said to him. "I need to tighten the strap."

He obeyed, and the man began to pull a length of leather attached to a metal cuff around his arm.

What are we doing? What's going on?

He's helping me put on my armor.

Armor? She realized suddenly he was wearing a breastplate made of some metal that gleamed like silver. The attendant grabbed another strap and cinched it tight. *What the hell does Ridgemont think this is—the thirteenth century?*

With a few twenty-first century improvements, yes, Cade thought, arching his chest to check the fit and nodding his approval at the assistant. *The armor is Ridgemont's design, made of a space-age polymer stronger than steel at half the weight. Not that weight means a damn to us.*

Why wear armor at all? Seems he'd want it as dangerous as possible.

Yeah. He just doesn't want it over too quick. And with our strength, it'd be easy for one of us to cut the other in half.

She winced. *Pleasant image.* A thought occurred to her. *Can he hear us?*

No, not in a deep link like this.

Finally Cade was fully armored from the gorget around his

throat to greaves that covered his shins. He flexed his arms and squatted, bunching his muscles, testing the fit, directing the attendant to tighten this or loosen that.

Nearby, Ridgemont was doing the same. The tension grew until it seemed to fill the air like the thick pine scent of the sawdust that covered the floor.

At last the ancient walked over to him, carrying a sheathed long sword in both hands. He presented it with a slight bow. "A new weapon. I think you'll find it satisfactory."

Cade accepted the scabbard and drew the sword from it with a quick, efficient hiss. It was four feet long, with an elegantly simple hilt and cross guard, both in the same gleaming metal as the rest of the weapon. The blade glinted in the bright overhead lighting as he sighted down its length, examining it for flaws, measuring its weight. Val felt his pleasure in its superb balance, the way it seemed to float in his hands. "Acceptable."

Ridgemont inclined his head again and stepped back.

"Cade?" the attendant asked.

Cade sheathed the sword and traded it for the helmet the man held. It was shaped like the helm of a medieval knight, but the visor was made of Plexiglas. He noted the change with pleasure, knowing it would give a better field of view than the slitted faceplate of his old helm, which had cut peripheral vision down to almost nothing.

Dangling from the helmet's conical point was a two-foot length of black horsehair that would reach halfway down his back when he donned it. *What's with the tail?* Val asked.

Ridgemont has a medieval man's taste for the gaudy.

He took the helm in his gauntleted hands and settled it on top of the arming cap he already wore. The cap's thick padding would protect him—at least in part—if Ridgemont landed a blow on the helm.

His assistant handed him his shield, a massive kite-like affair which wasn't nearly as heavy as it would have been if it hadn't been made of high tech alloy. Painted on its smooth silver surface was a wolf, done in medieval style and trimmed in black and red. Last, he picked up his sword.

I can't believe we're supposed to fight in all this stuff, Val thought, as he turned and moved back toward Ridgemont.

Just follow my lead. I'll keep us alive.

You'd better. I've just broken you in.

Ridgemont was dressed in black armor identical to Cade's, except for the dragon that curled on his shield. Val was once again conscious of the waves of power and evil that rolled off him. Her anxiety spiraled.

The power doesn't matter, Cade told her. *He lives, and that means he can die.*

But could they kill him? And what about that damn dream?

Hastily she suppressed that memory and concentrated on Cade, feeling what he felt as he followed Ridgemont to the center of the arena. He had very little fear for himself, and he refused to focus on his fear for her, both to avoid frightening her and to keep his mind on the job at hand. His entire being was focused on one goal: killing Ridgemont, even if he died doing it. Not for revenge or even for honor, but because it was the only way to keep Val safe.

You listen to me, Cade McKinnon, she told him, galvanized by his fatalism. *You are going to survive this. You just damn well make up your mind to that, because I need you, and I'm not giving you up.*

Ridgemont turned to face them in the center of the arena. His eyes flicked over Cade's face through the transparent visor of his helm, and his lips twitched. "It does my heart good to see all that grim, manly determination," he rumbled. "I didn't spend a century torturing you for nothing. As for you, girl—don't disappoint me."

"Oh, I won't," Val said in Cade's voice.

Ridgemont raised his sword in a salute Cade echoed with a short, choppy gesture. Then both men crouched, bringing their shields up.

Oh, God, Val thought, knowing that now they were all committed. It wouldn't end until one of them was dead.

With a roar, the ancient exploded toward Cade, swinging his sword like a scythe in a blow calculated to slice through his helm and take off the top of his head. Cade danced back and blocked. The shield jolted on his arms with a sound like a cannon shot, and the world pinwheeled.

He slammed into the arena floor with a teeth-jarring thud, but he instinctively tucked and rolled. When he bounced back to his feet, Cade saw the blow had knocked him a good fifteen feet. And there was blood on his armor. Ridgemont's sword had chopped through the shield and caught his shoulder.

That was like being hit by a car! Val thought, amazed and shaken.

"You can do better than that, gunslinger!" Ridgemont called mockingly—and leaped for them, crossing the arena in one inhuman bound.

Steady. Here he comes. Cade braced himself, and she desperately worked to reinforce his strength, building the power with him. They held against the second blow, only rocking back on his heels. Val threw all her force into his answering swing, but she was late, and it wasn't enough. The ancient caught the blow on his shield and returned it with an overhead stroke they barely blocked in time.

Ridgemont grinned at them, mocking. "Still not good enough, gunslinger. I've waited too long for this fight to be this easy. You'd better improve your concentration, or I'll go after that tasty little sister when I'm done with you."

Val mentally snarled and blasted more power into Cade's sword swing. It landed on Ridgemont's shield with a satisfying boom.

Then, finally, she stopped thinking, instinctively fusing with her lover until she was no longer conscious of her own existence at all. Instead she fought to turn herself into pure, raw strength, taking everything he gave her and feeding it back blindly, letting him do with it as he would.

The two men circled, feet scuffing in the thick sawdust, barely conscious of the creak of armor and the stink of sweat and steel. At first it was all Cade could do to keep Ridgemont from taking off his head, blocking with his sword or his shield barely in time. But the force and speed of his return swings increased steadily as he and Val fell into the rhythm of amplifying his power.

The taunting grin faded from Ridgemont's face.

Cade blocked a blow to his ribs and spun, Val seizing his power and volleying it back. The sword slashed out. Ridgemont tried to block, too late. The edge cut across his breastplate. He went flying like a Babe Ruth home run.

Bloodlust surging, Cade leaped after him, sword raised. Ridgemont, lying flat on his back, saw him coming and jerked up his shield, rolling into a ball under it. Cade landed on it with both feet and chopped down. But the ancient heaved the shield upward, tossing him like a poker chip, and the blow missed.

Cade bounced up again almost before he hit the ground. Ridgemont sprinted toward him, his face set and grim behind his visor. "It's not so much goddamn fun now, is it, you son of a bitch?" Cade sneered.

The ancient's answering sword stroke cut halfway into his shield. And stuck. The vampire's eyes widened. He fought to wrench the sword free. Cade grinned and swung for his head, but Ridgemont blocked the blow and slammed his shield into Cade's face so hard the bulletproof visor shattered.

Cade felt the tug of the sword pulling out of his shield just as he went down, blinded by blood and pain as jagged bits of plastic cut into his face. Desperately, he wrenched off the ruined helm, ignoring the jagged edges of the shattered visor that ripped his skin. He sensed more than saw Ridgemont's sword descending for his head. His shield was gone. He threw up his sword and parried, knocking the blade aside. Ridgemont chopped down at him again, but Cade rammed a foot into the master vampire's legs so hard his enemy went flying.

Cade scrambled up, mentally cursing the awkward armor that kept him from leaping with his usual vampiric agility. Still blinded by the blood streaming into his eyes from the deep lacerations, he backpedaled, not sure where Ridgemont was. He scrubbed at his eyes, smearing blood on his gauntlet, and managed to clear his vision just in time to see his sire's sword slicing toward his thighs.

He blocked, but Ridgemont reversed his stroke and chopped into his extended sword arm. The armor saved it from being hacked off, but the blade bit deep, shooting agony all the way up Cade's shoulder. He ignored the pain and stabbed for Ridgemont's ribs with all his strength. His sword drove into the black breastplate like a knife through tin foil, and Ridgemont howled.

The ancient grabbed Cade's blade in one gauntlet. Wrenched. The point snapped.

A chill slid over Cade as he looked down at his broken weapon. A third of its length still protruded from his opponent's black armor. Ridgemont looked up at him and grinned tauntingly, a smile Cade knew well from decades of torture.

Blinding rage swept over Cade. Snarling, he slammed his left fist into Ridgemont's visor so hard the plastic spiderwebbed. The ancient backpedaled, swearing, and Cade followed him. Ridgemont had to drop his shield to pull off the ruined helm. Cade used the opening to land another left cross that knocked him off his feet.

The ancient scrambled up and backed off fast, still dragging at his helm. Cade let him go. His injured arm wasn't hurting anymore. He could feel the heat of blood streaming down it from forearm to knuckles, pouring into the sawdust. Looking down, he watched the sword slide from his nerveless fingers. A scan with his vampire senses told him Ridgemont had hit something vital. He was bleeding out.

Oh Jesus, Val thought, recognizing the moment. *It's the dream! It's happening! We've got to block off that artery!*

It's damaged too badly. I'd have to divert too much of my power, Cade thought, distant and chill. *Ridgemont'll kill me on the next pass.*

Then I'll do it!

Get out, Val. It's over. We lost. You know yourself, he's going to kill me just like he did in your vision.

No! No, I'll figure it out. You are not *dying on me, Cade McKinnon!*

Drawing on his knowledge, she reached for the wound and sealed it, then worked to throw his body into healing the severed artery.

Meanwhile Ridgemont was coiling to leap for him. Cade managed to scoop up his opponent's fallen shield with his left hand. But without Val's reinforcement, he couldn't bring it up fast enough to block. The ancient's sword chopped into his breastplate. Something cracked. He hit the ground on his back and skidded in the sawdust.

Desperately, he struggled to regain his feet, but his legs buckled under him, and the lights of the arena spun around his head. Cade fell back, fought to rise again, but he'd lost too much blood. Numbly, he watched Ridgemont circle him, limping, his sword dangling in one hand. Blood smeared the side of the master vampire's ribs; he too, was badly hurt.

But not enough.

Cade had always known it would come to this. The son of a bitch was just too powerful. He'd sacrificed Val for nothing. He'd failed her, just as he'd failed all the others. He was going to die, and it was no more than he deserved.

No! Goddamn it, Cade…

Get out, Val. Go back to your body.

I'm not losing you. Damn you, I'm not going to lose you.

And she was gone.

For a moment, he couldn't believe it. He felt empty, powerless. But it was better than feeling her share his death.

Ridgemont grinned into his eyes. "You gave me a good fight, gunslinger. Hurt me, even. Rather badly. But it's not enough to save you." He tilted his head to one side and raised his sword. "I think perhaps I'll cut out your heart and keep it to remember you by."

"Sorry. I've already given it to somebody else." Weakly, Cade braced himself to fight as best he could.

"Get away from him, you son of a bitch!"

Ridgemont whirled away from him as Val raced across the arena toward them, stopping just long enough to scoop up Cade's broken sword.

Oh, hell. No.

She danced around Ridgemont in her blue jeans and T-shirt, ignoring her lack of armor, ignoring the fact she'd never held a sword in her life and the one she had now was broken. Ignoring the ancient's eight hundred years of power.

Ridgemont laughed in her face. "Go back, child. It's not your turn to die."

"It's not his either, you bloodsucking bastard."

Hell. Ridgemont's going to kill her. Cade shut his eyes and threw himself along the link.

Then he was looking up at his sire through Val's eyes, and the pain was gone. *What are you doing in here?* she demanded frantically. *You can't leave your body. It'll bleed out.*

Let it. He's not killing you.

Ridgemont grinned and shook his head, bringing his sword up. "You're a fool, girl. You don't have the power."

Cade lunged forward in her light, speedy little body as they threw all their combined energy into Val's narrow arms. The broken sword arched upward.

For just a split second, fear and realization burst across Ridgemont's eyes. Then the shattered blade bit into his neck, and his head spun away, his mind roaring a last outraged protest: *Not with a woman's hand, Cade!*

Val ducked back as the vampire's massive body swayed in a crimson fountain of its own blood. She didn't even watch him hit the ground. *Cade! You've got to get back!*

They rushed into his body just in time to pick up his stuttering heartbeat.

Epilogue

Val had no idea how long they worked to save Cade, repairing the injuries his body had suffered. Alone, he'd have been comatose for hours trying to undo the damage, but together they were able to speed the healing. At last they'd done what they could, and she left him to tumble into the healing sleep.

She reentered her body to the sound of weeping. "Val, please wake up," Beth sobbed. "I'm sorry about what I said. I didn't mean it. Please don't die. They won't let me call an ambulance."

"Good thing, too," Val said hoarsely, opening her eyes to see her sister kneeling beside her on the arena floor. "What a pain in the butt that would be."

Beth's reddened eyes widened with joy. "Oh, thank God! Can you walk? Let's get the hell out of here!"

Grabbing Val by the shoulders, her sister tried to haul her to her feet. Feeling weak and dizzy, Val batted Beth's hands away. "Wait a minute. Ridgemont's dead. There's no reason to go anywhere."

"But the other one's alive. I just checked him, and his breathing's better. I'm afraid he's going to make it. We need to get out of here."

Val sat up and took a deep breath as the arena spun around her. "Damn right, he's going to make it. And I'm not leaving him."

"But…."

"He just saved my life, Beth." Studying her sister's flushed face, Val said, "I thought you'd left."

"I came back." She took a deep breath, and shuddered. "Just in time to see you cut off Ridgemont's head."

"Actually, Cade did that."

Beth's dark brows drew down in puzzlement. "What are you talking about? He was out cold on the ground."

Val opened her mouth, then made a dismissing gesture. "Never mind. It'd take too long to explain."

"You know I didn't mean it, right?" Beth knotted both hands together in her lap, looking anxiously down into her face. "What I said before. You know I love you. This vampire thing doesn't matter."

Val sighed. Her sister's scent told another story. "Beth, you're still afraid of me."

"I'll get over it. We can go back to the way it was before. But you have to promise me…" She stopped and swallowed.

Wearily, stiffly, Val climbed to her feet. She rolled her spine to loosen it. "Promise what?"

Beth licked her lips and looked away. Her heart was pounding hard. "Promise me you won't kill anyone."

"Oh, for God's sake!" She didn't have the energy for this. All she wanted to do was crawl into a bed with Cade and sleep for the next two days.

"You could drink cow's blood or something. You don't have to feed on people."

Val laughed helplessly. "Baby, vampires don't have to kill anybody. We don't need that much blood. Ridgemont just did it because he was a sick son of a bitch."

"Oh." But Beth didn't sound convinced.

Val shook her head and reeled over to Cade, who lay sprawled on his back in a blood-soaked patch of sawdust. Crouching beside him, she started looking for the straps that fastened his armor.

"So we can go home now, right?" Beth said, moving closer with a wary glance at him. "I'll be starting to school in a few days. We've still got that money Ridgemont gave us, and I could get a part-time job. This time I could support you." She smiled, a little bit too brightly. "But if you really want to work, I'm sure you could find a job, too. Night shift or something."

"Don't worry about it." Val pulled free the straps and opened Cade's chest plate. She winced at the blood that covered his chest and tried to remember where he'd collected that particular wound. "I'll find something to do."

The bright smile faded as Beth watched the tender way she touched Cade. "You're in love with him."

Val looked up. "Yes."

"But he turned you into a vampire!"

"Yeah, well. It had to be done." She turned her attention to gently removing the rest of Cade's bloodstained, dented armor.

When she looked up again, Beth was watching her with wide eyes and lips that trembled. "I've lost you, haven't I?"

Val's heart twisted at the pain in her sister's eyes. "No. You could never do that. I love you." She looked down at Cade's peacefully sleeping face. "The fact that I love him, too, doesn't change that."

When she looked up again, she saw the fear and resentment draining away from Beth's gaze. "I'm beginning to see that. I love you too, Val." Her sister straightened her shoulders and looked down at Cade. Again, a trace of fear flickered through her eyes, but she banished it. "So, how can I help?"

Studying her, Val felt the knot of pain loosen in her chest. Her next smile was more genuine. "All I really have to do is get him cleaned up and let him rest. We heal fast, so his body will do the rest." She reached out and took her sister's hand. "But what about you? What do you want to do—go home, or stay in town a few days? I'd like to spend a little time with you before you start school."

Beth took a deep breath. "I really need to get home. I've got a lot of packing to do."

Val tried to banish the stab of hurt she felt. "Of course."

"But," her sister said hastily, "I can spare a day. Or maybe two. If you think you'll have time."

"I'll make time." She looked down at Cade. "I don't think I'd better move him right now, but I'd imagine you probably don't want to stay at the mansion overnight."

Beth shuddered. "I want to get the hell away from this place as fast as possible."

"I don't blame you. I can give you my credit card, if you want to get a hotel room. We could do breakfast." She grimaced. "If we can get a booth out of direct sunlight."

Alarm widened Beth's brown eyes. "You don't..."

"No, I don't burst into flames, but I burn real quick. I like to stay out of the sun as much as possible." Reaching into a pocket of her jeans, she pulled out a credit card and handed it over. "You need my cell to call a cab?"

Beth took it. "Nah, I saw a phone downstairs." She hesitated, then quickly leaned over and kissed Val on the cheek. Instinctively, Val wrapped her arms around her in a quick hug. After a pause, Beth hugged back, holding her almost painfully tight. They clung together for a long moment. When they drew apart, there were tears in Beth's eyes, and Val's were stinging. "I love you, Big Sis."

"I love you, too, baby. Nothing will ever change that."

"I'll call your cell in the morning. Have a good night." Slowly, reluctantly, Beth pulled back, turned, and walked away. Val watched her leave, feeling her heart lighten. They still had work to do to reestablish the trust between them, but they'd made a good beginning.

With a sigh, she looked down at Cade's unconscious body. "It's just me and you now, babe." She bent to pick him up. Despite his muscled length, he barely seemed to weigh anything as she turned and headed for the stairs with him.

When she glanced back one last time, she saw a group of Ridgemont's men were wrapping the ancient's body in a tarp. A cautious mental scan of one of them told her the old vampire had given them a compulsion to burn his corpse if he was killed. After that, they'd all be free for the first time in years. Val was relieved to note none of them had any intention of calling the cops.

Cradling her lover, she went in search of a bedroom that didn't smell like Ridgemont or Hirsch. With the last of her adrenaline rush fading, she didn't have the energy to leave in search of a hotel. Besides, both of them were covered in blood.

Val found a likely room and laid Cade down on a silky expanse of gold bedspread. Leaving him sprawled in all his bloody glory, she went looking for a shower. Fortunately, there was one in an attached bathroom. Fifteen minutes later she felt reasonably clean again, and wandered out, naked, to tend to him again.

Blood had glued the padded suit he wore under the armor to his skin, and she had to loosen it with gentle applications of a warm washcloth. He was so deeply comatose he never even stirred. Finally she had him clean and naked, the worst of his injuries healing nicely.

Then, with a huge yawn, Val crawled in next to his big, warm body, rested her head on his muscled shoulder, and fell instantly asleep.

When she woke, Cade's dark eyes were watching her, slumberous and hungry. A slight smile curved one corner of his handsome mouth. He looked so sexy Val grinned. "You do that on purpose, don't you?"

He blinked his long, dark lashes. "What?"

"That Wolf-to-Red-Riding-Hood-Come-Here-and-Let-Me-Eat-You look." She scanned his body, determining to her satisfaction that it was healed and whole again.

"Woof," he said, and pulled her head down to take her mouth. His lips felt like silk as they slid over hers in soft, liquid temptation. With a sigh, she leaned into him, burying the tips of her nipples in the tickling ruff of his chest hair.

They kissed lazily as he quickly grew hard, his erection lengthening against her belly. His hand drifted down the line of her spine and slipped between her thighs to find the lush folds of her sex. She gasped.

"Hmmmm," he purred. "'The children of the night—what music they make.'"

Val laughed softly, recognizing a *Dracula* quote. "And how long have you been waiting for an opportunity to use that joke?"

"Too damn long," he rumbled, and slipped his hands around to grip her bottom in both hands. He lifted her in his arms and rolled her on top of his body. Eagerly she straddled him as he slowly, lazily impaled her on his long shaft. She cried out in erotic surprise. "In fact, let's make some more music," Cade purred as he began to thrust slowly, deeply.

The sensation of his heated width filling her made Val shudder in delight. When he picked up the pace until he was shafting her in long, driving lunges, she whimpered in delight. Digging her fingers into his powerful shoulders, she hung on for dear life. The pleasure was so slick and demanding that she rotated her hips to grind even harder onto his delicious width.

With a low, feral growl, he fisted a hand in her hair and gently dragged her head down until he could sink his fangs into the underside of her jaw. Screaming in shock, she convulsed and came in a long, rolling orgasm.

Still drinking in deep swallows, Cade continued his ruthless possession of her tight, creamy sex as she writhed helplessly against him.

They lay tangled together on the bed, Cade's big body curled around hers, his head resting on her breast, both muscled arms wrapped around her body. It was, Val thought, a distinctly possessive pose. Not that she was objecting. Thoughtfully, she stroked one hand through the thick silk of his dark hair.

But in contrast to the atmosphere of peace, when she sought his mind, she found Cade was brooding. For a moment Val debated whether to let him hash it out on his own, then decided a little discussion couldn't hurt. "This thing with Ridgemont bothers you," she said.

Cade rubbed his chin back and forth over her breast. "He beat me, Val. I would rather have defeated him on my own—using my own body, I mean."

"You have to admit though, that wouldn't have pissed him off nearly as much," she said, grinning. "He was so outraged at being killed by a woman's hand."

He shrugged. "For a twelfth century man, that was the ultimate humiliation."

"Maybe to him, but it was actually ultimate irony. Think of all the women he's tortured."

"Yeah, I guess there was a certain justice that you killed him."

She lifted her head and twisted it to look in his face. "Cade, *you* killed him. Yeah, the hands were mine, but he'd have chopped me in two if you hadn't interfered."

His arms tightened around her as he met her eyes with a hard look. "Which brings up a very good point—what the hell did you think you were doing?"

"You didn't honestly expect me to sit there and watch you die, did you?"

"Not after spending as much time in your head as I have, no."

He was leaning down to kiss her when the smell of peppermint filled the air. They both jerked and looked around. Abigail floated beside the bed, watching them with solemn eyes. "Jeez, Ghost Brat, don't you ever knock?" Val demanded.

On what?

"She's got a point," Cade said. Then he stiffened. "Abigail...."

The darkness is gone now, Cade. You're free. The glow of the little ghost's face began to intensify. ***And so am I. I just had to see you one last time.***

"Abigail, don't leave me," he said, his eyes widening as he realized she wouldn't be coming back.

You have Valerie now. She'll take care of you, just as I knew she would. The ghost's smile was luminous. ***Your future is so beautiful.***

"So share it with us. Please...."

I can't, Cade. I can hear the Brightness calling, Abigail said, a soft wonder filling her eyes. ***It's like music. I've waited so long....***

Val felt Cade's broad shoulders slump. "Then go to it, darlin'. And remember I love you."

And I love you, Cade. I always will. Her little face lifted, took on such an expression of transcendent joy that Val felt her heart catch. Yes. Yes, I hear you. I'm coming!

The ghost's brightness flared, intensified until it flooded the room. Val's eyes filled with tears, and she heard Cade's breath roughen.

Slowly, slowly, the light faded away, along with the scent of peppermint. But as they looked at the spot where she'd been, they could hear the music, a long, rolling peal of it, high and glorious and so joyous not even Cade's grief could withstand it.

When the last note faded, his strong arms tightened around Val, and they lay together in a sweet cocoon of peace.

About the Author

Angela Knight's first book was written in pencil and illustrated in crayon; she was nine years old at the time. But her mother was enthralled, and Angela was hooked.

In the years that followed, Angela managed to figure out a way to make a living—more or less—at what she loved best: writing. After a short career as a comic book writer, she became a newspaper reporter, covering everything from school board meetings to murders. Several of her stories won South Carolina Press Association awards under her real name.

Along the way, she found herself playing Lois Lane to her detective husband's Superman. He'd go off to solve murders, and she'd sneak around after him trying to find out what was going on. The only time things got really uncomfortable was the day she watched him hunt pipe bombs, an experience she never wants to repeat.

But her first writing love has always been romance. She read *The Wolf and The Dove* at 15, at least until her mother caught her at it.

In 1996, she discovered the small press publisher Red Sage Publishing, and realized her dream of romance publication in the company's *Secrets 2* anthology. Since then, her work has appeared in four *Secrets* anthologies. She's tremendously grateful to publisher Alexandria Kendall for the opportunity to make her dreams come true. She believes her writer son, Antony, will one day follow in her footsteps.

Angela enjoys hearing from readers. You may e-mail her at **angelanight2002@bellsouth.net**. Check out her website at **www.angelasknights.com**.

Feel the wild adventure, fierce passion and the power of love in every ***Secrets*** Collection story. Red Sage Publishing's romance authors create richly crafted, sexy, sensual, novella-length stories. Each one is just the right length for reading after a long and hectic day.

Each volume in the ***Secrets*** Collection has four diverse, ultra-sexy, romantic novellas brimming with adventure, passion and love. More adventurous tales for the adventurous reader. The ***Secrets*** Collection are a glorious mix of romance genre; numerous historical settings, contemporary, paranormal, science fiction and suspense. We are always looking for new adventures.

Reader response to the ***Secrets*** volumes has been great! Here's just a small sample:

> *"I loved the variety of settings. Four completely wonderful time periods, give you four completely wonderful reads."*
>
> *"Each story was a page-turning tale I hated to put down."*
>
> *"I love* ***Secrets****! When is the next volume coming out? This one was Hot! Loved the heroes!"*

Secrets have won raves and awards. We could go on, but why don't you find out for yourself—order your set of ***Secrets*** today! See the back for details.

Secrets, Volume 1

Listen to what reviewers say:

"These stories take you beyond romance into the realm of erotica. I found ***Secrets*** absolutely delicious."

—Virginia Henley,
New York Times Best Selling Author

"***Secrets*** is a collection of novellas for the daring, adventurous woman who's not afraid to give her fantasies free reign."

—Kathe Robin, *Romantic Times* Magazine

"...In fact, the men featured in all the stories are terrific, they all want to please and pleasure their women. If you like erotic romance you will love ***Secrets***."

—*Romantic Readers* Review

In ***Secrets, Volume 1*** you'll find:

A Lady's Quest by Bonnie Hamre

Widowed Lady Antonia Blair-Sutworth searches for a lover to save her from the handsome Duke of Sutherland. The "auditions" may be shocking but utterly tantalizing.

The Spinner's Dream by Alice Gaines

A seductive fantasy that leaves every woman wishing for her own private love slave, desperate and running for his life.

The Proposal by Ivy Landon

This tale is a walk on the wild side of love. *The Proposal* will taunt you, tease you, and shock you. A contemporary erotica for the adventurous woman.

The Gift by Jeanie LeGendre

Immerse yourself in this historic tale of exotic seduction, bondage and a concubine's surrender to the Sultan's desire. Can Alessandra live the life and give the gift the Sultan demands of her?

Secrets, Volume 2

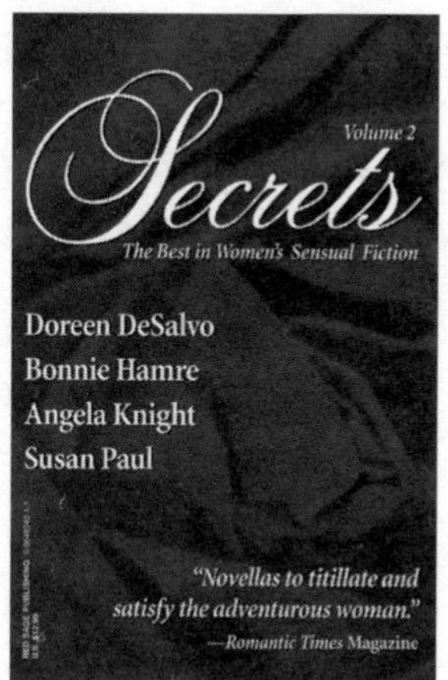

Listen to what reviewers say:

"***Secrets*** offers four novellas of sensual delight; each beautifully written with intense feeling and dedication to character development. For those seeking stories with heightened intimacy, look no further."

—Kathee Card, *Romancing the Web*

"Such a welcome diversity in styles and genres. Rich characterization in sensual tales. An exciting read that's sure to titillate the senses."

—Cheryl Ann Porter

"***Secrets 2*** left me breathless. Sensual satisfaction guaranteed...times four!"

—Virginia Henley, *New York Times* Best Selling Author

In ***Secrets, Volume 2*** you'll find:

Surrogate Lover by Doreen DeSalvo

Adrian Ross is a surrogate sex therapist who has all the answers and control. He thought he'd seen and done it all, but he'd never met Sarah.

Snowbound by Bonnie Hamre

A delicious, sensuous regency tale. The marriage-shy Earl of Howden is teased and tortured by his own desires and finds there is a woman who can equal his overpowering sensuality.

Roarke's Prisoner by Angela Knight

Elise, a starship captain, remembers the eager animal submission she'd known before at her captor's hands and refuses to become his toy again. However, she has no idea of the delights he's planned for her this time.

Savage Garden by Susan Paul

Raine's been captured by a mysterious and dangerous revolutionary leader in Mexico. At first her only concern is survival, but she quickly finds lush erotic nights in her captor's arms.

Winner of the Fallot Literary Award for Fiction!

Secrets, Volume 5

Listen to what reviewers say:

"Hot, hot, hot! Not for the faint-hearted!"

—*Romantic Times* Magazine

"As you make your way through the stories, you will find yourself becoming hotter and hotter. ***Secrets*** just keeps getting better and better."

—*Affaire de Coeur* Magazine

"***Secrets 5*** is a collage of lucious sensuality. Any woman who reads ***Secrets*** is in for an awakening!"

—Virginia Henley, *New York Times* Best Selling Author

In ***Secrets, Volume 5*** you'll find:

Beneath Two Moons by Sandy Fraser

Ready for a very wild romp? Step into the future and find Conor, rough and masculine like frontiermen of old, on the prowl for a new conquest. In his sights, Dr. Eva Kelsey. She got away once before, but this time Conor makes sure she begs for more.

Insatiable by Chevon Gael

Marcus Remington photographs beautiful models for a living, but it's Ashlyn Fraser, a young corporate exec having some glamour shots done, who has stolen his heart. It's up to Marcus to help her discover her inner sexual self.

Strictly Business by Shannon Hollis

Elizabeth Forrester knows it's tough enough for a woman to make it to the top in the corporate world. Garrett Hill, the most beautiful man in Silicon Valley, has to come along to stir up her wildest fantasies. Dare she give in to both their desires?

Alias Smith and Jones by B.J. McCall

Meredith Collins finds herself stranded overnight at the airport. A handsome stranger by the name of Smith offers her sanctuaty for the evening and she finds those mesmerizing, green-flecked eyes hard to resist. Are they to be just two ships passing in the night?

Secrets, Volume 6

Listen to what reviewers say:

"Red Sage was the first and remains the leader of Women's Erotic Romance Fiction Collections!"

—*Romantic Times* Magazine

"***Secrets*, *Volume 6***, is the best of ***Secrets*** yet. …four of the most erotic stories in one volume than this reader has yet to see anywhere else. …These stories are full of erotica at its best and you'll definitely want to keep it handy for lots of re-reading!"

—*Affaire de Coeur* Magazine

"***Secrets 6*** satisfies every female fantasy: the Bodyguard, the Tutor, the Werewolf, and the Vampire. I give it Six Stars!"

—Virginia Henley, *New York Times* Best Selling Author

In ***Secrets, Volume 6*** you'll find:

Flint's Fuse by Sandy Fraser

Dana Madison's father has her "kidnapped" for her own safety. Flint, the tall, dark and dangerous mercenary, is hired for the job. But just which one is the prisoner—Dana will try *anything* to get away.

Love's Prisoner by MaryJanice Davidson

Trapped in an elevator, Jeannie Lawrence experienced unwilling rapture at Michael Windham's hands. She never expected the devilishly handsome man to show back up in her life—or turn out to be a werewolf!

The Education of Miss Felicity Wells by Alice Gaines

Felicity Wells wants to be sure she'll satisfy her soon-to-be husband but she needs a teacher. Dr. Marcus Slade, an experienced lover, agrees to take her on as a student, but can he stop short of taking her completely?

A Candidate for the Kiss by Angela Knight

Working on a story, reporter Dana Ivory stumbles onto a more amazing one—a sexy, secret agent who happens to be a vampire.She wants her story but Gabriel Archer wants more from her than just sex and blood.

Secrets, Volume 7

Listen to what reviewers say:

"Get out your asbestos gloves — ***Secrets Volume** 7* is…extremely hot, true erotic romance…passionate and titillating. There's nothing quite like baring your secrets!"

—*Romantic Times* Magazine

"…sensual, sexy, steamy fun. A perfect read!"

—Virginia Henley,
New York Times Best Selling Author

"Intensely provocative and disarmingly romantic, ***Secrets***, ***Volume** 7*, is a romance reader's paradise that will take you beyond your wildest dreams!"

—Ballston Book House Review

In ***Secrets, Volume 7*** you'll find:

Amelia's Innocence by Julia Welles

Amelia didn't know her father bet her in a card game with Captain Quentin Hawke, so honor demands a compromise—three days of erotic foreplay, leaving her virginity and future intact.

The Woman of His Dreams by Jade Lawless

From the day artist Gray Avonaco moves in next door, Joanna Morgan is plagued by provocative dreams. But what she believes is unrequited lust, Gray sees as another chance to be with the woman he loves. He must persuade her that even death can't stop true love.

Surrender by Kathryn Anne Dubois

Free-spirited Lady Johanna wants no part of the binding strictures society imposes with her marriage to the powerful Duke. She doesn't know the dark Duke wants sensual adventure, and sexual satisfaction.

Kissing the Hunter by Angela Knight

Navy Seal Logan McLean hunts the vampires who murdered his wife. Virginia Hart is a sexy vampire searching for her lost soul-mate only to find him in a man determined to kill her. She must convince him all vampires aren't created equally.

**Winner of the Venus Book Club
Best Book of the Year**

Secrets, Volume 8

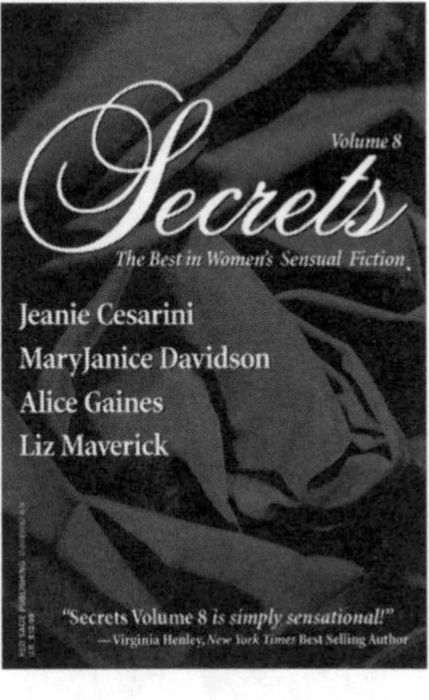

Listen to what reviewers say:

"***Secrets*, *Volume 8***, is an amazing compilation of sexy stories covering a wide range of subjects, all designed to titillate the senses. …you'll find something for everybody in this latest version of ***Secrets***."

—*Affaire de Coeur* Magazine

"***Secrets Volume 8***, is simply sensational!"

—Virginia Henley, *New York Times* Best Selling Author

"These delectable stories will have you turning the pages long into the night. Passionate, provocative and perfect for setting the mood…."

—*Escape to Romance* Reviews

In ***Secrets, Volume 8*** you'll find:

Taming Kate by Jeanie Cesarini

Kathryn Roman inherits a legal brothel. Little does this city girl know the town of Love, Nevada wants her to be their new madam so they've charged Trey Holliday, one very dominant cowboy, with taming her.

Jared's Wolf by MaryJanice Davidson

Jared Rocke will do anything to avenge his sister's death, but ends up attracted to Moira Wolfbauer, the she-wolf sworn to protect her pack. Joining forces to stop a killer, they learn love defies all boundaries.

My Champion, My Lover by Alice Gaines

Celeste Broder is a woman committed for having a sexy appetite. Mayor Robert Albright may be her champion—if she can convince him her freedom will mean a chance to indulge their appetites together.

Kiss or Kill by Liz Maverick

In this post-apocalyptic world, Camille Kazinsky's military career rides on her ability to make a choice—whether the robo called Meat should live or die. Meat's future depends on proving he's human enough to live, man enough…to makes her feel like a woman.

**Winner of the Venus Book Club
Best Book of the Year**

Secrets, Volume 9

Listen to what reviewers say:

"Everyone should expect only the most erotic stories in a ***Secrets*** book. ...if you like your stories full of hot sexual scenes, then this is for you!"

—Donna Doyle Romance Reviews

"**SECRETS 9**...is sinfully delicious, highly arousing, and hotter than hot as the pages practically burn up as you turn them."

—Suzanne Coleburn, Reader To Reader Reviews/Belles & Beaux of Romance

"Treat yourself to well-written fictionthat's hot, hotter, and hottest!"

—Virginia Henley, *New York Times* Best Selling Author

In ***Secrets, Volume 9*** you'll find:

Wild For You by Kathryn Anne Dubois

When college intern, Georgie, gets captured by a Congo wildman, she discovers this specimen of male virility has never seen a woman. The research possibilities are endless!

Wanted by Kimberly Dean

FBI Special Agent Jeff Reno wants Danielle Carver. There's her body, brains—and that charge of treason on her head. Dani goes on the run, but the sexy Fed is hot on her trail.

Secluded by Lisa Marie Rice

Nicholas Lee's wealth and power came with a price—his enemies will kill anyone he loves. When Isabelle steals his heart, Nicholas secludes her in his palace for a lifetime of desire in only a few days.

Flights of Fantasy by Bonnie Hamre

Chloe taught others to see the realities of life but she's never shared the intimate world of her sensual yearnings. Given the chance, will she be woman enough to fulfill her most secret erotic fantasy?

Secrets, Volume 10

Listen to what reviewers say:

"***Secrets Volume 10***, an erotic dance through medieval castles, sultan's palaces, the English countryside and expensive hotel suites, explodes with passion-filled pages."

—Romantic Times BOOKclub

"Having read the previous nine volumes, this one fulfills the expectations of what is expected in a ***Secrets*** book: romance and eroticism at its best!!"

—Fallen Angel Reviews

"All are hot steamy romances so if you enjoy erotica romance, you are sure to enjoy ***Secrets, Volume 10***. All this reviewer can say is WOW!!"

—The Best Reviews

In ***Secrets, Volume 10*** you'll find:

Private Eyes by Dominique Sinclair

When a mystery man captivates P.I. Nicolla Black during a stakeout, she discovers her no-seduction rule bending under the pressure of long denied passion. She agrees to the seduction, but he demands her total surrender.

The Ruination of Lady Jane by Bonnie Hamre

To avoid her upcoming marriage, Lady Jane Ponsonby-Maitland flees into the arms of Havyn Attercliffe. She begs him to ruin her rather than turn her over to her odious fiancé.

Code Name: Kiss by Jeanie Cesarini

Agent Lily Justiss is on a mission to defend her country against terrorists that requires giving up her virginity as a sex slave. As her master takes her body, desire for her commanding officer Seth Blackthorn fuels her mind.

The Sacrifice by Kathryn Anne Dubois

Lady Anastasia Bedovier is days from taking her vows as a Nun. Before she denies her sensuality forever, she wants to experience pleasure. Count Maxwell is the perfect man to initiate her into erotic delight.

The Forever Kiss
by Angela Knight

Listen to what reviewers say:

"***The Forever Kiss*** flows well with good characters and an interesting plot. … If you enjoy vampires and a lot of hot sex, you are sure to enjoy ***The Forever Kiss***."

—The Best Reviews

"Battling vampires, a protective ghost and the ever present battle of good and evil keep excellent pace with the erotic delights in Angela Knight's ***The Forever Kiss***—a book that absolutely bites with refreshing paranormal humor." **4½ Stars, Top Pick**

—Romantic Times BOOKclub

"I found ***The Forever Kiss*** to be an exceptionally written, refreshing book. … I really enjoyed this book by Angela Knight. … 5 angels!"

—Fallen Angel Reviews

"***The Forever Kiss*** is the first single title released from Red Sage and if this is any indication of what we can expect, it won't be the last. … The love scenes are hot enough to give a vampire a sunburn and the fight scenes will have you cheering for the good guys."

—Really Bad Barb Reviews

In ***The Forever Kiss***:

For years, Valerie Chase has been haunted by dreams of a Texas Ranger she knows only as "Cowboy." As a child, he rescued her from the nightmare vampires who murdered her parents. As an adult, she still dreams of him—but now he's her seductive lover in nights of erotic pleasure.

Yet "Cowboy" is more than a dream—he's the real Cade McKinnon—and a vampire! For years, he's protected Valerie from Edward Ridgemont, the sadistic vampire who turned him. Now, Ridgmont wants Valerie for his own and Cade is the only one who can protect her.

When Val finds herself abducted by her handsome dream man, she's appalled to discover he's one of the vampires she fears. Now, caught in a web of fear and passion, she and Cade must learn to trust each other, even as an immortal monster stalks their every move.

Their only hope of survival is…***The Forever Kiss***.

It's not just reviewers raving about *Secrets*. See what readers have to say:

"When are you coming out with a new Volume? I want a new one next month!" via email from a reader.

"I loved the hot, wet sex without vulgar words being used to make it exciting." after ***Volume 1***

"I loved the blend of sensuality and sexual intensity—HOT!" after ***Volume 2***

"The best thing about ***Secrets*** is they're hot and brief! The least thing is you do not have enough of them!" after ***Volume 3***

"I have been extreamly satisfied with ***Secrets***, keep up the good writing." after ***Volume 4***

"I love the sensuality and sex that is not normally written about or explored in a really romantic context" after ***Volume 4***

"Loved it all!!!" after ***Volume 5***

"I love the tastful, hot way that ***Secrets*** pushes the edge. The genre mix is cool, too." after ***Volume 5***

"Stories have plot and characters to support the erotica. They would be good strong stories without the heat." after ***Volume 5***

"***Secrets*** really knows how to push the envelop better than anyone else." after ***Volume 6***

"***Secrets***, there is nothing not to like. This is the top banana, so to speak." after ***Volume 6***

"'Would you buy ***Volume 7***?' YES!!! Inform me ASAP and I am so there!!" after ***Volume 6***

"Can I please, please, please pre-order ***Volume 7***? I want to be the first to get it of my friends. They don't have email so they can't write you! I can!" after ***Volume 6***

Finally, the men you've been dreaming about!

Give the Gift of Spicy Romantic Fiction

Don't want to wait? You can place a retail price ($12.99) order for any of the *Secrets* volumes from the following:

① **Waldenbooks and Borders Stores**

② **Amazon.com** or **BarnesandNoble.com**

③ **Book Clearinghouse (800-431-1579)**

④ **Romantic Times Magazine**
Books by Mail (718-237-1097)

⑤ Special order at other bookstores.
Bookstores: Please contact Baker & Taylor Distributors or Red Sage Publishing for bookstore sales.

Order by title or ISBN #:

Vol. 1: 0-9648942-0-3
Vol. 2: 0-9648942-1-1
Vol. 3: 0-9648942-2-X
Vol. 4: 0-9648942-4-6
Vol. 5: 0-9648942-5-4
Vol. 6: 0-9648942-6-2
Vol. 7: 0-9648942-7-0
Vol. 8: 0-9648942-8-9
Vol. 9: 0-9648942-9-7
Vol. 10: 0-9754516-0-X

The Forever Kiss: 0-9648942-3-8 ($14.00)

Red Sage Publishing Mail Order Form:

(Orders shipped in two to three days of receipt.)

	Quantity	Mail Order Price	Total
Secrets **Volume 1** *(Retail $12.99)*	______	$ 9.99	______
Secrets **Volume 2** *(Retail $12.99)*	______	$ 9.99	______
Secrets **Volume 3** *(Retail $12.99)*	______	$ 9.99	______
Secrets **Volume 4** *(Retail $12.99)*	______	$ 9.99	______
Secrets **Volume 5** *(Retail $12.99)*	______	$ 9.99	______
Secrets **Volume 6** *(Retail $12.99)*	______	$ 9.99	______
Secrets **Volume 7** *(Retail $12.99)*	______	$ 9.99	______
Secrets **Volume 8** *(Retail $12.99)*	______	$ 9.99	______
Secrets **Volume 9** *(Retail $12.99)*	______	$ 9.99	______
Secrets **Volume 10** *(Retail $12.99)*	______	$ 9.99	______
The Forever Kiss (Retail $14.00)	______	$11.00	______

Shipping & handling (in the U.S.)

US Priority Mail:		UPS insured:	
1–2 books	$ 5.50	1–4 books	$16.00
3–5 books	$11.50	5–9 books	$25.00
6–9 books	$14.50	10–11 books	$29.00
10–11 books	$19.00		

______

SUBTOTAL ______

Florida 6% sales tax (if delivered in FL) ______

TOTAL AMOUNT ENCLOSED ______

Your personal information is kept private and not shared with anyone.

Name: (please print) ______

Address: (no P.O. Boxes) ______

City/State/Zip: ______

Phone or email: (only regarding order if necessary) ______

Please make check payable to **Red Sage Publishing**. Check must be drawn on a U.S. bank in U.S. dollars. Mail your check and order form to:

Red Sage Publishing, Inc. Department FK P.O. Box 4844 Seminole, FL 33775

***Or use the order form on our website:* www.redsagepub.com**